TEXAS RANGERS ABROAD

The Combined Adventures of Texas Ranger Wayne Stephens and Scotland Yard Inspector Caleb Jones

J. STEPHEN MILES

ISBN 978-1-63903-489-5 (paperback)
ISBN 978-1-63903-490-1 (digital)

Copyright © 2023 by J. Stephen Miles

All rights reserved. No part of this publication may be reproduced, distributed, or transmitted in any form or by any means, including photocopying, recording, or other electronic or mechanical methods without the prior written permission of the publisher. For permission requests, solicit the publisher via the address below.

Christian Faith Publishing
832 Park Avenue
Meadville, PA 16335
www.christianfaithpublishing.com

Printed in the United States of America

The Texas Ranger of Scotland Yard Copyrighted 2014 by J. Stephen Miles

Lone Star Inspector Copyrighted 2017 by J. Stephen Miles

Texas Rangers Down Under Copyrighted 2018 by J. Stephen Miles

The Texas Ranger of Scotland Yard

Chapter 1

Chilled and gray, the night had slowly drifted by in London with such a dense fog in the streets that a man could hardly see where he was taking his next step. Inspector Jones of Scotland Yard was in need of a bit more visibility on this particular night in the early spring of 1885. Caleb Jones had been promoted to inspector less than a year ago and believed some still doubted his abilities and readiness for such responsibility. At the age of thirty-two, he was not the youngest inspector, but he had started later than some others in this career of combating crime. Since his promotion, he had felt the disquieting sensation that he was sort of on parole and that the powers at be were waiting to see if their decision was justified. The case that he was currently attending to was, in his mind, the chance to establish his value with the Yard.

It was his belief that among the cut-purses, petty larceners, and small con artists which were so typical throughout the streets of London, there was a broad alliance of sorts being formed which connected many of them to a common purpose. Such organization, while not unheard of, was deemed an extreme rarity and highly improbable by Jones's superiors. They reasoned that if it had existed, then at least a whisper of some head of industry would have come to their knowledge by this time, which it had not; and while they still allowed Jones a free hand to pursue his theory, much criticism existed regarding its success and the merit of the reasoning behind it. If tonight's excursion would bear a little fruit that Jones could sink his teeth into, then he might develop a lead that his superiors would have to listen to. If it didn't, then probably he would soon be ordered to give up the pursuit, if not something worse.

He shook his head to clear it; he would not allow himself to ponder the effects of failure. He must find a way to succeed. Jones had not been born high in London's social circles, but as the son of a well-respected retired military surgeon, he had been able to receive a full education, an education that included by association some small knowledge of medicine. It was medicine that had indirectly led in part to his decision to make a career in law enforcement. When the city coroner's office had fallen behind in its work due to an elevated volume of murder and crime, his father had occasionally been called on to assist with the workload. As a young man, he had sometimes been allowed to accompany his father as a sort of assistant. These experiences combined with some of his father's private cases had formed in him a longing for justice that he now attempted to satisfy. But wait… These thoughts and recollections couldn't distract him from the task at hand. He thought he could hear steps finally approaching on that dismal street, which was practically deserted these small hours before dawn.

Jones took his small pipe with the embers all but extinguished and tapped a few times lightly on the bricks of the doorway he occupied so as to alert the three constables accompanying him that the time might have finally come for action. A slight puff of wind began to sweep some portion of the fog down the alley and let the faint light of the streetlamp show the movement of a figure approaching at the end of the block. The patched trousers and dinted hat combined with a limping swagger confirmed the figure was Miller, a lesser bookie who in the past had been brought in several times connected with embezzlement cases. However, Miller had been surprisingly clear of trouble for some months now, and though his little back office still existed with roughly the same caliber of clientele, Jones had it on good authority that much larger sums of money had been passing through his office, and many of Miller's debts were being cleared.

To even be able to ask Miller questions in private, Jones had to arrange this sort of ambush to avoid various kinds of trouble on those streets. After having him observed over the last several weeks, it had been observed that Miller would sometimes travel along this route on some secret errand. Just maybe Jones would be able to finally discover what those errands were.

As Miller was about to pass the doorway, Jones took a casual step into the street and spoke softly, "I know you do business late into the night, Miller, but isn't this pushing it, even for you?"

Miller checked his stride but then continued a bit slower and answered, "It may be late for you, but there's no law I ever 'eard of that says a man can't take a stroll whenever he likes."

"That is very true, but why come down this way?" asked Jones. "By now, there's nothing you'd be interested in seeing along the river."

"Do I need any reason to go to the river if I 'ave a mind to?" Miller's reply was thick with resentment at his business being interrupted, and he had stupidly confirmed Jones's notion that the river had been his destination.

Miller simply didn't possess a higher level of intelligence, which was why Jones couldn't believe that after some twenty-odd years in his questionable and barely successful trade, Miller could suddenly be accumulating the kind of money he had been dispensing without having his crummy finger in a larger pie.

"You are quite right, Miller, but I can't help but have the idea that whatever your errand may be, it is going to get you into much more trouble than you're used to. Now I might be able to help keep you out of some of it if you would just play it smart for once." Jones had little faith that such an appeal would work, but he wanted to try before resorting to the rougher strong-arm methods common with some of his colleagues. Also, he wished he could get Miller to stop walking so as to better his chances.

They were getting closer to the end of this block where the fog was thicker and harder to see through. Miller could simply walk away from him if he didn't trip over his own big feet, and they were about to pass the point where his constables were stationed. Jones didn't like the prospect of being alone with the burly figure beside him without close help, but if his constables made an appearance to follow him, then Miller would take off and lose himself for sure.

Miller sneered at him and slowly tried to start widening the distance between them as they walked. "I ain't been in no trouble for a long bit, and now you're just trying to make some up for me."

"I promise that I'm not trying to make trouble for you, Miller, but you've been in trouble most of your life, and even you must see that what you're getting involved in is worse than anything you've faced before."

Miller still wasn't convinced, and his expression showed it.

"'Aven't you Yard birds got anything better to do than try to drag me back again, or are you just bored?" That last part came out slow and menacing, and before Jones could make any reply, Miller took a step toward him, and those big brute arms shoved against his chest with such force that his feet slipped and he went sprawling on the wet street. Miller dashed for the dark alley the fog had been drifting down and managed to plow shoulder-first through two constables who had come together to intercept him.

As a young inspector on a perceived trivial case, he had been allotted young and inexperienced constables. They were not yet accustomed to dealing with this kind of situation and had relied on the sight of their uniforms to halt the suspect. But their upraised hands had done nothing to deter the charging figure of Miller, except maybe make to him grin, and now they too were rolling on the ground while the third constable was trying to catch up from the other end of the street.

Jones was scrambling to his feet to give what he perceived would be a hopeless chase, for he had already reasoned that Miller would disappear once he got into the fog on a back street. He had just taken a step to begin to run when he saw something dark shoot out of the fog at the alley's opening and smash into Miller's face with a blow that crashed his head against the wall of the opposite building.

As Jones approached the unconscious fugitive, he peered into the fog to see a strange man emerge lightly, rubbing his gloved fist and staring down at Miller's unconscious heap.

"I don't know who you are, sir, but I appreciate your assistance." He held out his hand to the stranger, who took it and answered in a very distinct American voice.

"I'm glad to be of help. I just happened to see those two uniforms get plowed by this guy through a gap in the fog and figured that he wasn't exactly a model citizen. So I walloped him as he came up to me."

"Yes, I saw that," Jones replied. "Very impressive indeed. I am Inspector Jones of Scotland Yard."

Now the stranger looked up at him more closely, and a grin spread across his face.

"Well now," he said, "a Scotland Yard inspector is just the person I needed to find. My name is Wayne Stephens of the Texas Rangers."

Jones's look of appreciation turned to one of being flabbergasted at hearing this declaration. He must have looked terribly silly to the man shaking his hand, but the stranger actually seemed to take little notice and made no comment. Then Jones's astonishment at this announcement was interrupted by the blustering constables who had just arrived looking for orders. Jones quickly collected himself in front of his subordinates and gave orders for their coach to be fetched from the next street so they could convey the fugitive to the Yard.

"I'm grateful to you, Mr. Stephens," he said at last, turning back to the stranger, "and if you wish to speak with someone at the Yard, I'd be happy to escort you there."

"Thank you very kindly," said Stephens. "I do have business to discuss there, and the sooner I get it done, the better."

In a few minutes, the coach came to a halt next to the alleyway, and the three constables under Jones's direction slowly loaded the limp and still-uncooperative mass of Miller into a more or less sitting position on one of the seats. Stephens then mounted the coach at Jones's invitation before Jones and the constables took their places, and a light stroke of the whip started the horses trotting in the direction of Scotland Yard.

Chapter 2

As the coach rumbled on, Jones simply had to satisfy some of his curiosity, which was equally shared by the attending constable sitting next to Miller upon hearing the title Texas Rangers. Jones had heard something of that group over the last few years in connection with his own profession. They were viewed as a half-civilized militia who were working to assert themselves as a kind of police force in their rugged state. More accurate facts had never come to his ears. At length, he took the plunge.

"If I may ask, sir, what on earth brings you to London? From what little I know, the Texas Rangers never leave Texas."

"At least it's something that you've heard of us at all," said Stephens lightheartedly. "I'm glad you didn't assume that I was half savage. I met one great lady of your country on the ship over here who acted like she thought I would tear the boat apart when she found out I was from Texas, never mind my being a ranger. I was talking to the captain about my business the first day out when we came across this lord and lady on the deck. The captain made the introductions, and I tried to return the bows they gave me. When he told them who I was, the lady's eyes nearly popped out of her head, and she put her hand to her chest like she couldn't breathe. I think it relieved her a little when she discovered that my birth was on the other end of the ship. Texas is a big place, but we do occasionally stray beyond the borders when we feel it's warranted. I am here because I believe that a person I have been tracking and trying to lay my hands on for years is in this country."

"You're after a fugitive from your country, from your state, here in England?" Jones was even more astonished. He had seen American visitors in England before but always well-to-do families from the eastern seaboard. It would seem that a rough… Westerner would be rather obvious, at least here in London. Stephens had been watching his expressions and went on to explain as if he had deciphered Jones's bafflement.

"This man that I speak of is not a 'cowboy,' Mr. Jones, although he did for some years live very roughly in the South of Texas. What his exact origins are, I've never found out, but I know that he grew up in the northeast, probably in Pennsylvania. I doubt he would have a hard time adapting to English society in his own way."

"But why should he come here in the first place?" Jones asked.

"To escape from me," replied Stephens very flatly and with sternness.

There was no time for any more explanation as the coach pulled up in front of the Scotland Yard office. Jones just stared at the still sleeping Miller as the constables carried him into a cell and laid him down.

"I'll have to come back later in the morning to try and get something out of him. My soul, you'd think a prize fighter had gotten to him." Jones turned and looked at Stephens, still shaking his head.

"Not a prizefighter, Inspector, just an old Indian fighter. I thank you kindly for the compliment. Prizefighters have to save their strength and wear down the other fellow, but when you're fighting for your life against Indians that want to scalp you, then you learn to put out all you have."

As Stephens turned to walk back into the main office, Jones could just look after him in amazement. The more time that passed by, the more of a puzzle this ranger became. Following him into the main office, Jones collected his thoughts to discuss what should be done.

"I know I volunteered to bring you here, Mr. Stephens, since I gathered that this is where you wanted to come, but to be honest, it is just past 4:00 a.m. now, and the chief inspector won't be in until at least eight o'clock or so. There is really very little to be accomplished at this point in time. Come to think of it, why were you coming to the Yard at this hour?"

Stephens grinned slightly and drew a breath before explaining himself. "I've been on a ship for more days than I care to count, and though I'm used to spending hours in a saddle, I've always slept on something solid. It took me many of those days to adjust to sleeping on something that is moving. When I was finally able to get a whole night's sleep, I got three of them before we hit a storm that made sleep impossible for me and caused my boat to be three days late. I had everything packed and ready to come ashore later this morning, and then we docked five hours earlier than had been allowed for the storm. I wasn't going to spend another minute on that ship, so I got my bags and headed out to find a boarding house that the captain had told me about.

"Once I got there, the landlady was not happy at being woken up for an American border, but I got a room and got myself situated. I was still so wound up by the frustrations of the night that I couldn't sleep and decided to try and find the Scotland Yard office. If nothing else, I figured the walk would help me calm down which, combined with sharing in your little adventure, has worked, and I could sleep for few hours at any rate. If you can, why don't you come have breakfast at nine o'clock, and then you can bring me back here?"

Jones had hoped to get a little more sleep than that, but he hadn't planned on such a strange turn of events, and so he agreed and got the address before calling a cab to take Stephens back.

The next day, Jones arrived and had a satisfying, if humble, breakfast, after which he hoped he might learn more about his American colleague. He didn't have to wait long, for even though Stephens barely spoke during the meal, he seemed to grow a little more talkative after he had eaten, as men sometimes did.

"I apologize if I don't have very good manners as a host while eating, Inspector, but in the course of my life and career, there have been too many times that food has been scarce and long in coming. Habits formed when I was younger are hard to break. One of them is not losing time to eat while I have the chance."

The man did not look to be much older than Jones, yet he talked of being younger as a man of fifty or sixty. Also, this man did not appear to be the rough and uncouth brawler that stories had portrayed regarding people from his part of the world. He was dressed in a dark-gray suit that was plainly stylish after an

American fashion, and so far, he had been well-spoken in spite of his distinct Texas accent. Jones took the plunge at last to obtain his answers.

"I beg your pardon, Mr. Stephens, I don't mean any offense, but you aren't really what I would've expected in a Texas Ranger. We get very little information about that part of the world, and what we do hear makes it sound somewhat barbarous, as you hinted last night."

Stephens looked at him a moment, and he was not offended but considered what had been said to him, and at length, he answered, "To begin with, Inspector, drop the Mr., and just call me Stephens, that's what I'm used to. What you say doesn't surprise me since what you say isn't altogether false. The history of the Texas Rangers can be traced back to the early part of the century when American settlers first started moving into Mexico, and then they were officially established after Texas won its independence in 1836. Since then, the rangers have had more of a military role than that of law officers, and it has been a very hard and dirty business that has conjured up some of the stories that you may have heard.

"Up until recent years, rangers have been all that has stood between settlements, ranchers, and farmers and the hostilities of the Indian tribes and Mexican bandits. While those problems still exist, they are not on near the scale that they once were, and the rangers are starting to be molded more into a law enforcement group to deal with cutthroat outlaws and rustlers in the more spread-out part of the country. The general point of us is still the same: we chase down anyone who makes themselves an enemy of Texas and its people, so I guess that to a point, we are a little rough and uncivilized to your way of thinking. In fact, big cities like London and those in the Eastern states are very foreign to me. The stories and rumors you hear about us ain't entirely unfounded. It's still a hard country to be in, and it takes tough people to live in it. Many of those people don't exactly have the best manners, you might say.

"As for myself, I may not be exactly typical of a Texan or a Texas Ranger. My mother was a schoolteacher and had been well educated by her family in Maryland before her family decided to go West. My father was not quite so well educated, but well enough and came from Indiana. They married in Texas and opened up a general store before trying their hand at a small ranch. They've made a pretty good go of it too. My father ships supplies to a lot of towns and new settlements in the area, he has even hired a few freighters and extra wagons to help. The ranch is not nearly as big as some. Richard King down by Corpus Christi would probably laugh at it, but it's respectable with a few hundred head of cattle running around now and about a dozen hands to work them.

"I was born in 1850 and joined the rangers when I was twenty. With the upbringing that my parents gave me, it might be thought that I could've gone on to bigger and better things. After the civil war, things were very hard, and when I was old enough, the rangers seemed like a stable living. Plus, I didn't like being cooped up in the store all day taking inventory or being a nursemaid to cows fourteen hours a day. My parents wanted me to help with one business or the other. They didn't like the idea of me being a ranger, but try as I did, it just didn't fit me. So over the last fifteen years, I've ridden all over the state, mostly in the Southwest, and fought the Comanche, Apache, Mexican bandits, and outlaws of every kind."

Jones hadn't uttered a word but just sat like a schoolboy listening to this outlandish story. He hoped he might learn still more, but anything else, he would have to learn later.

Stephens looked at his watch and got up to get his hat and coat.

"Well, Stephens," Jones finally spoke up, "I don't know if I'll get to see you anymore during your visit, but I must say, I am glad to have met you and wish you luck with your business. I would like to warn you though that the chief inspector may not be… overly receptive. He has a hard time accepting anything that to him is out of the ordinary or unlikely. I've been trying to convince him for a couple of months now of a theory I have. In fact, it's the same case I was working last night, but he doesn't put any stock into it."

"Thank you, Inspector. I'll keep that in mind. I'm glad to have met you as well."

The two walked out onto the street and hailed a cab to take them to the Yard for the interview with the chief inspector.

Chapter 3

Back at Scotland Yard, the chief inspector sat quietly behind his desk and eyed Stephens for some moments as if trying to discern what to make of the ranger that had fallen into his lap before finally asking his business. Stephens had requested that Jones be allowed to sit in on the interview with the chief inspector since he had already been of assistance to him. Jones didn't argue when the chief inspector agreed and sat at the strictest attention so as not miss a word of the next part of the story.

"There is a man," Stephens began, "that I believe is in your country who is desperately wanted in mine for several years' worth of crimes that would hang him every day for a month. It's been some months now since he disappeared from Texas, but there were delays picking up his trail and then following its unsteady direction here."

Before he could say another word, the chief asked in a half unbelieving tone, "What such evil person could have brought a Texas Ranger all the way to England? And why not a federal agent if he is wanted by your country and not just your state?"

Stephens looked hard into the chief's eyes and replied, "A Comanchero."

The chief stared blankly for a moment. "A *Com-an-cher-o*? What in heaven's name is a Comanchero?"

"The term *Comanchero*, Chief Inspector," replied Stephens, "for more than a century has referred to men who trade and have dealings with the Comanche Indian tribe of Texas and Mexico. When I say 'trade,' I'm not saying it is the most honest and pleasant profession, but it caused little enough trouble until a few decades ago. The Comanche were getting ever bolder and making bigger, bloodier raids as a result of their territory being crowded by whites.

"Then Comancheros became even less saintly and started supplying guns and liquor and anything else they could get the Indians to pay for with money and valuables taken from white victims. The trade stopped, and an evil business of blood money started. So, there were not only Indians raiding the settlements but whites riding with them and adding to the carnage rather than detracting from it. In my early years, I was part of several raids to hunt down and stop small groups of Comancheros that still existed, but there was always one that got away—the biggest one, as the saying goes."

Stephens paused to catch his breath and looked away toward the small fireplace in the corner. His next words were less matter-of-fact and more disdainful. For the first time, his cool professional air seemed to melt away, and evidence of some passion peered out of the hard lines of his face. Jones guessed that whatever he was about to say had a more personal bearing on him that he was struggling to suppress. At length, he continued very coldly and still looking at the small fire.

"A man named Richard Shelby is the most dangerous, ruthless, and prosperous of the Comancheros that I have ever come across. As I told Jones here earlier, I believe he comes from the northeast of the United States and probably from a more well-to-do family, though what he or his family is and what brought him to Texas I don't know and really don't care. He was known to friends and enemies alike as Rico, I'm sure to sound more Spanish and fitting to that part of the country, but though he lived and looked as mangy as all the rest, there was no denying that he was more intelligent and clever than the others.

"He dealt guns and liquor, rustled horses and cattle, but also raided small settlements and the villages of other tribes and traded slaves to the Comanche. My father caught a bullet in his right leg during a raid on a new town he was delivering supplies to. The point is that this same man managed to escape from Texas just before one last raid that I led nearly a year ago and used his riches to cross the south of the country to the East Coast and took a ship to England. As I said, it has been some months before I could follow him, and he didn't exactly travel a straight line, but I wouldn't be surprised if he is still here in England somewhere and quite at home given his background and abilities."

He reached into his coat and produced a stack of folded papers that he handed to the chief inspector. They included a circular or wanted poster that described Richard Shelby and his crimes, as well as warrants for his arrest from the Texas Rangers and the United States Marshal's office and letters granting Wayne Stephens permission to pursue this criminal and requesting the assistance of Scotland Yard and any other authorities in this pursuit.

"This is all very intriguing," said the chief inspector, "but again, I ask why they have sent you."

"Because I know him best," answered Stephens. "Very few people have ever gotten a good look at him and lived to tell about it. I've seen him twice at a short distance and could recognize his features. Also, I've tracked and fought him and his gang long enough to recognize his actions. And my superiors know I won't stop."

Jones was all but hypnotized by this tale, and the chief inspector looked less doubtful, if not fully concerned.

"I suppose you came here to ask for assistance of my inspectors in trying to find this villain. I don't know whom I can spare that would be useful to you."

The chief inspector didn't really want to spare anyone. All his inspectors had plenty of work to do, and as dangerous as the ranger made this villain sound, the chief inspector could not see some Yankee yokel being any more of a nuisance than any other common low-life criminal wandering through the streets. He was on the verge of regretfully declining the ranger's request when his thoughts were interrupted.

"If you don't mind," said Stephens, "I'll take Jones here. I'm already acquainted with him, and I can tell that he's not the kind to give up easily."

Jones sat stupefied at this sudden statement concerning him. Fascination fell from him and turned to dismay in the face of being distracted from the case he had concentrated so hard on, a case that might solidify his position and reputation for ability within the Yard. He was about to protest, but before he could make a sound, the chief inspector started speaking again.

"He certainly never tires of annoying me with silly ideas about the grime of London starting to ally themselves together in operation, that's certain."

This hadn't occurred to him before. There was certainly plenty of other work that Jones could do besides chase shadows. Any number of cases that had been neglected due to the heavy workload would suffice to stem the flow of his annoying theories and possibly show him what it really meant to be an inspector. However, if he assigned him to the ranger, then that would potentially keep both of them out of his hair for the time being; he didn't doubt that this ranger would also prove to be a nuisance in his own way. They might even manage to scrape up a criminal or two of some sort in the process.

With these thoughts running through his head, he looked back into the eyes of the ranger. "You can have him."

"Thank you, sir," Stephens replied and got up to leave.

Chapter 4

As they walked out of the chief inspector's office, Jones's mind and emotions were whirling, but anger was gradually beginning to overtake fascination and wonder. As much as he had come to like Stephens in their short association, he resented someone, anyone, who so randomly and casually commandeered his time and energy. He had important work to attend to and a person of interest to interrogate, and he made his thoughts known.

"Now look here, Stephens," he said as they walked down the hall, "I appreciate your help last night, and I have greatly enjoyed your company and your conversation up to now, but you have overstepped your bounds! I have my own job to do and cases to pursue, and I can't spend all my time wandering all over the country on your wild goose chase when there are already enough domestic criminals for me to deal with. Now, I don't mind giving you some advice and maybe some pointers on how to go about your business here, but you…"

Stephens had turned to face Jones and calmly interrupted his tongue-lashing with a raised hand.

"Jones, you are right," he said shortly. "I'd be upset too if some stranger came up and borrowed me without so much as a by-your-leave, but I had to act before your chief inspector made up his mind against it. I see what you mean about his frame of mind, and he didn't act like he cared for the idea any more than you do. And what I said was true, I do think you would be helpful and unrelenting. The fact that you knowingly keep annoying your boss is proof of that. Now, I am going to get Shelby, if not here, then somewhere else, but nothing short of getting killed is going to stop me. But the world isn't going to end if I don't get him by this afternoon. So you help me if you can, and I'll try to help you if I can."

Jones's anger was now ebbing, and bafflement was on him again at what he heard. "I appreciate your understanding, and I appreciate your generous offer. Frankly, it's more than I've gotten from just about anyone else around here, but how in blazes are you going to help me?"

"I don't know," said Stephens. "I won't know what I can do until things start happening. To begin with, I assume that you're doing to talk to that skunk you brought in last night?" Jones couldn't help but grin at the ranger.

"Yes, I was," he said, "as soon as I had seen to you and the chief inspector, I was going to see if he was awake and ready to talk."

"Fine then!" Stephens replied. "Let's go shake him up and see what we can get."

"All right," Jones said, grinning, "but don't knock him out again. I don't want to have to wait another day to get at him."

"Ha!" Stephens said with a bigger grin, and they made their way toward the detention cells with Jones telling Stephens more details about what he knew and hypothesized.

All sorts of small crooks and lowlifes had been spotted infrequently and randomly interacting. Most just attributed this to unexplainable criminal behavior, but to Jones, it seemed that much more was going on. In large part, many of the criminals involved in these meetings would ordinarily never have anything to do with each other, either within their criminal trades or personally. Bookies like Miller, con artists, suspected forgers, pickpockets, and just about every other sort of crook was interacting at some point or another. And while they were still operating independently, it was not with the consistency or volume they had exhibited in the past. It was almost as if it were just a pastime or hobby.

Miller's debts, it was discovered, had been clearing up, and so it was suspected that large sums of money were likewise being dealt out to these others. Without such a need for money, most of these types were content to sit in their squalor and make merry until the money ran out or they wanted an extra bit of fun. It was hoped that enough information could be siphoned out of Miller to point Jones to the next clue in figuring out where this money is coming from and what it's for. It had taken five confirmed sightings of different criminals known to be taking part in these meetings frequenting Miller's betting hole to justify concentrating on him.

"Whatever part Miller is playing in this, he is still just a small fish," said Jones, "he's not nearly bright enough to be any sort of brains in this business. But if we can get him to let just a little information slip, then we might know where to look next. The trouble is that he is as stubborn as he is dumb."

Stephens thought for a second before commenting, "He may be dumb, but all the crooks I've ever seen have had some amount of pride in them, they almost have to in order to survive. Maybe with a little bit of fear and confusion, we can work that against him."

Jones pondered this for a moment. "I think I follow you," he said, "but how do you propose that we do it?"

Stephens conferred with him for a few minutes, and then they merrily made their way toward the detention block. When the two of them walked into Miller's cell, they saw him sitting on his bunk with his head in his hands. He lifted it when they entered, and they saw that there was a bump on his head and some bruising on his jaw. Stephens stood quietly and coldly in the corner of the room just staring at Miller while Jones sat down on the other end of the bunk to address him.

"Miller, last night, I only wanted to talk to you and try to reason with you about whatever new trouble you're getting yourself into, but now you've assaulted multiple police officers. You put yourself in this fix, but now maybe you can help yourself out of some of it. Tell me what you can about this organization of criminal meetings. I know you know what I'm talking about, and several of the criminals we've observed have frequented your place. Now please do yourself a favor and talk."

Miller had been looking at the ranger through most of this, but now he looked at Jones, and it was fairly evident that this appeal had been received much the same as the one the night before.

"What you think you know ain't no concern of mine, and my business ain't none o' yours. I don't care what other people do either unless they owe me money or get in my way. I ain't got nuttin' to tell ya." He turned himself away from Jones and crossed his arms to signify that he would say no more. Then he glanced at the ranger, who had very calmly reached inside his coat and pulled out his thin leather gloves and was carefully putting them on.

Jones put a hand on Miller's arm and tried again. "Don't you understand that this is bigger than you can imagine? And when it does finally crack, they'll most likely put everyone involved away for the rest of their lives. You'll never see beyond a stone wall as long as you live!"

Miller paused after he heard this, but then he rallied himself again.

"You ain't gonna bluff me, Yard bird," he said. "I may have to sit 'ere a few days for knocking over you and your coppers, but I got the time and the money for a fine, so just you go jump in the river and leave me be."

He didn't have to sit there for long. Stephens had come to life after this final denial, and with a couple of long steps, he reached and grabbed Miller by the collar, jerked him up, and pinned him to the wall. Stephens's face was growing red with impatience and some anger that this nitwit was getting in his way.

"I've had enough of this puffed-up horn toad!" he declared and began to shake Miller as he spoke. "You are going to tell us whatever we want to know, or I'll break your jaw this time and anything else I need to. We've got a job to do and much bigger fish to catch, and I won't waste any more time on an idiot like you, so whatever happens to you now is your own fault." He swung Miller around to the other wall and raised that same fist he had used the night before when Jones jumped into the mix.

"Stop, wait a minute!" Jones shouted. "He can't help that he's a buffoon. If you knock him out again, we'll just be that more lost."

"I'm not going to knock him out," Stephens replied, "he's going to be awake for everything I give him unless he goes to sleep for good."

Miller's face reflected his instant horror, and again Jones voiced his objection.

"If you kill him, then that will just make things worse, not better. I may be wrong all together about this. He's so stupid he probably doesn't have the capacity to be involved in anything so big." Jones turned away a moment and rubbed the back of his neck, then he turned back dejected. "I should've known he wouldn't know anything," he said. "Whoever is behind all this wouldn't rely on such a blockhead for anything important."

Jones put out a hand and took hold of Stephens's raised arm, and Stephens looked at him in mock disappointment.

"Come on," Jones said, "let's go find someone smarter to talk to, he's useless to us."

After a few seconds, Stephens relaxed his shoulders and lowered his arm and turned on one foot in reluctant submission. But then they were paused by Miller's voice. During all the dialogue between the two lawmen, Miller's fright had given way to indignation. Buffoon, idiot, blockhead, useless, and whatever a horn toad was, no one called him that, not even coppers, and he would have the last word yet. His pride asserted itself, and his voice rang as he spoke.

"Ha! You coppers think you're so smart, eh? Hehehehe. Call me stupid, will ya? I can tell you that no one else in jolly ol'

London would've thought of putting that new code into betting slips!"

Miller was grinning with his arms crossed again, and his chin held high when Stephens and Jones turned to look at him. Miller saw that they too were grinning from ear to ear, like a couple of schoolboys.

"Code," said Stephens.

"Betting slips," said Jones.

Miller looked at each of them, his countenance fallen, and then sank onto the bunk cursing himself. Pride and stupidity had won out, and now he was committed to talk whether he liked it or not. At this point, he could say nothing else and would still be labeled as a snitch and a traitor—Jones would see to that. So even Miller realized that now he must help himself all he could.

Chapter 5

Miller told his secret with a broken spirit. Random people would come to see him every couple of weeks or so and give him messages to give to other people whom he would be able to identify. The messages came to him in two or three pieces, and when he had them all, he would work them into a betting slip for the person who received it. The slip would have the supposed name of the bettor, supposed name of a horse, and amounts and odds for a supposed race. Large amounts of money were delivered to Miller for these services, and after the slips were handed off, he never knew anything else about them.

"I was told that last night the messenger wouldn't come to me, so I had to go to him. I was just going 'ome when you jumped me."

"Where did you go, and who did you see, Miller?" asked Jones.

"Just down to the docks," Miller answered. "I met a bloke named Thatcher, Gil Thatcher. 'E didn't say much, just made sure of who I was, took the paper, and told me to get outta there and go 'ome."

"What was on the paper?" asked Stephens.

"The name was Franklin, the horse's name was Shooting Star, the amount was 52, and the odds were 7-3," replied Miller.

Those were somewhat irregular numbers, and if that was the code for the organization, then heaven only knew what it stood for. In any event, that was all the help Miller could give.

"I'll check with some other inspectors and their sources and see what I can find out about this Gil Thatcher. If I come up with anything, I'll come for you," said Jones to Stephens.

"That's fine with me," replied Stephens. "If I'm not there, you can either wait or leave word with the landlady, and I'll meet you. I think I'm going to try to get a little more sleep—I still haven't caught up on what I lost on that darn ship—and then run an errand. On second thought, why don't you just figure on coming by around five o'clock, and we'll see what we have?"

Jones agreed, and they parted company.

That afternoon, Jones arrived at Stephens's boarding house a little before five o'clock and was told that he was still out. He had left around two o'clock to go to the shipping office to check their records. Supposedly, that was the errand he had spoken off. He didn't waste any time trying to find the trail of his fugitive, but the odds were probably against his digging up anything in that mountain of records books. Jones had gone up to Stephens's room to wait for him, but once he got inside, a very curious sensation came over him as he looked around the room. Whether it was the investigative nature he had developed or just his own nature curiosity about this whole happenstance, he felt incredibly nosy.

On the bed, a suitcase was laid open, and another one stood upright against the wall, and the door on the wardrobe was cracked open. He crossed the room and peeked inside the wardrobe first and saw another suit hanging up and a pair of old, tall boots. The suit was similar to the one that Stephens had been wearing, but was brown instead of dark gray. The boots, however, were not so stylish and in fact were very worn with age and hard use. Jones was usually a thorough man, but he was also in a bit of a hurry in this instance and moved back to the bed. If he had bothered to look inside the boots, he would've found a five-point cowboy spur in each boot, as well as a fair-sized knife with a keen edge and a stag handle. In the open suitcase was another pair of pants, a couple of white shirts, and few other usual items of clothing. All the grooming supplies, he saw lying on the washstand at the other end of the room—a razor, soap mug, comb, etc.

That just left the other suitcase, and slowly Jones stepped over, picked it up, and laid it on the bed. There were a few muffled clanks as he set it down. The clanks made him start for a moment. The strange noises heightened his curiosity still further, but it also roused his conscience. He had paused with the same anxiety of being heard and discovered that burglars must experience. Jones couldn't believe what he was doing; it was unprofessional, intrusive, and offensive. He also felt a twinge of disloyalty. Stephens was a guest in the country and a fellow policeman of sorts, and in the last twenty-four hours, he felt he had already developed a close friendship to the ranger as well. But even that did not stop him; he had started his examination and he would finish it.

When he opened the second suitcase, the first thing he perceived was a large-brimmed gray hat. At least, it looked like a light gray or maybe sandy-colored; it was certainly faded from its original color, as well as being badly battered, bent, and beaten. It was inside a slight wooden frame that protected it from any further damage inside the suitcase. Folded beside the hat frame was a faded-red bibbed shirt that must've been a bright crimson at one point in time. Also, there was a pair of black pants in similar condition that were made of a thicker, tougher material than the suit. Jones carefully pulled these out and set them on the bed. Underneath these he found what had caused the clanking. He perceived the parts of a dismantled double-barreled shotgun: the butt stock and action, the fore stock, and the barrels. But these barrels had been shortened. They couldn't have been much over one and a half feet long, much shorter than the guns Jones used for hunting.

Also, inside the suitcase were two drawstring canvas bags. Inside one of two bags he discovered Stephens's pistol, an 1873 Colt Peacemaker as he would find out, with a barrel just over five inches long and inside a holster and belt that were cared for but still showed years of hard use like the boots. The belt looked to hold a couple dozen cartridges, and there was also a full box of cartridges marked Winchester .44 WCF. In the other bag was another box full of twelve-gauge shotgun cartridges and two sets of heavy shackles, one set for wrists and the other for ankles, which had also contributed to the clanking. If Stephens ever did find this Shelby character, he was taking no chances of him escaping. All this had been padded on a long, faded-white overcoat or duster that was split up the back so as to be worn while riding a horse.

All these items set Jones's mind in a whirlwind. There was no doubt in his mind that these items and clothes when worn hid the polite, proper, friendly man that Jones was acquainted with and made him the real ranger that had fought and bled in the dust and sun of the wild Texas frontier. Or was it the other way around? Did the suits, small black hat, gloves, and other niceties that he had chosen to wear on his trip across the world help to amplify a more pleasant version of a wild adventurer? Every piece of regalia he saw and touched must have a dozen stories to tell, and his fascination was deeper than ever, but there was trouble in his mind also.

Why had these possessions been brought on such a long trip away from their origin and place of need? That question would need more time to be answered, but just then, the wheels of a coach and hooves of horses clattered outside, and Jones hastily but carefully put the room back to rights as he heard Stephens's footsteps on the stairs.

As he swung the heavy suitcase down off the bed to put it back in its original location, he accidentally pulled off one of the pillows from the head of the bed. He picked it up, and he noticed something that added to his jumble of curiosity: a small, black leather-bound Bible. Jones only had a couple of seconds to take it all in, but he noticed that true to form, it also was worn with use. The leather cover had infrequent dry cracks, and the pages were ruffled and appeared to be well thumbed. Then Jones threw the pillow back into place on top of it as Stephens entered the room.

Stephens and Jones sat across the table from each other, eating a small supper where they had eaten breakfast that morning. Jones remembered that it was better to wait until the meal was finished to talk, and when it was, he asked about Stephens's activities.

"I went to the shipping office this afternoon to see if I could rummage through their records and see if I could find the trail of where and when that snake Shelby came here," answered Stephens to the inquiry. "I had to try, but it was practically pointless. I don't have any definite idea of when he might have arrived or what of ship he came on, except I think it was what you call an Indiaman.

It was all I could do to find out that he came here in the first place. I read over records and passenger lists and tried to find anyone who might have some information when I was wasn't being quizzed about who I am."

He ended with a look of frustration, but he recovered quickly, and Jones took his cue.

"Well, cheer up," Jones said, "I've had a little more luck on my end. I've found out that this Gil Thatcher is a fairly prominent figure in the criminal community. He's virtually a thug for hire, very respected and feared by most who know of him, and he works for the highest bidder. He spends a lot of time around the river and the docks, but for the right price, he would go almost anywhere and do almost anything. If there is someone shelling out a lot of money for odd jobs, they probably wouldn't have much trouble recruiting him."

"Is there a way to find him and talk to him?" Stephens asked.

Jones looked at him sternly and answered.

"I understand that he likes to spend time down at O'Malley's tavern on the wharf, and most likely that's where he can be found if he's not on a job. But O'Malley's isn't a very savory place, in fact it can be bloody dangerous for police if they're not in force. Also, Thatcher is nothing like Miller. He's cold and hard and a very dangerous devil in his own right. We would probably have to raid the place to lay our hands on him, and even then, we would never get anything out of him."

Stephens had listened carefully to what he was told, and now he spoke very deliberately. "Who says we would have to announce ourselves as lawmen when we go down there? If we want to hire him for a job and can get him away, then we might be able to shake something out of him then."

Jones's eyes had grown large as he heard this idea and was very reluctant with his answer, but he must say it.

"I don't want you to think me a coward," Jones began, "but this might be going too far. The risk of going down there alone and trying to lure him away is enormous. One mistake and our bodies would probably be fished out of the Thames next week. I desperately want answers to our questions, you know that, but I don't think it justifies braving that viper's nest. And even if we did, we would still have to be able to make Thatcher talk. There must be another way to go about this."

"None that I can think of," Stephens replied. "And I'm sure we would lose a lot of precious time trying to. I don't begrudge you for being mindful of the danger, but if I have to walk into a wolf den to get what I need, then I'm going, and they'll pay a high price to stop me."

Based on what Jones had just found in the ranger's room, he could well believe it. In the end Jones relented and agreed to go that evening and went home. A few hours later, he reappeared in Stephens's room. He had tried to rough up his appearance a little, and Stephens had changed into his brown suit and made similar modifications to aid them in their excursion to O'Malley's tavern.

Chapter 6

The two lawmen had taken a cab most of the way to their destination, but as they neared the general area, they alighted and continued on foot. When they got close to the tavern, they saw the glowing light through the windows and could hear the singing and laughing of men having their good times. After a pause and a deep breath Stephens opened the door, and the two of them walked in. A few people who were scattered around close to the door stared at them and mumbled as they came in, but all the rest seemed to take no notice. They made their way over to the bar and waited on the bartender. When he finally turned his attention to them, he considered them a moment before asking their preference.

"We'll just have a couple of beers to start off with mate," said Jones, putting a little more *street* into his voice.

"You're strange around here, aren't ya? I don't remember serving up for you before," said the bartender guardedly as he sat down the mugs.

"Yeah, we just came up the river this morning. Had some ideas for some new business ventures to try here in the big city. To that end, we've got a job that needs doing to get things moving, and we heard we might find a bloke in here that would do it for us," answered Jones, trying to be as cool as possible.

"Oh really," replied the bartender, "and just who might you be a lookin' for to do this job?"

"A fella by the name of Gil Thatcher," replied Jones. "The word is that he would do anything for those that would pay him proper."

The bartender had stepped back a pace, and the room had grown more silent at the mention of that name. Jones and Stephens looked around the room in innocent surprise, and then a tall, lean, hard-looking man stood up from a back table and strode toward them with heavy boots hitting the floor.

Stephens and Jones stared at the man as he came to a stop in front of them.

"Who gave you leave to speak my name?" he asked in a very rough and demanding voice.

"I take it you are, Mr. Thatcher," replied Jones.

"Of course, I am," answered the man, "now who the devil are you, and what do you want?"

Stephens had kept silent up to this point, allowing Jones to do as he thought best, but now he took his turn to speak, and there was no hiding his distinct American accent.

"Who we are ain't important right now," Stephens answered and matching Thatcher's tone. "This ain't a social meeting. What matters is we got a job to get done, and we were told that you're the guy to get it done. Now we're willin' to pay what it costs if you're interested. If you are, then maybe we can start giving details."

Thatcher's mood did not improve at this, and he glared at the ranger. "And just who was it that told you about me Yank?"

"Your reputation is well-known around here," replied Jones. "It didn't take much asking to find out about you."

"Yeah," said Stephens, "a big name with a big price, which we'll pay if it's worth it. Do you want it or not?"

Thatcher clinched his fists and roared at the two strangers in front of him. "Look here, you. I do what I want when I want, and nobody, especially a stinking Yank, is going to come in here and try to boss me. And if you can't tell me who sent you, then you ain't worth my time. Now get outta here both of yas before I break your necks!"

"We didn't mean no offense, Mr. Thatcher," Jones hastily replied before Stephens said something to make a tactical retreat less possible. "If you should change your mind, we won't be hard to find."

"I doubt he has much of a mind to change," said Stephens as he grudgingly walked behind Jones toward the door. Then with a thud, a knife stuck into the wall about a foot in front of Stephens's face.

"That's just a reminder, Yank, not to be sticking your big nose where it don't belong."

Jones turned around to look at Stephens, and what he saw made him more afraid than he had been. The ranger's eyes were ablaze! He stood stiff as a board, and Jones saw something of the frontier fighter awaking inside those eyes. Stephens very calmly and deliberately reached out and jerked the knife out of the wall. Then he took a few steps just as calmly toward Thatcher and let out a small laugh.

"Well now," he said, "I thank you kindly for the warning. Would you like to have this back?"

"Sure," answered Thatcher, "just put it on the table there and then be gone." Thatcher was leaning against a pillar in the middle of the room and raised a mug off a table to take a pull from it after he spoke.

Stephens stared at the man intently. Every step he had taken toward that door to leave had gone against the grain. To run from a situation like this was not in him; he had been forced to fight against all odds all his life, but this was not his home, and he had yielded to Jones's lead. However, now there was no backing down from this miserable weasel. The insults would not be swallowed, and satisfaction, as well as information, would be had. While Thatcher was speaking, Stephens had been weighing the knife in his hand, and as Thatcher lifted his arm to drink, Stephens raised the knife and sharply flung it toward Thatcher. The point sank into the pillar an inch and a half below his arm and pinned the bottom of his shirt sleeve to the wood.

Stephens had no illusions as to what reaction this would cause. He knew what would come, and his hot blood lusted for it in indignation. Everyone in the room sprang to their feet, and as soon as the knife hit the pillar, Stephens grabbed a bottle from the table in front of him and crashed it into the bartender's head to eliminate any surprises from behind the bar. Then the charge came, and all restraint was lifted in Stephens's mind.

There was a wall behind him, the bar beside him, and tables in front of him. The attack was not concentrated, and one after another, enemies met with fists, knees, and feet. For every blow that managed to reach Stephens, he dealt out three in return. Fists met jaw, nose, and belly; knees met belly, chest, and face; and no action needed to survive was withheld. One man passed Stephens's guard and tried to cover his face with a hand so as to give his friends an advantage. Stephens managed to put a hand behind the man's neck to brace him, and he brought down his other elbow with a crack into the man's collarbone, and the man fell out of the fray with a cry.

Jones had not been standing idle during all this, for he had seen as clearly as Stephens what must happen and would happen. He could've done nothing to avert it, so he set his feet and prepared for the storm to come. He had boxed some in school and had competed for the championship. That skill now served him well as he sent one assailant after another to the floor in his own defense, but most of the brawlers were concentrating on the ranger, and from the glances that Jones stole of his partner's defense, he marveled.

A lull came in the storm as everyone collectively paused for breath and rest before the second wave. It didn't take long for the enemy to collect themselves, and now every man who was still able to fight or had not yet made it to the front line of battle collected with any weapon he could get. Thatcher stood in front with a bleeding mouth and his knife in his hand and started to signal the attack when Stephens threw up his hands in mock surrender.

"Wait a minute now, fellas," he said lightly while still breathing heavy and wiping a drop of blood from his own lip. "Let's talk this out a minute, maybe we just got off on the wrong foot, is all."

The men of the tavern didn't know what this Yank thought he was doing, and they didn't care, but they would be entertained by his bargaining before they finished him. Neither did Jones understand what Stephens was doing, but he figured that any stall was an advantage.

"You know," Stephens continued, "I have a bad temper, and sometimes silly little things just set me off before I know what I'm doing."

In a very carefree manner, he reached and pulled aside his jacket with his left hand and casually reached for his vest with his right. He was reaching for the string of a tobacco pouch, and in an instant Jones wondered to himself. He could not recall the ranger ever smoking or chewing tobacco, and he had not smelt it on him, so he watched with the others.

"I've learned," went on Stephens, "that sometimes to get what you want you just have to sit and talk things out."

His hand had reached the string, but as he said these last words, his hand shot past the string into his jacket and in the blink of an eye reemerged with a pistol at full arms' length, pointing inches from Thatcher's forehead. Every person in the room heard their own heart beating, and the room reverberated with the loud clicks as Stephens cocked the hammer and Thatcher's knife fell and clattered on the floor. The pistol was just like the one Jones had discovered earlier, except that it was shorter by a couple of inches and had a smaller curved grip.

Now Stephens addressed Thatcher with authority, "Your party here is over, Thatcher. Now you're coming with us out into the street for a nice long chat, and if I smell one whiff of trouble from you or the rest of these stinking coyotes, I swear I'll blow your puny brains out."

Chapter 7

Hot and cold battled in that instant. Thatcher's own hot blood and hot temper still blazed, but at the same time, the cold chill of fear entered him. He was in disbelief at this turn of events. Not for years had anyone dared to so oppose him like this. He had built a reputation of ability, of strength and of fear, and his very name had become a weapon. Now this Yank and his friend had directly opposed him and fought him with odds that he himself would never bet on. As he very closely viewed the cold, dark, metallic eye that held him captive, he looked beyond it into the eyes of the man that held it and perceived their still-smoldering passion and resolution. This man was no quivering farm hand or dock worker that was trying to rally a drop of courage in desperation; this man was a fighter, and Thatcher knew that the man meant what he said.

"Who the devil are you?" Thatcher hissed out of his clenched teeth as he struggled to suppress himself for his own good.

"I'm a Texas Ranger!" Stephens announced in defiant pride. "I've come a long way to finish something that's a heck of a lot bigger and more important than you, and I've dealt with too many of your kind to let you stand in the way of our progress."

Stephens then stepped forward, jammed the muzzle of the gun under Thatcher's ribs, and grabbed his collar to drag him outside.

Jones had taken half a second to take in what Stephens did and believe it before he reacted in kind. He had whipped out his own small revolver he always carried. He had needed and used the thing so little since his days of training that he mostly went about in a state of forgetfulness about its existence, but now he was grateful of its presence as he trained it on his half of the room.

Thatcher let himself be rousted outside, and Jones backed out the door to cover their departure. They were making for an alley that pointed in the general direction they needed to go to get back to the more lawful part of the city when a shout arrested them. Some ill-guided friend of Thatcher's had thrown open the door of the tavern and yelled out, "YANK!" while brandishing an old harpoon that he had yanked off the tavern wall.

All three watched in the light of the open door as the silhouette of the man took his stance to throw the thing when, with a fluid and natural motion, Stephens swung his arm out, took half a second's aim with the short pistol, and squeezed the slender trigger. The hummer struck, a small explosion erupted, and a .44-caliber bullet whizzed out and carved a trench along the outer side of the man's left thigh.

The harpoon rang on the cobblestones, and the man sank down, clasping his bloody leg. The trio had no more trouble from the tavern and proceeded down the alley. They went several blocks in the darkness before Stephens stopped and put Thatcher up against the brick wall of one of the buildings around them.

"All right now, Thatcher," Stephens began, "We know that your people have been going in and out of Miller's place to get betting slips. We also know that the slips are actually codes for some sort of organized operation. And you should know that when we bring this organization down, no one that is found to be a part of it will have much chance of ending their days in the free world. Now, what is the code? What does the information on the slips tell you?"

Despite what had happened to him, Thatcher did not believe that this ranger would kill him in cold blood for not answering a question. No one in his right mind would risk being shot in the head by someone whom he had practically tried to kill, not even Thatcher. But now that danger was gone, and so was part of Thatcher's high standing in consequence of him somehow allowing himself to be hauled out like a child. For his own sake, if nothing else, he must at least try to salvage his own opinion of himself. He assumed his own defiant attitude to make his reply.

"You may think you know whatever you like, but I don't make bets with that fool Miller. He doesn't know his head from his…"

Stephens had looked away from Thatcher in irritation as he perceived the denial, and now with a loud *smack*, he slapped Thatcher like a horse's rump with his left hand.

"I thought I had made it clear that I don't have the time to waste with your rubbish," Stephens said. "Now save all of us some time and aggravation, and tell us what the code means."

Thatcher rubbed his already-sore jaw and glared at Stephens. "You think that just like that I'm going to roll over and tell you something that would cost me my life if it was discovered? Go figure it out for yourself!" Thatcher had just uttered these last words as Stephens, in ever-growing aggravation, swung his left hand back in the other direction and backhanded the other side of Thatcher's face. The thin leather glove did nothing to soften the impact of the knuckles that briefly skidded across the skin of Thatcher's cheek.

Jones stood rigid and watchful while Thatcher held the other side of his face with clenched teeth. That last blow had thrown him off balance, and a fresh drop of blood ran from his mouth.

"I'll try one more time, Thatcher. What in thunder does that lousy code tell you?"

"It tells me where you can go roast yourself!"

With that comment, Stephens swung his right arm, and the top strap of his pistol was buried into Thatcher's stomach, and he crumpled down to his knees, coughing and gasping for air.

"You don't seem to understand that you're worried about the wrong people right now," Stephens said. "Now, what in blazes does that code mean?"

Stephens was still in his fierce mood, and Jones was getting worried that he might lose control altogether. Jones was not an advocate of these rough-and-tough methods that he had seen used in the past, but he could not deny that sometimes in situations such as these, they were necessary and useful. However, this was a very irregular situation.

Thatcher was finally getting his wind back, and he growled at Stephens, "I'm not going to tell you a bloody thing, you filthy cowboy!"

Then he spit on Stephens's boot. Jones saw that Stephens was about to go off on him again and quickly stepped in.

"You could be a dead man either way, Thatcher," he said. "I'm a Scotland Yard inspector, and just for what you've done here tonight, I could probably push for a death sentence for you and the others back there. And once we do break down this organization, then your part in it will just make it that much more certain. So if you want to salvage what little bit of your life that you can, then tell us what you know. Otherwise, prepare yourself to do the hempen jig!"

At last Thatcher's countenance fell a little, and he started to give thought to his own future. After a minute's pause, he limply sat back against the wall as if the last of his strength were drained from him, and he started to talk softly.

"The *Shooting Star* isn't a horse but a ship, the name of the horse is always a ship. The name of the bettor is the name of a contact onboard, and the odds are the numbers of crates we're supposed to take off. I was waiting for a contact to come tell me when the ship was due in and where I could find it. I would get some mates and go out before dawn to get the cargo."

This was a very clean business. Merchandise was being stolen off ships in the middle of the night, no one knew anything specific until the last minute, and no one knew more than was absolutely necessary to fulfill their personal role. And everyone was paid so well that they didn't care or ask questions. That was about all to be accomplished that night as it was too late to find out anything about the *Shooting Star*. So they got Thatcher to his feet, went a few more blocks, and then hailed a cab to take them to the nearest constable's station to deposit Thatcher until morning.

As they stepped back out onto the street, they paused, and Stephens almost shyly looked at Jones before speaking.

"You handled yourself very well back there," he said. "That turned into a very sticky situation, and at the time, I wasn't sure how it was going to turn out."

"Well, you didn't exactly encourage a happy ending," Jones replied.

"Yeah, I know," said Stephens. "I try to remember that I'm not back home, but I've seen Thatcher's in every bar room and trail herd from Galveston to El Paso, and I'll guarantee you that no ranger would put up with that trash. I'm sorry for putting you in that spot all the same, and I hope you don't think of me as a troublemaker."

Jones just looked at him. He hadn't been sure what to think. Stephens was intelligent and certainly capable, but he could display a different nature that could be frightening. Nevertheless, Jones knew that Stephens was a good man and knew his worth, and now that he had returned to his normal temperament, Jones could not be upset with him.

"No, I don't," Jones said. "You're rough and tough, but you're good, and we've made more progress in the last two days than I've made in a month. Look, it's been a long night, and we both could use some rest. I'll drop you off, and then in the morning, come to my house around eight o'clock and have breakfast."

Stephens, despite his tough exterior, had actually been somewhat anxious about what this inspector thought of him, as a colleague and as a friend. He had become even fonder of Jones in light of the scuffle in the tavern and didn't want to lose his confidence, but Jones's words gave him comfort, and the ranger gladly accepted the invitation.

Chapter 8

The next morning Stephens arrived at the address Jones had given him, and he tapped on the door with the figurative brass knocker. It was a nice, cozy-looking little town house that seemed to fit Jones in Stephens's opinion. He was still thinking this when the door opened and instead of Jones Stephens found himself facing a very handsome woman who was smiling at him.

"Yes?" she asked.

For a second Stephens paused in confusion; he was sure that the house number and street were what Jones had scribbled and almost started to pull out the scrap of paper when good sense reasserted itself. He must look ridiculous to this woman who was still smiling at him.

He wiped the silly look off his face and hastily removed his hat. "Oh, I'm sorry, ma'am," he said. "I thought I was at the house of Mr. Caleb Jones." He almost hadn't remembered Jones's first name.

"Indeed you are," the woman replied cheerfully. "I'm Mrs. Emily Jones. And you must be Mr. Stephens, judging by your speech. Please come in."

Stephens let himself be ushered into a nice little sitting room and sat down on a soft, velvet padded armchair in turn after the lady.

"I'm sorry, Mrs. Jones," he said again, "you just caught me off guard. Jones…that is, Caleb…never mentioned that he had a wife."

Mrs. Emily Jones was about thirty years old, five feet four inches tall, and had luscious auburn hair and a natural kindness and familiarity that quelled Stephens's awkwardness after a short time.

"I'm not surprised," she replied. "And please, call me Emily or Emma if you like."

"Very well, Emma," said Stephens.

"When I was a little girl, my grandmother always called me Emma," she said. "No one ever really knew why, but she did, and so that's what I've always been called. You may not have heard of me, Mr. Stephens, but I've heard of you. You are all Caleb has talked about for two nights, and I've looked forward to meeting you myself."

Stephens actually blushed just a little and was wondering how to continue the interview when Jones came in the door.

"Emma," he was beginning, "I've gotten what you needed. Do you think…" He stopped short when he saw Stephens. "Good morning," he said. "We're running a little behind on breakfast, and I had to go get a few things."

"That's just fine," Stephens replied. "Your charming wife has kept me entertained."

Jones handed the bundle under his arm to his wife, and she went into the other room.

"I sent a message to the Yard about Thatcher," Jones said, "and they should've picked him up by now, but they won't go to the tavern until we've checked into Thatcher's story."

They hypothesized for a quarter of an hour about what was being stolen and the aims of the organization when Emma came in to announce that breakfast was ready. They sat down, and as usual, Stephens said very little until he had finished. Jones had warned his wife of this habit beforehand, and so she just continued to smile and only spoke to ask if he wanted this or needed that.

"A very fine meal, Mrs....Emma," said the ranger in complete honesty.

"Indeed it was, my dear," Jones agreed.

"Thank you both," she said. "And now after the table is cleared, maybe you boys can tell me the full story of what happened last night."

Emily Jones worried about her husband in his dangerous profession as any good wife should, but she was encouraging and had enough imagination to enjoy adventures. So when the table was cleared, she sat and listened to the full tale of their expedition to the tavern, confrontation with Thatcher, consequent battle, and the ultimate breaking of his defenses.

Emma shared her husband's fascination of the ranger, and after her internal chill had passed from hearing of last night's episode, she decided to probe him.

"A few years ago, my sister and her husband traveled to your nation's capital to visit some relatives who work at the embassy. While they were there, they met an Army officer who had served in Oklahoma, I think it was, and he told them of some events he had heard of in Texas at the time. It was something about one of your captains who went to Mexico."

Stephens smiled wide as he realized what she was referring to. "You mean Captain McNelly," he said. "He was in command of the special company that patrolled the Nueces Strip next to the Rio Grande. Now, Jones, that was a man that you wouldn't know what to think of. He didn't let anyone or anything stand in his way, including the government. He was after a particularly vicious gang of cattle rustlers and murders lead by King Fisher, or so he was called. McNelly chased him all over creation and wanted him so bad that he finally crossed the border into Mexico and attacked Fisher's ranch. He caught him and some of the worst with him and brought him back. What that officer probably heard was that he almost caused an international incident with Mexico in the process. I wasn't allowed to be in that company because he didn't want native Texans to flinch from possibly having to shoot other Texans who were in the gang."

For the next half hour, Stephens told about Captain McNelly's escapades and then about how a small group of rangers went all the way to Florida to bring back John Wesley Hardin. perhaps the most-feared and most-wanted gunfighter in Texas. Both Joneses sat in close attention to the tales until finally Stephens had to pause for breath. Then Emma could help herself any longer and followed her female inclinations.

"Do you have a wife and family back home, Mr. Stephens?" she asked.

Jones almost rolled his eyes since no one was looking at him, but Stephens just grinned slightly and glanced down as if recalling more memories.

"No, I don't," he replied, "I've never found the woman that could put up with me long enough to get married. Oh, I've had my share of romances over the years, I suppose, but nothing I could ever manage to tie down and hang on to."

"Do you have no one but your parents back home then?" Emma asked.

Jones had already told her all he knew of the ranger.

"No, not quite," Stephens replied. "I suppose the next thing I have to family is Kina."

Now both Joneses looked their curiosity at him—Emma, in her natural female thirst for knowledge about what she supposed to be a female name, and Jones, in surprise since he had assumed that what Stephens had already told him was all there was to know about his personal life. Their glances were almost pleading, and Stephens took a deep breath and indulged them.

"In 1874, I was one of four rangers accompanying a cavalry troop that was chasing a small band of renegade Comanches and Comancheros. We chased them to a small village by a stream about fifty miles from San Antonio, and the Army captain in command decided to raid the village. I was still a young ranger and didn't much care for the idea, but I did what I was told, and so we charged. I tried not to shoot any more than I could get away with since I could hardly see a soul much older than fifteen and very few men at all. Whether the renegades had missed the village or pulled out earlier, we didn't know, but we could make little sense of the mess afterward. I was rummaging through the furs and belongings around a half-fallen teepee when this girl popped up and started to dart off toward the stream. I just barely caught her wrist and had to wrestle her down to make her stay still. She was about ten years old, I figured out later, but she was as full of fire as a full-grown warrior.

"Now I'm not an Indian hater by any means. I respect them for the most part and have even become respected by a few of them, including Quanah Parker, their chief. But there was one ranger there who hated them with a passion, probably for some past tragedy that he couldn't get over, and at the sight of her, he raised his rifle. I pulled her around behind me, and when he didn't stand down, I pointed my own gun at him and would have shot him if he hadn't finally stormed off. This girl knew that I had protected her and so wasn't really an enemy. Her name is Tosa Tabukina, which means White Rabbit. When I looked at her face, I could tell that she wasn't all Comanche and also her eyes were hazel instead of dark, but her hair was still as black as a raven's wing. She must have been a half-breed from a white captive or a trader.

"I brought her back, and she stayed with me, when I was around, and my parents. It started out to just be temporary until I could arrange to give her back to her people, but it was a long, dangerous way to their territory, and I couldn't take her along on patrol, so she stayed. It was interesting, to say the least, trying to get her to wear white people's clothes, learn English, and going to school was a battle," he paused and laughed.

"I remember once, a few years later, when I came home from a patrol with the Army, the first thing I heard was that she had thrashed a couple of boys that were picking on her and her friend. Being a ranger, I guess I understood her as a Comanche a little better than my parents did. They were furious that a 'young lady' would behave that way, and they scolded her until her ears nearly bled from what she told me, but all I could do was laugh! One half-breed Comanche girl beat the daylights out of two dumb boys her same age." He laughed some more to himself, perhaps recalling more details in private and then continued.

"When she was eighteen, we told her that if she wanted to go back to the tribe, we wouldn't stop her, but she stayed. To the surprise of many people, she had come to love us as much as we loved her, and we were overjoyed at her decision. Now Kina is twenty-one and a more beautiful and charming young woman than you would find anywhere. I'm not really sure how to consider her, but I love her as if we shared the same blood. She was doing well when I left, but I'll be awfully glad to see her again."

They all sat silent for a moment as Stephens seemed to grow more melancholy at the end of his tale in spite of the glowing adoration he proclaimed. Finally, Jones broke the silence.

"Well, we can't just sit here all day. We've got to get to the shipping office and find out when that ship is due in that Thatcher talked about."

Stephens hastily got up, graciously thanked Emma for the meal and her hospitality, and expressed his hope that he might see her again, before they stepped onto the street.

Chapter 9

As they walked into the shipping office, the two investigators presented themselves and their business to the clerks who were busy at their desks scribbling on lists and record books and were promptly shown into the office of Mr. Somers, the manager. He showed a sign of faint recollection at the sight of Stephens since he had seen him the day before when Stephens came to peruse the shipping and passenger records. He seemed to be the kind of person who could easily forget things if they weren't immediately in front of him.

"How nice to see you again, Mr., eh, Stephens, yes." He was a good-natured red-faced man who rarely stayed still for long periods of time in his endeavor to maintain his busy office. "I'm sorry," he said in earnest, "but we haven't had the time to research the man you were seeking yesterday."

"That's all right, Mr. Somers," Stephens replied. "We've come on different business today."

"Oh, have you now? Then please, please be seated and tell me how I may be of assistance to you gentlemen."

They sat, and then Jones explained their business. "Mr. Somers, we're here to inquire about a ship that has come up in a case we're investigating, the *Shooting Star*. It only just came to our attention last night that it may be of interest to us."

Before Jones could finish his sentence, Somers was already out of his seat, fluttering around his office and sifting through stacks of papers.

"I know I just had it not a half hour ago," he said half to himself. Then, with a shout of triumph, he pulled out a stack of papers and laid it before Jones and Stephens. "I knew I had them close," Somers said. "The *Shooting Star* anchored last night, and her cargo was unloaded the very first thing this morning. I knew I had finished her paperwork not long before your arrival. She was part an East India convoy out of Calicut carrying military supplies."

"Mr. Somers," Stephens began, "according to our information, the people we're after are interested in a particular portion of cargo. Do the numbers 52, 7-3 mean anything to you? They may be in a different order."

Mr. Somers picked up the stack of papers and began to ruffle them in close scrutiny with much muttering and whispering.

At last, "Ahh, here we are. Those numbers correspond to lot 52, crates 3-7 of military stores for the West Yorkshire regiment newly returned from India."

"Can you be more specific about the contents?" asked Stephens.

"I'm afraid not," replied Somers. "The army packs and organizes their stores themselves, we just get general information to ensure the correct numbers reach their destination."

"Would it be possible to find these crates?" asked Jones.

"Possible, I suppose, but very problematic," replied Somers. "By now some of the crates may already be on their way to the regiment, and the rest are scattered throughout the docks. If you really want to find them, you would probably do better to go to the garrison yourselves and meet with the commander."

"That would make things less complicated, I suppose," replied Jones. "If we catch an earlier train, then we could be there tonight. When will the last of the cargo arrive at the garrison?"

"Oh, the last of it will most likely arrive by tomorrow afternoon sometime, but of course, there is no certainty," answered Mr. Somers.

"Well, if these crates haven't arrived before us, then we'll wait," declared Jones. "For all we know, the information could've still be passed along and other agents on their way to collect them."

"Entirely possible," Stephens agreed. "We need to get moving if we want to get there first. I can't see a setup like this not having a backup plan. Thank you again for your help, Mr. Somers, and if you should happen to find a trace of the information I need before I get back, I would be obliged if you would send me a wire. Good day, sir."

The three shook hands, and the two investigators made quick time in preparing to leave for West Yorkshire. Stephens had all his gear packed and ready to go in ten minutes, and after they collected a bag for Jones, they arrived at the station in time to make the eleven-forty train to their destination. During the journey, Jones managed to squeeze a few more stories out of Stephens about rustlers, bank robbers, Indian fights, Mexican bandits, and all sorts of tidbits about his career and life.

Now Stephens was busy regaling him with the history of the Parker family and old Fort Parker. How the parker family had built it the same year Texas had won its independence from Mexico and the circumstances that led to Quanah Parker now being chief of the Comanche. Young Cynthia Ann Parker had been kidnapped during an attack on the fort and adopted into the tribe. She grew up to become the wife of the then-chief Peta Nocona, and then Quanah was born as next in line to lead the tribe. This was all fascinating to Jones, and the talk of adopting the girl made him remember Stephens's behavior that morning. He decided to cast a line.

"Tell me more about this young lady you mentioned, this Tosa Tabukina." Stephens continued to look out the car window as it rumbled along, and it was some moments before he turned his head to answer.

"I'm not sure what else to tell other than what I already have. She's a white Comanche half-breed that I saved and helped raise after her family was killed, and she is now a dear member of my family."

Not ready to give up Jones's cast again, "You said you would be glad to see her again, but you acted as if she were a deceased relative."

Stephens started at this, and Jones instantly feared the rage of an unintended insult, but momentarily Stephens seemed to concede the validity of the statement and responded, "She certainly is not dead, my friend, but she was very ill for nearly two months before I started my journey. That's why I was so far behind Shelby. I couldn't and wouldn't leave Kina until I knew she was out of danger. Then, once I did, I had a devil of a time picking up his trail and following it. I had Indian scouts to help me track him in the open country, and I sent telegrams and letters to every sheriff and lawman I knew to try and get a line on where he might have gone. I walked while he ran, all the way to the East Coast, and now here I am. Kina was much better when I left than she had been, but it still grieves me to remember the state she had been in."

Jones was still curious, but he more than suspected that he should let the matter rest. After a brief pause, Stephens decided to take his turn at fishing.

"You know, when you invited me to have breakfast with you this morning, you might've told me that you had a wife. I felt like a dunce just standing there when she told me her name."

Jones looked at Stephens in his own surprise.

"I guess since everyone else I know also knows about Emma that it just didn't occur to me to mention her to you. That, and I didn't expect you to arrive during the brief period I was gone. Did she really catch you off guard like that?"

"She did indeed," Stephens replied.

Jones grinned silently, but the grin was enough to translate that he wished he had been there to see the ranger's consternation.

Stephens grinned back in fair play and then continued, "You have a very fine woman there, Jones. She is beautiful, seems very capable, and has a strong spirit. I'll bet she would give some of our Texas women a run for their money. You are incredibly lucky in my opinion, I only hope I may be as lucky someday."

"Well, I...thank you," Jones ultimately answered after absorbing this great compliment.

After that, the events of the last twenty-four hours began to catch up with them, and the general conversation died away. The two settled themselves into comfortable positions on the leather seat covers and dozed for the remainder of their trip, which lasted late into the night. When the train finally arrived at their destination, the two disembarked and made their way sleepily to the local inn and got a large room for the night. The next morning they would make their way to the garrison of the West Yorkshire regiment to discover what they might.

Chapter 10

Around ten o'clock the next morning, the twain's hired carriage rumbled through the gate of the garrison post, and a smart-looking young sentry snapped to attention as they passed. Stephens grinned at the boy and threw a casual solute to him as they passed by. The carriage came to a halt in front of the regimental headquarters, and the two dismounted and strode in to ask the indulgence of the commanding officer. Upon stating their business, the clerk at the desk in the front room excused himself through a side door, and a moment later an officer emerged ahead of the clerk. As he approached, he reached out and shook their hands with a firm, confident grip.

"Good morning, gentlemen," said he. "I am Major Gerard, the executive officer of this regiment. How may I be of assistance to you?"

Both men shook the officer's hand in turn, and as he ushered them into his office, Jones began to answer his question.

"We came to speak with the commanding officer about some of your regimental supplies that followed you from India. We have reason to believe that a smuggling ring operating in London has an interest in some of the crates, for what reason, we do not yet know."

"Indeed," said Gerard with a more concerned countenance, "I'm afraid that Colonel Davenport isn't on the post. His wife and daughter lived on post with us in India, but they returned to England a month before us. Since we've returned, he has been anxious to spend time with them. They're out riding this morning, and I don't know when they'll return. I would happy to assist you in any way possible if you could tell me more about this circumstance."

With that, Jones and Stephens both took a deep breath and plunged into the long whole tale of events from the night of Stephens's arrival, the questioning of Miller, the expedition to the tavern, Thatcher's information, and the visit to the shipping office the previous morning, until finally they had appeared in the regimental headquarters. The two had told the story in turn and were grateful to reach the end. Gerard shared the same mixture of wonder and curiosity as others when Stephens's full identity was clarified to him and was taken in by a schoolboy fascination at the sequence of events which his practiced military demeanor labored to disguise.

When the tale was finally told and the lawmen caught their breaths, then Gerard refocused his mind toward the serious concept that dangerous mischief was enveloping his post.

"And you have no idea whatever about what is so valuable about military stores to these smugglers?" he asked.

"No, sir," replied Jones. "But if we could examine the crates corresponding to the numbers in the code, we might be able to figure something out."

"That should not be a problem," said Gerard. "Let's step over to the quartermaster's office and see about discovering which crates they are."

"And where they are," said Stephens. "There were wagons coming in ahead of us, and it looked like there might've been more trailing behind us, and according to that Mr. Somers, it may be this afternoon before all your freight shows up."

"That is true," replied Gerard. "But all we can do is look and find out for certain. I do believe that the majority of it has arrived, so the odds are in our favor that we won't have to hunt far."

The three men rose and were walking out of regimental headquarters when a clatter of hooves through the gate announced the arrival of the commanding officer and his female relations. The small troop approached headquarters with the ladies' dresses flapping like flags in the wind of their haste, and the colonel's buttons and orders shone bright in the morning sun. The party drew to a halt in front of headquarter, dismounted, and came up to the exiting search party still smiling and laughing at their morning amusement.

Colonel Davenport was a stout man, slightly taller than Gerard, with a strong, good-natured countenance and a self-sufficient attitude that had greatly aided him in becoming a successful soldier. Stephens had been a ranger for fifteen years; the colonel had been a soldier for twenty-five. He had followed old family tradition and gone to the academy as a young man and earned his commission near the top of his class. In the years following the Indian rebellion, the military's ranks had swelled, and he had climbed the ladder of rank quickly. Consequently, he had married within the military as well. Between his natural kindheartedness and the creation of his own family, he had become a sort of father figure to the men under him. This in turn earned him and his regiment renowned for their loyalty and their ability, as no soldier ever had to be asked for his best. Only a slight limp from an old wound chinked his powerful demeanor.

Mrs. Davenport was a gracefully matured woman who still possessed much of the charm, elegance, and beauty that belonged to her in her youth—a seemingly fitting match for the colonel. She had originally been Ms. Martha Atwell, the niece of Davenport's own colonel when he was a second lieutenant. She had visited her uncle's regiment when they were home from India and had met her would-be husband. He courted her along with half the junior officers while they were home, but her own share of grace and charm melded with his, and soon there was no question who the winner was, or any resentment, as everyone knew Davenport's value. A year later, they were married, and three years later, they had their daughter.

Young Ms. Davenport must have just been in her late teens and seemed to embody the prime characteristic of her parents. He was bold, confident, charming, and beautiful and commanded devotion from those who spent any time in her presence. She had grown up in this regiment since her father had been executive officer and knew the names of half the men in it. The men had half raised her themselves as she was always running about as a child, asking questions and trying to fit into what she perceived as her extended family. She was what Stephens would've called a tomboy back home, but that did not diminish her feminine qualities. She naturally treated men in a brotherly fashion and had yet to meet one that could make her feel closer than that.

"Good morning, gentlemen!" proclaimed the colonel in high spirits after a ride with his family. "I wasn't aware that we were expecting visitors today, Major."

"We weren't, sir," replied Gerard respectfully. "These gentlemen, or one of them at least, is from Scotland Yard and have come to investigate some potential trouble with our supplies."

Now it was the colonel's turn to assume a look of concern.

"Very well," said the colonel. "Let's step into my office and discuss the matter more thoroughly. Would you ladies excuse us while we conduct this business? But if only one of these gentlemen is from Scotland Yard, then who pray is the other?"

"My friend here is a visiting law enforcement officer from America," replied Jones, "a Texas Ranger."

At that announcement, the retiring ladies stopped short and turned, and all three Davenports gazed at the ranger. Deep in his subconscious, Stephens was beginning to feel like a carnival attraction.

After this discovery, the ladies would not be refused, and all six of them adjourned to the colonel's office. Then, with a deeper breath than before, the two investigators retold their story from beginning to end in detail. When it was concluded, the colonel shared his subordinate's concern for their post, and the two ladies were alight with fascination and excitement. Once again, the whole party adjourned and paraded out of headquarters and across the yard to the quartermaster. On rounding the corner of one of the first barracks, they came into view of some wagons and freight being transferred, and Stephens stopped short with a jerk. One wagon separated from the rest was attended by two men who seemed to be loading rather than unloading the cargo around them, and one of the men limped and periodically rubbed and petted his left thigh.

"Jones!" exclaimed Stephens pointing his finger. "Those men were in the tavern with Thatcher!"

"No doubt of it," replied Jones. "I believe that's the one you shot!"

They both drew their pistols and ran toward the wagon. On seeing their approach, the two men dropped the crate they were carrying into the back of the wagon and leaped toward the seat.

"Stop!" yelled Stephens.

"Halt!" yelled Jones.

Both the fugitives turned to face them, and the glint of their own weapons was visible in their hands. The two lawmen stopped to take aim when two shots rang out from their opponents. A shriek and a scream issued from behind them, and the two lawmen opened fire.

Bang! Bang! Pop!

Stephens's attention was immediately drawn from the fight by this additional noise. While Jones continued to fire, the ranger's mind began to fly through a lifetime of memories as he looked around him. That smart young sentry at the gate, roused by the noise and general alarm, had fired his Martini rifle at the fugitives and was reloading. That pop had not been loud enough for a rifle, but it had gone off almost simultaneously with the pistol shots. The fugitives, apparently unhindered, were on the wagon now and wheeling toward the gate. Jones fired again, but Stephens was still thumbing through his thoughts. The wagon approached the gate, and the sentry raised his rifle to fire again at close range. In that instant, Stephens hit upon the memory from years ago that he searched for.

He stretched out his hand and yelled, not at the fugitives, but at the young sentry, even though he was almost a hundred yards distant.

"Don't shoot!" he started to yell, but only got out "Don—" when the sentry pulled the trigger of his rifle, and it exploded in a cloud of orange sparks and black smoke. The wagon rumbled through the gate, and Stephens watched men yell and run in every direction to secure the garrison.

Chapter 11

Stephens knelt over the mangled body of the young sentry—very young, very eager, and growing very cold. The face of the boy had been sliced open with shards from the rifle barrel, and now he stared at the ranger with unseeing eyes and his face painted red. Stephens reached down and shut the boy's eyes solemnly. Unfortunately, it was not the first time by any means that he had seen such a young person lose their life needlessly or in such an ugly fashion. On the contrary, his career and the history of his state and country had been filled with such images. He remembered settlers that had been burned out by Indians or outlaws and young rangers who had joined younger than he had and had not had time to learn much more than this young sentry before their lives were prematurely snuffed out. It was a ridiculous thought, he knew, but he thought it nonetheless: whether or not his own presence here in this place had somehow influenced these events. He wondered if in some twisted way, he had brought the violence with him.

The surgeon had been rapidly summoned, not for the sentry for whom it was obvious that he could do nothing, but for Ms. Davenport. Apparently, one of the fugitives' bullets had pierced her arm after missing whichever one of the investigators it was meant for, and she was unconscious and bleeding. Men carried the young lady to the infirmary and had to half carry Mrs. Davenport, who was hysterical at the sight of her daughter's condition. And even the stout and hardy colonel, who had guided his men from the front through every dangerous and dismal duty they were allotted, was still a father, and nothing could've fortified him against even a slight shedding of his own daughter's blood.

Stephens stood up with all this going on around him as Jones and Gerard approached him.

"The garrison is officially on alert and will be closed," said Gerard. "None of the freighters that remain will leave until they have been checked. A search party is getting mounted now to pursue that wagon, but if they get to the crossroads, I doubt we'll find them."

"Or if they hide the wagon in the woods and take the horses," commented Stephens. "I've seen that and similar tricks pulled many times."

"Yes, that is very possible," replied Gerard. He was crestfallen at this turn of events. He was as fond of the colonel and his family as anyone, and his professional pride was more than pricked at fact the he and his men had not given a better performance in the conflict. They were all so glad to be home and had also assumed they had left all such terrible things behind them in a wilder place.

"Young McPherson will be honored for his gallantry," Gerard proclaimed. "He was a new recruit that had just been given to us. He didn't come from India with us but had just barely been trained before being transferred with a small group last week."

"That would explain his not perceiving what happened with his gun," commented Stephens.

"What do you mean?" asked Jones. "Do you know why his rifle exploded?"

"I have a pretty good idea," Stephens replied.

"And so do I," said Gerard. "Let's get to the quartermaster."

The colonel understandably stayed with his family in the infirmary after giving general orders to his first officer, which he instinctively knew was all that was necessary. After Gerard had issued the elaborated orders to the other senior officers, he accompanied the investigators to the quartermaster. The sergeant quartermaster quickly reviewed his records and invoices concerning the crates that were mentioned on the betting slip.

"Here we are, sirs," he said. "All those crates have been received. Some arrived yesterday afternoon, the rest arrived this morning."

"And what's in them?" asked Jones.

"Martini-Henry rifle ammunition, sir," replied the sergeant.

"Has any of that ammunition been issued?" asked Stephens.

"Yessir," replied the sergeant. "Just this morning I had to open one to finish filling poor young McPherson's requisition for guard duty. It was the first of those crates that had arrived."

"So not all his ammunition came from that supply?" asked Gerard.

"No, sir, only about a third of his allotment," replied the sergeant.

"We need to look at those cartridges," said Stephens. "Where is that crate, Sergeant?"

"Here on the table, sir."

They all crowded around the table with the crate of cartridges on it, and with tools provided by the sergeant, they began to open up the rifle cartridges.

"This isn't good gunpowder," said Gerard. "Some of it has started turning gray and brown."

"I'm not so sure it is gunpowder," said Stephens. "It doesn't look, feel, or smell right, even for old stuff. Now I know what happened to McPherson. The round in his rifle to begin with was one of these bad ones. When he shot it, the force from the primer pushed the bullet into the barrel but not out the other end. When he reloaded, he put in a live round, and when he fired it, the two bullets collided under pressure, and the barrel blew up."

"I saw something like this a long time ago in my first year as a ranger," Stephens continued. "A small group of us had picked up a few survivors that had been burned out by Apaches, and one of them was a boy about fifteen that had his grandfather's old army musket. On our way back, we got attacked and pinned down by one of their raiding parties, and the boy was trying to help fight. He was scared and still a little out of his head from losing his home. He had fired and reloaded his gun when an arrow hit a man right next to him. He panicked and loaded his rifle with a second charge. None of us could really pay attention to him at the time, and when he pulled the trigger, that old cannon busted wide open like a watermelon.

"In McPherson's case, he was young and inexperienced, as you say. He was also excited by what was happening, and with him firing at almost the same time as us, the pop of his primer was enough for him to think he had fired and missed."

"And because someone put the wrong kind of powder or bad powder in these cartridges, young McPherson lost his life needlessly while performing his duty," said Gerard with anger kindling in his eyes.

"Are you sure this is one of the crates from the group we mentioned, Sergeant?" asked Stephens.

"I'm almost positive, sir," replied the sergeant.

He reached over and picked up the lid of the crate leaning against the table to reexamine the label, and Stephens started and stood stiff as a board for about two seconds before he reached and grabbed the lid from the sergeant's hands.

On the underside of the crate's lid in the corner was traced a large Indian arrowhead, and inside it was traced a coiled rattlesnake with its mouth open and a drop of venom coming off its fangs. Stephens glared at the symbol wide-eyed and disconnected from what was going on around him. From the look on his face, the others thought he was going to smash the lid into kindling, but then he simply dropped it and finally spoke.

"Shelby, you dirty, rotten, miserable, poisonous devil! You…" And he continued to growl under his breathe for another few moments.

From what he had said, Jones began to get a horrible realization and continued to study the bad powder.

Major Gerard still focused his attention on the ranger, and when Stephens noticed his attentiveness, he quickly explained.

"That symbol, Major," he said, pointing his long finger at the lid, "is the symbol of the heathen that I came halfway around the world to find. That symbol is his calling card that he would leave on anything he did so that people would know him and fear him.

I don't know how he's done it, but I'd bet you a month's pay that he has worked his way up into this smuggling gang, if he ain't at the head of it, which is entirely possible. And it makes the whole situation twice as dangerous, I know what he's capable of."

"From what little you've told me, I can well believe it, Mr. Stephens," said Gerard. "But what can you do about it now?"

A slight grin now spread itself on the ranger's face, and he almost seemed strangely happy, which to the major's way of thinking was absurd given what had just taken place in the last hour. The major's expression must have translated his thoughts.

"This is hopeful for me, Major," Stephens replied. "This means that I'm close to that lunatic, closer than I've been since I started. He hasn't moved on to parts unknown but has set up house in this country somewhere. He hasn't gone to India, I can tell you that for sure, and for certain, he's not an errand boy. No, he's here where the money is, where he can run things and watch things. Jones and I have literally been on the same trail without knowing it, and as soon as I can get some clue as to where he is or where those crates are going, then I'll deal with him."

The ranger's own mind was influenced by his speech and was whirling with the possibilities of what might come, making rough plans for what to do when they did, and yet still working to absorb the fact that he was so close to having Shelby in his hands. For all he knew, Shelby might be within a day's ride of where he stood. But on the other hand, England was still a big place, even if it was an island. All these things and more ran through his head in the few seconds after he stopped speaking.

"That's all well and good, Mr. Stephens," said Gerard, "but we're still left with this mysterious gunpowder and have no idea of what purpose it serves." Jones had been deep in thought about the gunpowder through all this discussion. He had examined it as the others did but also went so far as to taste a few grains of it. He bit a small kernel of the stuff between his teeth, and after a second or two, a glimmer of recognition came into his mind. He then tasted a few more to double-check his conclusion. If this was what he thought it might be, then this whole mess went far beyond smuggling. Finally, he looked up from his concentration with a new light in his eyes and spoke.

"This is not gunpowder in these cartridges, Major, or any other kind of powder. What we have here, protected and preserved inside of these brass casings, is dried opium poppy seed!"

Chapter 12

The ranger and the major stared at Jones for a second before venturing to speak.

"Are you sure about that Jones?" asked Stephens.

"Very," Jones replied. "My father was a doctor, and I recognized the taste of the seeds. My father would sometimes have to mix his own laudanum to give to patients, especially while in the service, and I became familiar with the smell and taste of the stuff."

"Well, why would they be smuggling opium into the country?" asked the ranger. "I didn't think it was illegal."

"It's not," replied Jones. "The possession and use of opium is quite legitimate, but the mighty East India Trading Company has a monopoly on the import of opium from the East. It would go very hard with someone trying to cut into the company's profits."

"That it would," put in the Major. "The East India Company takes this sort of thing very seriously, and their customs enforcement is very severe. This tactic of smuggling out opium seeds in cartridges is one of the cleverest ideas I've ever seen."

"Shelby is a very clever customer, Major, although I hate to give him the credit. Who knows how much of this stuff he's brought in already? This seems to be the only crate mentioned that the thieves didn't get away with, and this is a good bundle by itself."

"That's true," agreed Jones, "and there are military transports and merchantmen in constant flow to India and Afghanistan."

"But there are not always troops or supplies coming back," interjected the major, "that couldn't make for a very consistent rate of delivery."

"Maybe not," said Stephens, but how hard would it be to damage or compromise a crate of cartridges and have them sent back? And who knows what additional means of smuggling they may be employing. However, there's something much more fantastic that I may suspect also. These seeds are dried and preserved as Jones has said. What would be the chances of growing opium plants here in England?"

"Very slim at best!" replied Jones. "England is much too wet and altogether cool to compare with India's and Afghanistan's hot and dry climates. What would make you think of that?"

"The one good trait that Shelby seems to have," replied Stephens, "is that he has a green thumb. Settlers and wagon trains that Shelby bushwhacked would carry seeds for farming, and when we found his camp, we saw that he had grown his own garden, quite a large one, with a mix of different plants, and many of them didn't come from anywhere near Texas."

"That may be so," said Jones, "but opium comes from the other side of the world. To try to grow it here would be ridiculous."

"It doesn't matter how ridiculous or crazy or stupid the idea may be, it just has to be different, and Shelby will try it. I often think that that's what draws him to these kinds of schemes, and you can't argue with the fact that to date, he's been pretty darned successful."

"Even if that is the case, it doesn't get us any closer to finding him," said Jones.

"Something will turn up," Stephens replied, "and I'll get Shelby yet, don't you worry on that score."

Just then there was a commotion outside as the mounted pursuit party returned, and the major was informed that they had a body with them.

The party went out into the courtyard and saw that thrown across the back of one of the horses was a dead body. As the major and the lawmen approached, the troop dismounted, and the body was pulled off and laid on the ground before them. Closer inspection revealed it to be Thatcher's misguided friend whom Stephens had shot two nights before. There was a slight bloodstain on his left pant leg where his bandaged wound had bled and soaked through, and now there was a fresh wound low in his right shoulder. His shirt under his coat was soaked with blood, and Jones surmised that the bullet probably nicked an artery.

"That was probably one of your shots, Jones," Stephens said. "I only got the one shot off, and if I had hit him, then he probably wouldn't have made it out of the gate."

"He also has several lacerations on his face," Jones added. "Probably caused by fragments from McPherson's rifle barrel, he was sitting on that side of the wagon."

The lieutenant of the search party reported that the body had been found on the side of the road where it turned to the left. There was no sign of the wagon, and it had evidently reached the crossroads where there was no way to determine its direction amid the myriad of tracks and trails of the local populace intertwining.

"This thief here," Stephens began, "was just thoroughly unlucky. He already had one wound in his leg, then got shot in the shoulder and had a gun blow up at him. He was losing blood fast and just managed to hang on until that turn in the road. Then I'll bet he fell off during the turn and bled to death, if he wasn't dead already. His partner was in a powerful hurry and didn't have a mind to do anything for him. That's often the way of it with outlaws."

Major Gerard dismissed the lieutenant and his party as Stephens and Jones continued to examine and search the body. Jones pulled a partially stained piece of paper out of the man's inside coat pocket, read it, and then grabbed Stephens's arm.

"Look at this!" he said. "It's a train ticket to Brighton stamped for the two twenty this afternoon." He looked at his watch. "Two seventeen, no wonder they were in such a hurry. We couldn't catch it if we had wings."

"Where in thunderation is Brighton?" asked Stephens.

"It's in the most southern part of the country," replied Jones. "It'll take some time for them to get there, they may even change trains."

Stephens thought he sensed a possible idea in Jones's head.

"It would probably be possible to wire ahead and have someone waiting for the train at its next stop," Stephens said. "But I'm not so sure that would be entirely wise."

Jones stared at him questioningly.

"We might be able to catch him and bring the opium back, and we might get a little more information out of him, but he probably won't know much more than any of the others. Remember that everyone only knows as much as they have to. I think it would be better to follow after him to Brighton and start nosing around to see if we can follow those crates to their final destination."

Jones saw the sense in this reasoning and agreed, and they spent the rest of the day going over everything that had happened and examining all the evidence again.

Before leaving the post, they went to the infirmary to check on the Davenports. The colonel was more collected now, similar to how he had been earlier that morning, but he still gave orders and heard reports inside the infirmary rather than his office. He would not leave his wife and daughter. The wife was still a little less than composed but calmer since it was assured now that her daughter had taken no permanent damage. The daughter's arm was bandaged and immobile, and she slept deeply as a result of the medicine she had been given. Just outside the door, the two investigators met with the colonel and briefed him on everything that had happened and what had been discovered. The old soldier almost shook with fury when he had absorbed all the details.

"These thieves and brigands dare to compromise the service and my own garrison!" he growled to himself, straining his self-control. "They smuggle and steal and cause the death of one of my soldiers and this harm to my little girl. Promise me, gentlemen, that you will hunt down those who are responsible for this. I promise you that you have but to ask, and I will summon all the favor and influence that I can to aid you. Even then I will still be in your debt, but please give me justice for this day!"

"One man has already paid his debt in full for this day, Colonel," said Stephens. "But the man behind all this owes a greater debt to many other people, including myself, and I swear to you that I will find him and make him pay it." The ranger looked straight in colonel's eyes with a hard stare that confirmed the sincerity and severity of his statement. The colonel silently shook his hand and then Jones's, and they parted.

The next day was Sunday, and the two investigators returned to the military post to attend a special service held in the chapel in honor of young McPherson. Stephens had his little Bible with him and solemnly thumbed through various pages as the parson spoke. It was the first time that Jones had witnessed Stephens making use of it, even though its condition testified to its avid employment, and as Jones stole glances at his partner, he revisited past thoughts and questions he still had. Stephens seemed to be within himself and not really listening to the service, and as he would mouth the words, he presumably read on one page and then another, his face contorted itself into a strange mixture of expressions. Jones had seen the ranger in anger and had a glimpse of him in sadness, but those and others emotion danced around the ranger's face as if he wasn't sure what he was feeling, or trying to decide.

After the service, they once again visited young Miss Davenport. She was now wide awake and still tended to by her mother. Despite her wound, her natural high spirit asserted itself, and she was charm itself to the two visitors.

"I'm glad I got to say goodbye to you, Mr. Ranger," she said. "I wish you and Mr. Jones every good fortune in your quest. If I were well, I feel as if I could come along and help you hunt your quarry."

Her mother gasped a little at this unguarded behavior, although by now she should've been accustomed to her daughter's general familiarity. The girl looked intently at this foreigner that seemed to possess so many of the same traits as her father and of other men that he, and so she, respected and admired. This was not meant to cast a shadow on Jones or his qualities, but it was evident that he was the policeman and that Stephens was the fighting man. Not just a fighting man, but what her young, romantic imagination perceived as a sort of righteous knight on a quest.

The ranger would have laughed if he had been privy to this comparison, but as it was, he smiled at the young woman, sharing her sense of fellowship. He reached inside his coat to pull out his wallet. Out of it he pulled out the detached top two inches of what seemed to be a bird feather stripped with brown and white.

"Here, this is for you, Ms. Davenport," he said, handing her the token. "This is the end of an eagle feather. The Indians where I come from greatly respect the eagle as a sacred symbol, and this particular feather was given to me by another charming young lady of spirit like you. I think if she were here, she would want you to have it."

The immense pleasure and gratitude was evident on the young woman's face, and it marked one of the few times in her life that Ms. Katrina Davenport was momentarily speechless.

After this visit, farewells were said to the colonel and major, and the two lawmen went back to town and packed for their return trip to London that afternoon.

Chapter 13

The next morning Stephens showed up a second time at the Jones household to enjoy another most scrumptious breakfast. While the ranger had endured and survived with some very lean and unappetizing morsels over the years, and probably because of this, he greatly appreciated good home cooking. His current landlady's cooking was tolerable in his opinion and better than some he could remember, but Emma's cooking had won his heart and stomach, and he would've begged and tricked his way back for more, even without Jones's invitation. Emma in turn was delighted to have the ranger as her guest once again and insisted on him and Jones telling her the whole story of their trip—again, since Jones had already summarized it for her late the night before. Stephens mannerly and eagerly ate his fill and showered her with praise before beginning the tale.

Emma listened attentively and looked up sorrowfully after the description of young McPherson's death and with energized sympathy after the wounding of Ms. Davenport. She stopped Stephens long enough to vow that she would write to the poor girl and reassure her of the inevitable capture of these murderers.

"I have every faith in you two," she said, "and I want this poor child to feel the same."

"I doubt you'll have to put much effort into that, my dear," Jones commented with a grin at the recollection of the exchange between Ms. Davenport and the ranger. The story continued to the discovery of the opium and Shelby's mark and the examination of the retrieved body.

"I want to know why Brighton happens to be their headquarters, if it is their headquarters," Jones asked. "They could bring those seeds straight to London and have an enormous market and distribution right at their fingertips."

"If they had managed to get it off the ship as planned instead of chasing the stuff up north, then it might have stayed in London," remarked Stephens. "But there may be another possibility that I am not ready to give up on. The extreme South of the country, though still a far cry from India, is at least marginally warmer than anyplace else and might aid the growing of the plants if that's what they're trying to do."

"I guess anything may be possible at this point," Jones replied.

"Whatever they're doing with it, I'll be glad when you stop them," said Emma. "I know it's not illegal to have opium, and Caleb has informed me of its positive uses in medicine, but my Uncle Clarence became addicted to opium some years ago. I loved him and still do. When I was a girl, I absolutely cherished going to visit him and Aunt Amanda with my sister. They were the most loving relations, and they always had fun things for us to do. They have a small bit of land in the country. Not an estate, but it's big enough for a couple of girls to spread their wings and stretch their legs. We would help Aunt Amanda in her vegetable garden, and her flower beds were the most beautiful thing in spring time with every color of the rainbow. Uncle Clarence would take us out in a little boat on the lake, and he would tell us fairy tales and fish while we let out imaginations run to the heavens. The images of the fields and the trees and the friendly neighbors who would visit and play games will always live in my memory.

"Then, some years ago, Uncle Clarence somehow began smoking opium. At first it was just an occasional indulgence, like going to the theater or the club, but then it became more common, and the opium seemed to almost completely replace the tobacco in his pipe. Now he will disappear for hours, or even a couple of days, to indulge himself and come back the most pitiful mess. I pray for him and hope they can find help before they are ruined altogether. It would break my heart if somehow they had to lose their beautiful home because of it. He is not the same man that I remember as a girl, though I try to always keep that memory. My aunt is in shambles also as a result of worrying about him out on his binges and then worrying about how to bring him back to his senses and keep it as quiet as possible. I feel so sorry for them both."

Jones gripped his wife's hand and patted it, and Stephens looked her straight in her moist eye. "I can't change the laws here or make your uncle quit his habit," he said, "but I can promise like I did to Ms. Davenport that this gang will pay. That's a fact. And you already said that you have faith it will come true."

"Yes, I do," she replied with a grin. "So now the two of you had better get busy and save the world. Off with you!" She ushered them to the door and wished them luck before putting them out onto the street.

The pair looked at each other for a moment after their rapid exodus and chuckled.

"Well, how long does it take to get to Brighton, and when can we start?" asked Stephens.

"Not so fast," replied Jones. "Before we go anywhere, I have to report to the chief inspector. I received a message this morning shortly before you arrived saying that he wants me to give him a report before proceeding further. He'll probably want to talk to you too, so let's get a cab and get it over with."

They hailed a cab and were soon at Scotland Yard and ushered into the chief inspector's office. He sat looking at the piece of paper in his hand and peered over the top of it as they came in.

"Come in, come in, you two, and sit down."

They did as they were instructed and waited for him to finish reading. At last he looked up at them.

"You two have been incredibly busy and somewhat destructive," he said, looking blankly at them. "I have a bookmaker in one cell who admits to passing coded messages to smugglers. I have an infamous hired lug covered with bruises in another cell who admits to stealing the goods. I have a report of a brawl in a tavern down on the docks that was completely wrecked involving a pair of men who remarkably match your descriptions. I have a report from a regimental commandant praising your skill and courage. And I have the body of a man one of you shot while stealing contraband from said commandant's military post which is due to arrive this afternoon. Is there anything else I should know about?"

Jones and Stephens looked at each other. Stephens was suppressing a grin, and Jones was dreading the anticipated reprimand.

At length Jones took the plunge and began filling in the details of all that had occurred since they had last been in that office, with an occasional injection from Stephens. At the end, Jones took a deep breath and braced himself; his past experience with the chief inspector had not been altogether pleasant. But to his astonishment, the chief inspector allowed a grin to escape him. Jones could be justified in his anticipation and dread of this encounter, but he had reckoned without adding in the variable of success. Up to this point, Jones had unfortunately had very little of it since his promotion, but now despite all the collateral damage that had ensued, he was making genuine progress that even the head strong chief inspector had to take note of.

Finally, he spoke. "You've done good work!" he said. "Indeed, bloody good work. Now we have to see it through to a conclusion. A conspiracy such as this one poses a threat to even the national economy with the East India Company being drawn in. Colonel Davenport assures me that a complete investigation will be conducted by the military's inspector general, and that they won't rest until the eastern end of this business is crushed. He is incredibly impressed by your behavior and has proclaimed his admiration and confidence in your abilities, as well as his ardent hopes that I will aid your progress. So now it is for us to see to the English end. How soon could you two travel to Brighton?"

"We could presumably leave this afternoon," replied Jones, overcoming his wide-eyed surprise.

"Very good. I'll telegraph the authorities there and instruct them to assist you."

This turn of events and the change in the chief inspectors attitude gave new heart to Jones and encouraged him more than ever. It would've been nice if the chief inspector would've openly admitted that Jones had been right in his previous suspicions, but that was too much to hope for. He knew the chief inspector believed him now, and that was all that mattered. The twain left the Yard in high spirits and once again parted company to prepare for another trip.

In less than two hours, they had met at the train station and were on a south bound train, and Jones was the picture of happiness.

"This is fantastic," he said as the train rolled along. "Finally, the chief inspector believes what I've been trying to tell him, and what's more, he complimented me—I'm sorry, *us*—on what we've accomplished. I've felt sure he would try to get rid of me if he could, but now I may finally be able to establish myself in the Yard. Emma was thrilled when I told her how we turned out. If only this good fortune could hold out until we find Shelby. Do you think he'll be in Brighton?"

"I don't know," Stephens answered. "I hope for both our sakes that he is and that we can wrap this up quickly. But if he's not, then we will find him wherever he is. How do you want to start when we get there?"

"It'll be late again when we arrive," said Jones. "We'll start in the morning by checking the freight records at the depot to see if we can trace the crates and where they might've gone."

"All right," agreed the ranger. "I don't know how long you think this smuggling has been going on, but it wouldn't hurt to find out who is new to the area."

Jones nodded. "Like I said, I just hope our good fortune will last a little while longer."

Chapter 14

The next morning, Brighton lived up to its name with a very bright and beautiful day, and the two lawmen were out early to visit the train station freight office. They showed the ticket from the dead smuggler to the clerk, who said the train that ticket would've been for had arrived the afternoon of the day after the ticket had been sold. The clerk had been there when the train arrived, and after the crates were described and the numerical markings told, the clerk remembered them. He shuffled back to review his logbook before he answered them definitely.

"Yes, yes, I thought so. Those particular crates were picked up and signed for by a Mr. Kelly."

"No one got off the train to escort the crates?" asked Jones.

"No, sir, not that I know of," answered the clerk. "They were just unloaded with the rest of the freight, and about half an hour after the train came in, Mr. Kelly appeared, signed for the crates, and asked to have them loaded onto his wagon."

"Have you lived in Brighton long?" asked Stephens.

"More than half my life," answered the gray-haired clerk.

"Then you would know if there was anyone knew to the area?" Stephens continued. "Someone who might stand out to residents like yourself?"

"Brighton is not a small place, sir, and there are scores of people who travel through for one reason or another."

"Yes, but I mean someone who may have shown up say a year or so ago and stayed."

The clerk pondered for some moments.

"There have been a number of families move into Brighton and round about during that time," answered the clerk, "but this Mr. Kelly didn't belong to any of them. He may be a new man on Lord Mallory's estate."

"Who is Lord Mallory?" asked Stephens.

The clerk's eyes grew wide.

"Lord Mallory is a nobleman of an old established family in this region," interposed Jones. "He is most known these days for training excellent race horses."

"That's right, sir," affirmed the clerk. "That's about all he does. To my understanding, he lost all interest in business when his son died of fever in India several years ago. He lets his bankers and staff worry about that, and he just raises horses. There are some who have wondered if that would change since his nephew turned up."

"What nephew?" asked Stephens in surprise.

"Well, I don't know if he's a nephew so much as a cousin. To my understanding, he's the son of some far-off relative of his lordship, most say that he is a nephew. He showed up near a year ago and took over management of the estate. I don't know the truth of it, but some say his lordship found him and sent for him. His lordship is old and not a well man. He never leaves the estate, and few ever actually see him, so I hear."

"Well, thank you very much for your cooperation," said Jones, and the two walked off.

"Our other smuggler could've gotten off at any number of places and let the freight continue," Jones commented as they walked along.

"Most likely," Stephens agreed. "And this Kelly may work for this Lord, or someone else, or he may just be another random mule being used to take the crates on the next part of the trip."

"Still, it might not hurt to look around Lord Mallory's estate," Jones continued, "there could be several new faces floating around, and His Lordship may not even be aware of any of their activities."

"It's possible, and I suppose we have to start somewhere," Stephens said, and they turned to walk toward the livery stable to hire a cart to take them to the estate.

The Mallory estate was extensive and impressive to say the least. The mansion, for that was what it seemed like to Stephens, was three stories tall and made of stone. The immediate yard around it was encircled by a waist-high stone wall with an opening on all four sides. The surrounding buildings included what appeared to be employee lodging for those that didn't serve in the household, barns, and storage for livestock, crops and supplies, and some very extravagant stables. The stables also had a similar stone wall, but with wider opening, separating them from the rest of the grounds. This compound was entered through a metal gate attached to stone pillars, and from the pillars ran a very tall and thick hedge of brush and shrubs with the occasional intertwining of small trees. This hedge ran most of the way around the compound until it tied in with some woods in back of the main house.

Only to the west was there any open access to the lands around it, which also belonged to Lord Mallory, for many miles. On these lands were tenants, crops, hunting preserves, and open fields for training his horses.

Jones and Stephens observed most of this as they rolled through the open gate and made their way up to the front doors of the great house. Jones rang the bell, and it was answered by a butler who showed them into a lavish sitting room where he asked them to wait. They sat, and a maid appeared a minute later with a coffee tray and poured them each a cup. They were still sipping it a few minutes later when a fairly well-dressed man in riding boots came into the room and held out his hand to them.

"Good morning, gentlemen," he said. "I'm Jonathon Hendricks, the manager of the Mallory estate. What can I do for you?"

"I'm Inspector Jones of Scotland Yard, and this is my friend Mr. Stephens," began Jones. "We were curious whether any crates were brought to the estate in the last few days. Evidence in one of our cases indicated that some illegal materials may have been shipped into the area of Brighton, and His Lordship's estate seemed a likely place to begin, considering how many people are working here."

"That's true enough," said Hendricks. "We do have quite a bit of goods coming in and going out. Just a couple of days ago, we brought in several boxes of miscellaneous stores for the household."

"Do you have anyone in your employ named Kelly?" asked Stephens, speaking for the first time.

Hendricks looked questioningly at him before he answered. "No, sir, the only Kelly we have here is little Kelly Singleton, the daughter of one of our maids. Why do you ask?"

"The particular crate we're looking for, if our information is correct, was said to have been picked up by a Mr. Kelly," answered Jones.

"He could've easily given a false name," said Stephens, "and his general description given by a very busy clerk could easily match any number of people I saw as we came in. This is a very busy place."

"It is that," agreed Hendricks. "Old Lord Mallory is by no means a well man and mostly stays in his chamber. His nephew has entirely taken over the management of the estate. My duties now really only involve supervising the development of His Lordship's race horses."

"As ramrod here, you don't have any control over the personnel?" asked Stephens.

"I'm sorry, sir. *Ramrod?*"

"My American friend means your role as the estate manager, as you told us," Jones explained.

"I have some control over them, but Master Reginald has a finger in every pie and interposes his own thoughts and preferences regarding the people he employs."

"I take it that Master Reginald is the nephew we heard about?" asked Jones.

"That is correct, sir."

"And I also take it that you do not entirely approve of his preferences?"

"It's not my place to approve or disapprove of the master, but I've worked for His Lordship for many years, and I don't believe that he would approve of some of the characters Master Reginald has brought in. But he claims that they have distinct talents that are of use. The horses have been taking up so much of my time lately that I don't have time to worry about it." Hendricks revealed a look of exasperation as he said this.

"Are you having trouble with the horses, Mr. Hendricks?" asked Stephens.

"As a matter of fact, yes, I am. Master Reginald also had the idea that breeding some of our thoroughbreds with wild stock will improve their abilities. He somehow managed to acquire some brumbies imported from Australia, and we haven't been able to do a thing with them."

"They're not broke?" asked Stephens.

"No, although they don't really have to be to breed, but they're completely unmanageable!"

"Show me," said Stephens.

Hendricks looked at him again with more curiosity, then rose and led them out to one of the stable yards.

A group of men were attempting to wrangle a dune-colored stud with little success. The three of them looked through the fence, and Jones looked at Stephens in surprise when he noticed the look of admiration in the ranger's face. The animal was a mountain of strength, healthy and toned from his wild living. They watched the horse confound his opponents for some moments, and then Stephens turned to Hendricks.

"Would you mind if I tried something with that horse, Mr. Hendricks?"

"I suppose not, sir, we can't do anything with him, and if you can, I would be indebted to you. But do you know anything about wild horses?"

A huge grin appeared on Stephens's face. "Indeed I do, Mr. Hendricks, indeed I do. When we were arriving, I thought I noticed a creek or stream running not too far away, how deep does it get?"

"Not terribly deep, sir, a couple of feet, maybe three in spots."

"What's the bed of it like?"

"Mostly mud and sand, with some stone here and there."

"Uh-huh, good," Stephens replied smugly.

Stephens entered the corral and shooed away the men so that the horse would stand still; they did so upon receiving an affirmative nod from Hendricks. Stephens gently took hold of one of the reins and firmly held the horse's head down close to him, talking softly to the horse the whole time. He reached in his pocket and brought out a large red handkerchief that he quickly threw over the horse's eyes and tucked into his halter.

"Lead the way to the muddy part of the creek, Mr. Hendricks," Stephens ordered, and the whole company walked down to the creek.

Stephens threw his coat to Jones, who happened to notice Stephens's little pistol now revealed in his shoulder holster for the first time in public, and led the horse out and down into the creek. As foretold, it was about three feet deep or so and very muddy. There was not a saddle on the horse, but that made no difference. Stephens gripped both reins behind the horse's neck as well as a double handful of his mane. He took a deep breath and swung onto the horse's bare back. The horse started and shook and snorted but dared no movement while he couldn't see. Then Stephens yanked the handkerchief off of the horse's eyes.

Now that the horse had his sight, it fully intended to do everything it could to remove the burden on his back, but it had an unexpected problem. The horse's weight, and that of Stephens, was forcing its hooves down into the mud. It jerked and snorted and did its worst to buck Stephens off his back. Occasionally, it did manage to get either its front or back feet loose and would throw itself into the air, but Stephens could not be dislodged. The struggle of the horse to rid itself of both sources of irritation went on for several minutes. It eventually began to worry less about Stephens and focus on the mud. It struggled mightily to free all its feet at once without success, and Stephens always kept the animal's head yanked around to one side or the other so that it couldn't ease its way out of the creek. At last, after about fifteen minutes, the horse gave up on moving altogether. A minute later, Stephens gave it a kick and slowly steered it out of the creek onto dry land.

The horse breathed heavily and pawed at the hard ground it was now on to reassure itself of its stability. Stephens wiped his face with the handkerchief and looked triumphantly at his awestruck audience. Then, with a shout, he kicked the horse again, and the animal charged out of the circle of onlookers. The horse ran like the wind for its rider, and Stephens rode him around the entire perimeter of the compound. When he finally returned several minutes later, the horse was completely winded and tame, and Stephens looked like a child on Christmas. He surrendered the horse to Hendricks's men and spoke between breaths.

"That is a fine animal, Mr. Hendricks, very fine indeed. If you ever did get a colt out of him, I'll bet he'd outrun the wind. Thank you kindly for letting me have some fun with him."

Hendricks thanked him in turn for his help, and the two investigators bade farewell and started their return trip to Brighton.

Chapter 15

"That was quite an exhibition this afternoon," said Jones as they entered their rented room. He had left Stephens alone in his exalted state during the drive back, grinning and recollecting half to himself the good points of the horse and comparing it to some he had owned or seen back home.

"I suppose it may have been, but I couldn't help myself. I've spent more than half of my life on the back of a horse, and I haven't been on one since I left home. First, there was all that time on the ship, and then once I got here, all we've done is walk or ride in coaches and carts. It felt good to be in control again, and he was a beauty."

"At this point it comes as no surprise to me that you could tame that horse," Jones said, "it's just a little curious how you did it."

"I learned that trick from a man I knew when I was growing up. He and his brother used to catch and break horses. He actually figured it out by accident when a mustang he was on threw him off and ran into a muddy creek and got hung up. He jumped on the horse when he saw how much trouble it had moving in the mud and sand, and by the time he led it out, it was as tame as a dish rag. Of course, there's not always a creek handy, and you have to do it the hard way, but when you can find water, it makes life a lot easier for both of you."

"From what I saw today, I can imagine it does. You probably would've earned the wage of every man there if you worked for Hendricks."

"Maybe so, but for my part, the debt would be satisfied if they could cough up some useful information on our case. Nobody seemed to really know much of anything out there, which is suspicious in and of itself. This new nephew is either hiding something or is just plain paranoid."

"He might be at that," Jones agreed, "or else he just has very definite ideas of how he wants things done. I heard stories from my father about new officers who took over commands coming in and turning everything on its ear. And I've seen it myself at the Yard. Some people just must have things the way they want, whether the old system works or not."

"You ain't wrong there, my friend," Stephens agreed.

It was late, and Stephens had taken off his coat and vest and was preparing to clean up and shave after their busy day. It still bothered him that everything was so secretive at the Mallory estate, and he wished desperately that he had more information.

"I don't suppose you managed to get anything else out of Hendricks or his men while I was on that stud, did you?" asked Stephens as he poured water into the basin and began to splash his face.

"Not so much," Jones replied, sitting at the desk to write out a message to have sent to the Yard. "Most of them just watched you and commented that you would either end up taking a plunge or breaking the horse's leg. Hendricks really didn't know much more than what he told us. He commented some more on the unsavory characters that the nephew has hired in the last several months. He did say that the nephew is fond of gardening and that a good deal of supplies for building greenhouses has been purchased."

"That place already has a greenhouse. I saw it on my ride around the perimeter, along with the fact that there's a lot of thick hedge rows and brush surrounding it, as good as any wall. I guess that gate we passed through is meant to close it up."

"Probably so," agreed Jones. "I've seen many estates like that. And English people are very keen on gardening, perhaps Master Reginald wants to grow more varieties of flowers."

Stephens put down his towel and turned to him, "Or perhaps some exotic Eastern plants," he said with a meaningful look.

"I suppose that's not altogether impossible, but I doubt it," Jones replied, looking up from his task at the insinuation. "Many people have seen him in the current greenhouse tending flowers and shrubs. Some guess that he does it for his health to keep from getting sick like his uncle."

"Is he *that* paranoid?" Stephens asked dramatically.

"I don't know, but he must be scared of something. They say that he keeps medicine in a bag around his neck, although no one has actually seen him take any. I would guess it's something he keeps for emergencies."

Stephens had been mixing lather in a mug with a brush and covered his evening beard with the foam to shave. He had just lifted his razor to begin when Jones's words froze all his motion. Jones was still looking down at the desk and paper and didn't notice the ranger's change in demeanor. Stephens looked at himself in the small mirror with hard, fixed eyes for several seconds before finally speaking. He made an effort to sound as natural as possible.

"He wears a medicine pouch around his neck? What's it look like?"

"I don't know," Jones responded, "Hendricks didn't say. Apparently, it's only been seen a time or two by happenstance, since he keeps it under his shirt. It's probably small since they say you wouldn't know it was there just by looking. Apparently, one of the servant's children happened to see it one day and asked him what it was. He just replied that it was his medicine."

Stephens had laid down his razor but still gazed into the mirror still as stone. He propped himself on his hands as he stood with his blood starting to rush faster and faster. Thanks to the foam on his face, Jones did not see how red Stephens was becoming as he stood up from the desk with his finished message.

"Right," he said. "I'm off to the telegraph office to send this to the Yard and see if I have any messages. When I get back, we'll make a plan for tomorrow."

"Fine," Stephens replied shortly but softly as if he were tired.

Jones shut the door, and Stephens heard him go down stairs. Once Stephens was sure that Jones was gone, the statue came back to life and sprang into action. He splashed the foam off his face and dabbed it with the towel before throwing off the remaining pieces of his suit. Then he reached for his unopened bag in the corner of the room and laid it on the bed.

Meanwhile, Jones casually made his way to the telegraph office and paid to have his message sent to Scotland Yard.

"Have any messages come in for me today?" he asked the clerk.

"No, sir, not that I know of." Then a second later, "Ah, I just remembered, sir." He reached under the counter off to the side and pulled out a small packet. "This was brought over from the train station this afternoon, sir, and I was told to give it to you if you came in."

"Thank you." Jones tipped the clerk and returned to the room in a lighthearted mood, until he opened the door.

Stephens was nowhere in sight and did not answer when called. Jones quickly looked around the room and found pieces of clothing scattered in all directions. Jones was pondering to himself what on earth could have happened when he looked at Stephens's bed and realized which of the two bags was lying on it.

The bag that had contained all of the ranger's old clothes and equipment was empty except for the frame that had held his old hat. Jones looked around again and accounted for all the pieces of Stephens's gray suit and his shoes, and his hat that he had worn since his arrival still hung by the door. Jones yanked up the ranger's other bag and opened it. The brown suit and all the extra clothes were still inside. Jones could only think of one thing that would make his friend behave this way. Something said during their last conversation must have meant something to him that it didn't to Jones. They had only talked about things at the Mallory estate, so presumably that was where he was going, the rest of the mystery would have to be unraveled later. He started to race out the door when he saw the packet he had flung onto his own bed. Quickly he ripped it open to review the contents. One piece of paper was a letter from the chief inspector, and he read it first.

> Inspector Jones,
>
> Included with this letter is another which I received this morning from the United States Federal Marshal's office. It was sent on a different ship than Mr. Stephens and just arrived. It confirms all that Mr. Stephens explained to us about his purpose here and the villain he pursues. Shelby is indeed a very sinister and devious character of much resource. I urge you to take the utmost precaution in your investigation, but there is more. Mr. Stephens was not entirely forthcoming in his reasons for his personal pursuit of his man. I have forwarded the letter that you may read for yourself. I advise you not to let him out of your sight if you feel you are close to your objective. I wish the both of you the best of luck.

Jones reread the letter and then quickly opened the other letter in turn. It read:

> Authorities of Scotland Yard,
>
> This is to inform you that we have sent Texas Ranger Wayne Stephens to your country on an

important errand. He is in pursuit of the wanted criminal Richard Shelby, also known as Rico. This man is extremely dangerous and devious and has avoided capture for many years. He is wanted on multiple charges of murder, armed robbery, assaults against women, arson, and fraudulent activities. Ranger Stephens is highly acquainted with the case and was the optimum choice to send on this venture. It is hoped and asked that you give him as much support as he may require to secure Shelby and return him to the United States for trial and punishment. However, this message is sent independent of Ranger Stephens as he also has a personal account to settle. His adopted sister was grievously assaulted by Shelby, and we are not entirely confident that Ranger Stephens will attempt to bring back Shelby alive. If possible, please take precautions to ensure that he does. We are very grateful for your cooperation in this matter.

United States Federal Marshal's Office

Jones's heart jumped up into his throat. That was at least a partial answer to the riddles, and Jones had no doubt that the marshal's office was correct, but there was no time to ponder that now. He grabbed his hat and darted out the door. He hurried to the livery stable to find out about Stephens.

"Yessir, he was here," the farrier replied to his question, "I only just recognized him from this morning. He was dressed differently, very odd indeed, and he had a fiendish look in his eye, so he did. I was almost afraid to talk to him. He spoke low and quiet and told me to saddle him a good horse. I did as I was told, and he threw the two bags he had across the animal, and then he took off like the devil himself was chasing him."

"It's more likely the other way around," Jones muttered to himself. "Did he say where he was going?"

"No, sir, just that he would bring the horse back in the morning."

That would certainly give him time to reach Mallory's. Jones next stop was the constable's station, where he ordered six constables and two coaches to accompany him to the estate. Jones sat silent inside the first coach as it rumbled on the road. He kept recounting everything that had been said and couldn't determine what was significant. As they drew closer to their destination, he spent half his time wondering what was going to happen and the other half praying that he would not be too late to prevent the worst.

Chapter 16

The moon was just shy of being full and still cast plenty of light to see by when it was high in the star-lit sky, but on the ground, a slight fog had begun to swirl in spots and was growing. The white glow of the moon on the mist could make some eerie images if one didn't keep his imagination in check. On guard at the now-closed gate of the Mallory estate, two of the unsavory characters belonging to the master stood an uneasy guard in such an atmosphere.

"This 'ere would be a fittin' night for All 'Allows Eve if it were the fall months," one said to the other.

"Aye, I don't mind the fog so much, but those shadows make me t'ink of a hangman in a village square."

"Why do we 'ave to sit up at this bleedin' gate anyways? Don't the master think 'e's got enough muscle to take care of any problems that come up?"

"How should I know? They say he's been wound up tight as a fiddle string all day. I just do as I'm told, but I wish I were back in bed."

"Why should 'e be acting cracked? The goods 'ave been comin' in easy as you please."

"There was sumt'n' wrong with the last shipment, there was supposed to be four boxes, and we only got t'ree. Maybe them two blokes that were here before had…"

At that moment, they both started and look out into the fog.

"Wot was that?"

"Sounded like a horse."

The sound of horse hooves got louder and nearer, maybe thirty or forty yards. Then they stopped, and a few seconds later, a different sound was heard—the slight *tink tink tink* of small pieces of metal hitting each other. Now that sound got closer—*tink tink tink tink*—until it was maybe twenty yards away, but the two guards could still see nothing through the mist. Then the tinking stopped too. The guards waited, and after a minute or two, they became curious. They opened the large gate with many loud creaks and scrapes and whines and walked out a few paces. Then the tinking resumed, and then what seemed like a ghostly figure appeared about eight or ten yards in front of them.

The florescent light of the moon made the ranger's white duster seem to glow, and with the black pants he wore, he seemed to float toward them, despite the tinking of his spurs with his steps. This frightful image had a powerful, what we would now call psychological, effect on the two guards, who honestly didn't know what to do or believe at that moment. Then the fantastic figure spoke in a strong, normal voice.

"I don't know who you are or what you've done, and I really don't care. I've come for your master, and my best advice to you is to run as far away from here as you can, while you can." The ranger's arms hung down at his sides, but his left hand clinched a large handful of his duster.

Upon hearing his speech, one of the guards slowly came to his senses and yelled out.

"That's no ghost, it's that bloody ranger! Get him!"

They would've done better to have taken his advice, but instead they both reached for whatever weapon they possessed—but too late.

The ranger lifted his left hand to waist-level, still clutching his duster, but now the duster fell limp from his hand and revealed that under it he held his now-reassembled double-barreled shotgun. Quick and smooth as glass, he grabbed the grip with his right hand, slipping two fingers into the trigger guard. The two guards had no time to think before he squeezed both triggers, both hammers snapped forward, and both barrels vomited out flame and dark smoke that contrasted with the mist. Both guards were flung backward onto the ground in a hail of buckshot. The ranger reached in his pocket and pulled out two more shells as the empties hit the ground. He reloaded and stepped over the bodies as he continued his walk into the compound. Cool-minded as he was now, he had to think fast; the shotgun blast had alerted the household, and he could hear men running around and yelling in confusion.

The ranger marched on, looking for the next onslaught, and he found it when he stepped around the corner of an outlying shed. There four men rushed at him, and he fired one barrel and then another. One man went down, but the other three dove for cover behind a tree or rock wall. Stephens let his shotgun drop to the ground, and he pulled both of his pistols that he now carried. At least one man had a gun and fired at him as he ducked back behind the shed. After a few splintering shots, the firing ceased, and Stephens jumped out into the open and fired both pistols alternately as he saw targets move.

Thank goodness for that nice, fat moon, he thought to himself. Only one more shot flew in his direction, then all three remaining foes lay in the dirt. But there were still more coming.

Stephens retrieved his shotgun, reloaded it, as well as his pistols, and headed for the stables. A way off, Stephens heard chattering and a woman blubbering and servants yelling questions at the men running around, but all they got in reply were orders to shut up and to get back inside. Stephens had come to one of the stable buildings and this time rounded the corner and came face-to-face with a partially dressed Hendricks carrying a lamp and a massive club.

"Who are you, and what do you want?" Hendricks asked defiantly.

"It's me, Stephens, and the devil is exactly what I want."

The voice helped Hendricks to recognize this recent acquaintance through his gruff exterior.

"What in blazes do you think you're doing?"

"I've come for your Master Reginald. Whatever kind of lord he may be, he's a low-down, stinking scoundrel that I've come halfway around the world to find. I have no quarrel with you or your people unless you get in my way. Tell all the honest ones to get under cover until this is done."

Without another glance, the ranger pushed past him on his way, and Hendricks, after a moment's consideration, did what he was told.

When the ranger got to the second building, he heard the voices of his enemies hissing to each other to listen. Then Stephens realized why and quickly bent down to unbuckle his spurs. He then moved over to a rear door of the stable and hung the spurs by their leather straps under a low shingle and stepped inside the dark doorway. The slight breeze blew the spurs, and they tinked once more, but without the regularity of footfalls.

"There it is," someone said, "come on!"

A moment later, a man appeared from each back corner, moving toward the spurs from opposite sides. They were almost to them when the men spotted them hanging from the roof, then it was too late. The butt of the shotgun swung and crashed against the side of one's head, while the other got caught between the stable wall and Stephens's fist.

Stephens opened the door, and once inside he moved toward the front of the stable and listened. From the murmurs, he guessed that eight or ten men were waiting for him. He gripped his weapon tighter as if trying to squeeze inspiration out of it on how to get out of this new predicament. As he looked around, he realized that this was the brumby stable, and the horses were very nervous with all the noise and excitement. They were restless in their stalls and wide-eyed; something wasn't right, and they couldn't escape. Then the ranger had his inspiration. He quietly went to each stall and unlatched all the stall gates, then went back and unlatched the big front doors.

With his foot he shoved the big doors, and they swung outward while he ran back to the inside corner out of the way. When the doors opened, all the men outside tensed up in preparation to rush this intruder, but then there came two more great blasts from the shotgun, and the doorway and yard without were filled with wild, half-crazed horses with men diving for cover in every direction. One man was caught too far from cover and was trampled by the small herd. When the horses had passed, the men peered through the dust, and the floating ghost appeared again out of the door way, and two points of flame erupted again and again as shots flew at the disoriented horde of minions. He kept walking forward, clearing his way.

The last shot he fired rang out, and all the figures that had opposed him were down or crawling off, except one that he missed. This one jumped up from behind a section of wall and dived headfirst into Stephens. They both went down to the ground, and the attacker was pawing and hitting at his enemy like a bear. In such a position, it was all Stephens could do to block the onslaught. When the opening finally came, he grabbed the man by the shoulders and rolled him over on his back, and then was rolled again by the man. This human wheel made two or three revolutions before Stephens rolled the man over onto something sharp that made him cry out, either a rock or maybe a discarded weapon. The ranger pulled free and got to his knees as the man did the same, and as they came to face each other, Stephens swung his arm, and an imprint of his pistol barrel was left in his opponent's skull.

Now as the ranger caught his breath, he didn't bother to go back for his shotgun but raced up the hill toward the big house with what speed he could muster. As he neared it, one more small group of men came around the far corner, and two more burst out of the front door. Stephens aimed and fired once more at one of the two from the door, but that was all; that was the last bullet he had between his two guns without reloading. No matter though, the ranger thought, it was a small obstacle to jump over, and the pistols were still heavy hunks of metal in his hands. His enemies still hadn't learned that he didn't care about their numbers, and as they closed with him, he blocked whatever blow or weapon came at him with one hand and bashed the head of the assailant with the gun barrel in the other. Finally, with his ears just barely picking up the moans, groans, and cries from behind him, he walked up the front steps to the mighty double doors.

Only now did the ranger have time to breathe and think. Shelby must be in the house somewhere, but Stephens was sore and tired and ached. It had been impossible to block all blows dealt to him during this night's work. Some had landed on various parts of his body, and it was possible that a knife blade had managed to touch him a time or two. A part of him desperately wanted to sit down and rest, to collect a few more ounces of strength, but that would give his adversary more time. He would have time to count the blood spots on his clothes later, but now his moment had almost come.

He pushed open the great doors, and they silently opened to him. The inside was lit by dozens of candles from various spots all around him and by a chandelier from the high ceiling. He was in the hall with suits of ancient armor and generations of portraits lining the wall to watch the show. Various rooms and entryways alternated before him, and he slowly walked forward until he came to the first step of the great staircase.

Here Stephens paused and wondered whether he should go ahead and check all the rooms downstairs or head on up to find where Shelby must be hiding. If Hendricks had done what he told him, and he had, then all the innocent servants must be hidden out of the way by this time; but in a house this size, who knew what was on each floor. Stephens had only been shown to the small sitting room earlier that day, which meant he hadn't seen even a quarter of the first floor. The ranger looked back over his shoulder at the open door. Faint sounds resulting from his invasion could still reach his ears, but nothing to suggest that another attack was to be feared. He had just about made up his mind to systematically search each room on each floor when a new noise arrested him: the soft thump of booted feet slowly coming down the carpeted stairs. Stephens looked up at the highest point he could see on the turning staircase, and there on the second landing there appeared the legs, then the body, and then the head of the master of the house.

Chapter 17

Stephens saw his quarry and clinched his teeth, but he put all his effort into staying calm. He had never seen this man this close before, but there was no doubt in his mind.

"Did you finally get tired of running, Rico? It only took a few thousand miles for you to get your belly full."

Shelby looked at him with a sly smile on his face. "I suppose I should be flattered that such a crude, self-righteous brawler like you would actually come this far to get me, Mr. Stephens. Of course, I know of you from the Texas frontier."

"And I know about you too, none better, as you should know by now. But I am curious as to how on earth or under it you could've managed to weasel your way into this cozy cabin?"

"Oh, Lord Mallory was my uncle, distantly on my mother's side. That part was easy enough, an estranged relative wanting to reconnect with the family. Throw in the fact that I'm the same age as his son would've been, and I'm the master."

"*Was* your uncle?"

"Oh yes, the old boy died a couple of weeks ago. I just thought it more advantageous to let these silly people believe he still lived."

"Well, it doesn't matter now anyway. You'll be able to wave goodbye to him soon enough on your way down to the firepit."

"One of us will, I don't doubt, Mr. Stephens, and perhaps you will be able to catch a glimpse of your little squaw again as well."

"Oh, I'll see her again, when I go back home. You see, you didn't finish the job like usual, Shelby. Why do you think it took me so long to come after you? I wouldn't let them send anyone else, and I would've caught up to you a lot sooner if she were dead. There's a live and healthy witness to all your crimes now, not that we really need her for that at this point. All of your old gang gave you up when I found your hideout. I'm sure I don't even know half the people you've hurt in your wretched life, but your reckoning is coming."

Stephens peeled off his duster and let it fall to the floor, and the encircled metal star on the left side of his chest reflected the light of the candles. Shelby's smirk had dropped, and now his lip curled into a snarl as word of his failure reached his ears.

"Well then," he said, "let's get to it!"

Then he pulled his own pistol out of his pocket.

Stephens's shotgun was lying in the hay in the stable, and he hadn't taken the time to reload his pistols again, but he didn't care. He threw the smaller pistol at Shelby's head and made a lunge up the stairs, ducking low as he did. Shelby also ducked and let fly two shots off hand. One buried itself in one of the great doors, and the other entered a suit of armor to judge by the metallic thud. Stephens tried to get within arms' reach of Shelby, but as he came up from ducking, Shelby put his boot against the ranger's chest and shoved him back down again. Recovered from dodging the mass of metal thrown at him, Shelby reaimed to shoot again, but

Stephens had grabbed the handrail part way down. Swinging himself back up again, he kicked in his turn and knocked the gun out of Shelby's hand.

The two men finally came together and grappled with each other like mountain lions on the first landing of the staircase. Both men were equally matched in strength and determination as they both knew the consequence of failure. In an instant, Shelby, using the ranger's strong forward force against him, spun him around and thrust him back against the rail. The ranger was in danger of losing his balance and released his loose grip on Shelby's clothes to catch himself from falling. Once free, Shelby raced up the rest of the stairs to the second floor with Stephens at his heels. Shelby came to a stop in front of a display of medieval weapons and had just put his hand on one when he was tackled to the floor by the ranger, but he had his weapon, and Stephens just had time to see it.

He had grabbed a small one-handed ax, similar in size and shape to the tomahawks used by the American Indian. As they sprawled on the floor, Stephens just had time to glimpse it as the candlelight shone off of it and roll out of the way as it came crashing with a thud into the floor boards. Stephens sprang to his feet and reached into his boot to bring out his own sizable blade. The two gripped their weapons and circled each other like big cats back on the prowl, waiting to strike at the other's weak spot.

Shelby moved first, lunging and swinging the broad blade. Stephens jumped back with his hands raised to keep them out of the way, and then he attacked while Shelby was still stopping the ax's momentum. The ranger sprang forward and made a powerful slash from left to right at Shelby's torso, but also to no avail. Shelby all but fell out of the way but escaped harm. Both men had had too much experience with Indians to be taken lightly in such a scrap as this. They took their turns slashing and lunging and trying to feint the other out of position for some minutes. As the two squared off again, Shelby decided to indulge in a few evil memories and see if he couldn't shake the ranger's concentration.

"It's too bad for you," he said, "that you didn't take that squaw for yourself instead of adopting her. They're the best at giving sport, you know, especially when they fight back like yours did."

Stephens perceptibly grew redder than he was already, trying to beat down the images popping in his head that he had hidden from for nearly a year.

"She couldn't understand why you didn't come to her rescue. The big, mighty ranger couldn't help her anymore."

Stephens had faced that accusation of himself every day since he had found Kina in the hideout just two days after Shelby had lit out, more than half dead and senseless. He had cursed himself as an incompetent fool for letting her go alone on that trip to the new settlement and for having taken so long to find her when the buckboard she was driving wandered in. Now this verbal reminder made him wince, and he momentarily shut his eyes.

The ax sang in the air as it swung at him again, and Stephens actually fell and rolled to the side to avoid its bite, but Shelby had anticipated that. Stephens rolled out of the way of the blade as he had before, but as he started to stand back up, Shelby quickly reversed the direction of the swing, and the long point on the back of the ax struck and scrapped up along the ranger's left shoulder. Stephens fell back to the floor with a deep cry and grabbed his left arm with the handle of his knife still in his hand.

Shelby stood back and anticipated the victory he was about to accomplish. This ranger had dogged him for years all over Texas and then across a continent and an ocean. He had all but ruined his opium enterprise before it could take full swing, an operation he had been secretly arranging for years when it was obvious that he had no future in Texas. This ranger threatened his very life, but he would have his first.

"You should've stayed home and chased your coach robbers and rustlers. This isn't your world, and you won't see your own again. Maybe your squaw will forgive you when you're dead."

"She already has," said Stephens softly, propping himself on one foot and one knee. "My face was the first she saw when she woke up, and she told me the fault wasn't mine. I didn't believe her for a long time, but she was right. I didn't kidnap her, violate her, and abuse the daylights out of her. That was you, and all she asked was that I bring you back to pay. I might not fully keep that promise though."

"Enough, you've had your say!"

With that, Shelby drew back the ax with one hand to bring it down in one more crushing blow, but right as he started to bring it forward again, the ranger seemed to convulse his whole body. Every part of him moved somehow so as to give his right arm maximum thrust, and with that power, he threw his knife underhanded in Shelby's direction, and it buried itself into the ample meat of his right leg. Shelby cried out, and that leg, with the added weight of that side holding the ax, collapsed, and Shelby became a wiggling mass on the floor.

Stephens slowly worked his way up on his feet and walked over to him. He knelt back down again and smashed his closed fist into Shelby's head before he put his knee and weight on Shelby's chest, then he reached around and jerked the knife back out of its resting place. Shelby cried out again and moaned with pain. Blood seeped out of the wound, but not enough for him to bleed to death quickly.

Too bad for him, Stephens thought to himself.

He faced Shelby and stared at the rotten piece of humanity he perceived. He grabbed Shelby's graying hair with much effort from his throbbing left arm, and with his right, he put the bloody knife to the edge of his hairline.

In that instant time stopped. Seconds seemed like hours as the ranger's mind flew through years of memories of what this man had done, the pain and suffering he had caused so many, until he reached the last ones that were personal to him, and he remembered all that he had sworn toward this man, a man without mercy, without conscience, without remorse. Stephens's mind flooded with emotion—fear of loss and the despair at the sight of Kina that day, the anxiety and condemnation that he had lived with every day of her recovery, and anger at the source of all his grief. His wrath and resolve were redoubled in those few moments, and every dark carnal passion in him screamed for vengeance.

It was at that moment when the first drops of blood emerged from the laceration he was slowly making in Shelby's scalp that Jones appeared at his side.

"Stop!" he cried. "What are you doing?"

"Dealing out justice," Stephens answered. "Anything this beast gets is better than he deserves."

Jones didn't dare move or try to touch the ranger in his most dangerous state of mind.

"You're supposed to bring him back for trial and proper punishment. You wouldn't tolerate someone else doing this back in Texas, would you?"

"The people of Texas would thank me for doing this, they know what he's done." His hand moved slowly another half inch, and a fresh trickle of blood ran down Shelby's forehead. Shelby winced once again but was half dumb with fatigue and the loss of blood.

Jones's mind was whirling. He knew what the ranger said was probably true, but he could not possibly allow this to happen. He liked this hard man that had dropped into his lap a week ago. He had helped him so much and shown him so much. It was because of him that Jones's standing at the Yard had soared over night. It was because of him that Jones had finally been able to crack the biggest case of his career. And already he could almost be called a close family friend. But he could not let this happen, and he slowly reached his hand into his pocket and secretly gripped the handle of his small revolver. In his mind, he prayed that he would not have to use it, for who knew what this ranger was capable of if interfered with.

He had to make one last appeal to the only soft spot he could think of. "Would Kina want you to kill him?" He saw a quick play of emotions on the ranger's face.

"Kina would be glad to know he's dead, and a score of others I could name."

"Yes, but would she want *you* to kill him here and now? You're not a murderer, Stephens, you know it, I know it, and Kina must know it. She and all the people he's injured deserve to see justice for themselves."

The struggle on the ranger's face was plain and ferocious as he was torn between his deep-seated sense of duty, and his own natural human desires.

"She asked me to bring him back, she did, but I can't help it. He doesn't deserve to draw any more breath than what he can manage in the few minutes I've planned for him."

"Is butchering this man really how you want to show your love for Kina? That would make you the same as him in her eyes, I think, and you would break your promise to her and your oath to your people. Don't turn your back on all that you believe in, all that you have honored."

Stephens's resolve, and body, were weakening. Deep down he knew that Jones was right, had known it from the beginning. His heart had carried him through the night and the battle with a powerful vigor, but now his mind was taking hold again.

Jones watched him intently and almost didn't dare to believe that he saw the ranger's face softening. He watched and was shocked when he actually perceived a drop of water run down the ranger's dirty face and then another. Then suddenly Stephens flung his bloody knife away, clattering down the hallway. He fell back against the wall, exhausted and hurting, with his face in his bloody hands, and Jones put a soft, reassuring hand on his friend's shoulder.

Chapter 18

Stephens and Shelby were both taken back to Brighton to receive medical treatment, and considering what all had occurred, Jones had no less than four constables guarding the hospital hallway that both of the men's rooms were in. Still more constables were called out to the Mallory estate to make sense of the shambles that remained after the battle. In the end, every one of the men Shelby had hired had a criminal record of some kind, from petty theft to being wanted for capital murder. Many of these Stephens had dispatched during his storming of the estate, and the few that remained that hadn't been able to run off were locked up until the full extent of charges were discovered that could be brought against them.

Following information Stephens related to Jones, Lord Mallory's body was discovered in a corner room on the top floor, which only Shelby had had access to. All the windows had been kept open to lessen the chances of servants below sensing the corrupting body. The servants told Jones that Lord Mallory had been moved into that room about a month prior, supposedly so that he could look out over all his lands. Over the next few days, further investigation discovered that in the heart of the estate, far from any tenants or prying eyes were the supplies and early progress for at least three new greenhouses. Evidence of recently dug earth was apparent in several spots around the building site, and no less than fifty crates were found containing military ammunition and several other commodities capable of being vessels for the opium seed that had been smuggled in.

There was much being done at the Mallory estate. Another inspector had come to help Jones coordinate his efforts with constables running around all over the place, collecting evidence and getting statements from all the original servants about all that had been happening over the last ten months. A search was being conducted throughout the house to see if any secret ledgers could be found to account for the actions of Shelby's organization. Lord Mallory's accountant and attorney were also summoned and consulted to try and ferret out Shelby's dealings, as well as an actual heir to the estate since Mallory was dead and Shelby would soon be going back to America. It was decided that the closest relative was a second cousin of Mallory's that lived in Herefordshire.

All this hustle and bustle was going on when Stephens stepped back into the great house a few days later. So far, his advance from the gate had been unhindered, but as he stepped over the threshold, a constable on his way out stopped him with a raised hand.

"Here now, where do you think you're going? Only the servants or those on official business can come in here. Who are you?"

Stephens was back in his gray suit, cleaned up, with his left arm in a sling under his coat, but he only had to say one thing to make his way clear.

He smirked at the constable's high-handedness, and as he looked him in the eye, Stephens declared with his distinct voice, "I'm the ranger."

Everyone in the house who had heard this looked on as the constable gapped and swallowed.

"Go right in, sir!" he said and hastily went out the door.

Jones had stuck his head out of the side room that served as his temporary office and tried to keep from laughing at the spectacle.

"Welcome, my friend," he said and escorted him to the same sitting room they had occupied on their first visit. He called for the maid and ordered coffee for them as they talked.

"You've been busy," Stephens said as he looked around him.

"I have to be to keep up with you. You know, when I wired the chief inspector that you had barged in here and shot up the place, his first response was that I bring you back in chains, but after I explained all that we had learned and discovered here afterward, he was ready to give you a medal. The East India Company may give you one too when they figure out how much profit you saved them."

The two smiled for a moment, and then Jones leaned forward. "You know, this was a very messy business, much messier than I ever want to see again, but you did some bloody good work here."

"*We* did some good work out here," Stephens retorted. "Don't you try to give me any glory. I have my prize, and that's enough."

"Yes, I suppose it is. The chief has sent a message to America through the embassy, and they should be sending some marshals to escort Shelby back, seeing as how you're hurt and all."

Stephens grinned, "You know dang well that by the time they get here, I'll be recovered, and Shelby will be too. You just don't want to take a chance on me."

Jones grinned back at him. "Maybe so, but I think you be happy for the extra security. Now then, don't you think it's finally time you tell me the whole story?"

Stephens nodded and started to talk.

He explained how about a year ago, Kina was taking some special supplies to the same young settlement where his father had been shot a few years earlier. She had also wanted to visit her friend, who had moved out there to help teach school. As near as could be told, she was about a mile and half away when Shelby's gang had ambushed her and carried her off. The buckboard horses bolted and went on into the settlement. Soon after, Stephens was informed and led a group of rangers to track Shelby down for good.

With the help of some Comanche trackers, they finally found the hideout a week later. By the time they got there, Shelby was gone, and Kina was all but dead with abuse and beatings. Stephens had nearly beat a couple of Shelby's men senseless before they all started pouring their guts out, telling everything they knew or could remember going back for years. It took days for Kina's fever to break and a few more before she woke up. Stephens had coordinated with rangers and marshals to get leads on Shelby and arrange assistance in his pursuit, but it wasn't until a couple of months later when Kina was moving around the house with something of her old high spirits restored that Stephens finally set out. From there he had already told Jones about his chase across the continent.

This was the crowning tribute to the ranger's esteem in Jones's mind, and at the end of the tale, all he could do was meekly reach across and shake the ranger's hand. Then he remembered something else.

"One last thing," he said. "What was it that we learned that told you that Shelby was here?"

"The medicine pouch you mentioned is an Indian medicine pouch that warriors wear into battle. It's not really medicine but more of a spell cast over them by the medicine man. Inside the pouch are ingredients that are somehow supposed to work together to protect them from harm. It's kind of hard to believe that Shelby would actually believe in such a thing, but he's by no means a normal person. Kina told me about it and said that he never took it off."

Another couple of days saw the end of all that could be accomplished by Jones's presence, and the two once again boarded a train with two constables to take Shelby back to London. Even in his weakened state, it was insisted that Shelby wear the heavy shackles that Stephens provided. When they arrived in London, Shelby was securely locked up at Scotland Yard, and the two investigators returned to Jones's house. It was an evening full of storytelling and grand adventure as, for the third time, Emma was regaled with all that had happened in Brighton and all the missing pieces were linked together. At the end of the night, despite Stephens's objections that he was fine and fully capable of taking care of himself, which Jones fully believed, Emma would not hear of Stephens staying anywhere but their spare bedroom.

This visit turned into an indefinite stay as Stephens awaited the arrival of the ship with the marshals. During that time, spanning some weeks, he and Jones were celebrated for their success at the Yard as they continued to tie up the remaining loose ends of the case and more, smaller henchmen were picked up. Also, during this time, Emma induced them to rest more than work, and they showed Stephens the sights and wonders of London while he continued to heal. Time passed, and finally the day came when the ship was due with the marshals. Stephens started to pack all his belongings that morning, but Jones persuaded him to wait until later, and they headed out. Stephens was thanking them for their generous hospitality and claiming that he needed to buy another bag for all the miscellaneous items he had acquired to take back to his family as they pulled up to the dock.

The ship had been moored and the gangplank put up from the dock to allow passengers to disembark. Several people came down before Stephens noticed a pair of men appear and start their way down. Even without seeing their badges, Stephens recognized them by their bearing.

They came down, and he heartily shook their hands and started talking to them about the trip home when Jones came up to his elbow and said, "Who is that?"

Stephens looked up at the ship's side again and froze. Standing there smiling down at him with a wide grin and shining eyes was Kina, in the best of health. She wore a fine lavender dress, and her glossy black hair flowed behind her as she hurried down the gangplank and threw her arms around Stephens. He held her tight for several seconds; so glad was he to see her, before he remembered his dignity and that he was surrounded by his peers. Jones grinned big at actually seeing the ranger embarrassed, and Emma laughed outright, but they laughed because they knew how much joy was wrapped up in that meeting.

It was discovered that the next ship sailing for America wouldn't set sail for another week, so after arrangements were made the quartet of the ranger, the inspector, Emma, and Kina all made their way home to the Joneses' residence. In the coach, Stephens eyed Jones suspiciously, remembering past comments made to him.

"You are a conniving character, Caleb Jones!" he declared. "You knew that Kina was coming, and that's why you wanted me to wait and not pack."

"I confess that I sent for her when I sent for the marshals. I thought that you and she both deserved a reunion.

Stephens slapped Jones's leg in mocked anger, but grinned as big as ever with his arm around his adopted sister.

The next week was an absolute pleasure. Jones took a week's leave, and they embarked to make the most of the time they had. Kina and Emma put the kitchen through a workout with new recipes, and they retraced many of the steps Stephens had taken waiting for the ship to arrive. It was a bittersweet occasion when they all appeared on the docks once more. Shelby had already been escorted onboard the ship and secured, and now it was time for the ranger to go home.

"I don't know if it would ever happen," he said to Jones and Emma, "but if you two are ever able to come to Texas, we would love to have you."

"We would be thrilled to visit you," Emma answered. "Who knows what the future will bring."

She and Kina hugged, and Jones and Stephens shook hands heartily as the last call to board was given. The quest was finished, the victory was won, and a lasting friendship was forged. Now Wayne Stephens was finally heading home, having completed his adventure as the Texas Ranger of Scotland Yard.

Lone-Star Inspector

Chapter 1

Sea salt was strong in the air as a brisk breeze blew inward from the Gulf of Mexico in April of 1887. Texas Ranger Wayne Stephens breathed it in deep as he paced to and fro, up and down the wood planking that constructed the porch and sidewalk immediately outside the shipping office on the dock of the Corpus Christi pier. For seventeen years now, he had had more occasions than he could remember to be nervous—sometimes he had been, and others he had not—but this occasion stood out as incredibly nerve-racking to him. He should be happy. He should be excited. Most likely he was happy and excited deep down, but these emotions were overshadowed by nerves. After two years of writing and receiving what must have amounted to possibly hundreds of letters, he was about to reunite with the man who probably was the best partner he had ever joined up with: Scotland Yard Inspector Caleb Jones.

Not only was Stephens about to see his old friend for the first time since they parted two years ago on the London dock, but also he was going to be *hosting* them, or rather, his family was. It had been months in the making, sorting out details and timetables through correspondence that spanned an ocean. Now the day had finally come, Caleb *and* Emma Jones were arriving for the long-anticipated visit. And now Wayne Stephens was nervous! He had almost been overwhelmed by the vastness of London and the advanced, centuries-old civilization that existed there in contrast with the wild Texas frontier that he had worked to help tame. Of course, he never admitted such a thing to Jones at the time; he just casually referred to that profound location as foreign.

He had been a guest in their cozy and charming London home and had done his best to not seem like a dumb rustic. Now they were coming to be his guests, and he was grappling with the impossible concept of how he could somehow transform Texas into something other than what it was. He was being silly, he would realize later. His whole family had done their best to explain and describe in their letters what the Joneses could expect upon their visit. Texas was worlds ahead of the primitive state it had been in half a century earlier when the revolution occurred. Also, Jones was a man of brains and sense, as Stephens well knew. He would be able to adapt and contend with whatever conditions he encountered. And Emma was a spirited, practical woman that would not swoon and shrink away from slight hardships like some of the fragile creatures he had encountered.

But what about the extra guest? Late in the planning, Jones had asked if they might bring along one of their cousins who had begged and pleaded to come on such an exciting trip. Whether Jones was for once being absent-minded and unthorough, or was being mischievous with his friend, Stephens didn't know, but Jones had neglected to provide any details about the cousin. Was it a man or a woman? On which side of the family did this cousin come from? Was the cousin the same age as the Joneses, or older, or younger? Either alternative in the extreme could be a great irritation, but Stephens had not dared to refuse and risk ruining the whole thing. Now as he paced back and forth, he wondered if he might not have rather ruined the whole endeavor to avoid embarrassment in front of his English friends.

Back and forth he walked with these thoughts racing through his mind and wrecking with each other. All the while he was only half conscious of the fact that he was being snickered at. Kina, his adopted half-Comanche sister, was seated on a bench against the wall of the shipping office reading a small book and glancing at her big brother with a wide, tight grin on her face. She had all but lost interest in her book, and she labored to keep from laughing at what she strongly suspected must be happening to Stephens. She possessed enough excitement and anticipation for the whole family at the prospect of this visit. She equally cherished the memory of the week she had spent with the Joneses before she came home from England with Stephens.

She knew everything that her big brother knew and sat confident in the conviction that there was no ridicule or embarrassment to be feared. She was also fully aware of her brother's pride and could not resist the opportunity to have fun with him. Finally, she spoke in a calm and jeering voice as he passed her for the umpteenth time.

"If you wear a whole in those planks and fall through, I'm going to laugh crazily."

He stopped, turned, and looked at her with squinted eyes.

"And I'll make sure you don't use your badge to get out of paying for it." She still looked at her book, grinning as he replied.

"It's sad that I don't doubt that for one minute. If I cut my leg wide open, you'd probably look to see if the blood made a stain before you went for help. Mom has rubbed off on you too much over the years. Just read your book and let me think."

She turned a page and spoke again, "You're thinking too much, which ain't surprising. I truly wish I could help you miraculously make Texas look like England so you don't have to put a gunnysack on your head."

Stephens squinted his eyes at her again and saw that her grin was somehow getting even bigger. "Remind me why I brought you along again? You'd be more agreeable if you were still running around in buckskins."

"If I were still running around in buckskins, I'd hit you over the head and make you be still. I may do that yet. You brought me along because you love me, and I asked to come, and you know that Emma will want a woman's companionship on the trip home."

Stephens let out a sigh mixed with a groan. "You better be glad that I need you, as it so happens that you're right."

"Wait, say that again. What am I?"

"I said you're a pest!"

"But I'm an adorable pest." Kina calmly turned another page in her book.

Stephens resumed his pacing as he continued to speak. "I just don't want Jones and Emma to look at us differently. Corpus Christi ain't London, and our home ain't Corpus Christi. You know I usually don't give a rat's tail what people think, but the Joneses ain't just anybody, you know that."

"Yes, I do. They are very special people, and they are our friends. They are very dear friends. What they are not is ignorant, they know perfectly well what they're getting into. You're fretting for nothing, and your fretting is making you grouchy. Is that how you want to meet them when they get ashore?"

"At this rate, they won't get ashore until next week! That ship captain is a pest too. It's been more than an hour since he came into the bay, and he still hasn't worked his way up to the pier."

"Wayne, have you ever driven a ship?"

"You know dang well that I haven't. What did you ask me that for?"

"So you would realize that you're being critical of someone for doing something that you couldn't do yourself. They'll get here when they get here."

"Pest," Stephens mumbled again to himself as he turned to pace back up the sidewalk.

A half hour later, with the help of some small boats, the ship that brought the Joneses to Texas finally came up alongside the pier. Stephens stood still now, with Kina standing next to him, although he almost shook with impatience as mooring lines were made fast to the dock and the gangplank was put against the side of the ship. The heads and then bodies of various passengers became visible as they came over the side of the ship and walked down the ramp. At last, after a dozen people went ahead of them, the figures of Caleb and Emma Jones appeared.

As soon as they reached the end of the ramp, Kina and Emma ran to each other and hugged. A moment later, Stephens reached out and shook Jones's hand heartily as he welcomed them to Texas.

"I still can't believe it. After all this time, you're actually here, y'all actually came to Texas."

"I can hardly believe it myself," Jones replied. "There were times I seriously doubted that we would ever make it, but here we are. The chief inspector said I could take as long as I wanted, as long as it wasn't too long."

"I would've been shocked if he had said anything else!" Emma exclaimed. "Since the day you two left, Caleb has hardly took the time to sit still. He has been working so hard in consequence of the esteem he earned on your case. Everyone has wanted his input when things became difficult. And he is still trying to catch the last few villains that got away from you."

"I'm proud to hear it. In another couple of years, you'll be running that place, and the chief inspector will be bringing you coffee," Stephens said as he laughed.

The whole group laughed, and the Joneses looked around at their surroundings.

"My goodness," Emma began, "you said that it was warmer here than in England, but I didn't quite understand what a change it would be."

If Stephens's hat hadn't shaded his face, they would've seen how red he turned as his previous fears rushed back to him.

"It's actually quite refreshing. I may not want to leave."

Kina actually laughed out loud as she perceived Stephens breathe out hard with relief and a smile.

"You may change your mind about that in a few days. Texas isn't England, as I was recently reminded." Stephens cut his eyes at a grinning Kina. "But we will try to make you as comfortable as possible. Just don't expect the ranch to be the Mallory estate."

"It may not be a good idea for you to mention the Mallory estate at the moment," a voice said, crisp and with a rebuking tone.

Stephens looked past Jones to see who had spoken. Jones rolled his eyes upward, and Emma looked startled.

"Oh my goodness," Emma exclaimed, "I'm so sorry, Katelyn. We got so caught up with our friends that I forgot to introduce you. Mr. Wayne Stephens and Kina, this is my cousin, Katelyn Stewart. She's from the northern part of the country near the Scottish border."

As she spoke, a very handsome woman stepped forward to receive the introductions. She had auburn hair similar to Emma's, but a touch brighter. She had eyes that were a mix of blue and green and a straight round nose that gave her a look of prominence without overshadowing her other features. Her mouth and red lips curved into a pleasant, attractive smile as she shook hands with Kina and expressed her pleasure. However, when she turned to Stephens, the smile flattened out, and she studied him before stiffly proffering her hand to him.

"So this is the man who made such a shamble of the Mallory mansion."

Stephens looked flabbergasted and then a little annoyed as she continued.

"Forgive me for beginning our association in such a way, Mr. Stephens, but I am an avid student of English history and antique architecture. The Mallory mansion is 130 years old and built on the foundation of the old house that stood there before it. I volunteered with members of the museum association of London to help try to restore portions of the house at the request of the family after your departure. I must say that I found such a lack of regard for personal property from a member of law enforcement, even American law enforcement, to be appalling."

During the speech, Stephens had grown perceptibly redder, despite his hat. Emma held Kina's hands tighter, and Jones had bowed his head with his hand over his eyes. If he wasn't already praying, it might've been a good idea to start.

Stephens took a deep breath and responded calmer than he might have, "Did the Mallory mansion blow up when I wasn't looking, or did it burn down after my ship set sail?"

As he waited for a reply, he gave the woman a look that translated his thought that she was close to being a lunatic.

Chapter 2

There on the Corpus Christi docks on what was otherwise a beautiful day, the ranger and the strange woman stared at each other. The cousin was not old or very young as Stephens had feared, but rather close to being Emma's age. Yet in the last ten minutes, the first ten minutes of the Joneses' visit, she was proving to be just as troublesome as he had expected.

At last, she responded, "Nothing quite so dramatic as that, Mr. Stephens, but given what I have already said about the house's age and importance, it can be said that a great deal of damage resulted from your 'visit' two years ago. For example, the handrail on the staircase was hand-carved as one of the last works of an aging craftsman when the house was constructed. The section of rail between the first and second landing is now cracked in three places and impossible to repair or hide without complete removal."

At this point Jones, tried to interject, "Perhaps we could discuss this on the road after we collect our baggage."

Neither the cousin nor the ranger took any notice of him.

"Did anyone bother to tell you," Stephens retorted, "that rail cracked under my weight when Shelby was trying to throw me over it back onto the ground floor?"

"Yes, after you burst through the front door. And then the door, which is ninety-seven years old, and one of the family suits of armor, which is three hundred years old, both have bullet holes in them!"

"Those bullets came from Shelby's gun, not mine."

"That he shot at you after you burst through the door."

"Kina, can you recommend a good restaurant or café where we can get some lunch before we start the trip to your ranch?" Emma asked.

Kina didn't have time to answer before Katelyn spoke again.

"Then there are the floorboards on the second floor. Those boards, along with most of the floors throughout the house, were shaped and treated to near perfection for more than a year by the craftsman's son through the course of the house's construction. And he hand-fitted the boards into place himself."

"Is there another way to fit floorboards into place?"

"There are no less than six places where the boards have been cleaved more than halfway through."

"The man was trying to cleave *me* halfway through with a medieval battle ax. I didn't figure the boards would mind taking the hits for me. Don't you think a giant bloodstain on the second floor would be more of a nuisance?"

"And finally, the stone walls around the house and main buildings have stood for centuries uncounted, with only the slightest maintenance to keep them in repair. They are now full of bullet holes as a result of your forced invasion."

"With all the civil wars your country has had since it's been a country, can you tell me of a stone wall more than a hundred years old that doesn't have a bullet hole in it? We've had one war so far, and that's enough. The scars that were left by it help to remind us that we don't want another. All this damage that you say I caused came about because I came to apprehend a criminal so vile that you can't imagine the depths of his evil. This is not the time, place, or company to go into detail about it, but I'm not sorry for anything you've mentioned, because in doing so, I dare say, I saved your country a wagonload of heartache."

The two glared at each other for some seconds before Kina's voice finally rang out.

"That is enough out of both of you! What's done is done and can't be changed, and it's not worth ruining the visit that we've all worked so hard for. Now, we girls are going to get something to eat and refresh ourselves. You men get the bags collected and loaded at the train station, and we'll bring you some food afterward."

With the glare of her Indian eyes indicating beyond doubt that the orders were not up for discussion, she whirled around and marched off with the other two women trailing behind her, leaving Stephens and Jones standing in the street.

As they disappeared up the street, Stephens commented to his friend while still staring after the women, "Next time I have to storm a hideout or a stronghold, I think I'll send her in first."

Jones looked meekly at the ranger, who finally looked back at him. "I'm so sorry about that. I don't know what to say. I knew she was upset about the damage, but when she wanted to come on this trip, I had no idea this is how she would behave."

"So she came across an ocean to give me a tongue-lashing about being too rough in the house."

"I can't believe that was her intention, no. But when she saw you, I can only guess that her passion carried her away. She has studied castles and fortresses and cathedrals and mansions for years and is quite the expert."

"Well, as I'm sure you remember, I know all about being full of heat and passion. If that's her sore spot, then I guess I can't blame her too much. I just don't want her to open up Kina's old wounds in the process."

"Nor do I. That was my primary concern when she started speaking, until I noticed that you're armed, then it became my second concern."

At that Stephens threw his head back and laughed hard. That made him happy to see his friend again, and they made their way over to collect the baggage and move it to the San Antonio Aransas Pass Railroad station. The Joneses were in luck, as Stephens related to Jones as they labored with the bags. Just that very year had the new San Antonio Aransas Pass, or SAAP, railroad been completed between San Antonio and Corpus Christi. If they had come to visit any earlier, then they would've had to take the stagecoach for most of, if not all, the way to the ranch. As it was, they would be able to ride on a train to San Antonio and only take the stage or travel on their own for the last segment of the journey.

After the civil war, many small railroad endeavors had tried to make their mark and fortune across the frontier. Some had succeeded, and some hadn't. The SAAP railroad was an endeavor to enhance San Antonio's commerce. For years, San Antonio businessmen had been forced to have goods imported to Galveston and had to deal with the railroad running from it. That railroad practically belonged to the mighty Southern Pacific line and did not make things cheap for the people that had little other choice but to use them. Now the SAAP railroad had been completed and gave competitive prices, as well as convenience. Corpus Christi was a lot closer to San Antonio than Galveston was, and now the SAAP line was giving it a chance to be a much more thriving seaport.

As the men set off to do their chore, the ladies made their way down the street and around a corner and came to the Royse Café. Kina had been walking quickly with a crisp stride, and the others struggled to keep up with her. However, the walk did much to alleviate her irritation, and she paused in front of the door to take a breath and wait for her companions. When they entered, they were quickly shown to a table and given menus.

Kina and Emma perused their options and quietly discussed what might be the best choices. Meanwhile, Katelyn was wondering, not what to eat, but what to do or say. Kina's outburst on the street had succeeded in quelling Katelyn's fierce passion over the damage to precious antiquities. Now the apparent cold shoulder she was receiving from both Kina and her own cousin made it all too clear that she had erred.

"E-Emma, what do you think of the special of the day?" Katelyn asked. "Do you think it is worth giving a go?"

"Whatever you want," Emma replied flatly without bothering to look up at her cousin.

The waiter came and took their orders and said it would be about ten minutes or so. Emma decided to take this opportunity to freshen up and stood up to excuse herself. Katelyn's heart sped up.

"Emma, may I come with you?" she said, almost in a state of panic.

"No, Katelyn, you stay right there until I get back. I won't be long." Emma turned and walked away with a slight smirk on her face.

Katelyn looked after her for a moment and then looked around to Kina, who also wore a smirk.

At last Kina spoke, "I understand your love for history and tradition, Katelyn, and your desire to protect it. I have balanced upholding traditions from two very different groups of people. I have been a part of them both, and both are important to me. It may interest you to know that the rangers have a history and tradition with the same goal as you: protection. For more than fifty years, they have fought to protect people who could not protect themselves. Yes, they may be a little rough and wild, but that is because they have had to adapt to the country and people they deal with. In fact, compared to some rangers I have met, Wayne is quite tame. I don't know if you know the whole story of his trip to England, so I'm going to tell it to you, and maybe you'll learn something new."

Kina was stronger than even her brother gave her credit for. While the events that she had experienced did take much effort to overcome, she was sufficiently above them to be able to convey the depth of the story to her audience. Emma could've been back at the table within a few minutes, but she held back and watched as Kina talked to her cousin. She could guess at the sort of conversation they were having and decided to leave them to it. She perused some pastries that were for sale by the door and even talked with another woman who was also eyeing them. It was about fifteen minutes from the time she left the table to when she saw the waiter loading up a tray with their food to bring to them. She got back to the table just ahead of him, and they all started to eat.

The food and Emma's arrival had halted the discussion of the other two, but more than enough had been said to convince Katelyn that she had misjudged Stephens, at least a little bit, and that her outrage was not nearly so justified as she had supposed. Now that they were all back on friendly terms, the three of them ate and talked about the voyage over and what they might do and see during the visit. They ordered more food to be made for the men, and when it had arrived and they were finished eating, Kina paid the bill, and they made their way to the train station to prepare for the next stage of the journey.

Chapter 3

Jones and Stephens had been sitting at the train station talking and laughing and regaling each other with stories of exploits since their parting. They were still carrying on when the ladies showed up with food and high spirits. The men eagerly accepted the food they were presented with. They each spread a napkin out on the bench they occupied and laid out their food before vigorously pouncing on it. Stephens's old habit of "eat first, talk later" remained intact, and he sank out of all conversation while they ate. Jones did exchange a few words with the ladies as he ate, but mostly they still talked among themselves. When the men finished eating, they led the women down the platform to the car in which they were to ride on their trip to San Antonio. They had already seen that their luggage had been loaded, so it only remained for the time to come for the train's departure.

The trip would take five to six hours, as opposed to the two or three days by coach, and it would be night by the time they arrived. Stephens had arranged for them to stay in a hotel that night, and they could continue their journey the next day or whenever they wanted. The trip was full of still more news and storytelling on both sides. Stephens told of cattle rustlers and bank robbers, murders, and all sorts of mishaps that he had been involved in resolving. Jones told about new cases that had come up in the last two years. He had his share of murders and thefts; most were relatively uneventful and routine, but sometimes he would get one that swept away the boredom. Just as the Yard had been abuzz with the exploits of Jones and Stephens over the Shelby affair, it had recently been abuzz over the unusual exploits of a private detective that had solved one or two bizarre cases that had been passed off as irrelevant.

At hearing the word *irrelevant*, Katelyn at last found her voice in the general conversation and addressed the ranger in a halting voice.

"M-Mr. Stephens, there is something I would like to say, and it isn't easy. I have been made aware of the full gravity of events that surrounded your trip to England, and it has caused me to realize that I was perhaps too harsh in my judgment of your actions. While I still very much regret the unfortunate collateral results of your arrest of the criminal you pursued, I must accept that they were inconsequential to the service you were rendering. To that end, I feel that I must a-apologize to you for my behavior upon my arrival."

The compartment they solely occupied had grown silent during her speech, and everyone one in it realized how hard it was for the cousin to make such an apology, no matter how deserving the recipient. Stephens looked at her blankly during and after her monologue for some moments before making a reply. He was probably the only person in the group for whom such an apology would've been harder, and it was the effort rather than the delivery that he appreciated.

"I accept your apology. Believe it or not, we operate out of the same motivation. Love, passion, and a protective instinct over what we consider valuable. I have a sense of duty to my profession and to my family and the families of multiple victims deserving justice. All that was intertwined in the circumstance that led me to your home. As passionate as you are about your history, it is nothing to what you feel when you're trying to protect people that are living, breathing, and hurting right in front of you."

The hush in the compartment grew even deeper, and all ears took in what was said.

"Now that all that is out of the way, let's get on with the pleasure of this occasion, and you, Katelyn, take your turn at fascinating us with stories of your life."

Katelyn's face broke into a smile, and she began telling about some of the less-known peculiarities of her home and history. One such bit of information that she thought the ranger would particularly enjoy was the history of cloven horseshoes. England shared one other affliction with Texas, at least at one point in time, and that was rustlers. Englishmen raised and sold cattle to be sold at no less of a demand. There was an instance where rustlers had fashioned special horseshoes for their horses that made imprints more akin to a cow's hoof. Using this artifice, they were able to drive cattle from one spread to another without their horses being tracked afterward. Such shoes that had been found were on display in a manor house that had suffered from their use.

The ranger's eyes actually grew wide at the thought of such a thing actually working. "Jumping Jehoshaphat! If any gang tried that here, I wouldn't know what to do. Trying to find horse track when the horse doesn't leave tracks like it's supposed to would even drive our Indian scouts batty."

Katelyn and the Joneses were pleased that the ranger had been impressed and the previous damage apparently had been undone. The conversation continued as different subjects arose, and the members of the group found strength to talk after such an eventful day.

That evening the train pulled into the San Antonio station, and the group rallied new strength to disembark. They collected the luggage and arranged for a porter to convey it to the hotel where they had reservations as the group casually strolled down the street. Street lanterns had been lit, and Stephens and Kina wanted their friends to see all they wanted of the bustling town.

"Doesn't this town have an important place in your state's history?" Katelyn asked.

"Yes, it does," Stephens replied. "It's the site of one of the great battles of the Texas revolution. If you want, we'll let you see the ruins of the Alamo mission tomorrow and pay our respects. The architecture there in the old part of town is largely Spanish. You may find it interesting compared to England."

Stephens was in San Antonio fairly often and knew a lot of people, but San Antonio wasn't small, and new people came and went between his visits. So when they walked into the hotel to check in, it didn't surprise him that he didn't recognize the man behind the desk. What did surprise him was his manners, or lack thereof. Stephens walked up to the desk and announced that he was claiming a reservation. The clerk looked in his book and found the name and gruffly asked the ranger to sign in. The clerk was a middle-aged man with thinning hair and a mustache. He hadn't taken much care when he shaved as his face showed nicks and missed spots. And he looked ill-fitted to the dress clothes he wore for his job. The ranger pegged him as the drifting type that took whatever job he could and didn't keep it for long. As he put the pen back in its holder, Emma spoke up, asking if they would get food there in the hotel or go to a restaurant. At hearing her voice, the clerk laughed a little and jeered.

"What's the matter, lady? Don't you think we can make decent vittles in the West? We know how to make tea, ya know."

He laughed a little more, and Kina glared at him.

"You don't get paid to be rude to your guests, sir. I doubt you would do well if you visited her country. I'll thank you not to make fun of her again, or we'll speak with the manager."

The clerk focused on Kina now for the first time, and as he looked, his irritation turned to disgust and anger. "You're a half-breed! I can tell. I know what an Injun looks like. Get out of here!"

Stephens slammed his hand down on the desk and did his best to remain civil. "Look here, you better hold that tongue of yours. It doesn't matter if she's a half-breed or not, she's no different than you or me. We've stayed here before, and nothing has ever been said. Maybe you ought to read the house rules again, if you can read at all."

"When I'm in charge of the desk, I make the rules, and I ain't lettin' a half-breed murdering savage under this roof."

Before he had finished talking, Stephens had reached out, grabbed the clerk out from behind the desk, and pinned him to the wall.

"Let me go!" he screamed. "You can't do this to me. I'll have the sheriff jail you!"

"Go on and send for him then. He'll get here in time to scold me after I rip out your windpipe, you stupid stack of cow paddies. That's what happens when someone insults my sister!"

"You ain't no Injun. How can you call one of them your sister?"

Stephens was about to take this man to his school on manners when the sheriff did show up. He had been sent for when the outburst first started and happened to be close by. He threw up his hands and shouted for everyone to settle down.

"Would someone mind telling me what in tarnation is going on here?" he said.

"Sheriff, this man's tryin' to kill me for no good reason!" the clerk exclaimed.

"Is that true, Wayne?" the sheriff asked. The clerk's face showed astonishment and fear at the familiarity.

"I wasn't going to kill him necessarily," Stephens replied. "I was just going to teach him how to treat ladies and what happens when he insults my sister."

"She ain't no sister, Sheriff. She's a half-breed Injun and don't belong here. You can't let him do this!"

"You're right, I can't, but I should," the sheriff said with a growling voice as he glared at the clerk. "She looks as much a lady as any, and if you want to call a Texas Ranger a liar on top of insulting a woman he says is his sister, then you're a bigger darn fool than I thought."

"Texas Ranger!"

"Yes, Texas Ranger, you darn ignorant fool. This is Sergeant Wayne Stephens of the Texas Rangers, and if anyone knows the difference between a wild Indian and a lady, he does. Now I can't keep you from fearing that she's going to scalp you, but until she actually tries it, you just do your job and show some respect. And thank your lucky stars that I didn't just walk out and leave you. Wayne, let him go."

Stephens pushed the clerk harder against the wall as he released his grip. The clerk ran off to the back room, and Stephens walked over to the sheriff. Sheriff Bill Driver was a man a few years older than the clerk, with slightly graying hair and an easygoing demeanor. Yet his chiseled features made it evident that in his younger years, he had been a man to stand aside from. He had helped Stephens's family after the war when everyone had been called on the help each other. He had worked the ranch, driven wagons, and done all sorts of jobs around the county as they presented themselves. He had even done a very brief stint as a ranger himself when the need arose, but he preferred to stay close to home. Then, about ten years prior to this night, the position of sheriff had opened, and Bill Driver won the election easily. Since then, he had performed his duties to most people's satisfaction, combining common sense with the rule of law. Now he welcomed his old friend with a strong handshake.

"Wayne, it's always good to see you, but you can come by the office to say hello. You don't have to start a ruckus to get my attention. Who are your friends here?"

"Bill, this is Caleb and Emma Jones and their cousin Katelyn. Caleb is the inspector I worked with a couple of years ago on my world tour. It took some doing, but we got them here for a visit. Although I'm afraid their first day may not be overly impressive."

"Stephens, what are you talking about?" Jones cut in. "We knew we would experience a different place and different people.

Nothing has happened to make us regret our decision. We're very pleased to be here, Sheriff."

"I don't take no mind of him anyway, Mr. Jones. I've known him for years, and he's always had a tendency to look down instead of up. That's why he's been conked on the head so many times."

"Bill!"

"We're mighty pleased that you folks have come to visit. If you need anything, just let me know."

Chapter 4

After the sheriff took his leave, the party made their way up to their rooms and had no further incidents that evening. They settled in, ate supper in the hotel dining room, and turned in early so that they would be fresh for the next day. The next morning was bright and beautiful, and it didn't take long for the Joneses to get percolating. They all met downstairs in the dining room again for breakfast and coffee, and when they had finished, they headed out to see the town. Stephens led the way to the old part of town as promised so that Katelyn could study and admire the Spanish workmanship. They visited the ruins of the Alamo mission, and Stephens told the story of the siege and the part it played in the Texas revolution.

After this, they just wandered. The ladies went inside a variety of shops while the men stood around and talked. At one point, the girls went into a shop that happened to be next-door to a gunsmith, and while they shopped, Jones and Stephens went into the smith's shop. Stephens showed Jones the fine points of the new Winchester 1886 repeating rifle that had come out the year before. It was the first repeater that could fire big buffalo cartridges like the old single shooters had been doing for decades.

"The old '73s we've been using are wonderful weapons, but they can't really reach out that far in wide-open country," Stephens said, holding the long elegant rifle. "I've got a reserve on one of the first carbine models that comes in chambered in 45-70. Then, even in a short rifle, I'll be able to hit a target a few hundred yards away easily and not have to creep up to just one hundred."

They finished examining the other firearms on display and returned to the girls. They made their way back to the hotel, and Kina revealed that she had arranged for a picnic basket to be prepared for them. Stephens went to the livery stable and returned with a double-seat buckboard. They all mounted the vehicle, and with a snap of the reins, the two horses began pulling the load. The party went just out of town to a peaceful and beautiful spot along the river that ran through town. The horses had plenty of grass to munch as the party spread out a sheet on the ground and began fishing food and plates and flatware out of the big basket. Grilled chicken, mashed potatoes, cream gravy, and apple pie in the sunlight of a spring afternoon gave them all a momentary feeling of utopian perfection.

When everything had been put back in the basket, the ladies began wandering along the bank, admiring the landscape and the literal sea of bluebonnets and other wildflowers that could be seen. Stephens pulled a couple of fishing rods out of the back of the buckboard that he had thought to throw in at the last minute. He and Jones rigged them up and stood on the bank of the river, hoping for some excitement while the girls walked and chattered. They got more than they would've imagined.

After only about ten minutes of fishing, their utopian setting was shaken by the sound of horses' hooves. Stephens looked up and saw three riders coming in a powerful hurry toward their picnic, and one of them was leading another horse with an empty saddle. Stephens set his pole on the ground and put his hand on his pistol, but then he relaxed when he recognized the man in the lead as Sheriff Bill Driver. The group reined in their horses at the buckboard, and the sheriff was taking a few deep breaths before he spoke.

Stephens spoke first, "I know that look, Bill, you didn't come out here to socialize. What the heck happened?"

The sheriff caught his breath and answered. "It's the stage, Wayne. The stagecoach on its way in from El Paso was held up. By all accounts, two men held it up about eight miles away. They got a right nice haul of cash and jewelry from the passengers, the coach was packed tight, and they took the mailbag. I guess they want to sift through the letters for more money."

"Uh-huh, and I can pretty much guess why you're here."

"Wayne, I'm sorry to bust up your visit with your friends. I truly am. But all my deputies are out making rounds in the county except for the one back at the office. These two have ridden out with me before and volunteered to do it again. They're good men, but I need more help, and with the federal mailbag being taken, the rangers will be called in anyway if we don't catch them in a hurry. Besides, the last the driver saw of them, they were headed in the direction of Bandera."

Stephens's squinting eyes widened, and his mind was made up. "Give me that horse."

The girls had seen the horsemen and had returned in time to hear most of what was being said. As Stephens swung up into the saddle, he looked apologetically at his friends.

"I'm awfully sorry, but I have to take care of this. Finish out the day here, and Kina can take you on to the ranch tomorrow. I'll be back as soon as I can. Y'all be safe."

With that he turned his horse and led the way to the northwest at a pace the others struggled to keep up with. When they diminished from sight, Jones turned to Kina.

"What's Bandera? At the mention of that, Stephens flew into that saddle like a bird."

"Bandera is a town about fifty miles to the northwest," Kina replied. "In 1880, Stephens's parents moved out that way to cut some of the distance off the freighting business. The ranch is about ten miles closer, near Pipe Creek. That's where we're going tomorrow, and that's why Wayne wants to catch them first."

"I see," Jones said. "Well, let's do as he would want and enjoy ourselves until his return. Why don't we go back to the hotel and figure out what to do next?"

The ladies agreed, and they loaded up and turned the horses back toward town. They discussed what they should do next, and the girls admitted that there were still a few shops that they wanted to visit before they closed. Kina, who was driving, smiled wide and tried to keep from laughing at Jones, who sat next to her on the front seat. At the prospect of chaperoning the continued shopping tour by himself, he shut his eyes and breathed deep.

"Why couldn't that sheriff have brought another horse?" he muttered to himself, and Kina cackled out loud as she snapped the reins to make the horses speed up.

Jones was not the best of horsemen. Stephens would attest that he spent most of his time walking or riding in a cab, but Jones would've gladly accepted an opportunity to improve his skills if it would've meant forgoing shopping. But he could not alter his fate now and made up his mind to soldier on through the hardship.

His attitude was lifted, however, when Kina told them that a group of performers had arrived earlier that week and were having nightly shows at the Grand Palace Theater. When their shopping was done, they would have time to refresh themselves and go see the show. The Joneses eagerly agreed. The afternoon progressed to the satisfaction of the ladies and with only slight damage done to Jones's mental state. As the sun began to set and the city lamps were being lit, they made their way back to the hotel. The ladies changed clothes while Jones read an issue of the San Antonio Express. At six thirty, they were sufficiently frilled, and they all briskly made their way to the Grand Palace to see the performance at seven o'clock.

The owner had certainly tried to make the theater live up to its name when he began building it four years prior. Much work had gone into the exterior alone, with bright colors and carved wood on the sign, doors, and windows. The brass handles on the doors had been polished to shine like gold, and the glass in them appeared to be crystal rather than the wavy frontier glass so common in years past. The foyer was bright with oil lamps lining the walls and a chandelier hanging from the ceiling. Somewhere, some sort of incense was being burned to help cover the cigar smoke, and it had a sweet scent that was almost hypnotic. The crimson carpet proceeded into the auditorium past rows of velvet-covered chairs to the orchestra pit at the foot of the raised hardwood stage. The walls were glistening like ivory with intricate gold trim, and red-and-gold-patterned curtain hung down at the foot of the stage.

The Joneses and Kina settled into their seats and listened as the musicians tuned their instruments and finally began playing introduction music. For the next two hours, with an intermission, the audience was enthralled with acrobatics performed by a team of Chinamen, a singing quartet that sang several old favorites along with new material they had composed, and a farcical play about a businessman trying to make his success while wooing his requiting secretary. It was a joyful evening that continued as the party reminisced about their favorite parts of the show over supper at the Yellow Rose restaurant. When they had finished, they began walking in a roundabout direction toward the hotel so as to walk off the meal and see a little more of the town.

They were just about to turn a corner onto the street their hotel was on when the whole block was shattered by the screams of a woman. The commotion seemed to come from behind them, and without a spoken word, they all turned and hastened in that direction. Several other people did the same and were clustering around the corner of a saloon at the end of the street. A man appearing to be a bartender was trying to comfort a sobbing woman that was clinging to him. It was obvious that she was a woman of the night that had already consumed a degree of alcohol, among other activities. The deputy sheriff that Sheriff Driver had mentioned arrived shortly after the Joneses and Kina, and he walked up to the bartender and his hysterical bundle.

"What's going on here, Pete?" he asked. "Why is Sally rattling every window in town?"

"I'm not sure, Danny. I heard the screams, came outside, and as I turned the corner to look down the alley, Sally nearly ran over me. I had to grab her to keep her from running off into the night, and here she is."

"We might would all have some peace and quiet if you had let her go," the deputy said with a scowl. "Is she drunk again? If she is, and that's why she's causing this ruckus, then she can sober up in a cell."

"I ain't drunk!" Sally cried out, speaking for the first time. "She's dead! One of the girls is lying dead as a butchered calf around back, and you're carrying on about me being drunk. It's horrible, Pete!" She began sobbing again and buried her face in Pete's shoulder.

"This is serious, Danny," Pete said, "I don't think she's making it up. Why can't you go check it out?"

With a sigh, Danny agreed and started ambling toward the rear of the building. Having heard the exchange with the rest of the crowd, Jones pushed his way to the front and up behind the deputy.

"Deputy, may I accompany you? I think I might can help."

"Who in thunder are you? You sound like a foreigner."

"I am, my name is Caleb Jones, and I'm an inspector with Scotland Yard."

"With what?"

"I'm a policeman and a friend of Texas Ranger Wayne Stephens."

"Oh, all right then, if you want to come then come on."

The duo walked down the alley to the back of the saloon, which was only dimly lit by a lantern by the back door. They began to rummage around, looking for a dead body, under the back steps, around the back side of a tree, even inside an empty whiskey barrel. The deputy kept muttering to himself as he wandered around, evidently still believing he was on a fool's errand.

"That Sally probably drained that barrel herself. I swear I'll lock her up, and she can choke herself on water and my lousy coffee."

Just then Jones stepped around the far side of a supply shed and stood stone-still. He stared down at the ground and put a hand up to cover his nose and mouth. The smell of blood and carnage that hit him was beyond stout.

"Deputy, you should come here."

The deputy sauntered over next to him and stopped short also. A second later, he turned away and hung his head over the empty whiskey barrel to call earl.

CHAPTER 5

The sight that Inspector Jones viewed behind that San Antonio saloon, he decided, must rank among the worst he had encountered. A relatively young woman, not yet approaching middle age, lay on the ground with eyes widened to the point of horror. Her face was white, as was the rest of her body, since most of her blood now pooled on the ground. The remains of her scant clothing were tattered and torn and, like the dirt around her, were stained crimson.

There was a long diagonal cut across the woman's stomach, and components of the human body that very few peaceful people had ever seen had gushed out in a jumbled mess for all to see. As Jones knelt down to get a closer view, he also noticed that the woman's earlobes had been cut off. Despite the abundance of blood all over, there was no blood that had run from the cuts on the ears. To Jones's combined experience with medicine and crime, this indicated that the ear-docking had been done postmortem.

A bustling noise from the direction of the alley announced the arrival of a gray-haired old doctor who had been sent for. He carried his little bag of instruments and medicine and cast a questioning glance at the deputy who was still studying the bottom of the whiskey barrel. Jones took the initiative.

"I'm afraid there is nothing you can do here, Doctor, except perhaps provide some information."

The doctor walked over to where Jones was kneeling and reacted similarly to the sight.

"Lord in heaven," the doctor rasped out. "I haven't seen anything like this for nearly ten years, since the Indian wars were going strong. What on earth happened?"

"I don't know exactly. We heard that other woman screaming and came to investigate. She said someone was dead, and the deputy and I came back here to discover this poor unfortunate. It is plain, however, that this was no accident."

"Despite her profession, it's a cryin' shame that something like this should happen to a lovely creature like that. I'll have someone send for the undertaker to come take care of her." The doctor started to walk off when Jones stopped him.

"I'm sorry, Doctor, I hate to impose on you, but would it be possible to take the woman to your examining room? Just for the night, of course."

"If you can get someone to take her there, then I suppose so, but why would you want to do that?"

"My father was a doctor, and I've learned that sometimes examining a body can tell you something about the crime."

"What happened seems pretty cut and dry to me. I beg your pardon, poor choice of words. But if you want to examine her, I have no objection as long as you clean up after yourself."

"Thank you, Doctor. If you'll wait for me to get some help, you can lead the way."

Jones went back to the crowd and gave a brief account of what they found and recruited a couple of men to help convey the body. The deputy had recovered enough to lend a hand as well. The doctor led the way to his office, and the sheet they had put the body in for transport was set down on the table. The doctor supplied an extra couple of lanterns to light the white-walled room and took his leave. Jones had taken off his coat and hat and was rolling up his sleeves when Kina, Emma, and Katelyn appeared in the doorway.

"Don't come any closer," he said as he waved them away. "This isn't something you should see."

Then he took the time to look at Emma and saw the mixed look of pain and anger that even on their holiday, Caleb couldn't keep from working.

Finally, he spoke again, "I'm sorry I left you like that, my dear. I just had to do something. This isn't a simple murder, and that deputy is…less than competent."

Emma took a deep breath and set her jaw. "I know you have to do this, it's who you are. If Stephens were here, he would probably be in the middle of it as well, although if he were, then the sheriff would be here, and we could enjoy our holiday."

Jones could say nothing and meekly looked his apologies.

Then Kina joined in, "If Wayne were here, I'm sure he'd be involved, but there's something I need to know. Does that girl have dark hair and look to be a little younger than Wayne?"

"Yes, that's about right."

"Does she have a scare on her left wrist that sort of looks like a check mark?"

Jones picked up the girl's left arm and studied the wrist. The skin was so pale it was difficult to tell, but when he was almost touching the arm with his nose, Jones could see scare tissue in a ragged form that could be called a check mark.

Jones sensed some deep connection and slowly turned back to Kina and replied, "Yes, she does. Who is she?"

Kina shut her eyes tight at the confirmation and took a moment before answering. "Her name was Judith Mercer, and she used to be a real close friend of Wayne's and mine. It's going to hit him hard when he comes back."

At this announcement, they all dreaded a moment that previously they had eagerly awaited. Sooner or later, Stephens would be back, and no one relished the thought of having to give him the news.

"Well then," Jones spoke at last, "I need to get to work. He's going to want to catch her killer, and I want to have as much information as possible to give him. Why don't you all go back to the hotel? It's getting late, and it will be some time before I'm finished."

The ladies did so and waited restlessly until he returned shortly after midnight.

Meanwhile, that same night about seven miles from San Antonio, Wayne Stephens and Sheriff Bill Driver sat talking around their campfire. The day had not lacked for stimulation. Figuring that these highwaymen might be similar to the pair that had plagued the San Angelo area a few years prior, the lawmen decided to search for a trail where the robbers might have looped back toward San Antonio. The chances were always good that thieves might be local to their hunting ground. Sure enough, making an arc that crossed the thieves' northwest trail, the lawmen came across another trail going back the opposite way. They had come up on the thieves under a bundle of trees that shaded them from the evening sun. It appeared that they had finished divvying up the cash and valuables from that passengers, and were about to start going through the mail, when they had an untimely interruption.

The sheriff and one volunteer had looped around to come at the thieves from the glare of the sun. Stephens and the other volunteer approached from the north, so that if the thieves got away, they would head back toward the San Antonio area. Stephens and the volunteer slowly walked their horses toward the two men under the trees. It was always possible that these weren't the men they were after, but it was unlikely. When the two men noticed them, they sprang up with their rifles in hand. The ranger and his partner stopped and raised their hands slightly, but not too much.

"Hold on there," Stephens called out, "don't get antsy. We were just looking for a decent campsite for the night. It looks like you beat us to it. Do ya mind if we settle down in the neighborhood?"

The two men looked at each other hesitantly and then slowly lowered their guns. The ranger and his partner touched their horses, and they started advancing again. They had closed to about fifteen yards when one of the horses to the west gave a loud, unwanted neigh. Instantly fearing a trap, the thieves brought their guns back up and let loose. One fired into the sun's glare in the general direction of the hidden horse and the other at the two uninvited guests. The ranger and volunteer wheeled their horses around and ducked as they drew their guns and returned fire at the thieves, who were trying to get on their own horses. Fast, widespread cover fire was most effective for keeping heads down, which was the lawmen's reaction to the thieves spraying bullets on the run, but cover fire was not accurate, and none of the outlaws' bullets found a mark.

Once on their horses, the outlaws forgot shooting and concentrated on making fast tracks. The sheriff and his partner were hurrying to give chase as Stephens yanked the carbine out of its scabbard on the saddle, jumped to the ground, and took a knee. He made himself breathe slow and easy and tried the judge elevation and what little breeze there was. After a couple of seconds, he squeezed the trigger until the gun boomed. When the smoke cleared, he saw that one of the outlaws' horses lay motionless on the ground and its rider was scrambling to his feet. The outlaw had only taken a few steps when the sheriff knocked him down again and put him in handcuffs. This meant that the second outlaw got away, but it was better than bagging no outlaws at all. As it turned out, the mailbag, still untouched, was attached to the dead horse. So they had recovered half the outlaws, half of the loot, and the federal mailbag that made it unnecessary to involve more rangers or any federal officers.

So that night the ranger and the sheriff sat by the fire and chewed their last morsels of food while the two volunteers stood watch over the prisoner and the open country around them, lest the other outlaw should come back. Stephens had told Bill more about Jones, Emma, and Katelyn and how the visit came about. They discussed old times and swapped stories that ultimately brought around the subject of women.

"You may not admit it, Wayne, but I know somewhere in that stone head of yours, you still think that something might could happen. It won't. I'm sorry, but it won't."

"You're a fortune-teller now, are you? I notice that you haven't found a woman dumb enough to settle down with you yet either."

"I ain't lookin' for one. And you may not be lookin', but don't say you ain't waitin'. You know it ain't gonna happen. You've watched her for years, and you know your chance is gone. It doesn't matter how close you think you are, she's beyond that now. Besides, you'd have to put up with a lot of ignorant people's reactions that can't forget times past if you did get her for a wife. Remember that knothead last night?"

"I don't care, a person can be something different than what they are. You've seen it happen, and you know I've seen it happen. I've helped it happen."

"Yeah, I know, but that doesn't change the problem. When you first ran into her years back, there may have been a chance, like I said, but that's long gone now. She doesn't want you, she doesn't want anyone. You've watched her become who she is, and yet you still don't get it. There's plenty of women sittin' over in that town right now besides her, and you got the whole state to choose from after that. I'm sure there's been some ladies in all your ranging that you haven't mentioned before."

"That's none of your business, you nosy busybody. I won't give up on her yet. Maybe since I have this vacation, we might have a chance to make things different. She may still have a little spark left for me and just don't know it."

"You may be a ranger, Wayne, but you're also a hopeless romantic. I think that's what they call it. And in this case, you're just plain hopeless. I don't know why I waste my time with you."

"I don't know why you waste your breath either. I'm quite warm enough without your contribution. And it doesn't change my mind. Judith Mercer is back in San Antonio, and now that I have some free time, I'm going to try to bring back who she was when I met her. When we get back tomorrow, we'll see how she reacts to my devilish charm."

Chapter 6

Stephens and the sheriff had alternated guard duty with the volunteers, and when dawn broke, all of them were in a hurry to return to town, except maybe the outlaw. They all nibbled on some cold biscuits and washed them down with canteen water. No one wanted to take the time to light another fire and cook when they could be back to civilized comforts in a few hours. With a rope tied to the outlaw's handcuffs, the sheriff and ranger led him toward town with the two volunteers bringing up the rear. The outlaw's horse was dead, and the sheriff would not take the chance of letting him ride double with one of them and the outlaw trying to steal the horse and running. He wanted a hot meal too, but the sheriff would take the time to walk his prisoner in.

The sun was high and bright by the time they did arrive back in San Antonio, and everyone was about their business. There were some onlookers as the party paraded through town toward the sheriff's office, including a woman who helped run a café not far from the sheriff's front door. When the party reached their destination, the sheriff and the ranger marched the prisoner inside while the volunteers took the horses to the stable. The prisoner was locked in a cell, and the two lawmen had come back out front, when the café lady entered carrying a tray loaded down with coffee and an assortment of vittles, all steaming-hot.

"Upon my soul, Maudie, you're an angel on earth. I don't care what your help says about you in your maturing years."

After paying such a compliment, the sheriff hastily grabbed the tray and set it on his desk before Maudie took it away again. Maudie jammed her hands on her hips.

"Bill Driver, one of these days, I'm going to put something in that coffee that will make you appreciate my civil contributions."

"Umm hmm, I know," Bill muttered with his mouth already full of food.

Stephens grinned big at the exchange between the two reprobates.

"I would sure love to see that when it happens, Maudie, but please wait to do it when I ain't sharing the coffee."

She turned her hawk eyes on the ranger.

"No one said you had to share it now. If you would stop wandering all over creation and find yourself a good woman, then you wouldn't have to worry about it."

"It's funny you should mention that. Bill and I were just discussing settling down last night."

"You two would make a cute couple."

"No, no, Maudie, it's you. We were fightin' over who would get to court you first and who would get to kiss you good night. Ol' Bill there is pretty darn confident in his ability to make you swoon."

"Why you…" She pinched some bacon off the tray and hurled it at the ranger before hurling herself out the door.

"That bacon is coming out of your half, Wayne," Bill muttered as he kept chewing. "If that's the technique you plan to use on Mercer, you're a dead duck."

Stephens shrugged. Bill finally finished chewing and sat back in his chair.

"Now where is that old varmint that I left to watch this mess?"

"Who'd you leave behind?"

"Danny. I told you, everyone else is out in the county."

"You left that wing nut in charge of the town while we were gone? How come there wasn't an explosion?"

"Would you have rather had him with us?"

"Heck no."

"Well then, what else did you want me to do with him? We were only gone one night, and someone had to be here."

"Then make him the janitor. But take that star away from him before he pokes his eye out with it."

Just then Danny shuffled through the door. He looked at the two lawmen with bleary eyes, and his chin sagged as he helped himself to a cup of coffee.

"Morning, Danny," Bill said. "Was there any excitement last night?"

"Yeah, there was, Bill, you could say that."

"Well, what happened?" Bill looked at Danny with wide, expectant, patient eyes, and Stephens began counting knots in the boards of the walls.

"Well, Bill, it was awfully ugly." He paused to take a big drink of coffee.

Stephens sighed, and Bill prodded.

"Broken nose, broken arm, or missing teeth? Did the mayor's mother fall off the sidewalk again?"

Danny swallowed a big gulp of coffee and looked up at Bill.

"Naw, Bill, one of the girls down at Fred's place is dead."

Both lawmen now sat up straight and looked at the deputy.

"It was terrible, Bill, whoever did it cut her open. It made me lose my supper." He paused to take another drink.

"Dang it, Danny, what happened?" Bill asked raising his voice.

"Sometime after ten last night, I guess it was, ol' Sally started screamin' and cryin', and half the town came runnin'. She said that a girl was dead around back. When we found the girl by the shed her, innerds were all over." The recollection made him set down his coffee cup and grab his stomach.

Bill hung his head, and Stephens took off his hat and rubbed his forehead.

"This ain't good," Bill said. "I guess I better get to the undertaker and have a look before he puts her in the ground."

"Oh, she ain't at the undertaker's, Bill."

Bill settled back into his chair and looked up at the ceiling.

"Where is she, Danny? What did you do with her?"

"Well, when I pulled my head outta that empty whiskey barrel, that foreign-sounding Yard fella that was with me told me and some others to put her on a bedsheet and take her to Doc Lewis's office. The doc told him he could use the place."

Stephens was on his feet now, knowing exactly who Danny was talking about, and sailed past him and out the front door. Bill scrambled to keep up with him as they hurried across town to the office of Doc Lewis.

Jones had managed to sleep well. The previous day had been full of activity, despite the disturbing end of it, and now he stepped onto the street. He, too, was heading toward Doc Lewis's office to see if he could find more clues in the daylight before time ran out. Soon that body would have to be buried. It was with this urgent excuse that Kina, Emma, and Katelyn had grudgingly allowed him to leave them again. They were supposed to head to the ranch anyway. What difference would a couple of hours make?

As he walked, he saw two men riding down the street leading two more horses with empty saddles. Jones looked closer and suddenly realized they were the same men that had ridden off with the sheriff and Stephens. If they were back, it wouldn't take long to hear about the murder, and Stephens would want to be involved. Jones quickened his pace. He wanted to get to the doctor's office before Stephens did and prevent the bad news from being discovered accidentally.

Jones came to a point across the street from the office and was crossing to it when he glimpsed Stephens and the sheriff coming down the sidewalk on that side of the street. Jones called to them and hurried across to meet them.

"Am I glad you're back. This is a very messy affair."

"I'm glad we're back too. Thanks for looking after things."

"Yes," said Bill, "thank you for stepping in last night. I know Danny isn't the most capable person, but I have to use what I have."

"You are most welcome, Sheriff. I'm glad I could be of assistance. But, Stephens, there's something I need to tell you."

"I'm sure you have a lot to tell me, and I want to hear it, but first let us take a look inside." He kept walking toward the office door.

"Yes, I know you want to look at the body, and so you should, but there's something I should tell you before you do."

"Yeah, we know about her being cut up. Danny did manage to tell us that much," Stephens said, pausing in front of the door. "It's a pitiful thing to happen, even to one of Fred's girls. We'll have to get this sick son of a gun in a hurry before people start to panic." Stephens walked through the door into the front room of the office.

"I agree," Jones replied. "But there is something special about this case that you should be made aware of," Bill cut him off.

"Wayne, I wouldn't think it possible after all this time, but with the mutilation, do you think it might be an Injun killing?"

"If it is," Stephens replied, "it would be the work of one renegade. A raiding party wouldn't come so close to here. But like you, I just don't think that would be possible now."

They kept walking toward the examination room. Jones practically yelled at him now.

"Stephens, you know the victim! You know who she is, and I think you should take a minute before you go in there, because…"

He was about to explain what he had learned from Kina the night before when Stephens interrupted him.

"Jones, I've rangered and wandered around this county and beyond since I was a boy. I know more people than I can count, and though I don't enjoy the idea that one of them has been killed, I have to always accept the fact that something can happen to someone I know. I wouldn't be good at my job if I couldn't come to terms with that." He stepped up to the table and put his hand on the sheet that covered the body. Jones was about to jump out of his skin.

"Would you please listen to me for one minute, you big oaf!"

It was too late. Stephens lifted the sheet to look at the face before looking at the rest of the damage. He didn't get that far. His eyes saw the once-vibrant green eyes; the wavy, dark hair now lying in tangles; the small, round nose; and the pale, full lips of Judith Mercer. Stephens's movements and blood froze. Anyone who had ever wanted a free shot at him would've had their chance at that moment. No one else existed as he stared at the once-lovely face he remembered so well. His hand that held the sheet tight began to shake and then dropped the sheet. His mouth also dropped open but produced no sound. And after standing like a tree for a few seconds, Stephens more than half fell in to a chair against the wall with his face in his hands and his hands in his lap.

Chapter 7

Bill and Jones stood silent as they looked at Stephens crumpled in the chair. Having known Stephens for so long, Bill had seen him hurt, but he didn't imagine that anything in their history could relate to this shock. Jones was half in shock himself. Kina had told him that she and Stephens were friends with the victim, but obviously, there was much more to their story than that. The inspector eagerly wanted to know the whole story, but the friend dreaded what the telling of it would do to the ranger. Yet he was a ranger as they both knew, and it only half surprised either of them when Stephens straightened up in his chair a few minutes later and stood up a minute after that and walked back to the table. He lifted the sheet again and called to Jones.

"Jones, what can you tell me about this?"

Jones and Bill huddled around the table, and Jones gave them a more detailed account of what had happened the night before.

"From the condition of the eyes," Jones described, "I'd say she was drunk, or very nearly drunk, at the time of death. That may have saved her some pain. But unfortunately, the cause of death was disembowelment. The only other wound to the body is the docking of her ears, and without more equipment and resources like we have back at the Yard, I can't detect the presence of anything but alcohol in her body."

"Why were her ears docked?" Stephens said with just a slight quiver in his voice. It was apparent that he was fighting desperately to keep a straight face. "That couldn't have been an accident that both of them are gone."

"No, I don't believe so. There was no bleeding from the ears, indicating that they were cut after she was dead."

"Why in heaven's name would someone do something like that?" Bill asked.

"There have been cases were criminals commit a series of murders, serial murderers we've come to call them, and they oftentimes will take…trophies," Jones said this last part hesitantly.

"Trophies?" both the other lawmen said at once.

"Yes, trophies. Reminders of what they've done, of what they've accomplished. Doctors tell us that there is something wrong with these people. Either they were born with such a predilection or were formed to it. They're not insane necessarily, but there is something wrong with them. The ears are not the only oddity, close inspection of the large wound seems to indicate that the incision was made by a jagged instrument."

"Jagged instrument?" Stephens echoed. "What do you mean?"

"Well, the flesh isn't cleanly cut, as it would be if it had been cut with a scalpel or a sharp knife. The flesh is torn and ragged as if it had been cut with a saw or a blade that was uneven and damaged. In any event, the attacker most likely grabbed her when she went to the rear of the building, there were no signs of a fight in the alley, and used his weapon to kill her before she had too much time to react."

Stephens stood silently, taking all this in, when the doctor came through the door and was shutting it as he spoke.

"Young man, I hope you have completed your examination because I have sent for the undertaker. That body must be buried quickly, and if patients were to show up right now, I would have no place to examine them."

As he spoke, he had walked to his office and set down his bag before truly looking into his examination room. He did this at the end of his sentence and realized how full it was.

"Oh, hello, Bill. I didn't see you in there. Is everything all right?"

"Doc, you're a good sawbones, but you'd be a bad sheriff. If you've seen this body, then you know everything ain't all right. It's looking like we have a ruthless, heartless murder on our hands. But we do seem to be finished here, if that will make you feel any better."

Bill turned back to his two companions, and the doctor turned and shuffled indifferently into his office.

"Is there a chance this could've been an Injun like we thought before? It's been years, but the only time I've seen anything like this before was after an Injun attack."

"Bill, I don't see how it could be," Stephens replied. "Most of the hostile Indians have been so far removed from around here that none could take off and make it this far without us hearing about it. There have been no other attacks, no telegraph wires have been cut, no livestock butchered… The signs just ain't there. And the rangers haven't got any reports of runaways. Something about this was personal, and I'm going to find out who did it!"

A deep glare formed on the ranger's face as he said these last words, and without another word of explanation, he walked off in a long stride out the door and onto the street in the direction that would bring him to Fred's place. Jones and Bill looked at each other for and instant and then rushed after him.

They had both seen the ranger in this mindset before, on different occasions, and so they both had a pretty good idea of what was to come. It would do more harm than good to try to stop him, but they might at least moderate the results. Down this street and then that street they followed the quick pace of the ranger until he eventually came to a halt in front of Fred's place. It was just approaching noon, and the saloon had just recently opened, but there were already enough employees and regular customers inside. The ranger stared at the front doors, and his friends stared at him. Dressed as he had been in only his shirt and vest, no jacket covered the pistol that was belted prominently around his waist. As a ranger, he did not have to abide the common Texas town law of not carrying guns in town; this was one of the more obvious ways of spotting them aside from their demeanor. As Stephens stood there, he reached over and unlashed his pistol from the holster and then continued his long, heavy steps up to the doors of the saloon. He grabbed the nob and pushed the double doors so that they opened before him. With the same slow, heavy, loud steps, he marched into the saloon, and just as he wanted, every eye turned toward him, and he spoke.

"Last night, a killing happened around in the back of this stinky waterhole. Anyone who even thinks they might know something about it, come forward now. I'm asking nicely."

Ranger though he was, none of the occupants were causing any trouble and so expected none, and none of them considered the murder of the previous night to be overly serious. They muttered a little, and few grinned at each other. It was evident that they didn't take the ranger seriously when he asked about the murder of a mere harlot. At this, Stephens gripped his pistol and pulled it out of his holster with a familiar rubbing noise that made the crowd give him a second glance. When they heard the reverbing clicks of Stephens cocking the hammer, they gave their full and undivided attention. The ranger's eyes scanned the room to decide whom to question first when he heard the voice of Fred Terrell come from the other end of the room.

"No one here knows any more than you do, Mr. Stephens, I'm sure." The proprietor walked easily toward the ranger, trying to look and sound the gentlemanly part that in no way suited him. "None of us knew anything about it before the wild clamor that forced us all to give up our time to listen to Sal's drunken sobbing. I still can't figure out why she got so upset, she barely knew that other petticoat."

Stephens's eyes widened even more than they had been, and he stared hard at Fred.

"'Other petticoat.' She was a human woman who was not only killed but mutilated. I thought even you would've thought that worthy of a little sympathy, you miserable ol' buzzard!"

"I'm a businessman, Stephens, not a preacher. The only thing that concerns me is that I've lost a portion of my potential profits.

But since upstairs, girls are a dime a dozen, I'll find a replacement soon enough."

Stephens, despite his best efforts, was about to boil over in Fred's direction. Other rangers would already have thrown punches at anything less than submissive cooperation, but Stephens tried not to be that way. Another ranger might not have thought much of a harlot dying either except for the gruesome way it happened and just left it to the sheriff to handle. He tried to remind himself that he couldn't let this get personal, but his shocked mind could only do so much. As he struggled to whip his mind into obedience, another voice chimed in from a corner table.

"If she was tore up so bad, then why don't you go ask your little dressed-up Injun what she knows about it? It sounds like the kind of thing they would do."

The statement came from the same clerk that had so inhospitably welcomed Stephens's party their first night in town. Not with all his practiced defiance would even Fred Terrell have made such a statement to Ranger Wayne Stephens. The clerk, however, was ignorant of the depths he was plunging into. He was sore because he had been disciplined after his behavior had been publicly censored the other night. And his deep-seated prejudice was as livid as ever.

Stephens was literally shaking, though the clerk had looked back to his glass and didn't notice. With a few long steps, Stephens was at the man's table, his hands were on the edge of the table, and then the table unceremoniously flew head over heels to the side and landed upside down. Now the clerk was up against the wall with the ranger's left forearm jammed up under his chin. A man standing nearby who was equally ignorant took a step to intervene but stopped short when Stephens leveled his pistol in the direction of the man's nose.

"You disgusting buffalo chip, who are you to judge? Huh! You're a hypocrite! You talk about savage Indians like you're a saint, but at the same time you scorn another human being whose life was cut short. A better human being than you are."

Even after these quivering, impassioned words, the clerk was still defiant. With his constricted voice, he taunted the ranger further.

"Oh, you must be a saint, you love all the dirty undesirables. First an Injun squaw, and now a drunken whore. How many more do you have? One for each day of the week? Do they all know about each other?" The last word he said sounded louder as the constriction was released from the clerk's throat as Stephens took a step back.

He stepped back to give himself clearance as he swung his pistol and laid the barrel across the man's jaw. He fell to the floor with a cry and put his hand to his face. He looked up and then ducked down as he saw the ranger raise his hand for another blow, but then Bill was there, wrapping his arms around Stephens and dragging him back.

"No, Wayne, no! Settle down now, settle down!"

"Sheriff," the clerk croaked, "this is your town. Why don't you throw him in jail for disturbing the peace or something? He's dangerous and shou—"

Bill looked toward the clerk, and the words died on his lips as Bill's eyes blistered him.

"You shut up! The only reason I'm grabbing him and not you is that you're the one about to get yourself killed. I don't know what happened in your past, but it doesn't excuse your behavior. And if you refuse to stop being ignorant, then you deserve what you get. I would've thought someone like you would at least understand when someone is in pain."

Bill released his grip, and he and Stephens turned and walked toward the door. As they approached, Stephens turned to face the room once more. His eyes swept the room and came to rest on a very-nervous-looking Fred Terrell.

"I'm going to find out what happened last night, and heaven help you if I find out any of you were involved or held anything back from me."

With that, he and Bill and Jones, who was standing by the door, all turned and walked out. Rather than return to the sheriff's office, Bill and Jones pointed Stephens toward their hotel. Neither of the ranger's friends would've insulted his fortitude and determination, but they were his friends, and they knew that he needed time to pull himself together. Also, it was in Jones's mind that the time was ripe for one of the ranger's profound storytelling sessions.

Chapter 8

When Jones and Bill arrived with Stephens back at their rooms, the ladies needed only a glance to see that all was not right with the world. Bill quickly excused himself, saying that he had to get back to his duties. As he walked out, he gave Kina a look that said plain as day, "Take care of him."

After his exertion at Fred's, Stephens had been quiet and half lost in his own thoughts. He had gotten little sleep the night before, had been shocked by Judith Mercer's ghastly murder, and had been on the verge of tearing Fred's place apart. Now he was tired.

With some soft nudging and encouragement, he made his way to the washroom to refresh himself and change clothes. While he was gone, Jones told all that had happened from the moment he had spotted Stephens on the street. He finished, and they sat and waited for Stephens to return. Jones was about to go check on him when he finally walked in. He had traded his soiled white shirt for a gray one, his vest and hat were dusted off, and his face and hair and hands were clean. He seemed a little more relaxed now; there was a hint of red in his eyes, but he smiled at them as he saw their worried looks.

"I'm fine. Y'all can stop looking at me like a bunch of chickens." He sat down in a felt-covered chair and returned their softened looks. "Jones, Emma, Katlyn, I want to apologize to you. You came across an ocean to visit friends and rest from work. But half your time has been full of interruptions, sidetracked plans, and dreadful occurrences. I was afraid that you wouldn't enjoy your time here, and now…"

Emma was on her feet. "Wayne Stephens, if you think we blame you for anything that has happened or that it is your fault, you are sorely mistaken. I thought you were smarter than to consider such nonsense. We do not regret coming here, and we do not want to leave. It is true that I wanted Caleb to rest, but now he has a chance to help you as you once helped him. I lament that poor woman's death, especially since she was close to you, but all the excitement that has happened since our arrival has added to our experience." She sat down next to Kina, who was now grinning from ear to ear. Katlyn also wore a wide grin as she sat next to Jones.

It was Jones that now spoke, "If you really want to make it up to us, why don't you start by telling us the whole story and filling in the blanks we have?"

Stephens nodded his accent.

"Judith Mercer's story is an all-too-common one, I'm afraid. Her father was a musician. He could play any number of instruments and was good. When the war broke out, he was a young man with a young wife and a young daughter. He joined the union army out of Massachusetts, I think it was, and became part of a military band that played at ceremonies and formal parties and the like. After the battle of Gettysburg, the Yanks needed men about as bad as we did. Mercer was converted to a stretcher bearer, like a lot of bandsmen were. They were responsible for carrying wounded soldiers off the battlefield. He survived the rest of the war, but his wife didn't. How or why she died, I'm not sure, but he returned to his daughter a widower.

"They stayed in their old home for some years trying to get life back to normal, but it didn't happen. He couldn't focus on his music with all the memories. So he packed up his daughter and began traveling South, hoping that the beautiful country he had seen absent of battle would help revive him. Over the next few years, they slowly drifted farther South with him performing solo or with other musicians and entertainers. His daughter grew, and as she did, she too learned the art of making music. They would perform together to the enjoyment of all who heard them, and they began to love life again.

"Then, about twelve years ago, while traveling from Dallas toward Waco, the group they were traveling with was hit by a party of renegades that the army and the rangers had been after. The raiding party wasn't even that big, but they traveled and hit fast. The traveling group actually fought them off fairly easily as Indian fights go. Maybe they were too hungry or ran low on ammunition, but as they were retreating, an unlucky bullet hit Mercer. He was one of only two casualties they had, and he died within minutes. Judith continued to Waco and did her best to find work. If not as a musician, then as a store clerk or seamstress or whatever honest work she could come by. Her best talent was still as a musician, but it had been much easier to perform with her father than to get a job entertaining on her own, and things were still recovering in Texas. She continued to drift finding work where she could and always looking for a better set of circumstances, but it never happened.

"Finally, the money ran out, and she found herself stranded at a stagecoach way station overnight. She had only enough money for a partial fare, and an unsympathetic driver told her she could go no further until she came up with payment for the rest of the trip. There was only one other passenger, and he had used the last of his money for his ride home. So out of necessity and despair, she resorted to the oldest profession and surrendered herself to the stage driver that night in the barn. From then on, when all else failed, she knew how to get money. For a time, she still tried to get by with honest work, but the world was against her, and she always ended up sacrificing herself for herself.

"That's what she was doing when I found her. She was in this area for the second time in her wanderings, though I hadn't been around for the first time to know it, and was all by herself near a beautiful place called Bandera Falls. I had hoped to show it to you before long. Anyway, I was on my way home on leave and was passing by the falls when I heard the sweetest music to ever reach my ears. I have listened to many a guitar, harmonica, and flat piano in my time, but nothing like this. She was sitting on a rock near the falls with her horse tied to a small tree and a little wooden case lying next to her. In her hands, she held a black wooden flute with little silver keys running all up and down it. It had been a gift from her father and the one possession she would never part with.

"As she held it to her lips and blew into it, such a sound came out to the accompaniment of the flowing water that it paralyzed me. I don't know how long I sat there listening to her before my horse shuffled, kicked a rock, and alerted her that I was watching. She sprang up, holding her flute like a club, and asked me who I was. I told her I was a ranger on my way home to Pipe Creek. 'Please don't stop,' I said. 'I could listen to you all day.' She relaxed and sat back down on the rock, and as she started to play, I got down and joined her. She must've played to me for a half hour before she stopped. As she put her flute away, I started talking to her, trying to find out who she was and where she was from. As you can imagine, she only gave me vague answers and seemed in a hurry to get away, but after I helped her onto her horse to leave, she looked down at me with a teary smile and said, 'Thank you for listening to me play.' Then she turned her horse galloped away.

"I didn't see her again during my visit home, but a few months later, I went with some other rangers to a saloon the next county over to unwind and relax. We were only there a short bit when I saw her come down the stairs, looking much different than she had that day at the falls. When she saw me, I could just barely see her turn red under all the makeup, and she acted like she would run back up the stairs before a grunt from the bartender made her reform and head out into the crowd. Then I understood the mystery of her elusive answers, and I pitied her. I watched as she wandered around the room from table to table and crowd to crowd, and when it looked like one dirty cow puncher was taking a shine to her, I flew out of my chair without thinking. I grabbed her arm, pulled her away, and said, 'Take me upstairs,' and off we went.

"When we got to her upstairs room, I put my hat on the dresser and sat down on the side of the bed. She turned around from locking the door with her head down and her hands clasped tight in front of her. Almost sobbing, she said, 'I'm sorry,' in her soft, shaky voice and began to undo buttons and hooks on her dress. 'No,' I said, 'don't do that.' She finally looked at me with a blank look on her face and said, 'What?'

"'Don't do that,' I said again. 'I'm paying for your time, I can use it how I want. Get your flute, and play for me like you did at the falls.' She broke down and cried when I said that, but she smiled at me, and said, 'All right, I'd love to.' She went to the dresser and took her flute case out of a drawer. She put it together, and for nearly an hour, she played all sorts of tunes that were an absolute pleasure to hear. The other rangers didn't believe me later when I told them what had actually happened, until another ranger that had been serviced in the next room showed up and confirmed it. Some of them laughed, and other shook their heads, but I didn't care.

"From that night on, I would visit her whenever I could, and at night I would pay her to play for me. We also talked, and I finally found out all that I've told you, but my interventions weren't enough to get her away from her nightly profession. At one point, I told her that I could try to pull a few strings and help get her a job somewhere else. I even offered to get her on as a cook on the ranch. But while she tried to keep as many shreds of self-respect that she thought she could, she was also acutely aware of the shame that she felt at her position in life. Try as I might, I couldn't get her away. One night I even said I would resign from the rangers and take her farther West. I could see clear as day the struggle in her mind through the look in her eyes, she wanted to say yes, and I wanted her to, but she said no. She believed that she was no longer worthy to be a wife.

"From then on, things digressed. She started drinking more and more as time went by. She became less interested in playing her flute, and when she did, it was always sad, morbid stuff. Later, she got to where she would avoid me when I showed up, she started becoming a different person. Then I got sent to another area to help some rangers who were shorthanded. When I got back a month later, I learned that she was gone, pushed on to a different town. I wanted to follow her, but I didn't. I knew it would do no good, and so I made myself move on.

"That was four or five years ago, since then I would hear about her from time to time in my travels, but I never came across her again. Just a few days before y'all were due in, I heard that she had come back, but I never got the opportunity to look her up. I had planned to find her today when Bill and I got back. We had talked about it last night, and even though Bill thought it was a lost cause, I was determined not to fail again. I was about to head out to find her when Danny told us about the murder, and the rest, you know."

The ranger finished his story and hung his head, and Kina crossed over to him and put her arms around his shoulders. Because of their relationship, she had also come to know Judith Mercer quite well, and Kina would've loved to have her as a sister, but she had realized sooner and more easily that it would never come to pass. A tear ran down Emma's face, and she felt in her pocket for a handkerchief. Katlyn and Jones were both staring at Stephens in consideration. Jones was aggrieved that such an occurrence had befallen his friend, and he was busily combing through all the things he had seen and all the clues he had found, trying to find a link between what had happened and why.

Though he was certainly no expert on Native American culture or some of the techniques they sometimes had employed in warfare, between what he had heard from Stephens and Kina and his own basic research in anticipation of their trip, Jones had to concur that for a rampant Indian to have done this act at this point in time was an extreme improbability. The massive wound to the victim's body was sloppy and messy; it had been done in such a way as to inflict the maximum amount of damage with that single incision. Also, there were the docked ears. Those wounds weren't messy at all but rather precise and clean. That was what cemented his belief that this was the work of a morally deficient murderer, and he would review and discuss these details further with Stephens when the time was right.

Katlyn was trying to solve a different mystery. She could not deny she had come here with some prejudicial ideas concerning this ranger and Texas people, ideas that were inflamed by her indignation over the damaged Mallory estate. Now she was confused. How could a man who had seemed so simple be so complex? How could a man who had been so hard and crude be so softhearted and refined—to be able to ignore a most basic and driven human desire to be soothed by fine music? Why was this man who was supposed to be so frigid and dull becoming so warm and interesting?

Chapter 9

A few moments later, Stephens managed to pry himself away from Kina, stood up, and picked his hat up off the dresser. He started toward the door, and this time Katelyn's voice rang out.

"Where are you going now?"

Stephens turned to her in surprise. "To find Bill, we've got work to do."

"Oh no, you don't!" Kina yelled at him as all three women seemed to surround him like wolves.

Stephens's face showed a mix of surprise and irritation, while Jones's face was overpowered by the grin he did not try to suppress.

"Don't look at me," Jones said when Stephens eyeballed his call for help. "If you think I can save you, then you need to go back to that doctor's office."

"That's right," Kina agreed. "You need time and distraction to help get you back to yourself. Our friends are here so we can enjoy ourselves, so let's enjoy ourselves, at least today."

"She's right," Emma chimed in. "You won't be at your best until you give your mind time to get through what you've experienced. We can help with that."

"I think I see something that might be a good first step," said Jones as he looked out the hotel window.

Stephens took the opportunity to escape and walked to the window. Down below could be seen the figure of the gunsmith they had visited the previous day pushing a cart loaded down with boxes of various sizes from the direction of the train station.

"Do you think your next rifle could be in that cart?"

"Maybe, but I don't have the cash on me to get it. We were just supposed to collect y'all and go home."

"Well, let's go look anyway. At least you'll be able to see what you've been waiting for."

Jones clapped a hand on his friend's shoulder and turned him toward the door.

"Dagnabit, make up your mind," Stephens growled as he moved toward the door. "First you people won't let me go, now you're trying to get me out. And people wonder why I like to be off on my own."

The others grinned as Stephens grumbled, and he and Jones stepped into the hallway. When the door closed, Kina turned to the other two.

"Well, what are we going to do with him? We won't be able to hold him for long." Her eyes came to rest on Katelyn, who was still staring at the door.

"Could we continue on to your ranch? I would think that being in his home with his family would be most beneficial."

"It probably would, but it's too late to start today, and by tomorrow he'll be out of our power. Even if he did take us to the ranch, he'd turn right around and come back here."

"Can we go back to that spot on the river?" Katelyn asked. "It was so beautiful and peaceful I doubt he could help but feel some pleasant relief. Besides, I want to take my paints and try to capture the sunset. The way the clouds are forming, I'm sure it will be a dazzling sight in a few hours."

Kina looked more intently at Katelyn and spoke slowly.

"It is certainly worth a try. Perhaps Wayne and Caleb could try fishing again. I didn't know you were a painter, Katelyn."

"I'm not nearly as talented as some. I just like to try to reproduce what I see. I'm better than I once was, I suppose."

"You are Katelyn, you are," Emma testified. "I've seen your work, and you are better than you give yourself credit for. When you finish it, you should show it to Wayne, I'm sure he would enjoy seeing it."

"If it turns out right, do you think he would like to have it?" Katelyn asked.

"I'm sure he would," Kina replied. "If you haven't already noticed, he has a particular appreciation for artistic things."

With that, the women began preparing for an afternoon that, if oddly repetitive of the previous day, would prove equally as soothing.

While they did this, Stephens and Jones went down the stairs of the hotel, out the door, and down the street toward the gunsmith. When they walked through the shop door, they saw the smith still in the process of transferring boxes from his cart to their proper location.

When he heard them come in, he looked up. "Stephens, I don't know if your gun is here or not. The odds are good that it is, but if you want to find out anytime soon, then lend me a hand putting all this mess where it belongs."

Between the three of them, it didn't take long to sort and stock the pile on the cart. There were boxes of ammunition in numerous calibers, gun parts and pieces, new tools, and a modest assortment of new firearms. There were a few new Colts, including a double-action model similar to what was carried by Billy the Kid, as Jones was interested to learn. There were also a couple of Smith and Wesson number 3 Schofields and a few smaller pocket pistols. Then at the bottom of the pile were three long boxes. One contained the new Winchester lever-action shotgun, whose reliability some people were skeptical of and still preferred an old tried-and-true double barrel. The second box contained the 1885 High Wall rifle chambered in 45-90, a single-shot long-range gun that was second to none. And the last box, to the satisfaction of Stephens's restless eyes, did contain the carbine version of the 1886 repeating rifle in 45-70, which he had been waiting for. After a moment of glee, his eyes saddened again as the smith held it out to him.

"It's a beauty, but I don't have the money to pay for it right this minute. I didn't even expect to be in town. We were just supposed to be here for one night."

Jones looked at his friend and then looked at the smith with a pleading look. The look was unnecessary.

"Wayne, we both know that you're going to end up with it anyways. No one else has been hankerin' for one. Take it out for a bit, and see how she does. Then I'll clean 'er up, and she'll look good as new when you come back for her."

He shoved the rifle into the ranger's hands and then tossed him a box of ammunition. The ranger looked at him and just nodded his appreciation. Then he and Jones headed back to the hotel and arrived in time to load up for the second picnic.

This time their excursion was uninterrupted. The meal was delicious, the company pleasant, and the view dazzling. Once again, Jones and Stephens grabbed their rods and threw fish hooks into the water. They stood and talked as their hunks of cork bobbed on the river. Little by little, they migrated down the bank as the breeze blew their lines. While they did this, Katelyn unpacked her paints and brushes and a large pad filled with thick sheets of heavy paper. All these supplies, she had bought new for her trip across the world, and she was excited to get to use them. Emma and Kina watched as she laid her pad on a board in her lap, and as she sat on the bank of the river, the other two were more than impressed at the way she translated the view before her onto the paper. They watched as she began with the horizon and gradually began working her way in closer, filling in more details as she went. The paper was undeniably flat, but she made it look as if it had depth.

They were still watching when the men came walking up. They had three fish strung on one of their lines, two caught by Jones and one by Stephens.

"I'll bet the hotel kitchen could fry these up nicely for us tonight," Stephens said. "Whenever you gals are ready, we'll head back and get cleaned up."

"Can't we stay a little longer?" Katelyn asked. "I'm not finished yet, and if I don't finish it while I can see it, then I won't get it right later."

Stephens was thoughtful for a moment before he spoke.

"I don't want to be responsible for messing up your painting, but it's almost past six as it is, and I wanted to check in with Bill before we went to the show."

"Then let me stay, and I'll come back when I finish. I can wear what I have on now to the performance, and I can easily carry my supplies."

"I don't know about that," Stephens replied. "I know we're just outside of town, but we're outside of town, and there are still dangers out here."

"I'll stay here so she can finish," Jones interjected. "You take Emma and Kina back to the hotel and check with the sheriff."

Katelyn looked at Jones with a stern expression.

"I don't need a babysitter, Caleb Jones. I am perfectly capable of looking after myself, and I won't be able to concentrate with you standing around fidgeting and wishing I would finish faster. I would appreciate the peace and quiet, and I would complete my work that much faster."

Stephens grinned at her no-nonsense attitude.

"All right then, you can stay, but just long enough to finish. No matter what, make sure you are back at the hotel before dark. If not, I'll have Bill miss his dinner to come find you, and then you'll be on his bad side."

She returned Stephens's grin and was the personification of charm as she graciously thanked him and gave him a quick peek at her progress.

"My stars, you do have talent. Don't ever let anyone say you don't."

Her grin widened, and she settled back down to continue as the others loaded into the buckboard and returned to town. Back at the hotel, they once again unloaded their gear, and Stephens marched into the kitchen to ask about having the fish for supper later that evening. Stephens and Jones returned the buckboard to the livery stable and began making their way to the sheriff's office.

"Bill may have already gone home, it's late enough, but if he has, then I'll just wait 'til tomorrow."

"You don't regret this afternoon, do you? I thought you enjoyed yourself."

"I did, don't get me wrong. This afternoon was very enjoyable. It's just difficult for me to enjoy much of anything right now. Y'all's effort did go a long way toward bringing me out of the hole I was about to fall into. I'm grateful, Jones. I truly am, and I'll be all right once I catch Judith's killer."

They continued in casual conversation until they were about two blocks from the jail. The sun was down, and only the faint pink and purple light of dusk was still in the sky. Stephens was just commenting on how well the colors would fit into Katelyn's painting when several loud bangs reached their ears, and everyone on the street froze or ducked behind cover. The bangs were unmistakably gunshots, and they caused the two lawmen to run toward the jail. They were about thirty yards away when two men burst out of the jail and grabbed the reins of horses that were loosely tied to the hitching post. One was the stage robber they had brought in, without a doubt, which meant that the other was most likely his partner.

At the sight of them, Stephens shoved Jones onto the ground and drew his pistol. He fired and missed and took aim again when the outlaws turned in their saddles and shot back. Stephens crouched down and then sprang back up to fire again. Another shot missed the now-fleeing outlaws, but his third shot seemed to hit one of them as he jerked suddenly. He kept his seat and kept riding. Stephens grabbed the reins of the first horse he came to and jumped into the saddle to give chase. The horse's owner would have to deal with the temporary inconvenience. As he turned the horse's head, he heard Jones yell at him.

"Stephens, they're heading toward Katelyn!"

With the thought that the desperadoes might cross paths with Katelyn in his mind, he drove the horse as hard as he could to catch the thieves.

He shot down the street the same way the outlaws had gone and could see them as he gradually gained on them. They were approaching the edge of town, and Stephens let out a couple of more shots at his quarry with a skill only to be acquired through practice in a wild frontier. The outlaws began to weave their horses back and forth to avoid getting hit. Then the thing Stephens tried to avert happened. A carefree and happy Katelyn, satisfied with her finished work of art, was making her way back into town when the two strange riders seemed to suddenly appear before her. In a flash, they halted, and one jumped down and grabbed her with such a strong grip that the pain of it choked her resistance. The outlaw threw her into the saddle and jumped up behind her with a pistol to her head as Stephens came to a halt a short distance away.

Chapter 10

Stephens stared hard into the eyes of the outlaw that held Katelyn. The man seemed to be snarling back at the ranger like a cur dog and acted like one backed into a corner. His eyes were wide, and drops of sweat ran down his face and through the stubble that was caked with dust. He had swung his horse around to face the ranger, and he shielded himself behind her almost perfectly so that the ranger did not have a shot that he was willing to try. Switching his gaze to Katelyn's face, he could see the fear she felt—who wouldn't be afraid in such a spot? But she kept her nerve, to her credit and Stephens's admiration, which he would realize later. She sat still in the saddle and would grip the fingers on one hand and then the other, trying not to let herself panic. Lastly, the ranger looked at the second outlaw, which was the escapee and the one who had been shot. At a glance, Stephens couldn't exactly see where he was hit, but his shirt was red, and his face was sweatier than the others and showed his pain. As he looked back at the outlaw holding Katelyn, Stephens slowly lowered the hammer on his pistol but kept it at the ready.

The outlaw spoke, "Don't you come a step closer! We're riding out of here, and if anyone shoots at us again, she dies! If we see or hear anyone following us, she dies! If you leave us be, maybe we'll send her back, but if you cross us, you can look for the buzzards to find her."

Stephens's face was like stone as he continued to stare down the outlaw, then he looked back to Katelyn, who still held her nerve.

"Mr. Stephens, I'll be all right. Please go back and tell Caleb what's happened." Her voice trembled, but she succeeded in her struggle to not be weak before her captors.

Stephens just nodded and gently tugged the reins back toward his stomach. Still holding his pistol and always facing the outlaws, he slowly backed his horse away. After five or six steps, the outlaws wheeled their horses and took off, with Katelyn trying to look back at him while keeping her seat on the running horse.

Stephens kept up his end and did not pursue, but he watched them as they grew smaller and took note of the last clear spot where he could see them before the light grew too dim. Now Jones and Bill were at his side on heavy breathing horses, looking their astonishment. Stephens briefly told them what had happened and turned his horse and took off back to town. Jones and Bill followed and caught up with him on the street.

"How are we going to get Katelyn back?" Jones asked. "I've been involved in hostage situations before, but usually it involved a ransom. Somehow, I don't think that will be the case here. They won't want us to get anywhere near them."

"You're right and wrong," Stephens replied. "You're right that they probably won't want a ransom. That would be too risky for them after what just happened. You're wrong when you say *we* are going to get Katelyn back."

Jones looked more astonished.

"I am going to track them and bring Katelyn back alive, and those two, any way I can."

Jones grew red. "Do you honestly think I'm going to sit by and do nothing when my wife's cousin has been abducted by dangerous criminals?" He was almost shaking.

"No, I expect you to stay here and help Bill catch a murderer while I'm gone. I can move faster alone, and this is what I'm good at. Bill needs help with an equally dangerous situation here, and you're the best man by far for that job."

Jones began to calm down and seemed momentarily bashful. "Bill, you don't mind the company, do you?"

"Heck no, I'd welcome it! I normally have five deputies, but three are out on their rounds as I've said, though they should be back some time tomorrow, and I lost two in the last two weeks. One quit to get married and work on his in-laws' place, and the other broke his leg. I haven't been able to replace them yet. Old Danny is just a stand-in at night."

"Was Danny at the jail when this happened?" Stephens asked.

"He should've been. He was there when I left. Let's go see what he has to say for himself."

There was a small crowd of people in front of the jail when they arrived. As they dismounted, Kina and Emma ran up to them. Stephens again retold the story, and Jones held Emma as she labored to display the same fortitude her cousin had.

"Kina, grab that store clerk there and go get the supplies I need to last for a week. Tell him it's state business, and I'll settle with him when I get back."

Kina ran off to do her brother's bidding, and he walked into the jail. At first, the clerk wasn't very cooperative, state business or not, and didn't intend to let go of supplies on credit to a stranger. But when he saw the hawkeyed expression on Kina's face, and finally comprehended what would likely be the consequence of his stubbornness, he relented.

The same graying Doc Lewis was in the office looking at Danny, who was sitting in a chair with his shirt pulled up on one side. There was a little blood smeared around an area the doctor was dabbing at, and every time he touched the spot, Danny went, "Ooh, ooh, oooh, take it easy, Doc!"

The sheriff and ranger watched as the doctor finished bandaging the graze on Danny's side and then excused himself.

"Well, Danny," Bill said, "tell us what happened."

"Well, Bill, it was like this, you had just left, and I started to sweep the floor to get that out of the way. Then I started looking for the coffee to see if I had enough for the night or if I needed to run to Maudie's. I had to shuffle some things around and get the lamps ready for the night and all…"

"For cryin' in my canteen, Danny, tell us about the jailbreak!" Stephens hollered. His teeth were clinched as he glared at the so-called deputy.

Danny jerked and became wide-eyed with tension.

"Take it easy, Wayne, I was gettin' to it. I'm sorry they're gone, but they're gone. If we don't catch 'em again, then somebody else will." He rubbed the bandaged spot on his side as if it might gain him some sympathy. Stephens just glared at him harder, and Bill spoke up with waning patience.

"It ain't that simple, Danny, they took a woman hostage on their way out of town to keep us from following them. And if we don't catch them soon, then we'll probably have another murder to contend with. Now talk!"

"All right, Bill, all right. Let's see, I had just sat down from putting on the coffee pot when this feller came in the door saying that he had a complaint to file, and he wanted to put it in writing. I opened the desk drawer to get some paper, and next thing I knew, I was picking my head up off the desk in time to see the man and the prisoner headin' out the door. I stood up, I think I stood up, and pulled my gun and shot at 'em. My shot hit the doorframe, and then they both turned and shot at me. I guess they found the prisoner's gun, but it was the big feller that sliced my side. Then they were gone, and I heard yelling in the street, and then the doc showed up, and then you showed up."

Stephens and the sheriff looked at each other.

"What's the bond?" Bill asked. "You know as well as I do that a free-and-clear outlaw don't come back for a caught outlaw unless they have a reason."

"Yep, the one we caught was either the boss or they're related."

"Yeah, they're brothers," Danny informed them. "Right before I shot at them, I heard one of them say, 'Let's get outta here, brother.'"

Bill yanked off his hat and ran his fingers through his hair. Stephens threw his hands in the air, took a step toward Danny, from which Danny recoiled, and then turned and barged out the door.

"I swear to my soul, Danny," Bill said, "someday I'm going to thump that head of yours 'till it starts working right." Then he followed Stephens.

Jones had been standing just outside the door, listening to the interview. He didn't mind letting them deal with Danny while he held his wife. His brief experience with the deputy had convinced him that Danny was more distracting than helpful.

"Let me come with you," Jones asked again as Stephens and the sheriff walked up. "I have to protect my family, and I'm not incompetent."

"Jones, I know you're not. You are an entirely capable lawman, except for being able to keep up with me on a horse. This is what I've done for seventeen years, and I'm good at it. I'll bring Katelyn back, I promise. But Bill and I both need you to stay here. Solving strange crimes in a city is what you're good at, and Bill is the only lawman in this city right now."

Just then Kina led a horse to the front of the jail. It was saddled and carried saddlebags packed full, along with a big bundle tied on top of them. She had also retrieved his borrowed carbine and had it hanging by a string from the saddle horn along with two canteens. The livery stable could not supply a rifle scabbard with the saddle when Kina acquired the horse. The owner of the horse Stephens had used in the chase had retrieved him and gone home.

Stephens shook both the Joneses' hands and hugged Kina before climbing onto the powerful animal. Kina had picked him out herself.

"How will you find them in the dark?" Emma asked.

"I'm going to the last place that I could see them before the light failed. If I can find their trail, fine. If not, then I'll be in good position to start tomorrow. They won't go too far tonight with one of them hurt. I'll find them."

With that he turned his horse and headed out of town at an easy gallop. When the sounds of his horse's hooves died away, the others looked at each other, and then Jones spoke.

"We won't do ourselves any good just waiting and worrying about them. The best thing we can do is keep busy."

"I have several friends in town," Kina said. "Since we'll be staying here for a while instead of going on to the ranch, I'll take Emma around to meet them. We might be able to find some of them tonight."

Emma looked kindly at her friend and agreed. They said goodbye and started walking down the street.

"Sheriff, how do you want to proceed with the murder investigation?"

Bill considered the inspector's countenance and then replied.

"First off, Mr. Jones, just call me Bill. Second, don't worry about your cousin or that rogue that's chasing them. The rangers had a saying in the old days that they could 'track like Indians, ride like Mexicans, shoot like Tennesseans, and fight like the devil.' Wayne pretty much fits that bill, and he'll see it through to the end."

"I know, I saw the aftermath of him storming an estate in England where he was outnumbered about twenty-five to one."

"Really? You need to come inside and give me the particulars on that story. Wayne never gave me that much detail about that part of his trip. When you finish, then we'll start nosing around town. I hate to say it, but right now it's a waiting game for something else to happen."

Jones nodded his agreement. "Very well...Bill, I'll tell you what I can."

The two walked back into the jail, and after Danny sauntered through the door to go home, Jones settled down to telling the whole story of how he and Stephens had met two years prior and every detail he could remember of their adventures until the day Stephens left. In return, Bill gave an account of his life as far as he thought it would concern the Englishman. His grandparents were Dutch, and he had been born in Texas just before the Mexican War started. He told about his own brief stint in the ranger company alongside Stephens when men were few and Texans fought Indians on one side and bandits and rustlers on the other. The stories helped both to calm down and accept the long night ahead of them. They never would've guessed that their easy actions were being observed, as they had been since the jailbreak, by a pair of catlike eyes that were excited but patient to wait and watch and see what the night would hold for him when the sheriff and his friend weren't looking.

Chapter 11

The eyes watched and the ears heard all that was said from the time of the jailbreak until the sheriff and inspector retired into the jail and shut the door. Still, he continued to watch and wait to see what would occur. The act of the previous night had drawn much attention, more than had been expected in the ignorance of who the woman was that had been killed and who was in town at the time. If it could've been said that the perpetrator was in his right mind, then it would've been common sense to move to a different location to continue his crusade, if continue it he must, in a less threatening environment. But he could not be said to be completely in his right mind, as Jones had hinted. He must continue here and now. There were still too many guilty here to leave. Too many here still sowing and harvesting their seeds of corruption and destruction as they had in his own life. A stand must be taken, and in this target rich city, he would make his start.

He continued to watch from the dark alley where the light of the streetlamps couldn't reach him. Through the window, he could see the sheriff and inspector taking turns talking to each other, telling their stories like they were sitting around a dinner table. On and on they went, and still the observer stayed put and watched. The previous murder had taken place close to ten o'clock, so when

Bill saw that it was a little after nine thirty, he moved his feet off his desk and back down to the floor.

"Welp," he said, "it's about time to start a patrol around town. According to you, it's almost the time the first murder happened. Maybe if we let people see us and know we're around, this fellow won't strike tonight. And if we're lucky, we might spot something useful."

"I agree with you. I was about to say something if you hadn't. Shall we split up and take different areas?"

"If I had deputies here, I would pair them off and cover different areas, but it's just the two of us. No offense, Mr. Jones, but I don't want you or me accidentally coming across this scoundrel by ourselves. There's no tellin' what he might try to do if he thinks he's caught, even if we don't know who he is yet. And you're not familiar with all our streets. I think it better overall if we stay together."

"You're quite right, Bill, I just wanted to better our chances. If I were back in London, I would go to a constable station and commandeer the manpower to make a thorough search. But as you say, there are only the two of us now. So let's make the best time we can. May I make one suggestion?"

"Go ahead."

"Once we complete our round through the city, let's do it again. This villain may see us and wait for us to pass before he strikes, but he probably won't expect us to return quite so soon."

"My feet think your idea stinks, but my mind thinks you make a lot of sense. We'll do it."

With that they prepared themselves for their venture through the town and set off. Bill gave Jones a spare pistol that he kept in the office and a pocket full of spare ammunition. Despite all that Jones had been told of this country by Stephens, he was not accustomed to taking weapons on a holiday unless it was for hunting. So he had come without his revolver that he usually carried around the streets of London. Now he carried his borrowed pistol stuck into his pants and covered by his jacket.

The pair made their way toward the nearest saloon to the sheriff's office. Once there, they walked all around the outside of the building and checked every corner and shadow. Then they went in and wandered around the inside until they were convinced that there was nothing and no one out of the ordinary. They continued to the next establishment and repeated this routine with the same result. On and on to one place and then another they went throughout the city until every location of night life had been examined. Then they wandered back to the sheriff's office through the other side of town to make sure there were still none of the more common crimes being committed against the quiet populace.

Upon their return, they found a pie pan sitting in front of the door with a towel over it. Bill picked it up and uncovered a beautiful apple pie that was no longer warm, but nonetheless looked incredibly appetizing. They went into the office, dipped out two cups of water, and cut into the pie. The slightest hint of cinnamon could be tasted, and neither lawman had trouble eating a large portion after their long walk. With about a third of the pie remaining, Bill leaned back and stretched his arms and legs and glanced at the darkened windows of Maudie's place across the street.

"That Maudie is a fine cook and a fine ol' gal when she wants to be."

Jones smiled at the mock insult. Stephens had already relayed to him the ongoing love-hate relationship between the sheriff and the cook. He had said that it was only a matter of time before Maudie hit Bill over the head with a frying pan or a rolling pin and dragged him to a preacher before he came to his senses. This recollection made him laugh to himself but also reminded him that Stephens was at that very moment out in the open country trying to save Katelyn from two dangerous outlaws. He wondered where they all were and what was happening. Had Stephens caught them already and making his way back? Was he asleep waiting for daylight to continue the chase? Was he lying on the ground injured and praying for someone to find him? Was Katelyn still safe, or…? He would not let those thoughts plague his mind. Stephens would bring them all back if anyone could. It was time for new distractions.

"Bill, I don't like the prospect any more than you do, but now that we've caught our breath and had some refreshment, we need to go out again. The sooner we start, the sooner we'll be done and can get some rest."

"How is it Wayne never told me what a slave driver you are?" Jones crossed his arm and gave him a sly smile.

"If he were here, do you think he would be any easier on you?"

"No, by thunder! He'd have started over the moment we got back and would have dragged me along like a bad kid outta church. But I thought you were a kindhearted gentleman?" Jones grinned bigger at the sheriff.

"I am always a professional law enforcement officer first and foremost."

Bill grunted at him and still made no sign of getting up for their second outing. Then Jones had an idea. He reached toward the table and, before Bill realized it, had grabbed the pan with the remainder of the pie.

"Come on, Sheriff," Jones said as he opened the door. "If you can keep up with me, then you can finish the rest of the pie as we go." He walked out the door and onto the street with Bill gaping at him.

"You've been around Wayne Stephens way too much, I can see that now, you lousy sidewinder!" Bill hollered.

And with that, he grabbed his hat and took off down the street after Jones. They moved a little slower during this second round but did a quicker sweep of each establishment just to make sure that nothing had happened since the first. At long last, they finally finished without incident in front of the sheriff's office.

"That's all I've got," Bill said as he rubbed his knees. "We have to rest if we want to get anything done tomorrow. I'm going to sleep on the cot in that jail so I'm handy if anything happens before morning. You go on to your hotel and get some rest. I'll send someone for you if I need you."

Jones nodded, shook his hand, and headed toward his hotel.

Then Bill yelled after him. "And if you feel like I deserve to sleep in a little, feel free to let me!"

Jones kept walking, shaking his head and smiling to himself. Both men, for all their efforts, were still unaware that they had been followed and watched all night long and every step of the way. Now the catlike eyes glowed in anticipation of having an uninterrupted evening.

The eyes watched from the same position in the alley they had started out in. They watched Jones walk down the street and disappear. They watched the sheriff shuffle around in the jail until things were just as he wanted them to be, and then he laid down, turned the lamp down low, and went to sleep. The eyes were patient and still watched and waited in the dark of the shadows. While the brain of the murderer might not have been exactly as it should be, he was no fool and would not jeopardize his success by rushing his plans. He continued to watch for over an hour, and nothing happened. At last, he slowly moved from his spot, and checking to see that no one else was around, he crossed the street. He crept close to the window of the jail and slowly looked inside. He could see the sheriff lying on his cot with his hands resting on his stomach and his hat covering his face, as if it wasn't dark enough already. The sound of his snoring could be heard from outside the window, and it reassured the assailant that the sheriff would not surprise him.

Now the murderer made quick time. He silently but quickly made his way toward the part of town where most of the nightlife occurred. It was approaching two o'clock a.m. at this point, and most places were winding down their business as their patrons became too tired, drunk, or broke to carry on. The murderer would not go to Fred's place again after all the commotion that had been caused there by the ranger. But there were still plenty of other targets to choose from. He moved on to a place down the street that was actually Fred's number 1 competitor, not that the assailant knew that or would've cared. He just saw another guilt-rich bed of devils that needed to be executed, and tonight one would be. With his collar turned up and his hat pulled down low, he slouched into the saloon with a clumsy step that gave the impression that he had already ingested a fair amount of alcohol. He mumbled a request for a drink and slowly drank it as he stood and glanced around the room.

The room was close to empty at this point. The bartender had come out from behind the bar and was beginning to put up chairs. There was a poker game still in progress over in the corner. A man had his head down on a table a few yards from there with his hand still grasping a glass. A few more stragglers took their last sips, trying to summon the energy to go home. A woman was trying to coerce some attention from one of the men at the card table with only limited success. He had the biggest pile of money in front of him, and she no doubt hope to appropriate some of it for herself before the night had ended, but he was winning and wasn't going to let more winnings slip through his fingers for the sake of a cheap petticoat that could be gotten anywhere anytime.

The girl finally gave up the effort, exacerbated and tired after the night's festivities. Between her aggravation and the heat and stuffiness of the room, she fanned her face with her hand and borrowed a cloth from the bartender to mop her face and neck. The assailant could tell now that it would only be a matter of time before she went out for some fresh air. While the bartender was looking away, he picked up the bottle he had been pouring from and shuffled out the door. The bartender would not be able to tell whether he had been gone one minute or ten; the bartender would only see that he was gone. He continued to slouch and shuffle down the few steps from the door and down the sidewalk toward the corner of the building. When he reached it, he again swept his gaze all around to make doubly sure that no one could see him and then darted down the alley toward the back of the saloon.

Once there, he contemplated how best to situate himself. There wasn't a shed as there had been at Fred's place; this saloon had a storeroom built onto it. There was the usual line of barrels, but they were of no use. He would make do with a sapling of a tree that was growing a few yards away, barely big enough to support his weight when he leaned against it, but it would get the job done. He relaxed his collar but kept his hat low as he stood leaning against the tree, taking regular sips out of the bottle that barely touched his lips. A few more minutes passed, and then just as he had predicted, the girl emerged from the back door with a shawl wrapped around her previously bare shoulders. She walked out into the small space behind the saloon, looked up at the stars, then closed her eyes and breathed deep and loud. She stood still for a few moments, enjoying the peace of the outdoors, then shivered slightly as the cool of the early-morning hours began to make itself felt. At this the assailant spoke to her.

"Got a bit of a chill there, missy?" He continued to act and speak in a way that suggested the presence of alcohol without being drunk. The girl just stared at him. "I'll share this bottle here with you if you share something with me." This made her come alive again, and she looked her doubts at the stranger.

"Nothing is free in this world," she replied, "and half a bottle won't get you much around here."

After this proclamation, the stranger reached into his pocket and pulled out a handful of silver dollars that gleamed in the moonlight.

At the sight of the coins, her expression softened, and she shrugged. "A girl's gotta make a living," she said, and walked over to the man and allowed him to put his arm around her. He gave her the bottle, and she turned it up to take a big drink. They laughed, and after he took a fake drink, she turned the bottle up again. The girl was relishing the thought of making some good money, and as the stupefying effect of the liquor began to take hold, the stranger reached inside his coat and drew out his weapon.

Chapter 12

Wayne Stephens had little hope that he would be able to find much of a trail in the dark; he mainly wanted to have a head start on following the trail in the morning. He had little trouble making his way to the spot where he had lost sight of the outlaws, and now he sat against his saddle huddled in his blanket and staring off in the general direction the outlaws would've taken if they hadn't turned. He sat and followed various lines of thought since his mind refused to calm down enough to let him sleep just yet. The country around San Antonio rolled and wasn't as flat as the plains farther west, so it was entirely possible for them to light a fire in a secluded spot, and he would never see it, even if it were just few hundred yards away. Even so, he doubted that they were stupid enough to risk a fire and give away their position. He and Bill had been able to outsmart them and catch them, but that didn't mean they lacked brains. That brother had been cunning and bold coming to get his brother out of jail in the evening. He either knew or guessed that the sheriff would be gone, yet he risked it in the late hours of daylight so that they would be able to make a good lead before it got dark.

It was mere happenstance and good fortune for them that they had been able to grab Katelyn and use her a shield and leverage to hold off pursuit. But if they had any brains at all, then they must realize that they would be pursued anyway, just not as quickly as might have been, and that was all they wanted was a few hours to get themselves lost. Lost. How lost would they be, and would he be able to find them? How long would Katelyn be safe? That was a relative term to use; every minute she was with them she was in danger, but when will the outlaws decide she was more trouble than she's worth? When would she outlive her usefulness? And until then, how cautious would they be to keep her unharmed, if they even have that consideration? Stephens snapped his eyes shut and flinched as if in pain, trying to rein in his rushing thoughts. Once before he had been too late to save someone important to him, and the recollection of the consequence of that tardiness made him flinch again.

Katelyn might not be his sister like Kina, but she was Emma's cousin and so Jones's cousin. On that account alone, he would ride through blazes to save her. That is to say, he would put forth even more effort than he would to save a total stranger that needed saving, if that were possible. He was a career ranger and did not take his duty or people's lives lightly, but this was a special case. Besides being Jones's cousin, she was a visiting foreigner and his personal guest, albeit by proxy to the invitation to Jones, and whether he had said it out loud or written it down or not, in his mind there had never been any doubt that is was his responsibility to keep all of them safe in this strange place they were unfamiliar with and which was altogether more dangerous than what they were used to. Then, during these serious thoughts and while huddled in the open country chasing outlaws, he felt embarrassed, similar to the embarrassment he had feared from the beginning.

The Joneses had been in Texas just a few days, and a large part of that time he had been gone to perform his duty when he was supposed to be on leave. While he had been gone, the ladies had been exposed to a most horrid murder, which had drawn Jones away from his vacation plans, being the excellent lawman he was, and the only competent one around at the time. And now what, Stephens had left him to continue filling the roll of a lawman to help Bill with the murder while Stephens was gone again. It was for Jones's own good that he had something to distract him from worrying about Katelyn, and he knew Kina would take care of Emma. It was small comfort though when measured against the fact that the whole vacation seemed to be shot to the stars before it could even get into full swing. What had they done? Had two picnics with some fishing, and they had seen a show while he had been gone. And in there somewhere, they had had to put up with him while he was bent out of shape over Judith's murder.

That pricked his conscience doubly since he was secretly glad that he was out there on the trail and not having to console them over Katelyn's kidnapping. He had to admit it to himself that he dreaded the idea of trying to dispel Emma's panic and frightful worrying about Katelyn's safety and reassuring Jones that she would be okay, even though there was no way on earth that he could make that promise with absolute certainty. He would push tirelessly to catch them, but until he did, anything could happen. Sooner or later, all these thoughts and possibilities and what-ifs must come to a head back there, despite all the distractions, and he could not help feeling glad that he would not be around for it. They might end up blaming him for wanting them to come in the first place. While that might seem absurd and merely a hysterical symptom of needing someone to blame, he would not be able to rebuff such an accusation. He felt they might be justified in such a belief since he was practically accusing himself subconsciously. This provoked him to wonder how fast he could get them on a ship headed back to England once he got Katelyn back.

He was in danger of letting himself fall into a tailspin of guilt. By the reckoning of some, he could be considered a Texas hero, a man who had spent nearly half his life in service to the people of the state. He had succeeded in saving countless other people from hostile Indians, Mexican bandits, and outlaws of every kind. Those he hadn't saved, he had secured justice for, and so ought to be proud of himself as many other people were, but still he could not forget the guilt of his failures. He had felt guilty about not finding Kina in time a couple of years ago. He felt guilty about Katelyn getting kidnapped and would feel guilty about anything else that happened to her down to the smallest scratch. He felt guilty about ruining the Jones's vacation, possibly even ruining their friendship. And he felt guilty that he had not somehow managed to get to Judith and save her from a miserable life that got her killed.

Why did his mind have to bring that up? Judith Mercer had been a shining star in his eyes. She was beautiful, talented, and a gracious human being who deserved so much better than what had befallen her. The history of the world was filled with innumerable tragedies that had befallen mankind without cause or justification, but this was the one that he was personally involved in. Why hadn't he gone after her when she went away? She had made it clear that she didn't want him, but that was only because she felt unworthy and resigned to her fate. Why had he so doggedly been a gentleman and respected her wishes? He had been willing to approach her now, why not then? By now maybe she would've cooled down and changed her mind about things and welcomed the possibilities. But waiting had wasted valuable time and prolonged her suffering, and now she was gone. He could have tried harder to make her see reason. He could've hauled her off by force and kept her away from that life until it was cleansed from her system like a bad hangover. But would he have done it? Could he have gone through with such a scheme?

Such a drastic course might have worked and might have saved her and what they had. They could've had a home and a life, if he had only done what was necessary. Why hadn't he? He had been afraid. Afraid that resorting to such an underhanded act would've lost her to him forever. He had been afraid that such an act would've been so contradictory to the code of living that he practiced and upheld would have irrevocably compromised him. It might would've been the first domino to fall in a line that would lead to his ruin, and for what? He was afraid that for all his efforts, all his compromises, all his hopes and dreams, he would have still utterly failed. He could stand up to the meanest, nastiest, most dangerous villain in the world without flinching because it was his job and his responsibility, but he had been afraid of standing up to a woman who had proclaimed on no uncertain terms that they had no future together even though he believed otherwise. As he sat there in the middle of the open country, alone in the dark, with his rifle in his lap and a blanket around his shoulders, he called himself a coward.

But now the inquisition was finished. His mind and emotions had run so hard and fast that now he felt as exhausted as after a hard day's ride. He slid further down until only his head rested on his saddle, and he quickly fell into a deep sleep that was blessed to not have any unpleasant dreams that he could remember. The next morning, he awoke as the first faint beams of light touched the sky. He ate a few mouthfuls of jerky and hard bread softened with water, saddled his horse, and was following the now visible trail by the time the sun made its appearance.

The trail continued in the same northwesterly direction from the day before. That was also the direction they had headed in after the robbery before they looped around back toward San Antonio. Maybe they planned to get new horses at Bandera or someplace close to it. His parents' ranch would be a prime spot to get horses and supplies if they could get there ahead of him.

He had a choice to make then: either keep following the trail to make sure he didn't miss a change in direction, or act on his hypothesis and make his way toward the ranch and the area where the outlaws could easily resupply. If he followed the trail, it would cause him to go slower with him always looking at the ground, and they might go into an area where they left no trail to follow. If he were to make his own way toward Bandera, then he could make better time and possibly manage to get ahead of them. But following that plan involved the risk of being wrong and losing them altogether.

He kept following the trail for a while longer and came upon the spot that must've been their camp for the night. It was a little more than a mile from where he had camped, and they had built a fire. But it had been small, and there were scatter drops of dried blood that he almost didn't see. The brother from the jail had been shot and hadn't looked so good when Stephens had seen him at the edge of town. They must've stopped when it got dark and built the fire to heat water for doctoring. So they had probably stayed there the whole night for him to rest and might not be that far ahead, but they would still make better time than he would following the trail.

Erring on the side of caution, he still followed the trail and was glad to see that it did not seem to be wavering. He kept tracking as careful as ever and it paid off. As he passed by a clump of bushes, he very nearly missed the flutter of white. He stopped and got down to examine it and discovered that it was a piece of fine white cloth. It was ripped all over and looked terrible, but something about it still seemed a little too neat. Stephens stretched the cloth out and held it up to the sky, and there it was. Ripped in the cloth, as if with a sharp rock, we're the ragged lines to spell R-A-N-C-H. Stephens's heart jumped, and he swung back into the saddle and took off. His ranch was the biggest and nearest in the area. If the outlaws had said they were going to a ranch, then it was an almost-sure bet that was where they were headed. Going on that assumption, he could now through caution to the wind and head for the ranch as fast as he could with nothing to slow him down.

He was doubly hopeful, and his spirits high as the swift air hit his face. Not only would he now be able to make much quicker time than the outlaws with one of them hurt, but Katelyn was alive. At the very least, she had been alive that morning. On top of that, she had had enough wits about her to be able to make that message. That elevated her standing in his eyes. It had been growing a little since after the incident in Corpus, she had been as charming as her cousins. Now it doubled as she showed that she was not all wind. So she had lived through the night without taking any serious injury presumably. Hopefully, whatever she was doing to make herself valuable to them would keep up and help her stay alive until he caught up with them. That was another point to ponder. Should he catch up with them on the trail, or should he get ahead of them and wait? They would undoubtedly be watching behind them as they went and would see him coming. In that case, catching up with them would be no different than catching up with them outside of town, and now they might just say to heck with it and kill Katelyn before trying to kill him.

He wouldn't be much better off at night, unless his timing was just right and he was able to spot them at the end of the day without them spotting him. If he could manage that, then he could sit and wait for dark before going in to get them. They would always be alert, and unless he could contrive to get right up on them without a sound or anything giving him away, it would still be futile. They would still grab Katelyn up in the blink of an eye and kill her or hide behind her creating the same stalemate. If they didn't have a hostage, it would be worlds different than as it was now. He would risk a few pot shots to catch up with them, and he would simply rush their camp. He would have the element of surprise and be up against two startled outlaws, one of which may not even be able to fight. But they did have Katelyn and her safety had to be paramount.

It seemed evident then that his best strategy would be to push ahead of them and try to catch them in a spot of his choosing where he could hold all the cards. He would set up an ambush between here and the ranch where he would be able to take them without much fuss or put them down if necessary to bring Katelyn back. It was just a matter of getting there. These boys new the roads well and had pretty much been running parallel to it but out of sight of any traffic. His advantage was knowing the country. The roads ran as direct as they could from one place to another, but they were made to be easier for wagons and coaches. Single riders could take shorter paths if they knew where to go. They would probably follow the road until they neared the ranch and then change direction to reach it. He would have no problem cutting ahead of them and selecting his ground. And woe to them when they met.

Chapter 13

Oddly enough, to some people's way of thinking perhaps, Caleb Jones slept rather soundly that night after his rounds with the sheriff. Perhaps it was because of the physical exertion of walking all over town twice that he had been able to fall asleep rather quickly. Perhaps he was also spared what might have been a very restless, agonizing night by the fact that he could've wanted no one other than Wayne Stephens to be tracking the kidnappers of his cousin. To Jones's very pleasant surprise, he arrived back in his room to find Emma thoroughly unconscious. Heaven only knew what Kina and her friends had done to calm her down and put her in a state where she could sleep like that. Whatever the answer was, Jones would be eternally in Kina's debt for her help and friendship this day.

Jones was a loving and dutiful husband, and while he would've performed his duty to his wife with a vigor exceeding what he displayed on his job, he had shared Stephens's dread of facing such a chaotic flurry of emotion and panic that might be expected from any woman in Emma's position. The truth was that just as Stephens had submitted himself to brutal criticism in his cold camp, Jones had come close to doing the same thing all evening. The sheriff's cheerful conversation and the professional focus that came naturally to him when working a case had aided him immensely in not falling into the same dark spiral. If he had, he might have blamed himself for leaving Katelyn by herself, or for even bringing her in the first place. He might have regretted the whole visit, as it might've been Emma that was taken. Shots had been fired during the escape, and someone might've been hurt or killed. In such a circumstance, it wouldn't be hard for him to blame his friends for their invitation, even though Jones and Emma had both agreed to accept it.

The whys and what-ifs could be endless, and fretting about what could've been and what might be, but wasn't, would only make things worse not better. Jones was careful then not to let himself slip into such a trap, and his fatigue and relief over Emma aided his efforts. So he had returned to his room, undressed, and slipped between sheets that were particularly comforting. With a last glance at his borrowed pistol that lay loaded and ready on the small table next to the bed, he shut his eyes and knew no more until morning. In the morning, he would glad for his night of personal peace before having to deal with a second murder.

As he slept next to his wife, and while Stephens slept next to his rifle, the dreaded murderer sat huddled with one hand on his weapon and the other cupped around the shoulder of his eminent victim.

Still sitting under the small tree, the strange man sat with the young woman. He secretly gripped his weapon but forced discipline on himself to wait for the right moment. The woman continued to take sips out of the bottle and make the usual preliminary small talk, to which the man gave rehearsed responses. With every minute and drink that passed, the more the intoxicating liquor stupefied the young woman so that it did not occur to her that the bottle should've long since been emptied. She was just happy for the endless supply of the potent liquid and didn't care what was going on since she had a heavy load of new dollars in her purse. Eventually, she ceased talking at all and just fixated on the bottle while the man fixated on her. His mind was racing with thoughts and memories that this dirty woman was inciting in him.

The ragged and disgraceful state of her clothes and appearance were appalling. The now-stale smell of her cheap perfume was offensive to his nose and made him grimace. The ribbons of various colors that were somehow supposed to accent her appearance in some way were obviously faded and coarse, even in this dim moonlight. And the hair, which had become a tangled mess through the course of the evening, moved with her head and occasionally tickled his nose and face. He was absolutely disgusted with this wretched piece of humanity—one of the same order of miscreants that had succeeded in wreaking such havoc and misery to him. The longer he sat there, the angrier he got, and the faster the thoughts whirled through his mind until he felt that his head would explode. When he could stand it no longer, he acted.

The hand that was on her shoulder gripped it tight and pulled with a force that made her jerk as if she had been shot. He forced her to spin around where she sat and then shoved the back of her head to the ground. The impact disoriented her even more than she already was, and when her eyes finally regained some small degree of focus, she beheld the strange man kneeling over her with something pointed and dull-colored in his hand. Her now-handicapped brain was still trying sort through what she thought she was seeing when he put his free hand over her mouth, and her entire being went blank as the pointed object entered her abdomen. Any noise she made was muffled by his hand, and her wiggles and jerks were fairly easy to restrain. As had been surmised, the effects of the liquor that had made her so susceptible also now made the experience at least a little less agonizing.

The man pulled now on the weapon, which caused it to cut and tear the wound open wider. Now blood was able to escape freely since the weapon no longer filled the wound. Within a few moments, the loss of blood combined with the shock of the stabbing graciously caused her to pass out, and it wasn't long after that she expired from this world. The murderer saw her soul leave. He had closely watched her eyes every second to know that she was feeling something of the pain she had dealt out. Once she was gone, he proceeded to desecrate her as he had his first victim, and when he was finished, he very carefully stole away into the night and was nowhere to be seen when dawn broke.

Bright light was coming in through the window of Caleb Jones's room when he awoke the next morning. It took him more than a few seconds to reach full consciousness from when he first stirred. He stirred in the first place because someone seemed to be using his door for a drum. He didn't want to leave the sweet embrace of his bed sheets or his wife who was still unconscious.

She won't be for much longer if that infernal noise doesn't stop, he thought to himself. With that in mind, he tore himself away and threw on his shirt as he took long strides to the door. He threw it open to see a boy about twelve or thirteen standing there with his fist still in the air.

Jones had little patience for pranks and was on the verge of schooling the young varmint on the finer points of courtesy and manners when the boy blurted out, "The sheriff sent me to get you, mister. He says he needs you right away!"

A dark dread enveloped Jones as the realization came to his sleepy mind what the probable reason was that he was being sent for in this manner.

"Where is he?" he asked the boy.

"He's at Burt's place, mister. The sheriff told me to wait and bring you there."

"Wait here then, I'll be right out."

Jones shut the door again and began scrambling to get himself dressed and presentable again. All the while he was almost in a panic, not because of a potential new murder, but because he was being taken from Emma again. He had not been there when she went to sleep, and now he wouldn't be there when she woke up. But what could he do? Bill and Stephens, and indeed the whole city, were relying on him it seemed to help unravel this mess. He was still in turmoil when he opened the door again, his body operating out of habit despite what was in his head. There, talking with the boy, was Kina. She turned and looked at him with a somber but kind expression.

"Go," she said, "help Bill take care of this. Don't worry about things here. We'll be fine until you come back."

He breathed out hard and took her by the shoulders. "Oh! My dear Kina, you are truly and angel on this earth." With that, he gave her a kiss on the cheek and took off down the hallway with the boy following him.

Once they were outside the hotel, the boy took the lead and went as fast as he could get Jones to follow in the direction of the second crime. Jones walked with long strides but refused to work his legs any harder to gain speed. He would not arrive out of breath and struggling to focus on the job. Also, his newly awakened self was in no hurry to see such another gruesome scene. He discovered that his fears were well founded when they finally arrived at the back of the saloon. He came walking up to a huddle of men, and when he worked his way through, he found Bill kneeling next to the body with his hand on his chin. It was uncanny how this crime scene mirrored the first one. The position of the body, the cropped earlobes, the same ugly, ragged wound and spillage of bodily contents.

The victim had been dead for some hours now, and with the sun shining on it, there would not be the same opportunity for prolonged observation. Jones knelt next to Bill and started to focus his attention on various parts of the body. There was nothing different about the condition of the ears; they were almost identical to the first. No other wounds could be found on her head. Other than where she had been cut, there was no damage to her clothing. The cut itself was just as ugly as the first. It wasn't smooth as if it were done with a sharp knife; even a less-than-sharp knife would've been cleaner. It was as if a saw had been used. It wasn't a pleasant task, but his dedication to thoroughness dictated that he examine the wound as closely as possible.

The body being in the bright sunlight was a much better condition to examine it in than by lamplight in the middle of the night. He might have looked a little ridiculous to the onlookers, almost crawling around on the ground to look closer at such an unappetizing sight. Jones had no time or interest for what the crowd thought; it was his job to do what he could to stop this slaughter as soon as possible. He wished mightily to himself that he had a magnifying lens, but since he didn't, he got as close as he could and forced his nose to bear it. Using a small stick from the tree, he gently pushed on the severed flesh to see if there was anything hidden from plain view. Near the top of the wound it looked as if the weapon had nicked the bottom of the rib cage, and his poking revealed a small fragment of something hard caught in the soft tissue. Jones carefully reached down and managed to grip the object between his fingernails and pull it out. It was covered with dry blood and appeared to be a simple piece of rock, but since it appeared that the victim hadn't turned onto her stomach, another explanation had to be sought for its presence.

Jones pulled a handkerchief out of his pocket, and after wiping off his hands as best as he could, he wrapped up the fragment in the cloth and put it back in his pocket. For a few more minutes, Jones and Bill tried to look over every aspect of the crime before finally letting the undertaker have the body for preparation and burial. After Bill shooed away the crowd, he and Jones began walking back to the sheriff's office, discussing what had happened.

"One of Burt's boys came pounding on my door this morning, yelling that one of their girls had been killed," Bill said. "I'd hoped it wasn't what it was, but it was, and I sent for you. They found her when they were dumping the garbage from last night and getting ready to restock for today. What do you think?"

"The scene was exactly like the first one. A woman off by herself in a secluded back lot, the earlobes gone, the same horrid wound to the abdomen in the same position and at the same angle. This perpetrator knows exactly what he's doing. When we get to the office, I want to take a closer look at this fragment."

"Do you think there's anything to it? It seemed to just be a piece of rock."

"Yes, but how would it have gotten there when she wasn't on her stomach? There was no indication that she had been rolled over."

"That's true, but it could've flown up from under the murderer's feet as he ran off. There was dust and dirt from where it looked like she might have kicked around some."

"That may be possible, but this is the only thing I found within the wound itself and not on the surface of the body. We'll soon see, won't we?"

When they arrived at the office, Jones took the handkerchief out of his pocket and dug out the fragment. He got a small tin plate from Bill, added some water from the water barrel, and began sloshing the fragment around in the bowl like a miner fishing for gold out of a stream. After some minutes, the blood began to loosen a little. At Jones's request, Bill added a few drops of alcohol to the water. With this additive, the process went a little faster, and soon the piece of rock was pretty much clean of blood and anything else that might disguise it. It was rock, but not limestone, sandstone, or any of the other random rocks you might come across. As Jones held it deftly in his fingertips so that the sun could shine on it through the window, he touched it with his other hand. The light-gray rock was smooth and pointed, and with enough pressure from his finger, the very tip of it snapped. His and Bill's eyes both widened at the realization.

"Flint!" Bill said. "A piece of flint left inside a rough cut like that tells me that what we feared was true. An old Indian flint knife. I didn't want to believe it, and wouldn't 've if it wasn't for this. It's just too strange."

"Strange? How?"

Before Jones could get his answer, they were interrupted by the office door being thrown open, to herald the arrival of the two employers of the victims.

Chapter 14

Katelyn sat silent on the back of the horse behind the outlaw that had taken her hostage. They were riding at a brisk pace, but not so fast as to make the condition of the wounded brother worse. They were doing their best to make quick time in the direction of the ranch they brothers had spoken of the night before, and out of necessity, she gripped her captor tight so as not to fall off. She couldn't claim the excuse of falling off accidentally even if it were true. Earlier that morning, she had slipped off when they had slowed down to leaving that note behind. She knew she didn't have a chance of outrunning her captors, on foot or horse, but the diligence that the healthy brother was employing to make sure they stayed safe had not given her confidence that simply dropping the note would pass unnoticed. Also, there was also the chance that it would've simply blown away and never been found. So when she perceived her opportunity, she had slipped off and run as hard as she could back the way they came. Then she had pretended to fall on purpose when she came to the bush and jammed the strip of cloth into the small branches. With that done, she jumped up and took off again so that her captor would stay focused on her and not notice the strip of white.

The ruse had worked, and he hadn't noticed, but when he caught her, the craftiness she employed earned her a slap across the face and a warning not to make herself more trouble than she was worth, lest something worse happen to her. This recollection was running through her mind as they rode. She was proud of herself for having managed her secret feat, whatever fruit it might bear, since the night before she hadn't dared to move after her abduction. She was a strong woman when it came down to it, but she had never been in such a plight as this and would've never expected to be. The shock and panic that she had felt during the flash of events that overtook her outside of town had been immense, and she had gripped the very cause of her peril even tighter than she gripped it now, since it was at least something strong and steadfast. Once they finally stopped for the night; however, she distanced herself as far as she was allowed without reprimand.

The brother had declared that he could go on no more and had to stop, and while she sat and watched what little she could see in the dim light, her nerves began to steady themselves. The pride and obstinacy of the Scottish part of her blood began to assert itself, and her mind began to work clearly and quickly. The unharmed brother, which turned out to be the elder brother, had finally decided it was necessary to light a fire for the good of his brother, despite his firm sense of caution. He gathered up a few twigs and small branches and soon had a small fire burning. He took a tin cup from his saddle, poured in some water from a canteen, and set it next to the blaze to warm up. When it began to steam a little, Katelyn stirred from her seat and stepped toward the brothers. When the older brother saw the movement out of the corner of his eye, his instant reaction was to draw his pistol.

Katelyn froze, and her heart jumped into her throat as she heard the hammer cock.

"What the devil do you think you're doing?" the brother asked in his gruff voice.

Katelyn swallowed and tried to steady her voice.

"I...I can help him. My cousin is a doctor, and I know how to properly dress a wound."

Technically, it was Jones's father who had been the doctor, and she hadn't really gleaned anything from that association to medicine. But that inspiration served her in the moment when she needed it, and at any rate, she calculated that she could do a better job than this overly excited ruffian. The brother slowly put his pistol away and pointed his finger at her instead.

"Fine then, come do what'cha can, but no funny stuff. And you better not harm him."

He moved back and allowed her to approach. She knelt and studied the gunshot. It appeared that the hole was more or less clotted with blood, though a trickle occasionally escaped. The bullet was still inside him and causing him pain. Its flight had squeezed between the bottom two ribs and had slowed its progress enough that it hadn't been able to exit. Even with tools, Katelyn doubted that she could've gotten the bullet out, and she had no tools at all. After sizing the situation up, she decided to simply do what she had promised and bandage him. She reached for the universal supply of bandages when in female company, her petticoats, and with the help of a sharp rock, she cut off a wide strip all the way around. She then cut off a few shorter sections and dipped one of them in the steaming cup. She dabbed the wound with the hot liquid to clean it. She was relieved that older brother realized that the grunts and groans of discomfort that the younger brother made were not from an effort on her part to intentionally harm him.

Once the wound was as clean as it could be, she folded up another bit of bandage and pressed it against the wound. She told the other brother to hold him up so that she could wrap the bandage around him. That done, they had laid him down again next to the fire to rest and gave him water. The older brother grunted a grudging thank you to her and told her to lay down and be still. She did so and surreptitiously kicked the sharp rock as she walked so that it was close to her resting place. It was hard to get comfortable on the hard ground without so much as a blanket, but after a little bit of shifting around and smoothing out an area in the dirt, she finally achieved a semicomfortable position. From then on, she tried to stay as still as possible, and after some time, the younger brother croaked a question to the older.

"What are we going to do now? I can't ride hard."

"I know that, but we've bought at least a little time, I hope, with that extra fluffy baggage over there. I doubt they'll risk following us too close."

"We don't need to be careless though. That guy that chased us out…"

"What of him? He didn't have no badge. He was prolly just some busy body trying to play hero."

"No, he ain't. You know like I do that rangers don't usually wear badges, and that's what he is. I heard 'em talking when I was locked up. He's a friend of the sheriff and was in town to visit friends. You won't keep him off for long, and there may be more comin'."

The older brother grunted a bunch of angry oaths that Katelyn could not quite hear, which was fine by her. Then he resumed the conversation.

"It doesn't matter, we'll keep headin' toward that ranch. He won't catch us before we get there, and even if he does, we still have the girl. Once we get there, we'll get you patched up, get some fresh horses, and blaze a trail without her to slow us down. By the time he shows up and tells them who we were, it'll be too late. We'll mix in with the cattle trails and get ourselves lost from him. Now you lie quiet and rest, we have to move at dawn."

Between exhaustion and perhaps some aid from Katelyn's ministrations, the younger brother dozed off and lay still. The older brother stayed sitting up, facing back the way they came, gambling that he would be able to see something if there were anything to see. Though Katelyn faced away from him and the fire, she could tell by the sounds of both that they were losing energy. With less light for him to see by and his eyes getting blurry, Katelyn made use of her time. Slowly she fished a spare piece of petticoat out of the pocket she had slipped it into and then felt around for the sharp rock. Using all the force she dared without risk of making a lot of noise, she began sawing at the cloth with the sharp point. Some of the lines she was able to cut all the way through, while others she settled for lines being just worn away enough as to be visible. As quick as she could, she spelled out the word *RANCH* in the cloth, and when she was satisfied with her work, she thrust it back into her pocket. With her task complete, she concentrated on trying to rest herself. She was tired and needed sleep, and she felt relatively confident that the elder brother was too concerned with pursuit to be a threat that night. Without even realizing it, she too dozed off into a light sleep, and soon it was dawn and she awoke to the sound of the older brother packing up.

Shortly after, they were on the move again with her holding on tight to her captor as they went. They rode behind the younger brother so that the older could keep an eye on him, while frequently glancing backward. It was well into the morning before they eased their pace enough for Katelyn to put her plan into action. It was successful, but now her thoughts came back to the present and fact that now she would have to be doubly careful and obedient so as not to provoke the ill-tempered brother more than he already was. For the rest of the day, they pushed as hard as the younger brother could stand. They stopped once a little after noon as near as Katelyn could decipher, to give the horses a little rest and drink of water out of a hat. They only stopped for about ten minutes, and in that time they all wolfed down a stick of beef jerky, just as they had for breakfast, and switched horses. They continued the same as they had before until it was too dark to see.

The older brother built another small fire and had Katelyn repeat her doctoring. From the brothers' point of view, speed had been paramount, and they had made the best they could, but now the wound had paid the price. It looked as if the skin around the bullet hole had tried to start mending itself but had been burst open again by the vigor of riding. And whatever the skin might try to do, the insides were inflamed and poisoned by the presence of the bullet without medicine. When Katelyn pushed down around the hole, the brother screeched through his teeth, and a mix of blood and pus came out. She looked up at the other brother and started to give her opinion on his condition, but he cut her off.

"Hush! I know he's bad off and needs a doctor and medicine. Well, we're heading for the nearest one we can as fast as we can, so just keep him bandaged 'til we get there."

"If we keep going like this, he won't make it to a doctor. If you turn around, you can spare him the rough journey, and he can receive treatment…"

"I told you to hush! What good would that do? They'll just fix him up so they could hang him. If he's gonna die, then it's better he dies out here free. Just bandage him and be still."

She did as she was told and cleared another space on the ground to sleep on. She had made no attempt to escape the night before and had no intention of trying tonight. She was just as tired as the younger brother after a long day of hard riding that she wasn't accustomed to and wanted to rest. But now the older brother was taking no chances and tied a big knot around her legs with his lasso and tied the other end to a bush that he sat next to, still facing back along their trail.

"Don't worry, missy," he said just as she was about to fall asleep, "if you behave yourself and things go like they're supposed to, then by sundown tomorrow, you might be sleeping in a bed again." He spoke no more after that, and Katelyn fell asleep.

As she slept and the brother watched, neither would've guessed that Wayne Stephens was sitting in his own camp just out of sight from them. He didn't even know that he was just out of sight of them. He just knew that he had pushed hard through most of the day, harder than them without being encumbered by an invalid on one horse and riding double on another. Now he was slightly ahead of them and making excellent time toward his ranch. He had spent most of his time since he camped trying to decide where he should stage his ambush. What place offered the best cover for him and the clearest lines of fire? What places would be the best chance of catching them in the first place? Since they weren't actually on the road, but rather following along with it, there was nothing that said they would have to come by the place he chose.

This was what occupied his mind as he sat in another cold camp. It was a much better puzzle to sort through than he had the previous night, and far less tormenting, if still a little stressful. There were numerous spots that were advantageous for one reason or another; he just had to narrow it down. Some were too far out of the way; once they were close to the ranch, they would want to get there as fast as possible. Some were short but too difficult for a man who was shot and weak. Some were less known and traveled, mainly used by the ranch hands and people like him that traveled all over. The fact that they had followed the road was a strong indication that they knew nothing of these routes. That left three primary routes that were the most probable, and one of those he could eliminate as well. It crossed a bridge that gapped a large stream. The bridge had been washed out last month by a big spring storm, and they were still rebuilding it since it had taken so long for the stream to go down and the bank to dry out.

So then, that left two main routes. One was on open country and offered no resistance or cover. The other was only slightly longer and went through some rocky areas. Those areas would offer excellent cover for both himself and the fugitives. If he timed it wrong, it could still turn into a bad firefight, but he felt sure they would take that path to take advantage of the cover to seclude their presence and trail. That was where he would lay his trap and make his stand. Besides, there was no practical place along the other route where he could lay an ambush without being spotted some distance away. It was either wait for them in the rocks or push on to the ranch itself and risk having to wait another night if they didn't make it.

CHAPTER 15

The noise of the entrance of the two men into the sheriff's office startled Jones and Bill to the point that they almost reached for their weapons. The two saloon owners looked as if they were mad enough to fight, and they kept cutting their eyes at each other in a way that made it evident that they were ready to fight each other. Heaven only knew what sort of discussion had taken place between them before going there. Jones presumed from their manner, and the episode he had witnessed between Stephens and Fred the day before, that they were there mainly to avoid legal trouble if possible, rather than an adherence to peace and order in the community. They stood in front of Bill's desk, and Fred spoke first.

"Sheriff, I believe this man is responsible for the murders of the last two nights." He pointed a long finger at Burt, who had to lean backward to keep his nose from getting scratched by the fingernail.

He slapped the hand away from him and then pointed at Fred in his turn. "Sheriff, this is the man you want. You know as well as I do that he's capable of it."

Bill was on his feet with his hands raised and an unhappy look on his face.

"What in blazes are you two raving about this time? You are always squawking at each other about something. Why should I pay any attention to you now?" Fred answered him.

"You just said that you know we're at odds, we run competitive businesses, and Burt is always trying to put me out. I say that Burt is your killer! He killed one of my girls so that people would shy away from me and go to him."

"You're a dad-blasted liar!"

"Burt, shut up!" Bill hollered and turned back to Fred. "So you think that Burt killed one of your girls to steal your business and then killed one of his own the same way? Why?"

"Probably to make hisself look innocent."

"And drive away my own customers! It ain't even sundown, and I ain't got as many customers as you did yesterday!"

"How do you know what I had yesterday, you spying son of a…"

"People talk, you idiot, and nothing says they can't go to your place and mine. And the point is that at this rate, I won't even be able to break even tonight, and I'll have done it to myself if we believe what comes out of your ugly face."

Bill broke in again, "So now you're saying that Fred killed one of his own girls so that the next night he could kill one of yours and blame it on you, Burt?"

"I wouldn't put it past him."

"You good-for-nothin' piece of…" Fred made a lunge at Burt and grabbed his collar, and soon they would've been tearing each other apart, but Bill got around in front of his desk and yanked them apart. His increasing age had not yet affected his strength.

"You two stupid donkeys sit down and shut up! This is ridiculous, the both of you would say anything about the other whether you honestly believed it or not. For all I know, you each murdered the other's girl and are trying to get out of it now." Bill was beginning to lose patience; he was not in the mood to put up with the hot air that these two hypocritical buffalo chips were spewing into his office.

"Sheriff," Fred spoke at last, "that's just plain obsewed!"

"*Absurd*," corrected Burt, which brought a glare from Fred.

"Is it?" replied Bill. "The two of you just got done making a case why the other would've committed both murders. Why couldn't each of you have committed one?"

The anger of the two proprietors began to evaporate from their faces.

"Now, Bill…" Burt began to plead.

"Don't you 'now, Bill,' me. If the two of you make such great suspects, why don't I just lock both of you up until I figure this out? If the killing stops, then I may just split the difference and hang both of you. My life would be a lot simpler later on if I did!"

Neither man responded but just stood with blank expressions, waiting for what came next as though they expected to be locked up right then. However, Bill was starting to cool down now that he had vented his displeasure with the two men, and his face began to soften.

Seeing it, Burt started to speak again. "Bill, there ain't no call to pepper us like that. I'm just a businessman here trying to provide services to lawful citizens and make a profit. That's what the point of business is. It just ain't my fault if other people ain't as good at it as I am."

Fred's anger rekindled itself, and he turned a pair of clinched teeth and fists at Burt.

"Got some more insults now that you didn't think of before? I do more business in a day than you do in three."

"Yeah, but then it takes three for you to dupe people into coming back. I have loyal, consistent customers."

"I oughta give you consistent holes in your teeth!"

It looked like the brawl was about to start again, and Bill was getting ready to jump in when Jones's voice rang out.

"Enough! That is enough out of both of you, I can't take any more! I've seen your kind for years use up and destroy people, and you're no different. I wonder that the sheriff keeps stopping you from killing each other but that he's committed to his duty. Mob bosses, crime lords, unconscionable opportunists, and pimps, the lot of you! And the fact that those labels don't seem to truly bother you, by the looks on your faces, is a most sorry testimony in and of itself. We are concerned with two human souls that were grossly ripped from this world. However low they may have fallen, however dirty and tarnished they may have appeared, they were human beings who had the most precious thing ripped from them as their bodies were ripped open. And you two degenerates stand here squabbling and insulting each other over your lost business and profit. These two women were your employees, and yet you care about nothing but your greed and vanity. You're both the vilest hypocrites! If you didn't own bars, then you would be doing something else, legal or illegal, to fill your pockets, and devil take the poor unfortunates who get in the way or fall by the wayside. The sheriff threatened to put you both in a cell. Whether he does or not, I would threaten to shut down both your establishments for the safety of the people in them for the duration of the investigation, and the devil can have your profits. Now get out of here before I get hotter than I already am!"

The two men were awestruck by the passion and strength of the speech that had so aptly described them. Very rarely does anyone enjoy hearing the truth about themselves. After a few seconds' pause, they looked at Bill to no avail.

"Don't look at me, you dumb knotheads, get out of here before I can't hold him back. I'll let you know whether or not you'll be shut down."

Dejected, the two proprietors decided to be smart and retreated out the door and down the sidewalk without an argument. Bill turned and looked at Jones, who had his hands on the end of the desk, his head hanging down.

"I wonder how it is that Wayne never told me how eloquent you are. You may have chosen the wrong line of work."

Jones brought his head up, looked at Bill, and let out a short laugh as he grinned.

"Maybe, who knows? I don't know that I would be a good parson."

"Maybe not, but you put a cork in ol' Burt and Fred faster than anyone I've ever seen. You gave them a strong-dose truth, and I wouldn't figure that would sit well with them."

"It is what it is, and we have their kind in England as well. I've never behaved in such a way toward suspects before. I'm normally able to keep myself disconnected from a case, but for some reason, this one seems to be particularly enthralling. Maybe it's because I'm supposed to be on holiday, and yet I'm still having to match wits with homicidal maniacs and witless roaches."

Bill grinned big. "Perhaps. And perhaps sometimes a man reaches the end of his rope and has to unravel a bit. The best of us can only take so much of the evil in this world without pitching a fit. It helps keeps our minds inside our heads."

"That is so. And perhaps those two have given us a lead."

"What?"

"I was standing here, trying to fight down the ludicrous thought that I should've kept my family at home after all that has happened, when I was reminded of what I studied about this place. Stephens and his family tried to tell us as much as they could about Texas and this area in particular. In anticipation of our visit, I decided to do some research on my own, and from that study, I recollected that Anglo-Americans introduced many things to Native Americans, including steel. It's my understanding, stop me if I'm wrong, that the Indians were still largely living in the Stone Age before the arrival of Europeans. But since the Spanish-colonized Mexico and South America and Anglos pushed farther West, Indians began using many innovations that were superior to their traditional tools. To that end, Indians have been using steel blades for their knives, lances, and other weapons and tools. This indicates to me that if a flint knife is being used for murder, then the murders must be deeply steeped in tradition and ceremony, or it is someone trying to make it appear that an Indian is the culprit to protect himself."

Bill just looked at him as he took in what Jones had said, and a light came to his eyes, as the more he pondered it, the more it made sense.

"I think you're right. I can believe that much easier than I can believe that a single rogue Injun is sneaking into San Antonio every night just to kill saloon girls with a ceremonial knife. If this guy is messed up in the head, as you say, then he may also be using it for the pain. I'd hate to get stabbed with anything, but if I had to, I'd rather it be a smooth, thin, sharp knife, and not a big, rough, ragged piece of rock. But that doesn't get us any closer to solving this mess. We still have no clue who he is or where he is, and we don't know how to stop him. Patrolling the town for half the night didn't do any good, he just seemed to wait until we went home."

"Yes!" Jones said as Bill's statement triggered a realization. "Exactly. He waited until we went home. He's been watching us, following us, seeing where we are and what we're doing, at least at night."

"By the eternal, you're right! That miserable devil was probably within a mule's kick of us all last night, and I wore my ol' legs plum out for nothing."

"Well then, let see if we can't turn the tables on this rascal by playing his game."

"What do you mean?"

"We now know that he's following us, so let's use that to our advantage. We'll let a few words slip here and there about the fragment of flint and that the murderer might be an Indian. Then this evening, we'll go out again as we did before."

"You mean you're going to walk me all over town again, even when we know it won't do any good?"

Jones grinned at his new friend. "I'm afraid so, my dear sheriff, but some good will come of it. We will have our own people hidden before nightfall with orders to watch us. We will patrol the town again, but in a more erratic pattern. If the murderer is following us, then he will be the only person to show up wherever we go, with no other possible explanation for his presence. Then our spies will report who the person is they observed and where he can be found. He will still be watching us, but once we have put on a good show of retiring for the night, we will double back to his position and follow him. If he makes another attempt to murder anyone, we will be there to stop him."

"Brilliant!" Bill exclaimed. "I like it, and I'm seeing more and more why Wayne likes you so much. My deputies are due back from their rounds anytime now, and we'll have the extra manpower to pull off your plan."

No sooner than had Bill spoken did one of his deputies walk through the door. He was told all that had happened in his absence and the plan for that evening. An hour later, another deputy showed up to hear the tale, and they were both ordered to get some rest before the adventure began.

Chapter 16

The fugitives altered their course around three o'clock in the afternoon if anyone had been keeping track of the time. The elder brother had decided it was time to stop following the road and start making their way directly toward the ranch. He had been in that area some years prior and was trying to draw on his memory to guide his movements. He knew that there were easier ways to get there; the road they had been following would've led them to a track to the ranch, but he still wanted to avoid people as much as possible. He had heard about the bridge being out over that particularly deep part of the river, just as Stephens had. So if he wanted to maintain secrecy and keep the odds of running into someone as low as possible, he would try for the only other path he knew of—knew of because he had never used it himself. He had been riding with another man who had once pointed out the less-traveled path and told where it led. Now his objective was to find other landmarks that would help him find that area. Once he got in familiar territory, he was confident he could find his way to the path.

It wasn't danger that made the path less used. In fact, it was rather picturesque and forded the river at a point that was fairly easy to cross in all but the wettest weather. It was also close to some of the fall spots in the river, and the shade of the trees and the spring wildflowers made it a pleasant place to just sit and appreciate the beauty of nature, if you had the time. The Indians who made the original path probably did, but the cattlemen that occasionally used it were usually in a hurry. The stage didn't use this route because it wasn't the quickest and not the easiest for a team of four to six horses pulling a heavy coach loaded with up to eight or ten people plus their baggage. This made it an ideal choice for someone looking to avoid attention.

With a little bit of wandering and zigzagging, and him telling the others what he was looking for, the big brother was soon able to find his way. A crease made between two low hills that overlapped was partly hidden by a large clump of tall, prickly mesquite trees leading the way down the sought-after path. Down it they went as fast as they could manage, but they had been slowing down. The younger brother was getting weaker and paler. Ideally, he should've been treated by a doctor immediately after he was wounded and kept in bed. But, the outlaws had to take their chances and couldn't be choosy.

They pushed on, and the beautiful scenes around them made Katelyn struggle to see all that she could while still clinging to her captor. More than ever, she wished she had her paints and a day to explore her surroundings. She remembered the painting she had made for Stephens outside San Antonio just before all this insanity began. She had dropped it along with all her supplies when a gun had been pointed at her. She had not had the opportunity to give it to him, and who knew where it was now? Where was Stephens now, or Caleb, or Emma? They were now approaching the end of their second day of flight and the third night since she had been taken. She felt tired and dirty, and now angry. She had begun to feel more kindly toward the ranger, especially in his time of loss, and she had been anxious to be more agreeable in light of her impetuous actions at their meeting. Now, however, her fatigued mind was starting to heat itself up again. Everyone had praised Stephens as a great man and ranger, a law officer who had done great things, and yet he was nowhere to be found. She admittedly knew little about this sort of thing, but she was a woman of intelligence and understood that they had not been going as fast as they might if the younger brother were not injured. And she had left a note for him to find, if indeed he had come after her at all. Maybe he hadn't and had stayed to solve the murder of his friend. Maybe he had decided that she was trouble and was glad to be rid of her.

Her racing mind almost overpowered her sense, and she tried to think as logically as she could. Whether Stephens or anyone else was coming for her or not, they would most likely be at their destination by evening. Even though she had been treated well, she was still a hostage held by criminals. They were desperate criminals on the run from the authorities. Though there was presumably no law enforcement official at this ranch they were going to, there would be several men under the employ of Stephens's own parents. It would seem logical that no matter what story was given to account for her, she could scream her head off, point a finger at her captors, and be saved by sheer numbers. Would the older brother be willing to take that chance?

He might be a little ill-tempered—and given the circumstances, who wouldn't be?—but he was not a fool. His one objective was to get help for his brother and escape justice. Katelyn had served a purpose to that end so far, but the need for her was diminishing, and she was turning into a liability. If she were the outlaw, she would want her out of the way and unable to cause future trouble. She highly doubted they would give up a horse to simply send her back. They might just set her down here in the middle of nowhere to fend for herself. That might lead to her death by starvation or accident since she was ignorant in the ways of wilderness survival. Or she might eventually make her way to the ranch house on foot, by which time the outlaws would be long gone. But there was the possibility that at any moment they could happen upon some of the ranch workers that would be able to rescue her and overpower her captors, or get her killed trying.

The most logical choice for the outlaws would seem to be to do away with her as quickly and permanently as possible. Katelyn could only guess whether or not this same line of reasoning had entered into the big brother's mind. The younger brother was in no condition to help or hinder whatever the other decided to do, so it would do Katelyn no good to appeal to him. He wasn't in a condition to do much of anything and barely held on to the saddle horn as his horse plodded along. If it meant saving his brother from death, from his wound or by hanging, her captor probably wouldn't hesitate too much about sacrificing her life in exchange. If the young brother were to die before they reached the ranch, then the eldest would be able to make much better time unencumbered by either of them. Katelyn might have been wrong in her deductions and might never know differently, but all her reasoning indicated that in any scenario, her life was sinking deeper into danger with every passing moment.

Her mind was made up. Erring on the side of caution and following the belief that the big brother would inevitably try to kill her, she decided that she must save herself. She would wait no longer for the murder attempt or a rescue, but at the first opportunity that offered her an even chance of success, she would go on the offensive herself. Even if she failed, she was determined now to exact as high a price as she could manage from her captors. From that point on, her eyes ceased to appreciate the beauty of the Texas spring and began scanning for anything that could possible help her achieve her goal. The outlaw wore his pistol on his belt in a cross-draw holster and always kept it pulled around in front of him. Katelyn had figured out long ago that except through miraculous happenstance, she wouldn't be able to take his weapon. So she would keep looking and watching for her best chance.

On they went, and soon Katelyn could hear the sound of water. They were nearing the river, and the sound kept getting louder. Where this trail crossed the river was a short distance from one of the little falls that existed along it.

On the high ground where the water fell, Wayne Stephens lay in wait for the fugitives. He had arrived at the crossing some hours earlier and had used the time to consider his setup. There was an abundance of trees on either side of the river, giving plenty of shade that help conceal someone trying to hide. At the top of the fall was a rock that was just big enough to offer decent cover. Even crouching down, the ranger's body was not entirely concealed, but it would get the job done. This spot on the fall was a mere seventy-five yards of so from the crossing, which was easy shooting distance for his rifle and his eyesight, which had not begun to deteriorate.

Being careful not to leave any more tracks than he could help, he had scouted the position on foot, leaving his horse tied to a tree well out of sight. Reassured that this location offered him the best chance of success, he scouted back along the trail to watch for his quarry. While Katelyn was going over in her mind the possibility of her living on this earth another day, she came into view of the ranger. His heart jumped to see her alive and seemingly unharmed. He also had a moment of personal exaltation over the fact that he had been right and his quarry was headed straight for him. That was all the time he could spare, because now he had to get back to his shooting position.

A few minutes later, he was there, and in another few minutes, he would have his target in his sights. He held his rifle in readiness and did his best to slow his breathing and his heart. He had already reasoned that a preemptive strike was necessary to ensure Katelyn's safety, but with her riding behind his target, the ranger would need all his focus to ensure he didn't hit her by mistake. He closed his eyes, bowed his head, and took a deep breath to mutter a quick prayer that his aim be true when he heard the sound of the horses on the riverbank.

The horses felt their way down into the water that was running calm but swift within its banks. The younger brother sat hunched over on his horse, gripping its mane instead of the saddle horn as it stepped cautiously through the water. Midway out in the river, the young brother's horse stepped on or in something in the water that made him flinch and throw his head. The older brother spurred forward and shot out his hand to grab the animal and calm him, and as the horses stood still in the middle of the river, ranger and captive both saw their opportunity.

Stephens raised his rifle and steadied it on the rock and peered through the sights at the big man that sat in front of Katelyn. At the same moment, Katelyn observed her captor in as vulnerable a position as he was likely to be, stretched out and trying to control two horses at once. As they rode, she had kept hold of his belt to keep herself from falling off. Now she grabbed the belt with both hands on his left side as he was stretched to his right and jumped off into the river pulling him down as well. Right as they fell, Stephens squeezed his trigger and fired, but Katelyn had pulled away his target, and the bullet sent splinters flying from a tree farther down the bank. Stephens jumped up and started running toward the confused scene.

Katelyn and the outlaw were splashing in the water, trying to get on their feet and see where the other was, while the horses wandered out of the way of troubled water with the younger brother not having a clue what was happening in the world. Katelyn tried to stand up in her waterlogged dress, lost her balance, and fell again. Her hand that stretched out as she fell wrapped around a rock in the river about the size of a large apple. If that was all she had she would use it. As she tried to stand up again, the outlaw came stomping over to her in the water. He grabbed her other arm and yanked her the rest of the way, and as he did, she swung the hand that gripped the rock and hit the side of his head with it. The blow knocked the man back a few steps, and he yelled out in pain, but he was hardheaded and still conscious. Katelyn reared back to swing at him again, but this time he caught her arm in the air and slapped her so that she fell into the water again with a cry.

At the sight of the slap and the sound of Katelyn's pain, Stephens stopped and threw up his rifle again. As the man lifted his fist to hit Katelyn again in his rage, Stephens squeezed the trigger a second time, and as the outlaw stood wound up to strike, the bullet burst through his chest and threw him backward into the river. With all that had happened to him, the man never saw the ranger, so focused had he been of Katelyn, and the sound of the first shot had mingled with the sound of river water gushing over his head as he fell from the saddle. Now he would never hear anything again.

Stephens ran the rest of the way to the riverbank and pointed his rifle at the younger brother, whose horse had wandered to the shore. He needn't have bothered. The brother had expired in the saddle somewhere between the two riverbanks, and his body remained hunched over on the horse. Both outlaws were dead, and the danger had passed. Now Stephens plodded through the water to help Katelyn, who was working her way out in her heavy dress. He pulled her to shore, and with the solid ground under her again, she sat with her face in her hands and wept. Stephens knelt beside her and lifted her head to see her face.

"Are you all right?" he asked with sincere concern.

She didn't take much notice of the tone in his voice and just remembered her previous anger.

"What kind of tomfool question is that? No, I'm not all right. I'm sore all over, my face hurts like a dozen bee stings, I'm cold, and I'm tired." She stopped short of saying she had been scared for her life to the man that Jones had professed to be fearless.

However, Stephens could figure that part out for himself, and he knew she had a right to her frustration and kept his tone calm.

"I mean, are you not seriously hurt? Is there anything I can do?"

"You could've caught up with us sooner! If you had, I wouldn't have felt the need to try and rescue myself."

Now Stephens's temper was beginning to flare.

"Well, if you would've just sat still and not pulled him off, then I would've hit him with my first shot, and you could've avoided all this and still be dry."

"I didn't know you were here, and he could've killed me at any moment to keep me from causing trouble at this ranch place. I had to do something since you, Mr. Master-of-the-West, took your precious time coming for me. If you're as good as Caleb says, then why did it take you so long?"

"I'm good enough to have figured that this is where y'all were coming and got here ahead of you. If I were still following your trail, you might still be in the river." A smirk spread on her face.

"You figured? Did my note have nothing to do with it?"

"It said where you were going, not how you were going to get there. Or did you leave the rest of your petticoat scatter across Bexar County?"

The question was meant to be sarcastic and rhetorical, but not offensive. Yet referencing her petticoat seemed to make it so to Katelyn's hot English mind, and she swung to slap him. He caught her arm in the air, much like the outlaw had done, and they were still glaring at each other when a strong breeze hit them that rattled the trees. Katelyn shivered in her dress that was still dripping wet, and her discomfort made both of them realize that there were more important things to do than bicker before nightfall.

Chapter 17

Twilight was fading into total darkness on the banks of the river as Stephens sat down and tended to the fire he had built. It had been late evening by the time Katelyn had battled with her captor in the river, and the sun was making a quick descent when she and Stephens had stood glaring into each other's eyes. The temperature had slowly fallen with the sun, and the breeze that had chilled Katelyn was a precursor to the steady, cool night breezes they had been experiencing. If the outlaws had continued unhindered, then they might very well have reached the ranch shortly after dark, but now Stephens could not risk Katelyn's health by making her ride into the night soaking wet. For this chase, he had brought the barest necessities, which did not include a change of clothes. All he had was his riding duster and blanket that Katelyn now sat huddled in by the fire.

Normal practice was to only build a fire big enough to cook with and see to do nighttime chores, but this fire was a bit bigger. Stephens had scoured the riverbank in either direction within sight of where Katelyn sat for firewood. Now the fire roared big and bright for the purpose of warming Katelyn and drying her clothes, which were hanging over a rope that Stephens had stretched between two trees. Katelyn had been torn between drying her clothes and herself as she desperately wanted to do, and the embarrassment of having every stitch of her garments in plain view to this man that she either liked or despised, depending on her mood. Common sense won the war in the end, and while Stephens went to tend to the bodies of the outlaws, Katelyn had disrobed, hastily wrapped herself in the blanket, and sat by the fire.

Stephens didn't have the tools or the patience to bury the bodies in the rocky ground along the river. He merely laid the bodies on the bank far enough up so no surge in water level would reach them and covered them with their own blankets. Then he laid stones on the edges to keep them from blowing away. He caught the reins of the tired horses without too much trouble and hobbled them with his own. When he returned to the fire, Katelyn had quit shivering and was more physically comfortable, if not less self-conscious. Stephens draped his duster over her shoulders before he sat down. He poured some water from a canteen into a tin cup and set it next to the fire to heat. Then he took out his pocket knife and began cutting a strip of jerky into bits and dropping them into the cup. Next came the hard tack bread he had, which was double-cooked in such a way that it was hard as a rock, hence the name, and would stay good for long periods of time, but that also made it incredibly challenging to eat. Hard tack wasn't normal Texas Ranger ration, but in a pinch it worked, and he hadn't the time to fool with a pack horse and supplies.

It was not uncommon for hard tack to be dipped in water to soften it, and some left it in the water to gradually dissolve into a stew or thick soup. This was what Stephens did to make a decent meal for Katelyn that would further warm her up and fill her up. He stirred the brew with his knife blade until it started to steam, then he handed it to Katelyn without looking directly at her. She took the cup and instantly set it down to cool so that it wouldn't burn her tongue or her fingers. Stephens watched her and grinned.

"I know I'm not the best cook in the world, but you might at least give that a try before you put it away. It's better than going hungry."

"I will try it when it cools down a bit," Katelyn retorted impatiently. "I don't want it to burn my mouth."

"I wouldn't have thought anything could scorch that fiery mouth of yours. Ever since you got here, you've been trying to brand my hide with it."

Katelyn opened her mouth to give a stinging reply, then she stopped herself with the realization that she would substantiate what he just said. She closed her mouth and sat silent so as not to give him anything else to use against her. He was good at that, better than most that she crossed verbal swords with. That was one thing, along with everyone else's resounding praise, that made her rethink her opinion of him. She was rethinking it now. Despite her expostulation of rage after the battle, she had to admit to herself that he really didn't deserve it. She couldn't figure out which direction was which in this infernal country, whereas he had gotten in front of them, and probably would have rescued her without her intervention. She simply would've been mad at anyone she had seen at that moment for not doing something sooner, but her now-calmed mind realized that she had been wrong. She picked the cup back up and took a sip. The concoction wasn't something she would recommend putting on a restaurant menu, but it wasn't half bad and did make her insides feel better.

"This isn't so bad, for a ranger."

Stephens grinned slightly but stayed focused on poking the fire.

"You know, we had rangers in England once upon a time."

"Yes, I know, our own traditions can be traced back to them. They would roam a lord's forests and lands, mainly to keep his property and game safe, but they did some good works."

"By my faith, I honestly didn't think you were that well educated."

"Then your cousins didn't tell you everything, or you would've known that my mother was once a schoolteacher and the best you could find."

Katelyn looked a little dejected now. "Yes, they did tell me that in fact. I just assumed that it was a simple education. I…" She couldn't or wouldn't say anything else on the matter.

"Don't worry, most people only want a simple education if that's what it takes to get them through life. And I took it upon myself to find out other things when I wanted to know them. You are no guiltier than most of the world for underestimating people and assuming they are no more than what you see at first glance. The truth is that if I hadn't chanced upon Judith out here along the river that day, I probably would have just dismissed her as another common saloon girl." He hung his head at remembering what he had needed to forget and ignore the last few days.

"Was it here that you found her?" Katelyn asked

"Not too far away from here, the late morning of a pretty day like today was. The falls were close enough to accompany her playing, and it just captured me."

"Did you love her?"

Stephens was surprised at the direct question and wanted to feint anger to escape it, but he made himself answer it for his own sake.

"Yes, I do believe I did. And even though she didn't return it and it turned stale for many years, I believe some part of me still did, at least until a few days ago."

"You still do even now. Love like that doesn't die but goes on. If the years apart couldn't stamp it out, then not even death can take it away." Katelyn paused, self-conscious again.

It was unusual outside of particular company for her to give her romantic and philosophic ideals free rein. But it wasn't the first time they had stirred in her, and she decided to continue. Keeping a tight grip on the blanket, she scooted closer to him.

"She is gone now, and nothing can bring her back, as I'm sure you know, but that sort of love needs to be passed on and not smothered. You may meet another woman with qualities that you think are worthy of embracing."

Stephens turned a sly grin to her that was partially to hide his own misgivings. "Are you volunteering, Katelyn?"

The question took her by surprise, and the mocking tone it was made in almost sent her back behind her fiery defensive wall, until she realized that she wasn't sure what the answer to the question itself would be. This was ludicrous; she had met the man not quite a week prior, who had seemed uncouth by the standards she was used to, and had been indignant toward him for several past and present reasons. And yet, there was something in her that made the notion seem not so impossible.

Stephens, mistaking her expressions, rebuked himself and spoke again, "I'm sorry, that was rude and uncalled for. I just don't see me ever deserving a woman like that. If I hadn't been so… weak, so feeble toward her, then I could've saved her, from herself and murder, but I couldn't. It's just another one of life's injustices, I think, that some people don't get to have a family. It's my own fault."

"It was her own fault for not taking advantage of the opportunity when she had it. The day she met you, she could've changed the course of her life. But like you and I, she was too proud for her own good. Pride and honor are to help keep us from falling below standards. Once we do fall, they shouldn't keep us from rising back up. Stephens looked into her eyes with a renewed appreciation.

"Well, we'll see. Maybe someday what you say will happen. If it does, I'll let you know."

Now Katelyn had a mischievous look on her face. "What, first you ask me to volunteer, and now you're cutting me loose after five minutes? Do I fall beneath your standards, Mr. Ranger?"

Stephens, still caught up in the moment, took her seriously and looked up from the fire with a gasp as he tried to think of a fitting apology, but when he saw the sly smile, he relaxed and grinned in turn.

"No, someone like you would not fall beneath my standards. I'm just not sure if I could rise to yours."

"We'll see. Now then, what are we going to do next? Well…?"

This secondary inquiry was caused by Stephens's look of being dumbfounded at Katelyn's reply of "We'll see," and then it morphed into a look of slight hope that overrode the sound of the question. Stephens rallied his thoughts to answer.

"Well, the nearest bathtub and warm bed is at the ranch. If we go there first, we can get fresh horses or a buckboard, and you can recover a bit before going back to San Antonio. Or since that's our final destination anyway, I could just leave you there and go back for Jones and Emma by myself. But I don't know when we'd get back here if this murder business is still going on. The other option is for you to put your clothes back on and for us to head back to San Antonio from here. Without the limitations of riding double, tracking, or keeping out of sight, we'll get back in much better time than it took to get here."

"While I do want to see your ranch and more of this beautiful country, I'd prefer to get back to Caleb and Emma as soon as possible. We'll all enjoy it at the same time. And you need to get back to help Caleb and your friend catch that fiend that has hurt you."

"All righty then, that's what we'll do," Stephens said, slapping his knees and rising to his feet. He walked over to the clothesline and started to rearrange the clothes so that the reverse sides would be exposed to the heat of the fire.

Katelyn frowned at him. "Must you do that? Those are my clothes that you're not supposed to handle."

Stephens smiled as he continued without pause and looked over his shoulder.

"Do you want to stand up and do it?"

Momentarily forgetting that her only covering was a blanket under the duster, she began to stand up with an indignant look, then felt the breeze in exposed areas, and sat back down with a grunt. Stephens snickered and turned back to his task, but he was surprised a moment later when Katelyn appeared next to him, grabbed her ripped petticoat out of his hands, and pushed him out of the way. After nearly tripping over a rock, Stephens looked back at her to perceive that she was properly wearing his duster buttoned all the way up, with wavy strands of hair sticking to the back of it and the blanket tied around her waist. She smirked at him in her turn and continued to rearrange the clothes.

Stephens laughed. "By thunder, Katie girl, we'll make a Texan out of you yet!"

Katelyn's sly smirk turned into a big smile, and she repeated her earlier answer. "We'll see."

Chapter 18

Jones lay in the bed of his hotel room next to his wife and did his best to relax while he could. It was still early morning with the light of the sun barely glowing in the sky, and Jones would not move until he had to. But while his body was still, his mind was active. The night they had planned to catch the murderer, they had not. The two deputies followed Jones and the sheriff just as planned but were unable to catch sight of anyone who went everyplace they did. At first Jones thought that murderer had been too cunning and had either evaded the deputies on purpose or been too slick for them to find in the first place. Jones had dreaded the coming of morning as a herald that another body had been found, but no such word came. They had scoured the city in the morning as they had in the night and found nothing.

This might would be a joyful discovery to some, as a sign that the murderer had left, but Jones did not take it so. He was glad that no one else had been killed, but he was not happy that they hadn't caught the killer. Nor did he have any notion that the killer had left or quit. Something must've prevented him from going on the hunt that night, and Jones would be ready the next night all the same. That night had come and gone with the same result: nothing had been seen or happened before morning. The second night they had all three deputies watching over them, as the third had finally returned from his rounds the day after the other two, but to no avail. The absence of a fresh body did give Jones and Bill a chance to rest a bit and recollect their thoughts. Bill wanted to believe the trouble had past and could make himself live with not catching the killer if it meant no more deaths, but he was a man of sense and heeded Jones's profession that this was just a lull.

The reason for the lull would've been almost laughable to Jones if he had known it and if the circumstances weren't so grievous. The murderer had not been out because he had been stuck in his bed. He had been so exultant at outsmarting the lawmen and achieving another victory for himself that he had celebrated. He had gone into a restaurant after the excitement of the second murder had died away and ordered a big steak and a big glass of beer that was refilled several times. He had so much inner joy over his success that he lost all patience and ordered the steak brought to him in the rarest condition. He would've benefited from exercising patience and caution, for the underdone condition of the meat combined with the excessive amount of alcohol gave him an acute case of food poisoning.

So all that night and the next day, he was sicker than a dog in the little deserted shack he occupied a little less than a mile from town. The next evening, he was pretty much back to normal aside from a slight lingering queasiness. However, wanting to leave nothing to chance, he fought his passion to continue his crusade and stayed in another night. It entered his mind that he might have to try to make up for lost time, if he could manage it. So far as he knew, he was still in no danger of discovery. And he was right that no one knew of his existence or location. But by token of his absence from town, he had no knowledge of the recurring plan Jones had implemented.

Despite the grueling toll all this nightly exercise was having on Bill's legs, he agreed to keep trying a little longer to make sure the danger had passed. And Jones was hopeful that tonight he would finally see the fruits of his labors.

"Third time pays for all," he muttered to himself as he lay quiet in his bed. "I'll get this black-blooded monster yet."

One consolation of the killer not being active was that without new crime scenes to go over, and the deputies back in town, Bill needed less help, and Jones had free time. He used that time exclusively to console Emma as he had not been able to do since Katelyn was first taken. Jones's debt to Kina was such that he would never be able to repay it. She had worked wonders with Emma during this most trying time, and Emma was not nearly in such a sore state as Jones might have supposed. This was also a credit to Emma herself. No one would've blamed her for having a more drastic reaction than what she did to the crisis that arose. It's a further credit to her still that though she was not happy with her husband being away from her when she wanted him the most, she was gracious and forgave his absence. She was just happy that she was able to spend time with him now, until something else happened to drag him away.

Until then they had made the most of their time. They had crisscrossed and recrossed the city, taking in everything they could find—new foods, new sights, and new culture they had missed before, and Kina outdid the best hostess to be found in London at making this time as pleasurable as it could be. Emma was in such good spirits between the fun they were thrusting upon her and the assurances that Stephens and Katelyn would be back soon that she actually joked about it.

"If they don't come back soon, we'll have to go find them ourselves just to have something else to do."

Jones and Kina laughed, and to keep Emma from disappearing, they rallied a group of Kina's friends yet again and spent the afternoon playing games and laughing. Jones dreaded having to leave her again but at the same time was anxious to replay his plan one more time in hopes of catching the killer. So around six o'clock, he gave Emma a kiss and Kina a hug and left for the sheriff's office.

When he arrived, all was in readiness. All three deputies were present and ready to head out of the office as if going home, when in reality they would duck into prearranged hiding places. Once the sun was set, Bill and Jones would go on patrol, and the deputies would follow at intervals to watch for the murderer. They had taken turns napping in the office throughout the day so that they had rest for the night work.

As the last one left for his post, Bill turned to Jones, "Do you really think there's a chance he'll come back again?"

"Yes, I do. I have no idea why he stopped, but the attention brought on from the first murder didn't stop him, and our patrol didn't chase him off from the second, he just waited us out. Something is driving him, and I just feel strongly that he'll be back."

"Part of me hopes you're right so we can get him, but part of me hopes he's gone. I don't know if I want him gone just so the killing will be over or if I'm afraid we'll fail again and someone else will die."

"I know exactly what you mean, I want the killing to stop as well. It's just maddening though to think that the person responsible for such things should go free and unpunished. But 'once more unto the breach,' as they say, perhaps tonight will be the night."

"If not, I quit! The night patrols at least. After tonight, you can pick whichever deputy to want to run circles around this town with you, but I'll be home soaking my feet."

Jones gave him a sly smile. "Oh, come now, Bill, that's not the attitude to have. You've gotten more exercise this week than you've probably had for a year. By the time we're done, you'll cut such a figure that Ms. Maudie won't be able to keep her hands off you."

"That's what I'm afraid of! Either that or the doc will just cut my feet off, and then I'll have to put up with her pushing me around in a wheelchair and fussing over me like I'm a child!"

Jones continued to grin at him. "Well, there are worse fates. At least, you would never have to worry about going hungry."

They continued to bide their time in the office until after dark and then set out on their patrol.

They changed up the order of the places they checked every time so that there was no predictable pattern that the killer could use. If there were, then the killer might easily plan a murder in one spot when he knew the sheriff and Jones were someplace else. As it was, the plan worked, and the killer continued to follow them, leaving nothing to chance. He had heard that the sheriff's habit of patrolling at night had continued and that no one ever knew where he was going to show up next. Fine then—he outfoxed them once; he would do it again. But he would not let them stand in the way of what he had to do. So he crouched in the alley where he had been before and waited.

Bill and Jones finally emerged and began making their rounds. They crisscrossed through the lit-up area of nightlife, going from one place to another and then skipping some and coming back to them later. They did everything they could to confuse anyone who was watching them. They even went back to double-check some of the busier hot spots. Since two nights had passed without any major incident, the people were feeling more comfortable about going out. Round and round they went, and nothing stood out to the lawmen as being unusual. At last, Jones could not justify staying out any longer, and to Bill's immense gratification, they returned to the office to rest.

As soon as they arrived, Bill reached in a drawer on his desk and pulled out a small bottle that Doc Lewis had given him for pain. The soreness of his feet was more than enough to justify using it, and Bill turned the little bottle up and let a generous amount of the stuff slide down his throat as he sat in his chair. While he was doing this, Jones was staring out the window. He was watching and waiting for the deputies to come back with news, as he had the two previous nights. Both times the wait had been long and infuriating when nothing was seen that could help them. One hand held the opposite elbow as that hand rubbed his chin, and he occasionally bit his forefinger. Seldom had he ever been as anxious about a case as he was about this one, and he fought not to let himself become openly frustrated. Realizing, yet again, that staring out the window was making things worse, he initiated his other habit of pacing. He set himself into walking at an even, leisurely pace up and down the length of the room.

The first time he had done that, Bill had given him a flabbergasted looked and asked if he hadn't had enough walking for the evening. But now he gave Jones no more than a glance and leaned back in his chair with his eyes closed. He actually found the regular sound of Jones's footsteps strangely soothing and was dangerously close to snoring when the door burst open and a deputy appeared in front of them breathing heavily.

"Bill, I think we got 'em. There was one guy, kinda tall and always trying to hide his face as much as he could. He went ever where you did, usually showing up a few minutes after you and waiting the same before he followed you again. Sometimes he'd go in the front door and sometimes the back or the side, always managing to stay unnoticed by most folks. When y'all came back here, he followed and stopped a block or so up the street and watched you for near twenty minutes before he finally moved."

The deputy paused to catch his breath, and Jones nearly choked during the few seconds before the deputy resumed.

"We followed him back toward the strip, taking turns just like you told us, and he finally stopped in front of that lousy place of Gomez's."

"Who is Gomez?" asked Jones, seeing that the name had some meaning.

"Some say he was a Mexican bandit back in his day or that he struck it rich somewhere, somehow," Bill answered. "No one knows for sure, he just showed up several years ago with his pockets full and built that rotten excuse of a saloon of his. His place is worse than Burt's and Fred's put together, but the difference is, he don't care about any of it. He has money, that place is just his pastime, and he'll lie through his teeth to you just for the heck of it.

It's out toward the edge of town, and I've gotten to where if there ain't any shooting or a fire, then I don't bother with him. Everyone knows about his place, and if they're dumb enough to go in there, then they can deal with it."

"Well, that's where he went," the deputy continued. "That's why it took so long to get word back. He hung around outside for a few minutes, warbling around like he had been drinking, and then slowly ambled on up. I left the other two to watch him and then lit a shuck back here."

"Well, let's go!" Jones exclaimed. "If he's gone inside, then there's no telling how long he'll stay there before he tries to lure out a victim."

With that he grabbed the deputy by the arm and pulled him out the door to lead the way to their quarry, while Bill groaned as he made his feet work to catch up with them.

CHAPTER 19

Stephens and Katelyn had been riding quick but easy during the second day that Jones had been on a fruitless hunt. Trusting to the ranger's superior knowledge of the area, they had traveled in a straighter direction toward San Antonio. However, knowing that it would still take the better part of two days to return, they didn't make as much speed as they could have. Being in much more pleasant company, Katelyn wanted to take the time to enjoy the shapes and colors of the country they were traveling over. She had been sorry to leave the banks of the river in its spring attire when the morning sun had illuminated it. After she had gotten back into her dry, smoky clothes, she had wandered a short distance while Stephens prepared the horses. The orange, blue, pink, and yellow flowers, combined with the rich green grass offset against the stone castle rock forms that had been carved by time and water as the river, moved her mind into a state of fantasy.

She was in this enlightened mood when Stephens came to fetch her. He had stood watching her for a few minutes as she focused on one area and then another, and her hands fidgeted as if she wanted to do something but couldn't—presumably draw or paint something. He remembered back to times past when he had done the same thing, looking at the beauty that could never be truly reproduced, no matter how hard someone tried. That's what he had been doing on his way home the day he met Judith. He would tell Katelyn later that their camp was fairly close to where Judith had been sitting and playing her music. The bittersweet memory reminded him that they needed to get moving, and he broke in on Katelyn's thoughts to tell her so.

He got her in the saddle, and they were off, going back the way they had come the day before. Besides not having to fear for her life, Katelyn felt the freedom to talk and enjoy the trip as much as possible rather than be bored. So whenever Stephens eased their pace to let the horses catch their wind, she started asking him questions about himself and his past. He told her the same stories he had told Jones two years prior and even threw in a few more as he felt inclined. These were mostly about his younger days, making it through the rough years after the war, his early attempts to help run the store, childhood romances that he thought he had, and the time he and Bill first met and he had tried to fight him because Stephens's father started paying him more attention than him. He hadn't understood at the time that by virtue of age and size, Bill was able to do a lot more work than Stephens was able to contribute. In the end, the attempted fight turned into a string of lessons that helped prepare him for his ranging career and earn him a lifelong friend.

Fair was fair, and in his turn, Stephens began asking Katelyn about her life. She paused for some minutes before answering, as if trying to figure out which stories she should tell. She finally began talking about her father, who had served in a highland regiment during the Crimean War before she was born. As she got older, he began to tell her stories of the battles and the way of army life, and it sparked her deep interest in history. She plied him for more and more details about every little thing, until finally he had been on the verge of having to make things up. She had sensed that her source was running dry and began studying on her own—not just that war, but every aspect of English history as she made her way to it, gradually working her way back farther and farther.

It wasn't long before she had been hired as a governess for the children of a lord who had an incredible library. When she wasn't teaching the children, she was continuing to teach herself. And so she became a self-taught authority on history with a special interest in architecture. With the help of her lord, who recognized the potential in her, she began working with groups to help preserve pieces of their history that was disappearing. Thus, she came to be involved in the restoration of the Mallory estate after Stephens's incursion two years prior.

Katelyn's mother was Emma's aunt, and the two of them had spent much time together as children. She had been like another sister rather than a cousin, and they had remained close over the years into adulthood. It was probably due to this relationship that she had been able to finagle her way into coming on this trip. And now she admitted that she had come, not just for the opportunity to ring Stephens out for his destructive abilities, but also to expand her education even further. England was steeped in history and culture reaching back to the days of the Roman Empire. Old gray-bearded professors at universities were still trying to comb through all the details and discovering new information to fill in gaps in the history books, but Katelyn had been fascinated by the prospect of being able see and experience a different place in the world where such things were more vivid and not quite as settled as back home.

Few people enjoyed a good story more than Wayne Stephens, so when they were admiring the spring landscape and telling about themselves, they swapped tales, real or imagined, as the hours of their journey passed by. Stephens already knew the basic story of King Arthur, but now he let Katelyn tell it to him with more detail and her own flourish. She also told of real kings and lords who had done incredibly heroic or villainous things throughout history. Stephens in turn told more Texas stories, Indian legends, and various other tidbits he had learned from his parents or other people over the years.

The hours and the miles passed without notice due to these conversations, and if there hadn't been such an important reason for returning, then they might have very well just wandered over the countryside until want of supplies forced them back, not that they had much food to spare anyway. Such was the unimagined, and doubly unexpected, contentment that was conjured by these two while in each other's company in such a heavenly setting. It was one of those rare occasions that many people fail to take advantage of when worry, strife, evil, and hardship fade away and the joys of life and good companionship envelop you with a sense of peace. Stephens had not experienced such a phenomenon for some years, and when he realized that he had slipped into one, he was dumbstruck.

However, this state of bliss was still just shy of being absolute. No matter how wonderful the world might seem or how hard he tried, he could not forget the unfinished business he had left in San Antonio. It was an ever-present spark in the back of his mind that always kept the horses moving in the right direction and a little faster than he would've wanted otherwise. His sense of duty, both professional and personal, would not be silenced or ignored. Also, when he realized what a pleasant time he was having on their return journey, this recollection of reality brought him a pang of conscience. This woman that he had only met a week ago—and had stood toe to toe with in red-faced anger, twice—was beginning to stir up feelings in him that he had not felt since he had been with Judith Mercer, the same woman whose murder less than a week ago had crushed him. Much time had passed since there had been anything between him and Judith, but he had not given up until the end, and now to feel the way he was now pricked him as a betrayal of her memory.

All this had occurred to him as they sat for a few minutes to eat a few bites of food and let the horses rest. He had been in the middle of chewing when the avalanche of realizations and emotions hit him within seconds, and his mind was now in a turmoil. He had been having such a good time. How could he allow himself to do so when such a savage killer could still be on the loose? He was enjoying the company of a beautiful woman. How could he look at women when a woman he had loved had been so brutally murdered? He thought he had been feeling the rarest and best form of happiness. A few days ago, he had been devastated by the worst form of grief, death caused by murder of a person so dear to him, and then having to deal with thieves and kidnappers. So how could he dare to be happy?

Swallowing his food, he said that they needed to hurry if they wanted to get back before dark. Once in the saddle, he set them at a pace that was just fast enough to make casual conversation more than difficult. He wanted to be left alone to organize his thoughts and deal with his feelings. He wanted the happiness and the joy and, dare he think it, love. It might there; it might come to bloom. After years of conflict he might have found someone who might bring him some peace. Such a concept seemed foreign to him after so much time spent in self-denial of such luxuries. His rough and rugged career translated into an equal lifestyle that didn't easily allow for such things. And yet, it had a strangely strong appeal to him; otherwise he wouldn't have continued in it for so long. Would it be possible for the two sides to coexist with any degree of harmony, or would he have to give up on one or the other? He had been willing to give up his job once many years ago. Could he make that decision again? So many things circulated in another of his cyclone thought patterns that kept him occupied for some time.

Finally, when he felt a slight foam of sweat building up on his horse, he realized that he had gone over long at that fast pace. Without dire need, there was no reason to push a horse too hard, or else he might not have the strength when you needed it. And then, of course, Katelyn was still not used to this amount of horseback exercise, and when he brought them to a halt, she was panting and sweating. At first, the look on her face hinted that she was irritated and that they were about to have their third shouting match, but when she saw the expression on his face, her own expression softened. What she saw was a mixture of anxiety over her displeasure, aggravation from all the threads of thought he had been following, and fatigue from both the physical and mental effort he had been exerting.

"What is the matter with you?" she asked in a tone that revealed a mixture of irked confusion and concern.

He stared at her for some moments, trying to figure out what to say. He opened his mouth, closed it again, patted his panting horse, looked back, and opened his mouth again, but still no words came out.

"Wayne, what is it?" she asked again. She had begun using his first name.

He felt the same as if he were pinned down in a firefight, so his instinct kicked in as if he were going on the offensive, and he just blurted it out.

"I like you, Kate! It sounds nuttier than a fat squirrel, but there it is, I like you. We only met a week ago, and we want to kill each other half the time, but I can't help it. I've enjoyed the last two day with you more than I've enjoyed anyone's company in a long time. But when I did feel like this, it was with Judith, and she's been dead less than a week. It was over between us, and I had little chance of getting her back, but I still miss her. I'm a mess inside, and I don't know what to do about it. I'm on my way back to help catch her killer, if he isn't caught already, and yet we've been treating this trip like a long picnic. I try to keep things as black and white as I can, and it's usually pretty easy for me in my job, but right now I don't know how I'm supposed to be."

She sat staring at him in his consternation while she took in how much torment the ranger's mind must be in, while also realizing how much his thoughts echoed some of her own. She just hadn't taken the time to admit it to herself before. With a glimmer of moisture in her eye and a soft grin on her face, she nudged her horse up next to his so that she was only a couple of feet away from him. She reached across and touched her soft hand to his unshaven face, then gently tugged him toward her and gave him a kiss on the mouth. When she touched his face, the ranger's mind whipped itself up like a team of horses without direction. But when she kissed him, everything in the world came to a stop, and it seemed as if time itself was suspended for those few moments. Their eyes met as she pulled away, and she smiled at him.

"You go do what you have to do and take the time to get your mind straight," she said. "When you're ready, let me know."

Stephens smiled at her, and his smile got bigger the longer he sat there. Not only was he encouraged and comforted by her words, but he couldn't stop admiring the beauty of her face and hair as the sunlight made it glow. He nudged his horse, and they started off again at an easier pace. This allowed them to renew their previous conversations and make the most of the time they had left in private.

They were still going when night overtook them. Ordinarily they would've stopped, but Stephens knew how close they were and told Katelyn that if she could last a little longer, then she could sleep in a bed that night. She agreed, and they continued. A little more than an hour later, they came within sight of the town and could see lights shining in windows. Stephens stopped as they looked.

"There it is, civilization has found us. Jones and Emma will be thrilled to see you."

"Yes, and you can get back to your business, and we'll continue our visit, and things can go back to the way they were."

"Maybe not entirely." And with that he reached over to her and kissed her again, and she didn't resist. "Let's keep it to ourselves for now though."

"Absolutely," Katelyn replied with a mischievous grin.

They started their horses trotting and covered about another quarter mile when sounds that Stephens was all too familiar with reached their ears on the night air.

"Gunshots! And probably from that no-good Gomez's place off to the left. Katie, you blaze a trail to the hotel, find Emma and Kina, and stay there."

With that he kicked his horse and took off toward the outlying building that was lit up in more ways than one.

Chapter 20

The killer had watched Bill and Jones do their rounds throughout the city, just as he had the time before. He knew what they were doing and why their movements were so sporadic and unusual. It made him grin to think that they were doing all this to try to catch him when all they had to do was look behind them to see him mixed in amongst the crowd, not that they would know him to be the killer rather than any other person. Round and round, up and down, he kept up with them, always making sure of where they were. Finally, they had given up and gone back to the office, just as they had the night of his last murder. He knew they would. Try as they might, they had to rest sometime, and now he had freedom to roam. The first two saloons had given him good pickings, but that whole area was on the alert now, even though he hadn't struck in two nights. And if he wanted to increase his victims, he needed a location where it would be even less noticeable.

He had heard of Gomez's reputation for not giving a hang for what went on around his place, and it sounded like the perfect place to restart his crusade. In addition, his place was doubly alive tonight with many new faces from an outfit that had just been paid, and they were celebrating and living life as hard and as fast as they could. So he made his way toward the Gomez place after he had given proper vigilance to the sheriff. He approached with his usual low profile with a pulled-down hat and closed jacket. There were several men and women standing around outside, but none were by themselves. He started to go on inside but then decided to just hang around outside a bit longer in case one of the girls freed herself. It was while he was doing so that the deputy had gone running to fetch Bill and Jones while the others kept watch.

A few minutes later, while the deputy was still explaining to Bill what was going on, a very lovely young lady appeared around the corner of the building. She wasn't dressed like a woman of the night; in fact, she appeared fairly modest, but she went from man to man as she came up to them talking to them, and usually she was shooed away. Evidently, they didn't want to give up the partners they already had for this newcomer, so the killer decided to make a move. He wandered out onto the sidewalk and made his way to the corner of the building just before she reached it, and she came up to him.

"Excuse me," she said, "I'm looking for someone. I—"

He cut her off before she could say more. "Of course you are, and I can help you with that. Why don't you come with me?"

The girl seemed surprised at his response and allowed herself to be led down the side of the building.

"Where are we going?" she asked as he tugged her forward by the hand.

"Don't you worry, I'll take good care of you," the killer replied.

The girl suddenly had the horrible realization that she had been misunderstood, and she dug in her heels to pull against his grip.

"I don't think you understand. I'm here trying to find my brother. We think he came to town with some of our hands, and my Pa is away, so I came for him."

The killer still tugged her wrist. She wasn't the sort of woman he wanted, but if he let her go, she might tell someone about him. They might not care, but then again, they might cause trouble. He tugged harder.

"He may be back here all the same, so come on."

They were at the back corner of the building now, and the girl began struggling madly to get loose from his firm grip. He grabbed her other wrist and put his weight into dragging her further back. Now she began to scream as she struggled. There was a lot of noise coming from inside, but her screams were high-pitched enough that someone might hear them. He yanked her to him and wrapped a big arm around her arms and body, and as she wriggled in his clutch, he reached into his pocket and brought out his flint-rock knife. As he raised it to plunge it into his mistaken victim, the voice of a deputy rang out. They had been instructed not to confront the murderer if possible, but when they saw the man take the girl into the alley, one of them stayed to keep watch while the other crossed the street and made it to the back just as the knife became visible.

"Hold it!" he yelled with his gun drawn and pointing at the killer.

He swung the girl around between them as a shield, but the deputy thought himself a good-enough shot that he stared down the gun barrel at the man's head. The killer, reading his intentions and not wanting to fall prey to a luck shot, acted first. He slashed at the dress around the girl's stomach, and she gave out a cry of pain. This startled the deputy out of his concentration, and the killer shoved the girl toward him. He instinctively reached to catch the wounded girl, and as he did, the killer brought out his own pistol and shot at the deputy. He jerked and slowly slumped down until he and the crying girl were leaning against a row of barrels.

The killer started to run back up the alley to get lost in the crowd, but his shot had brought the newly arrived sheriff and inspector running down the alley toward him. Jones beat Bill to the yard, and as he took in the scene around him, he raised his weapon to aim at the killer, who had been surprised by these new adversaries. Jones needed no convincing that this man was extremely dangerous and beyond reason, and so he had no reservations about promptly pulling the trigger once his sights were aligned, but nothing happened. The gun didn't fire because Jones hadn't cocked the hammer. The gun Bill had lent him was the same 1873 Colt that so many Westerners carried, and it only fired if you cocked the hammer first. For years Jones had carried the British Bulldog double-action revolver and had no practice at cocking the hammer before firing.

The obvious failure to fire brought a grin from the killer as he grasped the opportunity to shoot first. An understandably dumbstruck Jones was staring at his pistol in panic and dread when he heard the killer cock his own weapon. Bill's arm shot out and grabbed Jones and yanked him down out of the line of fire, and the killer missed his mark, but he continued to fire blindly into the dark alley. Jones was still ducking down low when he heard a muffled moan beside him. He looked up and saw Bill's teeth clinched.

"Bill! What is it?"

Bill muttered and inaudible reply and clutched his left arm. A bullet and grazed along a barrel and lodged itself in his arm. Jones pulled a handkerchief out of his pocket and was tying it around the wound when the firing stopped. The killer had shot all his bullets, and now he broke his pistol open, dumped the spent shells, and quickly reloaded before he ran to the back door.

Jones tied a knot in the cloth, and Bill gripped Jones's arm.

"That's good enough, I'll live. Just get after him and remember to cock your hammer before you pull the trigger."

Jones nodded and cautiously went back up the alley. As he reached the corner, he heard the back door slam, and he ran up to and through it into the back room of the saloon. As he emerged into the main room, he saw the killer almost at the front door, and he pulled his pistol again and cocked the hammer. As he did, the two other deputies who had been left to watch the front in case the killer escaped appeared at the front door with weapons drawn.

"Stop!" Jones yelled above the roar of celebration in the room and pointed his pistol at the man again.

Seeing this, the deputies did likewise, and the man was cornered. Jones was beginning to feel the joy of catching his man when things took a different turn. The killer did not lack for imagination, and being caught in a room full of half-drunk cattlemen and bums of every sort, he appealed to their natural greed. He raised his hands and pointed at Jones and the deputies, and he hollered at the top of his voice.

"Murderers! These men are murderers! They murdered my family, and now they're after me! There's a one-thousand-dollar reward for them dead or alive!"

As the killer started to yell, all music and conversation died away, and his audience was struck with confusion and irritation at the interruption, but at the mention of such a large reward for the proclaimed murders, they reacted the way the killer had hoped they would.

In a mad scramble, half the room rushed at Jones and the other half rushed at the deputies. And in the middle of it all, the killer lost himself in the crowd, though he was having to fight hard to make his way toward the door with the speed of a snail. Jones, however, had no time to watch the killer at that moment. He was being rushed by a horde of men who saw him only as a valuable object to be traded in for money in whatever condition. He had his gun, but he didn't have enough shots to stop them all. And besides, they were innocent in this affair. They might be some of the lowest, despicable people in the county for all he knew, but they had done nothing so far that night to warrant a death sentence. Desperate to stop any violence, he shot a bullet into the rafters, hoping that would give the mob pause, but it didn't. They leaped at him, and he swung the pistol and his fist with all his might to beat off his attackers. Even the bar fight he and Stephens had been in at O'Malley's tavern in London hadn't been quite this one-sided, and he was in a worse position being cut off from the deputies.

Jones swung this way and that, trying to make contact with any part of whoever was close to him. To his credit, Jones was doing as well by himself as the two deputies were, but the mob was getting closer and closer. As his attention was taken up by two men trying to tackle him, something large, possibly a chair, smashed into his blind side, and he fell to the floor as his gun tumbled away. A man was coming toward him now with the sharp, pointed end of a broken bottle neck in his hand. "Dead or Alive" usually just meant dead to most people, as it was the simplest and least troublesome means of collecting reward money. Jones tried to reach for his pistol while still dazed from the blow. He watched the ugly man with countless years of hard living chronicled on his face lean over him. He put a foot on Jones's reaching hand and was about to commit unknowing murder when another shot rang out and threw the man backward against the bar with a cry of pain.

As Jones's head began to clear, he looked back behind him toward the door and saw Stephens with a faint whiff of smoke coming out of his pistol barrel. The rest of the mob paused at the sight of this newcomer, but figuring him to be another of the wanted gang, they rallied and rushed him as well. They had taken down the other one when he had a gun; they'd do the same to this one. They rushed at the ranger, and they began to fall. Stephens didn't want to kill people any more than Jones, but neither would he be so lenient with their greedy ignorance. Stephens had his second pistol with him now, and as they came at him or Jones, he shot into their legs, causing them to fall with cries of pain. Jones got back on his feet again and took on anyone who managed to get around Stephens's field of fire with a fury that he had never experienced before.

Someone jumped onto Stephens from the side, and the ranger began to wrestle with him until he finally threw him to the ground. As he did this, someone up on the second floor had come out with a rifle and took aim at the distracted ranger. Holding his reclaimed pistol with both hands, Jones fired at the would-be sharpshooter, and he fell back. Whether he was dead or not, Jones couldn't guess, but it was necessary to save his friend. Stephens heard the shot and had almost felt it, so close had it been, and he saw the man fall away. The mob was thinning and running now, rather than be shot into and oppose such a force as what Stephens and Jones emitted. With their way clear, they went to the aid of the two deputies who were still in a struggle. Between the four of them, the fight ended quickly, and they made their true identities know to those who hadn't run off. As the four lawmen walked out the front door, they met Doc Lewis and two other physicians who had been summoned in the wake of the great commotion, and Jones grabbed his arm.

"Doctor, go around the side of the building. The sheriff, a deputy, and a young girl are injured."

As the doctor hurried off with some men with lanterns, Jones sat down in a chair on the porch to answer the questions on Stephens's face. After the whole story had been recounted, Stephens let himself fall into a chair as well.

"We were so close!" Stephens exclaimed, putting his hands on his face and growling.

"I'm sorry," Jones said with a pang of guilt.

Stephens heard his tone and looked at him. "It's not your fault, you did everything a man could do. I'm truly grateful for that."

They sat a moment longer, then with a sudden realization, Jones sat straight up.

"If you're here, where's Katelyn? What happened to her?"

"Relax, my friend, she's fine aside from a few bumps and bruises. She should be at the hotel with Emma right now."

Jones let out a deep breath of air and sat back and closed his eyes. "Thank you. Thank you."

A few moments later, one of the deputies came walking up to them with another man they didn't know.

"Bill's going to be all right, Wayne, he'll just have to wear a sling for a while. The girl should be all right too, but she'll have a quite a scar. I'm afraid Ben is gone. He couldn't have lasted long after the bullet hit him. But I think this man here can help make things right."

Stephens and Jones looked at the stranger, and he began to speak.

"I was on the street heading home for the evening when I heard the first shots. I reined up and tried to see what was going on. A few minutes later, I heard the yelling inside, and then the brawl started. Next thing I know, a man comes running out, yells at me to get down, pulls me down off my horse, and takes off with it. I recognized the voice as the same one that had done the yelling inside."

"Who was it?" Jones asked.

"Where'd he go?" asked Stephens.

"I don't know who he is, but I've seen him before. A few days ago, when I was coming into town, I went a little off the main trail and spotted him outside the old Buford shack outside of town. At least I think that was him."

Stephens and Jones jumped to their feet, thanked the man, and left the deputy in charge as they took off toward the stable.

Chapter 21

Having reclaimed the horse Stephens had used, which had wandered back to the stables after he had jumped off him, and procuring another for Jones, they hurried toward the Buford shack where the murderer was supposed to be. The moon gave them just enough light to see where they were going, and it didn't take long to cover the distance to the shack, and soon they reined in their horses while they were still a ways off. They could faintly see the dim glow of a light, presumably a single candle or lantern, which made the window visible. They sat still and watched the shack for some time, trying to catch sight of the murderer.

"I don't like it," Stephens said. "He may not figure that we would've found out where he is yet, but why risk a light?"

"After that trick he pulled this evening to get that mob after us, I wouldn't be surprised at anything he might do," Jones replied. "But I doubt he'll make the first move. Let's move forward and see what happens."

With a grin, Stephens nodded his assent, and they nudged their horses into walking forward. Slowly they made their way toward the shack. At one hundred yards, nothing changed; seventy-five yards and nothing happened; fifty yards and closing without a sound; then a second later, the shack exploded with flashes, and the silent night was splintered with gunshots. Jones and Stephens jumped from their horses and flattened themselves on the ground and waited. A moment later, a few more shots rang out, and Stephens fired back at the flashes and then rolled a few yards to his left.

"Shoot at the flashes, and then roll away before he does the same. I'll go left, and you go right, 'til we have him in a cross fire."

Jones nodded, and when more shots came, they both returned fire and rolled away from each other.

They continued this exercise until they were almost at a right angle to the shack, and then the shooting stopped. After a few minutes of silence, Stephens was about to fire a few more rounds into the shack before rushing it when the killer fired again, and the two lawmen answered the shots. When they did, the light they had seen suddenly disappeared in the darkness, and a moment later, another light appeared and began to grow brighter. Something inside the shack was on fire, and it was spreading. Soon tongues of flame could be seen coming out the window. Stephens yelled to his partner.

"Jones, can you see anything?"

"Just the fire, I haven't seen our man."

"Come on then, we've got to find out if he's still alive."

Soon the heat would be so great that they could not get near it, so they stood up and began to run to the shack. Just then the whole place exploded, and the two of them fell back to the ground. They were both dazed—Jones for the second time that night—and they slowly began to get up. As they did, Jones began to sniff the air.

"Stephens, do you smell something odd?" Stephens took a couple of deep sniffs, and his eyes widened.

"Kerosene!"

"Yes. It could've been an accident, of course, but what if he set up a large container of kerosene to explode?"

"The skunk probably knocked the lantern over on purpose and took off while we watched.

"A flaming cloth hanging out of a closed container would provide an excellent explosion."

"Let's go!"

Jones's horse had disappeared in the night, but Stephens's horse stood a short distance away, just visible in the light of the fire. Whether he was just a good-tempered horse or just tired from the day's journey he had already completed was anybody's guess, but Stephens made up his mind that if that horse saw him through to the end of this episode, he was going to try to buy him. He grabbed the reins and led him around to the back of the burning shack where Jones was already studying the ground.

"I'm not a tracker, you understand," Jones said, "but I think he came out here to where his horse was tied to this lean-to, and it looks like he fidgeted before finally mounting."

"You might be a tracker and don't know it. I can't read it any other way myself. He probably waited until the explosion to jump on the horse and not risk being seen. By the time we got up off the ground, he was gone."

"Then what chance do we have of catching him?"

This wasn't the open plain of West Texas, but sound could travel if one listened hard enough. Stephens led the horse further away from the crackling of the shack and peered into the darkness in the direction the tracks went from the shack, but nothing came to his ear. There was one trick he could try; it wasn't foolproof, but it might work. He took his new big carbine off the saddle, racked a shell into the chamber, and pointed it toward the sky. He squeezed the trigger, and the gun boomed and echoed through the night. A second later the wind brought back the sound of a horse's whinny that had been surprised. Stephens smiled, threw himself into the saddle, and was reaching to help Jones up behind him when they heard another faint whinny that was higher-pitched. Jones got up behind his partner, and they took off as fast as the ranger dared push his tired horse toward the sounds they had heard. Both of them were surprised when, after a few hundred yards, they nearly ran over the body of the horse they were tracking. Lying motionless in the grass, the creature never twitched as the two lawmen jumped to the ground and walked around it from opposite sides with their guns out.

"My stars," said Jones as he looked at the beast's head and saw a gleam of faint moonlight on liquid, "his throat has been cut. Now I can smell the blood."

"His leg is broken. When I fired that shot, it must've threw off his stride, or maybe he stepped in a hole or something else, but a horse with a broken leg is the same as dead. The killer probably cut its throat to save the sound of a shot and keep it from making more noise."

"But where is he then?"

No sooner than Jones had stood up from kneeling and asked his question that a scream like a war cry sounded in the darkness, and their quarry leaped at them and hurled both of them to the ground over the body of the horse. Jones hit the ground with his pistol landing a few feet away. Never had his head taken such a pounding in a single night, and he slowly brought his arms to lift himself up, and as he did, the various bumps he had received let him know that they existed. He winced, put his hand to his head, and winced again. But the fog began to clear, as it had earlier, and he squinted in the darkness to see the dark figure of a man rolling around and grappling with Stephens. The ranger had retained his weapon after years of practice and now struggled to bring it into line with the killer's head. He thought he had, but just as he pulled the trigger, the killer jerked on him, changing his aim, and the bullet sang past his head. He hadn't known the gun was about to go off, and it surprised him, and the flash from the barrel temporarily blinded all of them.

Stephens renewed his effort to subdue the killer, but the man was by no means small, and it wasn't a contest that could be won easily. As Jones got to his feet to help, the killer managed to pull his and the ranger's hands apart and crashed his forehead into Stephens. The ranger fell, barely conscious. This did more than anything to bring Jones's mind back to clarity, and as the killer turned to him, Jones jumped at him with a flying punch to the killer's jaw. The killer recovered and took a swing at his second adversary. Jones dodged and landed two more punches before finally being hit himself; it felt like he had been hit with a boulder. While Jones's abused head recovered from this latest blow, the killer spit blood onto the ground and reached into this coat while stepping to grab Jones. He threw an arm around Jones's neck and drew back his flint knife underhanded. As he did, Jones threw his head backward and smashed into the killer's nose. He fell back with a yell, but as he did, he swung his hand up, and the stone blade scraped upward along Jones's side, cutting through cloth and flesh.

Technically speaking, Jones's rib cage prevented the blade from reaching any vital organs, but it didn't keep it from hurting any worse. Jones clinched his teeth in pain and sank to his knees. He had not felt pain so acute as this since he had broken both the bones in his lower arm as a boy. Now, as he struggled to contain the pain in his mind, the killer stomped back up behind him.

"You ruined everything! Those harlots don't deserve to live, they're a disease that should be destroyed. And you fight to advance it. Curse you!"

He raised his weapon to bring it down into the man who had thwarted him, when Stephens appeared and grabbed his raised arm, and the struggle between the two renewed. It was a battle of raw strength to control the movement of the knife, until Stephens quit. He allowed all the force that was pushing the knife downward to succeed and simply guided it down and into the pelvis of the man holding it. The yell of the man's pain sounded more like a wounded animal, and he fell to the ground. When he hit, the stone blade broke off at the handle, causing another yell to erupt. As the killer rocked around, holding his wound, Stephens stood over him.

"Why?" he yelled at the killer. "Why them? What did they ever do to you? What made you think they deserved to die instead of you?"

The killer looked at the ranger, struggling to restrain his pain as he answered, "I saved other people from suffering the same fate that I've suffered. Harlots curse those they encounter. They corrupt and devour the lives of honest men. They are not righteous. My family was happy—happy and content with the life we had. Until my father began to notice a woman in town. She was prettier than my mother, who had gradually been made plain by the labors of making a life in the wilderness, and for a price, this pretty woman could be had by anyone. My father was a good man, but he eventually succumbed to the temptation and went to the woman. One moment of weakness could have been forgiven, but he didn't stop. A long time later, he went back again, and then again and again. In the end, he spent more time in town than at home, corrupted by the woman's whisperings in his ear. Nothing my mother did or said could bring him back, and ultimately, he was killed by a past acquaintance of that horrid woman. I did my best to help my mother, but I was still a very young man, and we couldn't keep the place together. My mother passed away in her bed of despair, our home was lost, and I began to wander and take work where I could find it. And I decided that I would strive to rid the world of its oldest plague."

Stephens looked at this poor example of humanity with a face of stone.

"Your story is sad, but any sympathy I might could have for you is washed away by the memory of the pain you yourself have caused. That girl you attacked tonight was as innocent as you once were, and now she's scarred for life. The first woman you killed had a story just as sad as yours, but she was a woman and didn't have the same opportunities as you. Through it all, she retained her good heart, but you let yours turn black. The rope will be too good for you."

As he stood over the killer and spoke these last words, the killer's good leg shot up and kicked the ranger in the thigh with a force that sent him tumbling back to the ground. The killer pulled a small pistol from his pocket and aimed it at the ranger as their eyes met.

"If you were so fond of her, then I can arrange a reunion." He let out a soft, gargled cackle as he began to apply pressure to the trigger.

Then a flash of light broke from behind Stephens, and his ears rang with the boom of the shot that battered its way through the killer's body. The ranger snapped his head around and saw Jones sitting with one hand wrapped around to hold his side, while he held his pistol in the other. Stephens crawled over to him and looked at him, not knowing what to say. There wasn't anything in particular that Jones wanted to hear. They had succeeded in their duty, solved the case, saved some people while losing others, and they had dispatched the vile criminal while fighting the good fight. Now they just sat in the grass with the body of a once-good man consumed by hate. At last, they regained enough strength to get on the tired horse and slowly return to the people they loved.

Chapter 22

Jones and Stephens slipped back into San Antonio as quietly as they could. They and the town had had more excitement than they could handle already, and the lawmen didn't want to cause any more fuss just yet. Stephens led the horse with Jones on it to the office of Doc Lewis, who was none too happy about being woken up for the second time that night. But when he saw who it was and heard the abridged story while Jones was hobbled into the examination room, he threw himself into his vocation. Jones was laid out on the table and his coat and shirt removed. As the doctor collected his instruments and lit more lanterns, Stephens stood by the table.

"It was just a few days ago that I stood looking down on this table at your friend," Jones said and then bit his lip at a fresh resurge of pain. "I'm still sorry about that."

"Hush, what's done is done, and you helped make it right, more than anyone. She was already dead, but you're not. So keep still 'til I get back."

The doctor gave Jones a drink of something to dull the pain and help him relax and then began to clean the wound before he started stitching it. Stephens left and headed to the sheriff's office. He knew that once he went to the hotel, he would never get away from the flock of females that were ready to ambush him, especially when he walked through the door without Jones. So he made his way to the jail and reported to the two remaining deputies what had happened. One of them volunteered to take care of his horse, and Stephens began the long walk to the hotel. The whole way he tried to prepare his answers to the inevitable questions. When he walked through the door alone and in such a shambled state, Emma nearly jumped out of her skin, and all three of them jump out of their chairs.

"Jones is alive and fine," Stephens said in a hurry with a raised hand to halt their stampede of supposition. "He's a little banged up, but he's over at Doc Lewis's now, getting tended to."

With that, they all marched out and over to the doctor's office. There, Stephens and Jones recapped the entire ordeal to them and the deputy, who had come after stabling the horse. Jones stayed at the doctor's that night at the insistence of Lewis, so that the wound could start binding together without too much movement.

The next day, however, saw Inspector Jones walking out of the office slowly by his own, unassisted strength. As he walked down the street with Stephens and the ladies forming a line beside him, he was praised by passersby for the service he had performed in helping to rid their town of such evil. Without instructions to the contrary, the deputies had made no secret of what had happened between the inspector, the ranger, and the murderer, and now they were the talk of the town.

They stopped back at the sheriff's office to check in before going to breakfast at Maudie's. When they walked in, they found Maudie herself leaning over the side of the desk with her hand stretched toward a plate. Behind the desk and the plate sat Sheriff

Bill Driver with his arm in a sling and his face flushed with red anger as he slapped Maudie's hand away from the plate.

"Woman, leave me be. I can eat by myself and take care of myself."

She slapped him back on his good arm and then set her hands on her hips. "Bill Driver, I don't know why I don't grab that arm of yours and force you into your own jail to live on bread and water for a month. But for some ungodly reason, I want to see you whole again. So you sit there and shut up before I shove the whole plate in your mouth."

The whole group busted out laughing at the spectacle the two made and visited until Bill finished eating, and then they stole Maudie back over to her café for some breakfast.

That day was spent in easy leisure for Jones's sake. The next day, quite a few days later than originally planned, the group set out for the ranch that belonged to Stephens's parents. Two leisurely days later, they arrived to a hero's welcome. News had traveled fast about what had happened in San Antonio, and the parents were overflowing with pride, anger, and belated worrying over the various events that had occurred, even in their own backyard as it were. They were also elated at finally meeting the long-anticipated and celebrated Joneses. Katelyn's presence was an added bonus that inflated their joy beyond measure. The story of her kidnapping and rescue was particularly enthralling to them, even though they went into details about their bickering along the way. The parents gave each other meaningful glances as though they suspected the details that had been left out.

Every morning they awoke to the sounds of the ranch life that surrounded them. Some days were simple and leisurely; others were full of sharing in the work and experiences. They talked with all the hands on the ranch, hearing their stories and just enjoying the good company. Jones's wound healed quickly, and he and Stephens went on an overnight ride with some of the hands to find some steers that had lost themselves.

"When I get home, I'll be able to tell my colleagues that I actually worked cattle in Texas," Jones had said during their journey.

In repetition of Kina's visit to England two years prior, the ladies all put the kitchen through its paces and served up a different new dish to the family and hands every night.

Group fun was all well and good, but Stephens and Katelyn didn't forget each other. Several times Katelyn would go off during the day to paint a picture or write her personal record of the trip. Often, Stephens would find a way to disappear during these times to find Katelyn. Stephens adored Katelyn's paintings as much as he adored her, and the bond between them grew stronger every day. Those spring days were some of the best days Stephens could remember for his entire life. Ranch life wasn't easy, but good people and a good mindset could make it a good life for people who are determined. Being surrounded by family and friends such as these, it was impossible to imagine such evils as they had just conquered.

One day, early on, Stephens rode up to the road to wait on the stage that was due for Bandera, saying that there was something he needed to tend to. He wouldn't say anything to anyone about what the business was, and so they left it alone. After ten glorious days on the Stephens ranch, the Joneses announced that, much to their displeasure, they must soon be leaving. They had all sensed that the end was drawing near, but it was still a sad moment. That evening, Stephens flagged down another stagecoach, again without a word of explanation. That was the last night that they all ate at the Stephens table, and it was a long, bittersweet meal.

The next day, the troop once again loaded up and headed back to San Antonio. When they arrived, they had another day of bidding farewell to Bill and Maudie and everyone else they had befriended during their visit. After one more stay in the same hotel, minus the rude clerk who had since been fired and moved on, the party boarded a southbound train the next morning. About five hours later, the train came to a halt back in bustling Corpus Christi. This would truly be their last night together since the ship taking the Joneses back to England was sailing the next day. They explored as much of the town as they could, and they ate supper. Then Stephens and Katelyn excused themselves separately and as nonchalantly as possible. Once outside they walked next to each other down the sidewalk, unaware they were being spied on with unashamed eyes through draped windows.

"I don't know what to say," Katelyn said after they had gone a little way. "Tomorrow we're leaving, going back to England, and I don't know when I'll see you again. I would've never thought this before, that I would want to go somewhere else besides home, but I don't think I want to go."

"You have to go, you have a home, a life, and Emma to keep you out of trouble."

Katelyn gave him a strong tap on the arm and then dabbed her eyes with her fingertips.

"You and I both know you can't stay here, not now."

"Now? What do you mean now? What has changed?" She looked up at him with eyes that were fighting back feelings of fear and anger that something she wasn't aware of was about to be exposed.

Stephens stopped and looked back at her with a lump in his throat as he braced himself to say something that he never thought he would say.

"What has changed is that I love you, Katie. I never thought I would say that, to you or anyone, but you've dragged it out of me. I was a perfectly respectable bachelor before you showed up, but now I want you for my own. You have to go home now and make sure that this is what you want and prepare for it. People are expecting you back home, you have a life and responsibilities to tend to. But if you ever show your face in Texas again, don't you dare think that I'll ever let you leave."

The eyes that had stood ready to bore a hole through the ranger now burst into tears as she threw her arms around his neck, and he held her. They walked for another hour, telling each other anything they wanted to say until they could stay awake no longer and went to their rooms.

The final dreaded morning had finally come. In a few hours, the Joneses would be at sea, bound for England, and who knew when the dear friends would meet again. After breakfast, the party collected their bags and had them taken to the dock to be loaded. They were casually walking and talking in the area where Stephens had paced in anticipation weeks earlier, waiting for the call to board. Stephens seemed particularly anxious about something but wouldn't talk about it. He was on the verge of chewing his nails when Jones tapped his arm.

"Stephens, you better look at this." Jones was looking up the street at a row of five mounted men making their way toward them as a canter.

It was hard to be sure at that distance, but Jones could've sworn that the man in the center of the line stood up in his stirrups and looked at them as if he recognized them. Then he said something to the others, and they came at a gallop down the street toward them.

"Stephens…" Jones said as he took a step back and reached for Emma.

When he looked at the ranger, he was astonished to see him smiling. The five men reined in their horses just a few yards from the party, and as they did, one of the more spirited horses reared up on his hind legs and gave a loud neigh in protest.

"Whoa, son of a buck!" the rider yelled as he wrangled the horse.

They all dismounted, and the man in the center walked up to Stephens with his hand out.

"You ornery old coyote, I ought to kick your teeth in for dragging me all the way out here," he said with a grin.

They shook hands and looked at Jones, who was wearing an awkward expression.

"Jones, this is Texas Ranger Captain William Scott of Company F and four of his men."

Jones looked on wide-eyed at the tough-looking men that faced him. Due to obvious circumstances, Stephens was the only Texas Ranger Jones had ever come in contact with. Now he had five more standing in front of him who looked as if they could stare down a tiger.

"It is a pleasure to meet you, Captain," Jones said when he found his voice at last.

Introductions were made all around, and then Jones looked at Stephens.

"Will you ever become a captain?"

An instant later, Scott busted out laughing.

"Most likely never, knowing him."

Jones looked at the captain in surprise.

"He could've been a captain years ago. Heck, he could've had my job and been my boss, but he doesn't want it. Says he couldn't stand the paperwork and prefers to be left to himself. Sergeant is all he would take."

Jones looked at his friend. "You must be joking."

"Nope," Stephens replied, "the man speaks the truth. But they're not here to discuss my rank, they're here to discuss yours."

Now Jones was more astonished than ever.

"What on earth are you talking about?"

Stephens looked at Scott, who took out a folded piece of paper and read it:

12 May 1887

By order of the governor of the State of Texas, and in recognition of the duty he has performed in service of the state, I have the honor to appoint Scotland Yard Inspector Caleb Jones of England as an honorary Texas Ranger holding the rank of sergeant with all the privileges and responsibilities applying thereto, with the exception of wages.

> Lieutenant Governor
> Barnett Gibbs

Captain Scott folded the paper and handed it to Jones, who stood with a gaping mouth, along with everyone else. Stephens smiled big and stuck out his hand to him.

"Congratulations, Ranger Jones."

Jones took his hand and continued to be speechless. "Scott, do you do this to everyone you meet?" Stephens asked.

The captain glared at him and then looked back to Jones.

"I'm honored to have met you, Mr. Jones, and I wish you a pleasant voyage."

With that he and his men remounted and rode off.

Jones was still looking from the paper, back to Stephens, and back to the paper.

"I…I don't know what to say. I'm honored and dumbfounded and…"

"My friend, don't say anything except that this ain't the end."

"I'm sure it won't be, my friend, it won't be."

"I can guarantee that it won't be," Katelyn chimed in as she stepped forward to look at Stephens.

They just stood looking at each other; words weren't needed and would've been inadequate. Their eyes said all that needed to be said. A moment later, their gaze was broken by the call for all passengers to board. They looked back at each other again.

"You'll write to me, won't you?"

"You know dang well that I will."

Then, in front of God and everybody, Stephens pulled Katelyn to him and kissed her like there was no tomorrow—to the surprise of none.

Jones looked on in less-than-dry-eyed joy. For the second time since he had met this ranger, his life would never be the same again. They had had such an adventure as they could've never hoped for, but now it was time for the Lone-Star Inspector to return home.

Texas Rangers Down Under

Chapter 1

A fresh night breeze was blowing and clouds traveled quickly through the sky intervening in the glow of the moon. If anyone had been around to see, the glow would've revealed a small group of men mounting horses next to a secluded building in the heavy bush country of New South Wales. The mounted men turned their horses and raced toward their objective on a road a few miles away. The road was one that led to a railroad way station, and a wagon was traveling briskly to reach it on time.

It had been several years since the gold rush, and the time of the great bushrangers had reached their zenith. The gold rush had calmed to a steady industry, whereas the bushrangers had been gradually snuffed. Some still existed though. Those hard, resourceful outlaws that survived by their wits and skill in the wild bush of Australia died hard. But died they had, and history would recount that by 1888, they had already seen their best days. Yet some persevered.

These men urging their horses to speed were such men, and their goal was gold. Railroads and civilization continued to expand, but there was still plenty of open country, owned or unowned, where power belonged to whoever happened to be standing there.

The wagon on the road was an armed shipment of mined ore on its way to be refined. The trip was being made in the middle of the night and taking a lesser-known and lesser-protected path to save time. This gang of bushrangers had made themselves felt in recent months, and the owner of the gold was trying to get it on the train where it would be better protected as quickly and quietly as possible. Unfortunately, it hadn't been quiet enough.

Information about the gold had gotten to the bushrangers, and they were making their best speed to intercept the shipment. They closed the distance to a point in the road ahead of the wagon. The wagon was pulled by four strong horses with a guard sitting next to the driver and two more riding in the back with the gold. Even though the trip was being made in the middle of the night, no additional guards or escort had been sent so as to keep their profile as low as possible.

The wagon was still rumbling on through the woods when the bushrangers reached the road and selected a spot that suited their purpose. The wagon had no lantern, but in the moonlight the outlaws first heard and then vaguely saw their objective approaching. When the wagon reached the spot, three men urged their horses out into the road and fired off two shots. As the wagon came to a stop and the guards raised their weapons, three more outlaws appeared in the road behind them and shot into the air again. Finding themselves outnumbered and surrounded, the guards dropped their rifles and raised their hands.

"Get down from there," one of the bushrangers growled as he aimed his pistol at the head of a guard.

They did as they were told and were hustled to one side by two outlaws that had dismounted. They then climbed into the wagon, pulled off the tarp, and struck matches to quickly inspect their prize. Being satisfied, they nodded to the bushranger, who had spoken and got up on the seat. One of the guards who had been grumbling to himself found his full voice.

"How long do you think you can keep this up?" he asked indignantly. "This is four gold shipments that you've managed to nab in five months. There will be an army after you before long, and they'll have you swinging pretty. The days of Kelly and Hall are done."

This guard had been standing halfway behind one of his fellows, and as he finished speaking, he fished a small pistol out of his coat pocket and shoved his comrade out of the way to have a shot at the bushranger. The outlaw's pistol banged, throwing out smoke and sparks, and as the guard fell, his gun went off and sent an unaimed bullet at another outlaw. It hit with a metallic thud against the man's chest, and he grunted and growled as the guard rolled around on the ground in pain. The bushranger urged his horse forward a few more steps.

"Ned Kelly is gone. Ben Hall is gone. Thunderbolt is gone. But the bushrangers are far from done. Someday we'll make things different. The Iron Shirts will make a difference!"

His pistol boomed again, and the guard moved no more. The remaining three stood stock still in anticipation of being next, but the outlaw turned his horse and took off back down the road with his gang and the wagon following him.

*****

Texas Ranger Wayne Stephens was completely ignorant of these events, and why should he not be? He had absolutely nothing to do with Australia. He and the other Texas Rangers had quite enough to worry about in Texas and never gave a second thought, or even a first, about the troubles of other people in other places. For eighteen years now, he had worked long and hard to tame and safeguard the land he called home, and thoughts of his past efforts flowed back to him in random order as they sometimes did to interrupt his main line of thought. After all his wandering and fighting, he wanted to cash in on some of the rewards he felt he had earned. To that end, he now had much more prevailing thoughts on his mind as he patiently waited on the cobblestone street near a once-so-familiar door.

Meanwhile, Emma Jones and Katelyn Stewart, the wife of Scotland Yard Inspector Caleb Jones and her cousin, were walking down a similar street. The Joneses had been dear friends of Wayne Stephens since he came to London three years prior chasing a horrible outlaw. Jones and Stephens working their intertwining cases together had cemented their friendship and laid the groundwork for the Joneses' visit to Texas two years later. It was during this visit that Stephens had met Katelyn, and after a string of wild adventures, including kidnapping and murder, they had decided to love each other rather than kill each other. But now those memories were growing darker in Katelyn's mind as she walked with her cousin.

"I can't help but think it, Emma. I just can't," Katelyn said as they walked. "He's lost interest in me, I know it. I suppose it hasn't helped that he hasn't seen me in over a year, but I had such hopes."

Emma gave her a soft smile as she replied, "Katelyn, you don't know anything for sure. Just because it been longer than usual since he has written you is no reason to lose hope."

"It's not simply longer than usual, Emma. After we returned from Texas last year, the letters arrived steadily, one every two or three weeks as shipping allowed."

"Yes, I know."

"Then as the year drew to an end, he started writing less. Each letter was at least a month apart."

"Yes, I know, dear, but he is a Texas Ranger. He may be on a long assignment or stuck out in the middle of nowhere."

"I know all that, Emma, but you've known him longer than I, and you know that if there were any possible way for him to get letters to me, he would, if he wanted to. Summer is nearly over, and I haven't received a letter in over two months."

They rounded the corner and began walking down the street where Jones and Emma lived.

"Do you think I may have written him too often?"

"No, Katelyn, I don't. You may have come close, but I think you restrained yourself." Emma snickered to herself. "If you are that worried about it, then perhaps you should go back, find where he is hiding, and talk it out."

Katelyn turned her head to focus on Emma as she replied, "You know I would love nothing better than to go back and see him again, but I can't go back there by myself. I wouldn't know where to turn or what to do, and if I asked Kina for help, she would certainly tell Wayne. I can't go back to Texas alone."

They stopped in front of the Jones residence, and Katelyn stood waiting for Emma to unlock the door when a masculine voice arrested them.

"Then perhaps you'll go back with me?"

Katelyn's blood seemed to freeze for an instant before it began to race through her veins, and the fair skin of her face began to resemble the color of her hair as she slowly turned to look behind her. On the street, dressed in a black suit, stood Wayne Stephens. So focused had Katelyn been on Emma that her peripheral vision had dismissed him as just another figure on the street. Now he had her undivided, frozen attention. He and Emma both smiled at her.

"Well," he asked again, "would you like to?"

Katelyn still gave no answer, but she freed her frozen body and sprang forward to embrace him.

"Wayne!" she said as she wrapped her arms around him.

He held her for several seconds before she released her grip and looked into his eyes with joy. Then her smile twisted into a frown as she gripped his arms tighter.

"Wayne, what is the matter with you? Why haven't you answered my letters?"

Stephens continued to smile, and Emma laughed at the spectacle.

"Katelyn, the man has had a long journey. Let him inside, and I'm sure he will explain."

Emma swept open the door, and the three of them entered into the cozy townhome that Stephens remembered so fondly from his first trip three years earlier. As he and Katelyn passed in front of her, Emma's mind flashed back to equally fond memories of the previous spring when they had all traveled to Texas to visit

Stephens and his family. It had been remarkable that in one trip, however harrowing, that Stephens and Katelyn could've been changed so much and come so close together.

Emma grinned bigger at the recollection of Wayne and Katelyn's first meeting when they had argued so vehemently over the ranger's destructive nature. But now, even that experience could be used to show how compatible the two of them were. As they sat down, Katelyn's frown dissipated. She was too happy to be angry, but she was still curious and pressed Stephens for an answer.

"I'm sorry I worried you, Katie, honest, but I couldn't help it."

"What couldn't you help?" Katelyn asked with a penetrating look in her eyes.

"Well, how much time and opportunity I had to write and send letters. I've been busy with other things. I've got the rangers to let me do a little less roaming in favor of taking time to train new rangers. When my company gets some new sprouts that don't know anything, sometimes the captain will let me have them for a bit to line them out. I've been trying to stay closer to home as much as possible so that I could get more work done."

"Work done on what?" Katelyn asked.

"A house," Stephens answered with a large, sincere grin.

Katelyn started and softened her glance. "A house?"

"Yes, a house, a new house on the ranch. A little bigger and better than what Mom and Dad originally had. It sits close enough to their house to be handy, but far enough away to be private. It's a house for us, Katie, if you're still interested. I was afraid that if I wrote any more than I did, I wouldn't be able to keep quiet about it."

"If I'm still interested!" Katelyn threw her arms around the ranger again. To her, it was the happiest moment of her life up to that point.

As she squeezed a small amount of moisture out of her eyes, Stephens spoke again in a handicapped voice.

"I must admit though, I did go without writing on purpose before I came, just to make sure you were still committed."

Katelyn jerked away from him, looked at him a moment, and then slapped him hard on his arm. "You scoundrel!"

Emma, who had been drying her own eyes as she watched their exchange, now laughed at them.

"I couldn't be happier for the both of you. And I must admit now, Wayne, that your plan worked quite well."

Katelyn's head snapped around to her cousin, and her mouth gaped open in astonishment at this confession from her own cousin.

CHAPTER 2

Katelyn's mind was still trying to process how her cousin could've kept such information from her when the door of the house opened again and Caleb Jones came into his home.

"Emma?"

"In here, dear."

Jones appeared in the sitting room, and he reveled at the sight he saw.

"Stephens, by George, I'm glad to see you!" He stepped forward as Stephens stood up and pumped his hand heartily. "I hoped you would arrive today."

Emma stifled a laugh and covered her face.

"Arrive today!" Katelyn exclaimed in surprise. "Is my whole family a band of rogues conspiring against me? You mean, you knew he was coming here and didn't tell me?" Her gaze shifted from Jones to Emma to Stephens and back to Jones until her head started to swim.

Jones took her by the hands and eased her into a chair.

"Yes, my dear Katelyn, I'm afraid we did. Stephens wanted to surprise you, and we went along with it. We thought it was a charming idea. And if you're still disgruntled with us, then consider this a return for the endless hours of you romanticizing to us at every opportunity."

Katelyn's hot head now had to share her anger with her embarrassment. "Surely, it wasn't as bad as all that."

Jones's eyebrows rose high against his forehead in an expression that signified that she should know better. She slumped back in her chair as embarrassment began to overtake anger and might have lost the joy of the occasion, but Emma came to the rescue.

"Don't be so hard on her, Caleb," Emma said with a wide smile. "The girl is in love. Katelyn, darling, we don't hold it against you, we just needed to give our ears a rest from time to time. We are still extremely happy for the both of you."

The joy of the grand occasion of Stephens's arrival returned, and they spent the rest of the evening in eager conversation about news from both families. Stephens's parents were as well as ever and working hard to keep the ranch running like it's supposed to. Sheriff Bill Driver had finally retired from being the protector of San Antonio earlier that spring, though not because of any prompting from the public. The murder case he had worked the year before with Jones had brought him much esteem. He had just decided that after living through the civil war, the Indian wars, surviving wild days in the Texas frontier, and protecting a city like San Antonio for so many years, he was ready to have a more peaceful life.

Stephens's father had made Bill a partner and let him and Maudie oversee the freight business. Maudie, who ran the well-remembered café across from the sheriff's office, was now Mrs. Driver. Whether Bill had consented to this union or been forced was still debated by many, but his increasing figure was proof that he was reaping some rewards from it. This might have also contributed to his career decision. In any event, he seemed to have a comfortable home and seemed none the worse for the change.

Kina, Stephens's adopted half-Comanche sister, was helping teach school in Bandera and occasionally ventured to some other neighboring communities as the need arose, or if she just felt like it. Stephens sometimes wondered if there was another reason why she wanted to travel. If there was, Stephens knew he would have mixed emotions on the matter. Kina was young and very beautiful, and she deserved happiness as much as anyone, but could Stephens bring himself to trust or allow someone to provide it? He tried to not let himself get too embroiled in the notion since he had not been able to get any sort of confirmation from Kina on the subject. Since most of Stephens's spare attention had been on the new house; he would just have to wait for something to happen.

The house, as Stephens had mentioned, was bigger than the house his parents had started with at the ranch's birth, though they had since expanded it many times. It was a single-story home with a wraparound porch that encircled it. It sat about fifty yards from a little creek that ran to the river. The kitchen had a new stove, and the pump was sheltered by an awning just outside the back door. It was simple and spacious and had much potential to be made into a warm and welcoming home by its occupants. Stephens had received a lot of help from friends and ranch workers to get it built as quickly as possible. He wanted it done right and carefully, but like Katelyn, he didn't want their separation to last any longer than it had to.

He was not the sort to openly portray his feelings to just anyone. In fact, if you were not a close friend, chances were, you wouldn't know what was going on in the ranger's head. Katelyn had almost driven Jones, Emma, and others mad with her continuous rhetoric of love, passion, and tenderness. It was evident to the world that Cupid's arrow had hit her hard, and although Jones and Emma were close friends of the ranger, even they wouldn't have known that the ranger had been hit equally hard.

The experiences and adventures Stephens and Katelyn had shared during the visit the year before might have served to bring them together faster than they might have otherwise, but come together they had. Now Stephens wanted this woman, wanted to make her his, and had ever since their parting. Past relationships and the course of his life had brought Stephens to the belief that he was destined to remain alone, and he had resigned himself to this lonely life, to which he seemed particularly suited. Katelyn had given him hope, not just hope but a flame of determination that he could be happier than what he was. This mindset had flogged his efforts to their utmost, so that now he was ready to take the next step; he had come back to England to fetch Katelyn away. But first, since he was there, there were some people who wanted to see him.

The next day was a little overcast, but pretty. When Stephens returned to the Jones residence, Jones pounced on him. Before Stephens even had time to understand what Jones's rapid chatter was about, Jones had all but threatened to hold the ranger at gunpoint if he didn't go with him to the Yard. The chief inspector and others remembered Stephens from his excursion to track down Richard Shelby over three years prior, but many didn't. There were several who were new or had been busy elsewhere and had never met the "legendary man." All they knew were Jones's recounts, which they judged to be a little too fantastic.

Dressed as he was in his suit and vest, and portraying a more refined figure than had been expected, he took the awaiting spectators by surprise. Entering the Scotland Yard office, they passed about a dozen people, some of whom gave inquisitive glances, as Jones led the way to a lounge where inspectors would take their ease. Apparently, the handful of men in this room included at least part of the Doubting Thomases. They took stock of his American clothes and easygoing, confident demeanor. The ranger read the thoughts behind the expressions, and a mischievous grin grew on his face.

"Jones, did you bring me here just to make me feel like a carnival attraction all over again?" As he spoke with his distinct accent, smiles and giggles came from the crowd.

A young inspector stepped forward and spoke. "Inspector Jones, where did you get this play actor? Do you expect us to believe this is the immortal warrior of the American West you described?"

Stephens took his cue and walked up to the man and looked into his eyes with a hard expression. It was all Jones could do to keep a straight face. After considering the young inspector for a moment, Stephens turned back to Jones.

"Jones, if this young peckerwood is the best you've got to work with, then you're in sad shape."

The inspector, perceiving the minor insult, if not fully understanding it, changed his expression from jeering to angry.

"How dare you, sir!" the young inspector rasped out at the ranger. "I have half a mind…"

"I agree," Stephens broke in.

"I have half a mind to throw you into a cell and let you practice your rude comedy on our criminals!"

While Jones and the young inspector each turned red for opposite reasons, Stephens reached up and pulled back the left side of his jacket, exposing to all in the room his short-barreled pistol, ever present in its shoulder holster. The young inspector studied it as though trying to deduce whether it was real or not. As he did, Stephens pulled it out and slowly held it up while still pointing it at the ceiling. With a jerk and twist of his wrist, the ranger reversed the pistol and held it by the barrel.

Still standing stiff and silent, the young inspector stared at the pistol being displayed in front of his nose as if waiting for a magic trick. The trick happened when the ranger flicked his wrist again and thumped the young inspector on the forehead with the butt of his pistol. The blow had just enough force to cause him to lose his balance and fall backward into a chair.

While the young inspector winced as he held his forehead, and the others fussed over his mistreatment, the ranger holstered his pistol and turned to Jones. Jones looked as if he would swallow his bottom lip, so hard was he trying to keep from laughing at the spectacle. The ranger walked back over to him, grinning in turn. He turned back to face the young inspector, who was back on his feet, but before anything else could happen, a commanding voice made itself heard.

"Mr. Stephens," said the chief inspector from the doorway, "I heard that you were returning to our city. It is a pleasure to see you again, but I must ask you to restrain your destructive tendencies and not damage my inspectors. If you require assistance on another case, we shall be pleased to accommodate you, but otherwise, I must ask you not to detain my inspectors further as they are very busy men."

With this last statement, he turned his eyes to the group who fidgeted and made ready to leave the lounge. The chief inspector half turned to leave and then turned back, deciding to leave on a more courteous note.

"Enjoy your visit, Mr. Stephens, and convey my respects to your captain."

With that, the conference was ended, along with any further doubt as to the ranger's credentials, and everyone went about their business.

The boys returned home for lunch to not two but three very excited women. Upon entering the house, Stephens looked with a puzzled expression at the trio. Emma sat in a chair with her auburn hair, Katelyn stood next to another chair with her lighter shade of auburn hair, and in the second chair was a much more matured woman with whitened hair mixed with strands of bright red. The third lady was none other than Katelyn's mother, whom Katelyn had secretly sent for the previous afternoon after Stephens's arrival. With a sly look of success, Katelyn invited him to come meet her.

This was a moment that Stephens had honestly not looked forward to. But as when facing any potentially dangerous situation, he set his jaw and put his best foot forward toward the obstacle. With a few steps, he stood next to Katelyn, hat in hand, and stooped to offer his other hand to his would-be mother-in-law.

Chapter 3

"How do you do, Mrs. Stewart?" said Stephens with the utmost respect and sincerity.

The woman took the proffered hand and studied this strange man who had won over her daughter's heart so completely. For several silent moments, they just stared at each other, their eyes locked.

"It's Agatha, Mr. Stephens," she said at last and allowed her gaze to soften.

Stephens released the grip that they shared, and behind him, Katelyn released the deep breath she was holding. Her mother would not have given permission for her first name to be used if she had disapproved. Throughout her life, Agatha had many encounters and opportunities to interact with all sorts of people. This, combined with a naturally endowed talent of discernment, had honed in her the ability to peg a person's character very quickly. This had caused much embarrassment and aggravation to a younger Katelyn, but in later years, she had relied on her mother's intuition.

"Katelyn has, of course, told me volumes of stories about you, Mr. Stephens. But perhaps now you will elaborate."

"What would you like to know, Mrs. Stewart?"

"It is still Agatha, Mr. Stephens. Perhaps you can give a full account of the situation that necessitated you rescuing my daughter."

Stephens sensed that he was being further tested and considered his strategy for answering. Was she seeing if he would downplay the serious episode, take the opportunity to build himself up, or in some way challenge Katelyn's account? He had no intention of doing any of this, but he had to tell the tale in a way that made that plain. He was not so confident in his natural ability to set people at ease as he should have been when he wasn't performing his duty.

So after accepting an invitation from Emma to sit down, he began by telling how he had helped Sheriff Bill Driver catch the two thieves to begin with. Referencing Bill allowed him to throw in some comical comments without taking away from the story. From there, he described every event that had happened to him, from the jailbreak, to them making Katelyn a hostage outside of town, to tracking them in the direction of his ranch, to how he had laid his ambush for them, and how it coincided with what Katelyn had told afterward. By referencing back to earlier events that contributed to the kidnapping story, he was actually able to report most of his friends' entire visit before he finally drew the story to a close.

After Stephens caught his breath, he contemplated Agatha's face, as though he had not been staring at her for the last forty-five minutes. He and Katelyn were both pleased to see her smiling. He had succeeded in keeping her so enthralled with the excitement of the story that she was no longer concerned with Stephens's familial qualifications. He had found the right balance of honest detail and subtle embellishment, and he now sat in a more relaxed state of mind. While he leaned back more at ease in his chair, Jones announced that he must return to the Yard and that he must be told about anything that happened that evening.

Out of a desire to both rest his voice and return courtesy, Stephens asked Agatha to favor him with more details about her and Katelyn's family. Agatha obliged and began with her own history. She was the sister to Emma's mother, and they had grown up close to the Scottish border. It was no wonder then that she had married a young Scotsman that she met while helping her mother. They had worked with various organizations to help veterans of the Peninsular Campaign and the war against Napoleon Bonaparte who had returned maimed and mangled and unable to provide for themselves years before. It was during this time that she met Allen Stewart, named after the old Scottish hero from the previous century. He would come with his father, who had lost a leg and a few fingers at Waterloo, and soon they were taken with each other. They eventually married, and she worked as a seamstress while Allen followed after his father and joined the army shortly before the War of the Crimea.

He returned from the war in one piece, and a year later, Katelyn was born. He remained in the army for some years and then returned to civilian life as a blacksmith. This hardy life only added to the mystery of how Allen had managed to succumb to an outbreak of sickness in the area around their village, a sickness that manifested so quickly and viciously that without an adequate supply of medicine being readily available, Allen had passed away. Katelyn had been a teenager as the time, and in her eyes, her father was undoubtedly the best man that ever lived. It had crushed her heart to lose him, and every man that she encountered she held to his standard. This being said, it made Agatha doubly curious, besides being protective of her daughter, to meet the man that had been able to qualify for Katelyn's affections.

This explanation gave the ranger a fresh appreciation for the position he held in Katelyn's life and a renewed resolve not to fail in his duty to her. The solemn moment was observed and then passed as Agatha showed a new broad smile to Stephens.

"Now then, with histories exchanged, let's concentrate on the future. What's going to be done for the wedding?"

Stephens's eyes nearly bugged out of his head as he realized the severity of his tactical disposition. He was now trapped in a house with his fiancé, her mother, and her cousin—three excited women who were about to commence planning a wedding. He promised himself that Jones would pay for his absence.

As it turned out, Stephens didn't have nearly as bad of an afternoon as he had expected. Though Katelyn had become discouraged about her future with Stephens prior to his arrival, it was a recent and brief development. For many months before the trick that dampened her spirits, Katelyn had feverishly dreamed, and so planned, for the day when she would have her own family. Either with her mother or Emma or other friends who would take the time to listen to her, Katelyn had systematically pounded out the vast majority of the details concerning her prospective marriage. Now as Katelyn sat with her mother and Emma, Stephens just seemed to blend into the background as they talked in rapid speech about seemingly five different subjects at once. Occasionally, someone would break the circuit of the conversation to ask his opinion on a particular topic, and most of the time, he couldn't finish his thought before they were off on a new topic that had appeared in their minds.

So as the women worked through the logistics of the wedding, Stephens sat back and worked out in his own mind the logistics of getting all the people and freight home to Texas. He, too, had planned ahead for such events and now just had to figure the exact details. He was surprised when he asked Agatha about accommodations for her passage, and she declared that she would not be going. While she had escaped death with her husband, she had not escaped the illness itself. She had recovered and been able to resume her normal life, but her body had never been quite as strong as it should've, and though an ocean voyage was nowhere near the hardship it had been in centuries past, she did not think it wise to subject herself to it.

Katelyn already knew this was her mother's mindset, but it took Stephens by surprise. While her reasoning made perfect sense, it seemed unfair that she should be denied the privilege and right to see her own daughter get married. It was a problem that he felt he must solve one way or another.

"Agatha," he said, "I understand your concerns, but believe me when I say that you would be quite comfortable onboard the ship. You would have a nice stateroom to yourself, and if anything were to happen, there is an excellent doctor onboard to take care of you. Once we reach Texas, the climate may help you. I'm sure that Jones and Emma will attest that it's warmer and more vigorous than the foggy streets of London. It might be the pick-me-up that you've been waiting for."

Agatha looked at him with an appreciative expression. "Wayne, you may be absolutely correct, but favor me by not arguing. I've been on this island my whole life, and I have no desire to leave it now. As much as I would love to attend the wedding, I would rather not take the risk but rather do what I can to ensure that I am still here for my daughter for as long as possible, however many miles may separate us."

Stephens nodded in submission to her will and resolved to approach the matter a different way.

It was about that time when Jones returned home for the evening, and as he was hanging his coat on a hook in the hall, Stephens declared loudly, "Ahh, there's our flower girl now. Katie, do you think he would look better in pink or yellow?"

Jones turned and looked at the cluster of faces and replied:

"I beg your pardon, what on earth are you talking about?"

"Wasn't I plain enough?" Stephens replied. "You forfeited your right to be the ring bearer when you deserted this wedding party and left me to handle it all. So now I declare that you're going to be the flower girl. If you wear pink, then we'll get you a bonnet, but if you wear yellow, we'll get you a hat with a matching ribbon. Personally, I'm hoping for the bonnet so I can have extra lace sewn on so you don't scare people away."

Perhaps Jones's mind had been too occupied with whatever business he had left at the office, but for whatever reason, he was not seeing through the joke and kept the most confounded look on his face. At last, all three women busted out laughing at the spectacle, and Jones realized what had happened. A second later, he began to turn red as he considered how silly he must've looked for even momentarily believing the story.

"By all the saints, I don't know why I allowed you to come back here in the first place," he said to Stephens, who was grinning from ear to ear.

Emma ushered him into a chair, and while telepathically trying to exchange friendly insults with Stephens, he listened to an account of all that had been accomplished that afternoon. After dinner, Jones went out the door with Stephens to see him on his way to his boarding house, but first they made secret arrangements for the next day.

The following morning Jones, Emma, Katelyn, and Agatha were walking down the street on the pretext of doing some shopping for the wedding. At one point, Jones insisted they take a detour. None of the ladies could understand why, but they did as they were directed. A few minutes later, they came to a small protestant church whose minister Jones had known personally for years; he was none other than the minister who had married him and Emma. Outside of the church stood Stephens in his suit with freshly shined shoes and a fresh shave.

"Wayne!" said Katelyn upon seeing him. "What are you doing here?"

"Well, Katie," he said, taking her hands in his, "up 'til now you've just assumed there would be a wedding, but nobody seems to have noticed that you're not really engaged yet."

Katelyn stared off as she thought back and realized that he was right. As she thumbed through her thoughts, Stephens looked down and breathed deeply, then he cut his eyes at Agatha and saw her eyes widen as he lowered himself onto one knee and fished something out of his pocket.

"Katelyn Stewart, will you marry me?"

CHAPTER 4

Despite all her fantasizing, Katelyn was speechless. Her mouth was still gaped open as he slid a golden ring with a small cat's eye stone set in it onto her ring finger. Between working on the house and preparing for the trip, he had not been able to afford a precious stone, but when he had found this and cleaned it up, he felt nothing could be better. Evidentially, Katelyn shared his view because her mouth gaped still wider at the sight of the ring. Agatha and Emma both began to feverishly dab the tears from their eyes. Jones looked on in satisfaction and joy and pounded his fist into his other hand to signify it.

At last Katelyn lifted her eyes from the ring back to Stephens with her own eyes full of tears and exclaimed, "Yes!" She then tugged on him to get him back on his feet and threw her arms around him. "Yes, my love, yes!"

He held her for several moments before easing her back to speak again.

"Then marry me now."

"What?" Katelyn replied with a confused look on her face that was shared by the other women upon hearing his statement.

"Katie, we can still have a big wedding back home, none of your plans will be wasted, but Agatha won't get to see it. Right here, right now, let her see you get married."

Jones turned on his heel and walked briskly into the church to find the minister to whom he had sent a message early that morning, while Agatha's face wrinkled to a fresh onslaught of tears.

Katelyn went to hug her and again said, "Yes."

They began collecting themselves and turned toward the door as Jones opened it to usher them in. Stephens entered with Katelyn on his arm, and Agatha followed supported by Emma, with Jones bringing up the rear after he had shut the door. The minister and his secretary came out and presented papers that had to be reviewed and signed before they could proceed. Once this was completed, everyone took their place and a deep breath as the minister opened his book and began the ceremony. A few minutes later, Katelyn Stewart was legally Katelyn Stephens, and the true flood of tears began. The shopping trip was postponed, and the day was spent celebrating the marriage and happiness of the newlyweds.

Later in the evening, when Katelyn suggested that they should retrieve her things to take to Stephens's boarding house, Jones gave a surprising reply.

"Tomorrow we can go retrieve Stephens's things to bring back to our guest room with yours, but for tonight, I've already arranged for the two of you to stay at the Charing Cross Hotel. Consider it an early wedding gift."

Stephens's knee-jerk reaction was to protest against being treated so lavishly at someone else's expense, but his good sense saved him, and he realized that he should be grateful for the generous gesture. He reached out and pumped Jones's hand in gratitude, and a fresh flurry of conversation erupted between the women. The festivities lasted a couple hours more before Stephens and Katelyn were dropped off with one small bag apiece at the beautiful Charing Cross Hotel that had been built twenty-three years prior.

The next day it was afternoon before Stephens and Katelyn reappeared at the Jones residence. Two happier people could not have been found, and they had plenty of energy to finalize the plans for going back to Texas. Two days later, Stephens, Katelyn, Jones, and Emma boarded the ship that would carry them all back to Texas. The passage was completed without incident, and it seemed like hardly any time had passed before the ship was being moored to the same familiar dock in Corpus Christi.

Later that evening, they were once again guests at the same hotel in San Antonio and sat down to meal in the dining room with former sheriff Bill Driver and his wife, Maudie. Stephens joked that Bill's waistline had enlarged even more since he had left, and Jones cautioned Maudie not to make him burst open. Bill grumbled and growled, and the battle of insults commenced while the ladies laughed and talked about the upcoming second wedding. Early the next morning, the party mounted a stagecoach that would take them close to the ranch. As the last of their luggage was being stowed, Bill approached the coach door.

"At least this time you're sticking to your plan and not staying here to make trouble for me like you did last time."

Jones put his hand over his heart in an attitude of sarcastic shock. "My dear Bill, that smarts! We worked so well together last time, it saddens me that you would say such a thing."

"Yeah, it was smarts when I got shot in the arm too. If it hadn't been for that and Maudie being able to fuss over me afterward, I might still be a happy bachelor."

They all laughed and waved as the reins snapped and six powerful horses propelled them toward their destination. The great advantage of the stage system was that at the end of each stage of the journey, there was a layover station where travelers could eat and refresh and fresh horses were attached to the coach. New teams being rotated like this allowed the coach to maintain a fairly high rate of speed. In this way, the party reached a drop-off point near the ranch that evening rather than two days later. The spot where they dismounted was little more than a crossroads, but when they arrived, Kina and a ranch hand were waiting with a buckboard and a wagon to take them the last few miles. Jones and Stephens opted to ride in the wagon with the ranch hand and leave the women to converse in the buckboard.

After such a long journey, greetings by Stephens's parents were kept to a minimum that night. It wasn't until breakfast the next morning around the solid wooden table of fond memory that the details of what had taken place were told and plans for the future were described. Stephens's mother was thrilled at the revelation that he and Katelyn were already married, and as the other mother, she fully understood how it had occurred. She would still get to partake in the second wedding, so she had no complaints. After the general discussion had died down and the women had begun their preparations, Stephens borrowed his wife and took her to see their new home.

The house Stephens had labored over might not have won any awards in the London social columns, but to Katelyn's eyes, it was the most charming and cozy place to call home. Much love, as well as sweat, had gone into its construction, and that gave it a soul all its own that was evident. It was not a complicated layout, but simple and efficient, as Stephens had described. There was even a large bookshelf in what would now be referred to as the living room, and its shelves already had many occupants. Most of them were books that Stephens or his parents had obtained over the years, and they were books which Stephens felt he and Katelyn would enjoy. Outside, next to the pump, was a little fenced-off area that was freshly tilled, should Katelyn want to plant a fall garden.

"Oh, Wayne," Katelyn said as she twirled around and threw herself into his arms, "I don't think I could be happier. I love you!"

"I love you too, darling. I just hope you still feel this way a month from now or a year from now. It's one thing to be on a vacation, but to actually live here can make you see the imperfections you don't notice at first."

She gripped him tighter and looked deeper into his eyes. "I'm not letting you back out now."

She kissed him, and he kissed her, before taking her back to the planning party.

Stephens had three more days to wait before the day that would change his life forever…again.

It took that long to set up the wedding at the ranch, with a flowered archway to conduct the ceremony, a plank floor laid out for dancing, invitations to nearby friends sent and accepted, and all other manner of organization. During most of this, Stephens, Jones, and Stephens Sr. tended to ranch business and kept out of the way. One other ranger showed up with a couple of new recruits for Stephens to line out before they started their duty. He didn't know that the wedding was so imminent, but Stephens agreed to take them for an afternoon if the other ranger would stand next to him and Jones. Katelyn would have Kina and Emma by her side, so now they would be balanced.

So that afternoon, while the other ranger was getting cleaned up and preparing for the next day, Stephens and Jones took the two boys out on the range and instructed them on the finer points of shooting, riding, shooting while riding, tracking, hiding your tracks, and other skills that would be of use to them in open country. It was profitable to the young men and a good way to pass the time for Stephens and Jones. It helped them clear their heads and calm their nerves for the next day.

"Dang it, I'm already married. Why am I still nervous? It doesn't make any sense," Stephens pondered this conundrum half to himself.

"Don't ask me," Jones replied. "I only did it once. It's not my fault you have to do things bigger than other people."

Stephens gave his friend a lopsided glare. "Maybe it's because this is the big wedding where everyone is watching instead of a few friends."

He grinned at the ranger again, not being able to restrain himself. "In any event, I'll see that there is a horse on standby in case you decide you can't handle the pressure."

Stephens glared at him again and flatly said, "Thanks."

"What are friends for?"

"You mean what is family for, *cousin*. You better have two horses saddled so you can come with me, or else Katie will kill you."

They laughed over their jokes and waited for the next day.

When it came, it was quite the spectacle. A score of people came to witness the happy occasion dressed in their Sunday best. Bill and Maudie were there with his guitar freshly tuned, and he pushed and prodded for them to get a move on so he could start picking. Stephens and his men stood in front of the old country preacher along with Kina and Emma as Katelyn came walking up in her white dress lined with lace and accented with little flower buds. She stood before him and faced him overflowing with happiness. Even in this moment, Stephens could not forgo a joke.

"I've heard of people having dual citizenship in other countries, but this dual marriage-ship seems a little ridiculous."

Katelyn just smiled bigger and slapped his arm. "Wayne Stephens, you idiot."

The old preacher went through the ceremony from memory, and when Stephens and Katelyn kissed, the air was filled with whoops and hollers.

Katelyn and Stephens's second wedding day was perhaps the most thrilling day of their lives. Not to downplay the first wedding held for the benefit of Agatha, but this day was an exalted day. Since several of the guests had traveled far and were staying overnight, the festivities continued long after the happy couple had retired to their new home. The next day, they began working to make the house wholly their own, after bidding farewell to Jones and Emma, who unfortunately could not stay any longer. They unpacked all of Katelyn's things that had been brought over; they arranged and rearranged and made the transition from house to home.

Chapter 5

They made the most of their time together, but eventually Stephens had to leave her to do his duty with the rangers. Even before he left for England, he had tried to restrain how much time he spent away from home so that it would be an easier transition when he came back, but being a ranger still meant ranging. As a single, unattached man, he hadn't minded ranging. In fact, he liked it. That was why he had done it for so long, but now things had changed. Katelyn was a sensible woman and knew what she was getting into, but that didn't make it any easier the first time he had to leave. She had a nice house on a ranch with a dozen hands and their families if they had them, and it took less than ten minutes to walk to her in-laws', but she still felt alone in this strange country. She did plant a fall garden that had moderate success, she would keep the house and help cook for the hands, and she would still draw and paint and even work out plans for building new buildings and renovating the old ones based on her knowledge of architecture, but she was still lonely.

When Stephens finally returned a month later, she was overjoyed and wept, and she swore she would never let him go again. Of course, she knew deep down that sooner or later, she must, but at the time she meant what she said. Since he had returned to his old lifestyle, it wasn't as hard on Stephens as Katelyn, but it was still hard. He hadn't realized how much he would miss her and how anxious he would be to return to her arms. He pushed ever harder for more stationary duty, and he got what he could manage, but there would always be a call for him to travel.

This was a struggle they had to face, but in spite of it, they were still happy. Perhaps because of it, their time together was all the sweeter. Month after month came and went, then a year, and more months. Then one evening, as they sat on the west side porch watching the sunset, Stephens was calculating and thinking while Katelyn painted.

Finally, he spoke, "You know, the world is a lot different now than what it was when I was a boy. A lot has changed, and a lot has happened."

"Based on what I've seen and heard since I've been here, I can well imagine. And you've done much to make this world what it is, my love."

"I suppose you're right, but that's just it. There's still a lot of wilderness and unpleasantness in Texas, but maybe it's time to let someone else fight it."

She stopped painting and looked at him. "What do you mean?" She almost didn't dare to breath.

"I mean, maybe I've done my time. It's 1890, and I just realized a minute ago that in a few months, it'll be twenty years since I started rangering. That's a lot longer than most that join up, and maybe it's time to stop."

This was something that Katelyn had dreamed of hearing him say, but she kept her excitement hidden a little longer.

"What would you do then?"

"Well, I've actually thought about that some too. Fighting bad is all I've ever done, and I still don't think I'm cut out to be a full-time rancher. Lots of rangers have left to become sheriffs, marshals, railroad officials, and such. What if I became a cattle inspector?"

While he was talking, Katelyn had set down her paints, and when he asked her this, she could restrain herself no longer. She jumped out of her chair into his lap and kissed him.

"You have no idea how happy I would be if you did!"

He held her and smiled. "All right then, that settles it. Next week I'll have to leave out again, and I'll tell them that after that I resign."

They enjoyed the rest of the sunset and went to bed. A few days later, Stephens was packing to go meet up with other rangers when a supply wagon came in from town; it had a bundle of mail, including letters from Jones and Emma and Agatha. There was nothing unusual about that, and they took the time to read them before he finished packing. There was something odd though: the last letter written by Jones was specifically for Katelyn. He had a huge request to make of her about her husband that made her heart jump. After reading it, she carefully folded it back up and put it in her pocket. She thought it best not to burden Stephens with it before he left. She just wanted him to concentrate on coming back home. As he prepared to mount up, she walked up to kiss him goodbye.

"You be careful and take care of yourself, Wayne. If you get yourself killed, I'll come find you and break your neck to be sure."

"I don't doubt that at all. Don't worry, I'll be back before you know it."

"You better!"

She did her best to smile and put on a brave face as always, but she couldn't help her mouth trembling a little. He kissed her goodbye and rode off to the northwest. After she watched him disappear into the distance, she went back inside, sat down, and reread the letter. To receive this on the day that he left made it doubly difficult, and if Jones had appeared in front of her at that moment, she would've beat the daylights out of him. She stood up and walked back and forth through the house, asking the books and the furniture how her cousin could think of doing this to her. Was he insane? Was he joking? Had the world gone crazy? She marched outside, grabbed her garden hoe, and started hacking at the ground as if she were attacking a den of snakes.

The exertion helped to gradually cool her temper, and as her mind cooled, her rational thinking took over. Jones would not ask such a thing lightly. He would know from past experience and the letters she had written how hard a thing it was that he wanted her to do. The situation must be serious for him to take this step, and so she would make herself help him. She went back inside, sat at the desk, and began writing a reply. Allowing for the time it would take for the letter to reach him, he would have to act fast. If everything went according to schedule, Stephens would return in about six or seven weeks.

She sent her reply to Jones and settled herself into the routine she followed when Stephens was away. Summer was approaching, and there wasn't much of her garden left. She reread some of her favorite books when she wasn't cooking or helping her in-laws. Kina would return periodically from her scholastic travels and give her distraction for a few days and bring her new books, but the thought of the future was ever on her mind. None of the family was in contact with Stephens any more than she was, yet she kept Jones's request to herself. She knew Stephens wouldn't refuse the request. He might try. He might think he shouldn't go, that it was none of his business, that he was done with that life; but deep down, she knew he would not be able to resist. The call of a friend for help, the need for swift action, and the lure of adventure would draw him in, and he wouldn't be able to fight it.

Day followed day, and week followed week, and four days before Stephens would return home, Inspector Caleb Jones appeared once again on the Texas ranch. Stephens's parents were delighted at his return, and of course, Katelyn was happy to see her cousin, but the reunion was overshadowed by his mission, which he now openly declared to all. As could be imagined, the family was less than thrilled to hear Jones's proposal. For twenty years, Stephens had roamed all over creation, even to England, always running the risk of not coming back. They had hoped as Katelyn had that he would finally settle down to something quieter and safer. Now that that was his intention, Jones wanted to take him roaming again.

Jones could not apologize enough or overemphasize that for what he needed to go do, Stephens was the best man for the job and the only one Jones could rely on. They knew better than Katelyn that there would be no stopping Stephens from going and that all they could do was hope and pray, as they had always done, that he would come back to them safely. So when Stephens showed up four days later, they greeted him joyfully and then left them alone to conduct their business. Stephens was surprised to see Jones standing there when he got off his horse, but was also pleased, not knowing what was in store for him. After all the kisses and hugs were given, Stephens and Katelyn took Jones into their home.

Stephens dusted himself and put away his gear before finally sitting down at the table to enjoy Katelyn's cooking. While Stephens was eating was the best time to breach the topic of Jones's visit, since he would be less likely to argue with food in front of him. So as they finished discussing pleasantries and Stephens took his first mouthful, Jones took the plunge.

"Stephens, I don't enjoy saying this, but I'm not here for a social visit. I came to ask for your help with something."

Stephens looked at him and swallowed. "Okay, what is it? Do you need me to come train with those Scotland Yard sprouts of yours?"

As Stephens took another mouthful, Jones swallowed hard. "No. I need you to come with me, but not to England."

Stephens swallowed again and gave Jones a more serious look. "Where then? Are you working a case here?"

Katelyn set down a glass of tea in front of both of them and then sat next to Jones. Stephens took a drink out of the glass as Jones spoke again.

"No, not here either. I've come to ask you to go with me to… Australia."

Stephens's eyes bulged, and he gulped hard to keep from choking on the mouthful of tea. It would've been a comical sight if not for the seriousness of the conversation. He hung his head and caught his wind before looking back at Jones, and then at Katelyn, who seemed surprisingly unmoved by this.

"Katie, tell me that's some Gaelic word of yours." He looked from one to the other without reply. "That must be Gaelic for

Austin. If you want to go to Austin, we'll go to Austin. Katie, you liked it when we went last year." He shoved more food in his mouth.

"No, Wayne," she said, looking at him solemnly, "he means Australia."

Stephens swallowed and shook his head. "No, no, no, you must be talking about Arizona. I've never been there myself, but I hear there's some real pretty country out that way. Just say the word, and we'll go see it."

He took another pull from his glass as Katelyn, and Jones both raised their voices together and said, "AUSTRALIA!"

Stephens set his glass down with a thud on the table and swallowed hard before he spoke in a tone that was almost pleading.

"What in the world do you want me to go to Australia for? I don't know anything about that place except that it's on the other side of the world and not where I want to be!" He looked from one face to another, and neither showed any sign of relenting. His joyous homecoming was turning into one of the darkest situations he had ever faced.

Chapter 6

Jones and Katelyn looked at each other, and then back to Stephens seated across the table. Stephens kept shifting his eyes, looking from one face to another, and finally settled on Katelyn.

"Katie, I'd expect you to be in a frenzy right now. Why are you so calm?"

"I'm only calm on the outside. I don't like it any more than you do, but I knew what he was going to ask. He asked my permission first."

"He what?"

"I wrote to Katelyn to tell her about what was happening and to ask her permission before I asked you to help me. I knew what a toll it would take on her, and I wanted her to cool down before I actually showed up."

"Smart move," Stephens replied flatly. "So just out of curiosity, what is going on in Australia?"

"Well, Australia has been part of the British Empire for over a century. It started out as a penal colony, a place where we could send criminals to serve their sentence with less fuss than keeping them in domestic prisons. Also, the wilderness made it less advantageous for them to try to escape. Eventually, the continent began to be more alluring to settlers, people wanting to make a fresh start like here in your Western frontier. Colonists and convicts released from prison began making homes in the wild country, and it became not dissimilar to the American West with ranches, or stations as they call them, fledgling new towns, farms, and even gold mines.

"Another similarity it shares with America is outlaws. For some convicts, the threat of the wilderness was not enough of a deterrent, for several convicts still tried to escape. Many of those that did ended up dying in the wilderness, but some survived. Originally, the escapees were called bolters, but as time passed, other criminals took to hiding in the Australian bush country. Highway robbers, cattle rustlers, horse thieves, and murders all found relative safety in hiding in the wild. These men were given a new title—bushrangers, because they would range far and wide through the bush prospering and evading capture.

"Over the years, there have been some more notable and infamous bushrangers that have made their mark on history: men like Ben Hall, Fredrick Ward, who referred to himself as Captain Thunderbolt, Harry Power, and Ned Kelly, to name a few. Ned Kelly is said to have been the last of the bushrangers, or at least the last big name in their fraternity. He was captured and hanged in 1880, and the time of the bushrangers was thought to have ended, more or less. There were still a few rogues that roamed the bush country, but not to serious consequence.

"Then a couple of years ago, a new gang of them started operating in the state of Victoria. They operate like phantoms, appearing and disappearing, and to our knowledge, no names of any of the members have been discovered. They have concentrated primarily on gold shipments and have been a scourge on the mine owners and businessmen of the area. On one occasion, a gold shipment was sent overnight to a train stop with just a few guards, which no one knew anything about except the participants. The gang still got wind of the shipment and ambushed the wagon and killed one of the guards. Then, after they appear, they won't be heard from again for weeks or months at a time.

"This has been going on for nearly three years now, and it is calculated that the total amount they have robbed must equal something over a million pounds. The very economy of the state has become affected by this gang's operation, and so far, the authorities have been fruitless in their efforts to apprehend the culprits. People in the area have become quite disgruntled and restless with the government's lack of success. To that end, Parliament has instructed Scotland Yard to launch its own investigation, which means sending someone from England who is impartial and objective."

Jones spoke these last words with an exacerbated expression and let his eyes sink to the table as they envisioned other things. Stephens considered him and spoke.

"And that objective, impartial individual is you," Stephens commented.

"Yes, it is."

"My stars, I can't imagine what Emma must be going through."

"I can," Katelyn said quietly with her hands clasped.

Stephens looked at her, and his brow wrinkled as his mind began to grapple with itself. The story had succeeded in rousing his sense of adventure and duty, but now he was reminded of what else was at stake. He looked from Katelyn back to Jones as Jones began to speak again.

"She was very upset at me being given this assignment. Just the time that has lapsed since I left her to come here has been longer than we have been separated before. But the chief inspector made it very clear that if they were to send anyone, it would be me, because of my past record, which largely involves you. Australia is part of the British Commonwealth with British people subject to British rule, but it is a strange land with as much, or more, in common with your country. I don't believe I can resolve this on my own, and I would rather have you with me than any other inspector or constable. And so I asked Katelyn to share Emma's fate if you would agree to help me."

Stephens continued to look from one to the other as his mind worked to process all he had heard. At last, his eyes came to rest on Katelyn.

"Katie, you have a say in this. I think you know that for Jones, I'd go to help take care of this, but that will mean a longer wait for you than ever before. I won't do this without your blessing."

She brought her eyes up to meet his in an expression of mixed emotion. "Blessing! If I hadn't had a month to prepare for this, I would bless the both of you in the head with my garden rake for even thinking of it. And if it wasn't Caleb asking this of you, I still would, especially since you just decided to resign and stay close to home with me. But Caleb and a lot of people need you, so I reluctantly and unhappily approve."

Stephens reached across and took her hands in his as he spoke again, "I love you, Katie, and thank you. As soon as we clear this up, I'll be back to make you happier than ever. But I'm not resigned yet, so I'll have to check with Austin before I can go anywhere."

Jones started fidgeting again. "I have already taken the liberty of contacting them," he said guiltily pulling a folded paper from his coat pocket. "They have authorized your cooperation with Scotland Yard in this matter, should you choose to accompany me. We just need to send them notification of our plans."

Stephens rested his chin in his palm as he stared back at Jones. "You've thought of everything, haven't you?"

Jones couldn't help but smile at him now. "I tried to. Once upon a time, you didn't even give me a choice."

At the recollection, Stephens grinned and then laughed. Even Katelyn couldn't resist grinning at the irony.

"All right then," Stephens said at last. "Give me a few days to get things in order, and we'll head for California and a ship to Australia."

With the difficult part of their meeting done, everyone could relax and enjoy each other's company as night came on them. Katelyn and Stephens's mother cooked such a meal that they all nearly fell over with full stomachs before settling into a round of conversation and sharing of news. The next day, Stephens put a letter on the stagecoach to be conveyed to ranger headquarters, notifying them that he had accepted Jones's request and that they would soon be leaving for the west coast. Then it remained to gather all the supplies and gear that Stephens thought he might need. It was a simple task since he figured this excursion would be little different than the countless others he had taken over the years, just longer. Most of this gear he had just unpacked to be cleaned, mended, and stored, so he did so and repacked.

His duster and rain slicker were rolled up together in a bundle. In his saddlebags he had a complete change of rugged clothing; a small bag with bandages, salves, and one or two other medical items; another bag full of seasoned beef jerky that would stay good for a very long time; two fifty-round boxes of 44-40 ammunition for his two pistols; and three twenty-round boxes of 45-70 ammunition for his Winchester carbine. This was the same rifle that Stephens had acquired during the Jones's vacation three years prior, and it had served him well. He also included a tin cup, matches, and several other items that might come in handy in the wilderness. Stephens fetched a second set of saddlebags and packed them similarly for Jones to have.

"We'll be on a train most of the way to California," he explained to Jones, "and will be able to get what we need as we go. The same goes for the boat, and I suppose most of the places we'll be staying when we get there. But if something happens that we have to jump and run, I want to be able to grab these and go. We may not be able to grab suitcases in a hurry or pack them around with us if we're riding through the brush. And I don't want to be held up from doing the job by running around trying to find stuff we need."

"It's just as well that between us, you packed so much ammunition," Jones commented while watching the process. "The cartridges for your guns will be difficult, if not impossible, to find in Australia. The same can probably be said for my pistol also. Most people there still use weapons that use percussion caps, with the exception of the Martini rifles and some old converted pistols, but still nothing that shares ammunition with your guns."

With this speech, Stephens turned and disappeared into the bedroom and reappeared a moment later and held his hand out to Jones. In it he held an 1878 model Colt double-action revolver. With a gesture from Stephens, Jones took it and examined it.

"I picked that up some time back and figured I'd get it to you when I could. I've shot these things a time or two, and they just don't suit me, but considering the trouble you had with a peacemaker last time, I thought you might like it better. It's the same caliber as mine, so we can share the ammunition we've packed."

Jones's eyes lit up, and he grinned as he shook Stephens's hand in gratitude. He had only a passing interest in firearms, but besides being a gift from his friend, he realized the usefulness and effectiveness of having such a weapon on this trip.

They finished their preparations but delayed one more day before leaving. This was for Katelyn. Stephens had only been home a couple of days, and they had been busy with planning and preparation. This last day was solely for Katelyn and Stephens to spend together doing whatever they wanted, and from dawn until after dusk, Katelyn made the most of it. Katelyn was actually up before Stephens, painting the best sunrise picture she could muster for Stephens to take with him as a reminder to come home. While Jones spent the day with Stephens Sr. and the hands, Stephens and Katelyn wandered over the ranch to their favorite spots, even as far as the riverbank where they shared their first fire. The night passed with everyone getting an indifferent night's sleep before rising and collecting their gear. They flagged down the stage that was due to pass that morning and began their journey to the coast and to Australia.

Chapter 7

Jones and Stephens took the stage to San Angelo and connected with other coach lines making their way in a west-by-northwestern direction. Between the coach lines and railroad lines, they took the most direct path possible toward San Diego, California, and a week later, they arrived. Their trip to the West Coast was uneventful to the point of tedium. Stephens almost wished for outlaws, Indians, or bandits to show up and give the trip a little excitement. As it was, they talked to each other about whatever they could think of, except the case. While they were still in the United States, traveling through territory that neither of them had ever seen, they preferred to enjoy and discuss what they saw.

Once they arrived at San Diego, they arranged for passage on the next available steamship bound for Australia. Two days later, they boarded and departed on their next adventure. The first day or two was filled associating with the crew and other passengers, but after the pleasantries were past, the trip became a matter of patience, with only the occasional whale, dolphin, or flying fish to break the monotony. Now that they were at sea, they had all the time in the world to discuss the case.

Australia was divided into seven provinces or states: Western Australia, South Australia, the Northern Territory, Queensland, New South Wales, Victoria, and the large island of Tasmania. The state where the specific trouble was occurring was New South Wales, which occupied much of the southeast coast of the country. This state was also home to the thriving port city of Sydney, and it was to this port that the two lawmen were gradually making their way. On one particularly dreary day, when a gray sky and gray waves threatened to drench anyone who showed themselves with gray water, the duo seated themselves in the dining area with some warm beverages to discuss their mission.

"Tell me more about these bushrangers that you mentioned before. I was paying attention, believe it or not, but tell me some more," Stephens asked as they settled into their seats.

"Well, I've told you the basics of how they came to be. The whole situation of their existence in the later years could probably be best compared to your post-civil war outlaws. Jesse James and the like, if I have my history correct. While there was never a civil war as such in Australia, violence always threatened to emerge in the tensions between squatters and selectors."

"Squatters and selectors?" Stephens held a puzzled expression on his face.

"Yes, squatters and selectors," Jones replied. "You see, years ago when Australia was still in the early days of being settled, the term *squatter* probably carried the sort of derogatory context that you would expect. But land was plentiful if you could tame it and keep it safe from native raids. So many people looking for a new start did just that. They would settle or squat in an area of land to farm it or raise sheep or cattle. Those who were successful would gradually expand their territory at will. On the whole, squatters did well for themselves and flourished. Later on, however, the government intervened as more people came to Australia, and the remaining unclaimed land was divided into sections, and newcomers could select which available section they wanted. While this created widespread opportunity for a greater number of people to own a piece of land, individual sections could become landlocked quickly, and expansion was much more difficult than it had been for squatters.

"Few selectors were able to do as well as squatters had done, and they found it hard to make ends meet. On top of that, squatters were annoyed that the sections held by the government stifled their further expansion. So selectors were bitter with the squatters for having so much land and so limiting their own prospects, and the squatters were bitter at the selectors for getting in the way of their advancing empires. *Squatter* quit being a term for a vagabond and became the name of big, well-to-do landowners. The selectors even began calling them the Squattocracy, as if they had become the nobles of Australia. Very similar to your Southern plantation owners, again, if I'm getting my history right. In such circumstances of poverty, it's small wonder that the likes of Ben Hall and Ned Kelly and his brother turned to a life of crime. And for the most part, they committed acts against the squatters rather than their own selector people."

"I guess not," Stephens agreed, remembering the old confederate outlaws he had heard about in his younger years and remembering what a mess the South was after the war. "What else can you tell me about the bushrangers themselves? How did they operate?"

"Oh, about the same as most outlaws would operate. Like I said, all the big names of that fraternity have long since been punished for their crimes, and it was thought that bushrangering had dwindled down to almost nothing until this new gang began stirring things up. Ned Kelly was hanged in 1880. He was first caught as a young man selling stolen horses. After a few years in prison on account of it, he became more active, moving stolen horses and stealing from squatters.

"Things got hottest for him when he and his gang, which included his brother, killed two policemen that were in the same woods they were. One constable survived to tell the tale, and Kelly continued his career, becoming more political as he went. At one point, he crossed from New South Wales into Victoria, took a small town captive, and sent out a document he'd written denouncing the government. That situation ended peacefully enough, I believe, but Kelly was still on the run. He ultimately met his end when his plan to derail a police train was upset.

"He and his gang had contrived for a train carrying a police force to derail at a curve in the track. To do this, they had to take another small town, which was little more than a camp, captive. His downfall was in his kindheartedness, because he later let some of the people go, and one of them flagged down the train before it reached the curve, and the police force came after the Kelly gang. After a prolonged exchange of gunfire, three of the gang were killed in a small inn either before or after the building caught fire. Ned himself had fled off into the woods and was actually coming back at the end of the fight when he was fired on again. They had to shoot him in the legs to capture him for trial and punishment."

Stephens looked at him with another puzzled expression. "I'm sorry, I'm all for law and order, but if the man and his gang were in a big firefight with the law, why didn't they shoot him down in self-defense?"

"Ah! That is the most interesting part, they tried but couldn't. He couldn't be shot down because before this episode started, he had put on armor."

"What?"

"Yes, he was covered from his head to his thighs in a crude, probably homemade suit of armor that succeeded in stopping bullets."

"You must be kidding," Stephens exclaimed.

"I am not."

"I've heard some wild tales, but that takes the cake."

"I thought you'd like it."

"But what does all that have to do with the case we're on now?"

"Maybe nothing at all. You asked to know more about bushrangers. However, there may be a link to the Kelly story. One of the guards from the midnight robbery when another guard was killed claims that the guard who was killed shot one of the gang first, but the bullet seemed to bounce off, and the bushranger just moaned and groaned. He also said that the leader referred to themselves as iron shirts. Now maybe these new bushrangers have taken a page from Kelly's book and wear iron plates under their shirts."

"Maybe so," Stephens replied, "but that doesn't give us any clue as to how they've been able to be ghosts. Maybe they're that good, maybe the police are just that bad, or maybe the gang has an inside man."

"Or maybe inside men. There have been rumors that some police are corrupt. And depending on which side of the fence you're on, the police aren't always very impartial."

"What about the military? Do they still operate in the country, or are they just there in case?"

"It used to play a sizable part, but no longer. The military presence in Australia has dwindled down to almost nothing in the last twenty years. It is mainly made up of marines that augment the navy in defense of the colony as a whole. I doubt they have any involvement with this."

"Maybe not, but we might still get some useful information from them."

"Who knows."

This was one of many conversations they would have over the six-week voyage to Australia. The rest of the time, they occupied themselves as best they could. They would assemble with other passengers to play games of cards, dominos, or whatever other passengers had going on. It became known that Stephens was a Texas Ranger, and as he had come to expect, people began to ply him with questions about the rangers, Texas, Indians, outlaws, and even political issues in the state and country. Stephens had an affinity for telling stories and wild tales, as Jones well knew, and one night when the interviews were pushing Stephens to expound in ever more detail about his adventures, Jones tapped the ranger's leg under the table and rubbed his mouth nonchalantly as the ranger cut his eyes at him. He was reminding the ranger of what they had agreed upon before they set sail, that no one could know that Jones was a Scotland Yard Inspector and Stephens could reveal nothing of his past association with the Yard or their case.

When they had arrived in San Diego, they had no idea which ship they would embark on until they examined the shipping schedule. Once a ship had been chosen, there had been no time to research any of the passenger or crew; any of which might be connected with their business in Australia. So the two lawmen had decided to keep their purpose and Jones's identity a secret. The ranger had no lack of other juicy stories to tell his audience. Stephens had easily explained his presence onboard to his fellow passengers by declaring that in his travels, he had hunted many North American animals for food or sport, such as deer, antelope, bear, and buffalo, to name a few. Now he had the opportunity with the help of his English friend to go to Australia to hunt more exotic game, to which the presence of his rifle bore witness. Some of the gentleman passengers who were shooting and hunting enthusiasts asked to examine it since they had never handled an 1886 Winchester rifle before.

"Wouldn't it be better suited for hunting," one man inquired one evening, "if it were longer and heavier? I would think that would be better suited for hunting big game."

"You're right, it would be better for hunting animals if it were longer and heavier. Buffalo hunters for decades have used Remington and Sharps rifles that are time and a half the size and weight of this gun. The difference is they were shooting at huge animals at long distance that weren't shooting back. I have also used this carbine in my job to hunt and chase after many two-legged animals that wanted to get me as bad as I wanted to get them. In those situations, having a smaller, handier rifle makes a world of difference."

And so the voyage continued until the ship dropped anchor in Sydney.

Chapter 8

Sydney was no small place. It seemed to stretch on and on as the two lawmen stood at the handrail on deck as the ship made its way to its anchorage. There were countless three- and four-story buildings making up the vital areas of the city, and the hustle and bustle appeared like a disturbed ant bed with each person bobbing and weaving around the others, trying to conduct his or her own business, order looking like chaos. Rather than pulling up to the dock, the lawmen's ship dropped anchor a short distance from shore, and a small steam-powered boat came out to take the passengers off, while barges came alongside to collect the cargo.

Jones felt that he looked a little silly stepping on shore in his suit and small hat with a bag in either hand, all accented with the set of saddlebags Stephens had provided draped over his shoulder. Jones was not like Stephens and had never tried to be, just as Stephens had never tried to be like Jones. Jones was a policeman who worked in the big city, while Stephens was as much like a soldier as a policeman who traveled the wide-open country. They were each their own men with their own place in the world. So while Jones felt like a spectacle over this one aspect of his appearance, he could see nothing odd about it with Stephens, who wore his own suit and carried his bags with saddlebags over one shoulder and rifle scabbard over the other.

They walked from the quay into the town and so let the flow of passengers sweep away from them and dissolve into the rest of the crowd. After receiving a few well-wishes on their hunting trip, the duo was soon left to themselves, and they stopped to consider their next move.

"Well, this is certainly an interesting place. Not London perhaps, but still impressive," Stephens said as he looked all around him.

"It is that. I've seen drawings and a few early photographs of this land from decades past, and to see what it has become now is most impressive. Imagine what your Texas was like fifty or sixty years ago compared to how it is today. That was once the state of this country."

Stephens nodded his head at the comparison and turned to look at his friend. "So do you still want to play it quiet? It may make it more difficult to get answers, but might also be safer."

Jones nodded his head. "Yes, I believe I do. The chief inspector counseled the utmost caution, and with the enormous lack of information about this whole affair, I don't believe there is any such thing as secrecy except between the two of us."

"That's good enough for me. Let's get going with the usual drill then, drop our gear at a hotel and start looking for answers wherever we can track them down."

With that the two continued walking and navigating their way through the city. After a few general inquiries about lodging, they arrived at a decent, modest hotel. Jones had been given a very generous allowance of cash to conduct his business on the far side of the world, but there was no sense in wasting money they might be needing later. After depositing their gear in their room, they enjoyed a good meal in the dining room before heading back out into the city. Back on the street, they set out at a leisurely pace to explore the intricacies of Sydney. More than once they came around to the wide roadway that was George Street with scores of all sorts of people about various forms of activities. On one part of the street, a demonstration was going on with banners and signs denouncing the lack of laws regarding labor.

At the sight of the demonstration, Jones snapped his fingers and walked over to a paperboy on the sidewalk and came back with a copy of the *Sydney Herald*. It had much to say about the labor issues and the outcry it was provoking, which they were now witnessing. The Craft Union and Industrial Union had fought long and hard for their existence and victories in past years. Now the movement was broadening, it seemed, and less-skilled laborers wanted in on the advantages of union membership. They wanted regulation of pay, workdays, and better work conditions, among other things. Another article addressed the theft of gold from prominent mines and the outcry over such occurrences still transpiring after all the progress of recent years.

There was also an editorial on the subject that made Jones frown as he read over it. The author denounced the police, the military, the very government for not taking swifter, more decisive action against these raiders that threatened a crucial part of the economy. Though the article didn't say so directly, Jones detected a hint of rebellious undertone meant to influence readers to think they should take matters into their own hands. Jones showed the article to his partner, who also understood the meaning.

"That doesn't sound good," Stephens commented. "I wonder how many other such articles have been written lately?"

"Probably more than a few. Once newspapers take a side in a conflict, they hold on like a bulldog and carry on as hard as they can. Sometimes they may actually believe in what they're printing, sometimes they're paid, and sometimes they just print what will sell. In any case, they can be a devil of an inconvenience sometimes."

Stephens suddenly grinned wide. "They sure can. As I recall, the *Boston Observer* once gave you a fair bit of trouble."

Jones looked at him in confusion for a moment before realizing the reference.

"Yes, well, some still maintain that the American Rebellion should've never succeeded, but if it hadn't, then the rangers might have never existed, and then where would we be?"

The duo continued their wandering, and Stephens started talking half to himself.

"Papers are sometimes paid to print stories, and sometimes they print what sells. While you allow that everything must have some small element of truth to it, you also have to take everything with a grain or two of salt. Very few people know everything about any story, so some might get things wrong, and some choose to stay wrong if it works for them. For all we know, the editor of that paper may be biased or corrupt."

"That line of reasoning reinforces the rule that information gleaned from newspapers should be considered hearsay until it can be verified. Unfortunately, without revealing ourselves to the local authorities, we must do all the work to verify whatever we come across."

"Oh, I don't know," Stephens retorted. "Sometimes you can pick out a man that's a little too chatty." He suddenly stopped on the sidewalk and began to grin again. He also began running his fingers through the hair on the back of his neck as he stared forward.

A short distance ahead of them was a small establishment with a white-painted front and red spiral stripes painted around the columns in front of it. Stephens had not dared let the ship's barber anywhere near him on the voyage over, not with any sharp object while on a boat that could hurl him across the room without warning. He had managed to do his own shaving, but his hair had grown perceptibly since he left Texas.

Jones followed his gaze and then noticed his fidgeting.

"I assume you want to stop for a haircut then. I agree you look like you need one."

"True enough, but also can you think of anyone chattier than a barber?"

Jones now shared a big grin as he realized his friend's implication.

"Absolutely not! If everything is hearsay, we might as well talk to a master of hearsay."

Most everyone had to get their haircut and face shaved at some point, and it was a huge convenience to let someone else do it for you if you could. Barbers saw a vast variety of people, and it was one of those mysteries of nature that a person sitting in a barber chair had a tendency to talk and share news and gossip with whoever was present, especially the barber. A similar phenomenon occurred with bartenders, but since people in a barbershop are usually sober, they were at least slightly more reliable sources of information. So the pair gleefully walked the remaining short distance to the barbershop and stepped in to make a casual interrogation of a man who was most likely to know what might be, could be, and should be.

Chapter 9

A small bell jangled as the door opened, and the lawmen stepped in. It looked as if the barber had just finished his only customer and was receiving his payment. He was a tall, stocky man who maintained a very neat mustache but was practically bald on his head.

"There you are, Phil," the customer said, placing a few coins in the barber's hand.

"Thanks, Ed, I'll see you Friday."

"Yeah," Ed replied with something between a laugh and a snort. "If my investments in the mines don't make me go bankrupt. Cheers."

Phil shrugged, and the two lawmen stepped aside to let Ed exit the shop.

"Now then, what can I do for you gentlemen today?" the barber asked with a good-natured expression.

"I haven't had a clean shave for two days or a haircut for two months, and now I would appreciate both if you don't mind," Stephens answered with an equal measure of lightheartedness.

"A Yank by gad!" the barber strode forward and offered his hand to the ranger. "Pleased to meet you, sir. My name is Philip Rory. What brings you here?" Phil asked curiously as he turned and swiveled the chair around for Stephens to sit down and reached for a fresh cloth to drape from his neck.

The ranger took off his jacket and hung it on the rack in the corner. As usual, this left his short pistol exposed in its shoulder holster. The sight of a man packing a pistol wasn't as unusual in Australia, as it might be in England, but the barber still took particular notice of it.

"Bless me, you don't take chances, do you, sir?"

"No, Mr. Rory, I do not. Having grown up and lived in Texas my entire life, I've learned that men don't tend to live long if they take unnecessary chances. But don't you worry none. I've never had cause to kill a barber yet."

Stephens grinned mischievously at the barber, and a snicker from Jones confirmed the joke.

"Pay no attention to my friend, Mr. Rory, he's just a crafty old devil who wanted to see if he could make you squirm a little."

Rory grinned and pulled the cloth snug around the ranger's neck.

"It's a rare person that sits in this chair that I take too seriously, my good sir. Giving a clean cut is my primary concern. Now then, my good sir, how would you like your hair cut?"

Stephens had been studying a large piece of paper on the wall that illustrated various hair and moustache cuts to choose from. "I think I'll have the second-to-last haircut on the first row and a clean shave all around."

"Very good, sir, just sit back and relax." Taking his comb and scissors, he began snipping on the back of Stephens's head before speaking again, "You never told me what brought you to Australia."

"Well, my English friend there does some business in the States, and he insists there is game here worth hunting that would be a change from back home. He said he was planning a trip here, so I packed up my gear and came along to see what I could bag."

"Um hmm, um hmm," Rory said as he focused on his work. "Well, I don't hunt myself. As long as my wife can get good meat from the market, then I'm content. But I have customers that talk about hog deer, red deer, and sambar deer that are quite impressive throughout New South Wales and over in Victoria. Not to mention innumerous species of quail and duck. Or if you want something bigger, there are buffalo."

"Those deer sound nice, I'm not so big on the birds though," Stephens replied. "They're plenty good to eat, I'm sure, but you get a lot more meat from a dear, plus hides and antlers. Now the buffalo sounds pretty enticing. The big shaggies back home are almost gone. What about them funny-looking critters that hop around like oversized jackrabbits?"

"You mean the kangaroo. Everyone who comes here wants to see the kangaroos. They're plentiful enough. The red kangaroo ventures all over the country. I shouldn't doubt that you will find some."

Not wanting to seem rude by leaving Jones out of the conversation, Rory now turned his verbal attention to him. "And what business are you in, sir, that causes you to travel to America and now here?"

Jones saw his opportunity to start to probe, and he took it.

"I'm a business investor. I was looking to invest in ore mines in the western part of the American states and territories."

"Um hmm," Rory replied again, still snipping. "And does that make you a mine owner?" talking to Stephens again.

"No, I'm a rancher. I ran into my friend in Amarillo and tried to convince him to invest in cattle instead of gold. Mines will eventually run dry, but folks will always want a good steak."

"I can't argue with you," Jones replied, continuing the charade, "but like I've said before, the value of one of your steers is pocket money compared to the value of its weight in gold."

"Yeah, but in one year, I can take a thousand head of cattle to market. Each steer weighs several hundred pounds. Now how long does it take one of your mines to put out that much gold?"

"You have one ranch, while I'm invested in several mines."

"Bless me, it's just as well that you two are friends. I'm afraid you would make bitter enemies," Rory commented.

"Well, hopefully, we'll never find out," Jones replied. "He is right about one thing in that mines will stop producing sooner or later. That is why I'm always looking for new investments and why we have come here. I want to get in on the mining operations in Australia if I can."

Examining Stephens's forehead, Rory gave a final snip and then set down his scissors. He then picked up a mug, added a few ingredients, and started to stir it with a lather brush before he responded.

"Up until not long ago, I would've called that an excellent idea and wished you luck. But now I dare say that you might've wasted a trip."

"What makes you say that?" Jones asked.

Rory appeared to be satisfied with the amount of lather in the mug and began to apply it to Stephens's face as he spoke again.

"People have been mining for gold and silver for decades, and with the continual spread of the railroad and new machinery, it was becoming a real industry. But it seems the past will not allow it. The days of highwaymen and rogues ranging through the bush killing, stealing, and causing trouble were thought to be largely over. But now there are more of the vermin plaguing the country immensely, especially the gold miners, and they are managing to keep the old feud between squatters and selectors alive."

"But the country as a whole is making progress, isn't it?" Stephens asked. "We just read…" Stephens's statement was cut short as Rory put a finger to his chin and tilted it back to scrap the edge of the razor up his neck.

"What he was saying," Jones continued, "is that we were just reading about the success of the unions and the push to make things better for workers and families."

"That may all be for naught if the government can't control these tensions."

"How do you mean?" Stephens asked, now that he was unhindered.

"The theft of the gold has impacted many people, big and small, and some are starting to insist that the government do something to stop it or give up control to those who can and will."

"Yes, we read something about that too. What do you think of it all?" Jones asked.

Rory shrugged. "Supposedly, it's the government's job to maintain the economy, and the volume of gold that has been taken is starting to affect that."

"But even outlaws have to eat," Stephens said, "and I never heard of an outlaw that didn't like to spend his money. The gold ought to be making its way back into circulation somehow."

"I'm not an accountant. I'm just a barber, but from what I've heard, that is not the case. Perhaps these rogues are trying to store it all away like some sort of pirate treasure."

On a small stove in the corner, a kettle sat with a little wisp of steam coming out of it. Rory picked up the kettle and poured the hot water onto a towel he held with his fingertips and let the water run off into a large bowl. When the most of the water had dripped from the bottom corner, Rory turned around and applied the hot towel to Stephens's face.

"Mmmmm," Stephens moaned with the sensation that was a mixture of pain and delight.

"If you gentlemen want to learn more about the unrest or the prospects of your investments, I would suggest you talk to Mr. Conner."

"Who's Mr. Conner?" Jones asked as Rory pealed the towel off of Stephens's face.

"Mr. Jeffery Conner is a prominent mine owner and a man who has worked hard to help maintain civility and peace between the selectors and squatters."

"Which one is he?" Stephens asked.

"Neither, I suppose. His land is squatter land, but he bought it when the original owner died without any heirs. It was shortly afterward that gold was discovered there. That would be about four years ago."

Stephens got out of the chair, and Jones spoke as he stood up.

"Where can we find Mr. Conner?"

"He may be here on business, as he frequently is, or else he's probably at his home near Orange. If he's here, you might could find him through the Department of Lands building, or I hear he likes to frequent the Fortune of War Pub."

"Well, that's something," Stephens said as he fished some coins out of his pocket and put twice the posted price in Rory's hand. "Mr. Rory, that was quite satisfying. Next chance you get, eat a good steak."

He turned, and he and his partner walked back out onto the street.

Chapter 10

The two lawmen decided to go back to their hotel for the afternoon to eat and rest a bit. They had just gotten off the boat that morning and had already begun to work their case. As evening approached, they headed out to find the pub that Rory had mentioned with the hope of running into Mr. Conner. The Fortune of War was located in the Rocks District of town, so named for the fact that many of the buildings in that area of town were made out of sandstone. It had been considered a slum area for decades and until about ten years prior had been dominated by a gang known as the Rocks Push. But now it had settled down and had made peace with the rest of the city.

The Fortune of War boasted being the city's oldest pub since it was established in 1828, but in any event, it was a welcoming place. Jones and Stephens sat at a table in the middle of the room where they could see the door and signaled for service. After ordering some food from the list posted behind the bar, Jones probed the waiter.

"One more thing, my man, we were hoping to find Mr. Conner of Orange here this evening. We were told that he frequents this establishment, and we wanted to talk over some business with him. Was our information correct?"

"Oh, yes, sir. In fact, Mr. Conner has a room upstairs. He usually does when he comes to town and doesn't make a secret of it. I'm sure he'll be along soon."

So they sat and waited and began to eat when their food arrived. Every time the door opened, they looked at the newcomer and then glanced at the waiter, and every time he shook his head to signify that it was not Conner who had arrived. Honestly, half the time this confirmation was unneeded as it was some sailor or dock worker coming in from a long shift. They were all but done with their meal when the door opened and a tall man entered that grabbed their attention. He was tall and fit with what would now be described as dirty blond hair that looked to be recently cut and a meticulously trimmed goatee. He wore a fine suit tailor-made for his physique and shiny black shoes. A gold watch chain ran across his vest that glinted in the light of the lamps. He exhibited a perfect blend of sophistication without seeming fribble. Only his worn and weather-beaten broad brimmed hat, which he removed upon entering, detracted from his otherwise-polished appearance and seemed to reinforce the notion that he was not ignorant of or disconnected from the average working man.

Jones glanced at the waiter, who instantly gave a big nod of his head that this man was Jeffery Conner.

"That's our man," Jones said to his partner.

"I'd be surprised if he wasn't. Do you want to approach him now or wait?"

"Let him get settled. We still have to present ourselves as businessmen, and it would be rude to throw ourselves at him before he's even sat down."

Stephens agreed, and they proceeded to finish their own meal. Meanwhile, Conner walked past them, sat at a table ten feet away, and ordered his own meal. After the waiter had brought his drink, the lawmen decided to make their move. They stood up and casually walked toward Conner. Stephens stood slightly behind Jones so as not to crowd the man as Jones addressed him.

"Mr. Jeffery Conner, I presume?"

The man nodded and waited for Jones to continue.

"My name is Caleb Jones, and this is my friend Mr. Stephens. I was wondering if we could have a minute of your time."

Conner nodded and waved for them to sit down.

"What can I do for you, gentlemen?"

"I have come to Australia," Jones responded, "hoping to invest in ore mines, of which yours seems to be among the successful. I would like to help make it more successful by helping to supply new equipment, large and small, and anything else you may require. I have a great many contacts in England and elsewhere that could be of use to you."

"Do they not have newspapers in England, Mr. Jones, or do they just not care about our news? This would be a poor time for someone new to start investing in my or any other mine in this part of the country."

"We've heard of some trouble with bandits in recent times, but surely that wouldn't stop your entire business."

"That depends on if I can continue to get people to work for me. I can mine the gold easy enough, the bushrangers want us to get it out of the ground, but transport and refinement are troublesome to say the least when guards and workers keep ending up dead and the ore stolen. One of the more commonly told stories is of the wagon guard that got killed after a midnight robbery that revealed the name of the gang: the Iron Shirts. That was my guard and my gold that was stolen. And yet I am one of several prominent businessmen being affected by this monstrosity, but the English government seems unconcerned. It has been going on for over two years with local authorities being helpless to correct it."

Jones and Stephens were both surprised at the amount of passion that had erupted from Conner so quickly in the short conversation. It was natural that a man in his position would be distraught over the circumstances, but to be so quick to voice it and his dissatisfaction with the government was disconcerting. Their faces must've betrayed their thoughts as Conner's expression changed as he considered them.

"Forgive me, gentlemen, I didn't mean to lash out at you, but this is a most aggravating predicament."

"Are the police really so helpless as you make out? Jones continued.

"By all appearances, yes. They have not managed to kill or capture a single bushranger since this all started. Never before was there a group that was so elusive. They will strike, disappear for weeks, and then strike again on the opposite side of the country. No precaution or countermeasure has been of any avail."

"And the expansion of settlements and railroads hasn't helped to curb their concealment?"

"Hardly. Unless a group of track layers is going to stumble onto their camp in the middle of the night, then it doesn't help much. One downside of being a large landowner like myself, and there are several, is that it is impossible to keep an eye on all of it every minute. So there is still plenty of open country for them to occupy. Add to that, we have no names or descriptions. One of them could be sitting in this very room, and we would never know it. They can literally go anywhere."

"I see," Jones replied. "That still doesn't explain what we've heard about the old feud being rekindled between the squatters and the selectors."

Conner shrugged. "The old argument remains that the squatters take up too much land and the selectors don't have enough to make a decent living. To a point, I say, that depends on the individual, but it helps to have a little extra help. I began life as a selector, and now that I am in the squatter camp, I try to offer jobs and assistance to selectors as much as possible. But again, it doesn't help when they keep ending up dead. I'm afraid this is an altogether bad time for new investors seeking riches here, Mr. Jones."

Conner moved his glance from Jones to Stephens, who had not said a word so far in the interaction.

"And what is your interest in this? Are you some sort of investor also?"

"No, sir, my interest is purely academic. I accompanied my friend here from the States, when I couldn't get him to invest in my ranch, to hunt some of your Australian game. Tonight I'm just along for the ride."

"I see," said Conner, stroking his chin and considering the ranger intently as if he couldn't figure something out. After a few seconds, he gave up the effort and continued, "Well, I wish you good fortune, better than your friend is likely to enjoy, I fear."

"Then I gather you are not interested in taking on a new investor yourself?" Jones asked.

"No, I am not. I will not give up fighting for my property, but being responsible for your money as well as my own would add to my problems, not detract from them. Good night, gentlemen."

With that, the two lawmen left the pub and made their way back to their hotel to consider what they had learned.

"What do you think?" Stephens asked

"I don't know. I can certainly understand the man's frustration. I just don't like this common attitude that is forming against the government. Stopping these bushrangers is starting to look less like merely saving part of Australia's economy and more like saving Australia from possible civil war."

"Do you really think it would come to that?" Stephens's memories of the wartime and postwar years of his childhood flooded back to him in an instant, and he hoped that no such thing would transpire here, not if he could help it.

"I don't know. If you get enough people worked up enough, anything is possible."

"Well, everything we've come across here all seems to point in the same direction, so I don't see what good it will do to hang around here. Besides, cities bother me if I stay in them too long. Tomorrow let's start riding toward this Orange place and see if we can't stumble across something that Conner's track layers didn't."

"We might as well. I think even I would prefer to see the countryside more than the city. Ordinarily, I would say that since we've only been here one day, it's too soon to move on. But whether it's the fact that everything we've seen and heard points to the turmoil we suspected at the Yard, or just the feeling I get from being here, it seems that we would do better elsewhere."

Stephens nodded in agreement with Jones's gut feeling and began double-checking the saddlebags when he looked up again.

"Any idea why Conner looked at me so strange? I'm used to people looking at me weird when I get around you," Jones grinned at the slight. "But it seemed different this time. He didn't bother to ask where I was from either."

"To him, a Yank may just be a Yank. I don't know why he reacted like that, perhaps he was just too preoccupied with his own problems."

Stephens shrugged. "Oh well, I'll just be glad that I didn't have to explain myself all over again."

Chapter 11

The next morning, the duo got a little later start than they might have normally. Their hotel had soft, comfortable beds, and after more than a month on ship board, both men's usual habits were overruled, and each subconsciously waited for a knock on the door from the other saying he had to get up. At last, when the sun lit up both their eastern-facing windows to the point of blinding, they collected themselves. Out of their suits and in more rugged attire for brush-riding, the lawmen made their way downstairs and had breakfast. They then turned their keys in at the desk and made it known that they would be gone for some days.

The sight of men walking down the street with saddlebags on their shoulders was not an oddity, though maybe a little less common than in years past, but they drew little enough attention as they made their way to a livery to rent horses. Here, as in the States, the ever-expanding railroad decreased the need for large volume long-distance horse traffic. It was less than two hundred miles from Sydney to the Orange city and area, and taking the train, they could've ridden comfortably and continuously in a train car and arrived the next day. But they weren't hunting train robbers; they were hunting bushrangers that traveled as far away from people as possible and stole from more secluded locations to avoid detection and capture.

As hinted by Conner the evening before, this gang was good and smart. They had just appeared and started operating. No individual identities were known, and no faces could be described. Anonymity was always a friend to outlaws and was a most practical strategy, but some of history's more infamous characters never had that chance. Their careers might have started in circumstances where everyone already knew them, or it was easy for authorities to deduce who they most likely were afterward. Some outlaws used their name and reputation to their advantage. Pirates had let the fear of their past acts of violence fight for them and cause potential victims to give up without a fight in exchange for mercy. Post-civil war outlaw Jesse James had been similar to the bushranger Ned Kelly in that he had written articles to newspapers stating his purpose. In this way, he had endeared support from other Southerners as a sort of Robin Hood fighting back against the overbearing Northern victor of the war.

These were not the sort of outlaws the lawmen were concerned with now. Their ghostlike activity with such complete success was almost unheard of and would be of great interest if their methods could be discovered. To attempt to make headway with that discovery, the lawmen needed to travel the country as their quarry did. They did not obtain a pack horse with extra supplies but intended to move at a pace that would enable them to reach a different town or village each night. They obtained a map from the farrier and headed off in a more or less westerly direction to reach Orange. *Orange*. An odd name for a town, Stephens had thought and said so to Jones as they traveled.

"If I have my history right…" Jones started to say.

"Just assume your history is right," Stephens cut in, "your research seems to be pretty spot on so far."

"A British noble who lived that region had been an aide-de-camp to the Duke of Wellington during the Napoleonic War, along with the Prince of Orange, the Prince of the Netherlands. He named the territory Orange after the prince, and later the city grew in the middle of it. It wasn't too far from there that the first gold discovery was made that sparked the Australian gold rush."

"So the whole area has been built up around the mines, working in them and supplying them. More people have gotten rich in boom towns selling goods and services than the miners digging in the dirt. Take the gold out of the mix, and things start hurting," Stephens summed up.

"So it would seem. There are livestock stations in the area and businesses that will ensure the people remain, but gold has become vital."

"Has anyone stopped to wonder where all this gold is ending up if it isn't finding its way back into circulation? If they're piling it up into some sort of EL Dorado treasure, then how the heck are they figuring to get it out of here when they get their fill?"

Such questions filled their minds as they rode west. Their first stop was at the community of Penrith, which allowed them to stop and rest themselves and their horses as planned. As they sat and ate in a simple dining room, they kept their ears open to listen for any surrounding conversation of note. It was all similar to what had been heard before. Selector families were trying to do better for themselves as they had been trying for years, and while factories and industry offered some new opportunities, many felt little progress had been made. When one of them began to complain about the squattocracy always grinding them down loud enough for the whole room to hear, another man spoke up. Evidentially, he worked on a squatter sheep station and declared that the squatters had to work themselves up from nothing and the other man should do the same. Nothing was said about the enormous difference in situations between original squatters and later selectors, but the argument raged on.

The lawmen's ears perked still more when a third person in a calm voice mentioned Jeffery Conner and his efforts to help selectors. This man seemed to be trying to settle tempers but just flared others.

"What good is it to work for Conner or any miner when that work gets you dead by bushrangers?" one woman called out her response. "My Harry went to work for Conner for the better wages, and he only got paid twice before he was killed, trapped in the office where the gold was when they come to steal it."

Such talk and stories seemed to abound. The lawmen stayed as discreet as possible and didn't take part in any of the conversation if it could be avoided. This was to be their rule all along their journey. The next day they continued on the west road, which led them through a pass in the Blue Mountains toward a place called Katoomba. The Blue Mountains weren't altogether as tall as the Rockies, but they were mountains, beautiful with hints of snow near their peaks. The dense forest did not hide the monumental rock formations that adorned the land. Waterfalls and undercuts in cliff walls were a few of the sights the duo quickly took in as they rode on. Being in the southern hemisphere of the earth, it was actually Australia's cooler time of year, and the mountain air was brisk as they rode along.

They had started before dawn that morning, and it was well after dark when they arrived at their destination, and they welcomed the warmth of fires and lamps. They were not making their trip leisurely. They were pushing fairly hard to be able to make good time and ensure that they did stay in a town every night. Fortunately for Jones, he was not as inept at riding as he once was. He had little to no experience with riding horses when he had met Stephens five years ago, but subsequent adventures and experiences with the ranger had shown him the value of equitation. He had taken every opportunity to advance his horseback riding skills over the last few years, and now that practice was paying dividends.

The overall mood and attitude of people was little different in Katoomba as it applied to the bushrangers and public strife. Conner's name was heard mentioned again here and there, and one insensitive man said that as long as Conner had empty positions to fill, then who cares. Thankfully, others stopped the fight that almost erupted between that man and others that were friends and family of people killed in the mines, and the lawmen were able to stay inactive.

"Bushrangers or no, Conner has certainly established his good standing," Stephens commented as things settled back down.

The next day, they obtained fresh horses and were off again, winding their way toward the Orange area. Past the mountains, the landscape most closely resembled prairie land with some wood areas here and there. It was beautiful country that Stephens would've like to enjoy more if he had the time, but he didn't. Next, they headed for Lithgow and seriously doubted if they could make it before midnight. From Lithgow they made a shorter trip to Marrangaroo, from there they went to Yetholme, and from there to Bathurst. They steadily kept moving toward the Orange area, and the closer they got, the more the trees began to thin and become sparse. But there were still hills, not just hills, but hills of rock.

Now they were approaching the property of Jeffery Conner. While he was said to be from Orange, he was from the Orange area with his property being concentrated in an area called by some the Rock Forest, which was near Bathurst. Knowing this, the lawmen decided to take a day of rest in Bathurst and see if they could learn anything new. The day after they arrived, they were walking down the sidewalk observing the goings-on of the town as they had in Sydney, when they once again crossed paths with Jeffery Conner himself. He had arrived back at his home days earlier by train and had come into Bathurst that very morning to check on some new equipment he was expecting. It came as a surprise to him to see the two foreigners before him.

"Mr. Jones, isn't it?" Conner spoke less from trying to remember the name and more as if he were trying to deduce their presence, and his expression betrayed it.

"Indeed, it is Mr. Conner," Jones replied and waited for Conner to continue.

"I didn't expect to see you two again, certainly not here, not after the circumstances were explained."

"I'm not dissuaded so easily, Mr. Conner. I wanted to see the potential of a mine such as yours. If you're not interested in taking on an investor, there may be others who would, and I'd like to have as much knowledge as possible."

Conner's countenance lightened, and he stopped frowning.

"Of course, Mr. Jones. I doubt I'll have much time to spare for anything like a tour, but if you'll be patient, I'll send my foreman to find you and give you the information you want."

"Thank you," said Jones.

In the minute that it took for the short conversation to transpire, Conner's manner changed from deep annoyance to almost glee as Jones informed him of where they were staying. The rapid transformation baffled Jones and Stephens alike.

"Which is the bigger question," Jones asked as they continued to walk back toward their small inn, "why he was so sour at the start, or why he was so happy at the end?"

"The initial annoyance may just be because he's losing money and people, and we happened to get in his way. Or perhaps he didn't think he'd have to deal with us pesky businessmen anymore. If he had a fresh idea of how a wealthy investor could help him, that might explain why he got so happy."

"You would think in that case, he would make the time to speak with me." Jones's confusion was evident as they entered their room.

"Business is business, Jones. When it's round-up time on the ranch, nothing gets in the way of the job. It's probably much the same for him. He may want to talk to you after his man gives you more information to chew on. Besides, do you actually have a plan for talking to him like an investor for hours if he wanted to?"

"I hadn't quite planned that far ahead."

Just then a knock on the door heralded the foreman's arrival.

Chapter 12

When they opened the door, they perceived a tall, bearded man wearing fairly good clothes that were worn with use. He seemed unmoved at the sight of the two men he was sent to tutor.

"I'm Dobson," he announced, "foreman for Mr. Conner. Is one of you Mr. Jones?"

"Yes, my man. I am Mr. Jones, and this is Mr. Stephens."

"Fine then," Dobson said flatly. "Come with me, sir."

He turned and took off, assuming that the men would catch up with him, which they did after realizing there would be no formalities with this foreman. They followed him to the train yard where equipment was being transferred from the train to the ground, and from the ground onto wagons.

"Until now," the foreman began to speak, halting and pointing here and there as he went on, "we have been mining underground with picks, dynamite, and trolley cars. Mr. Conner suspects that the tunnels may be nearing the outside surface of the hills, so we're going to use this new equipment to attempt hydraulic mining. The boss figures he can save time and energy by washing away the outside of the hills instead of picking away at the inside."

"That sounds very innovative," Stephens commented. "But won't that require a good deal of water? If he diverts natural rivers and streams, he will affect a great many things besides his production schedule."

Dobson looked at him with a blank expression as he answered.

"In anticipation of this new process, Mr. Conner gave notice to all the surrounding area that he was going to dam up areas of flowing water to build up capacity. The water flow diminished somewhat until the new water level flowed over the dam. Then things returned to normal. Gates will be opened from the reservoirs and the water allowed to drain through pipes to the mine site. He will use the pent-up water until it falls to a certain level, then he will let it refill and continue mining underground in the meantime."

"Ingenious," Jones commented. "I would imagine that the water runoff would be collected at the bottom of the hill and allowed to flow along sluice boxes to filter out the gold."

"Yes, sir," Dobson replied, still with a blank expression and flat voice, but there was the slightest hint of annoyance as if he were irked that his pupils had skipped ahead in their lesson.

"But with sluices and water boxes running across the countryside, won't that make it all the easier for these bushrangers to attack the operation?" Stephens asked.

"If the bushrangers attack the sluices, then they'll have to filter the gold out themselves. They only strike when they know the gold is collected and they can steal it in a hurry. This just means that the gold will get closer to the station before it is collected. It's safer this way."

This was the answer the ranger had expected to hear; he had just wanted to hear how the foreman would say it.

"If having the sluices makes it easier to get the gold from A to B, and the new B is a lot safer than the old one, won't the sluices become a prime target for the bushrangers anyway? If they can disrupt them, then Conner will have to revert to the old methods until they are fixed, and that will provide new opportunity for your bandits."

Dobson now had a distinctive look of annoyance on his face, like a man beaten in a debate who was still unwilling to concede a point no matter how wrong he has been proved.

At last, he answered, "Mr. Conner will look after the sluice boxes. If he pays them enough, men will stick their necks out to protect what's his. And with the sluices running, he will have more men free to guard them."

That also was the answer the ranger had expected from a man who seemed to not care one way or the other about the success of his employer's new plans. Planning for the future was Conner's responsibility. Dobson would just continue to pass down orders until he stopped being paid to do so. If he didn't know the answer, he would either make one up or pass the buck to someone else. In this case he had done both at once. After they completed going through the train yard and discussing the finer points and purposes of individual pieces of equipment, they prepared to part company. Dobson passed on a message to the lawmen from Conner that if they would visit him at home the next day, he would endeavor to personally explain his future plans further. With that they made their way back to their room. For fear of not knowing who might hear them on the street, they postponed any conversation until they were behind a locked door.

"What do you think?" Jones asked after removing his jacket.

"I can't decide if that guy is just plain weak-minded or if he was trying to bore us into giving up and going away. He knew what he was saying because it had been explained to him, and who knows how many times it took, but he's not the type to make snap decisions when the boss ain't around. Either Conner's kind heart somehow snookered him into giving that guy a job, or maybe Dobson has some sort of drag on Conner's good graces."

"Perhaps his true purpose isn't to oversee miners but to do something else that Conner doesn't want known."

"Such as?" Stephens asked.

"There have been numerous cases where wealthy individuals wanted to shield themselves or others from harm who, having no confidence in the police, tried to work out trouble on their own. It wouldn't explain why he sent Dobson to us today, unless he were just handy, but what if Dobson is supposed to act as some sort of go-between for Conner? By all accounts, he had been trying to keep the peace between the selectors and squatters over the trouble the bushrangers have been causing. What if to that end, Conner intends to broker some sort of deal with the gang, a percentage of the take in exchange for no more violence?"

"That ain't a crazy idea. Instead of being robbed, he simply pays protection money. The problem with that game is, there's too much room for treachery. At any point they could start raising their price, or the go-between could get greedy and cause more people to be killed. And if Conner starts paying for protection, then it would open the door for other mines to follow suit or face worse consequences than they've suffered so far. For a momentary stretch of relative safety, they could be setting themselves up for greater danger down the line."

"I see your point," Jones said. "I wonder if you could make Conner realize it."

"Maybe, we'll see when we get out there tomorrow."

They slept soundly but with their weapons within reach. The night passed uneventfully, and early the next morning they made ready to ride to Conner's station. They mounted fresh horses and began traveling deeper into the hills. After a couple of hours, they entered into Conner's territory, and soon after as they peeked a hill, they stopped and looked. Through a small pair of brass binoculars that Jones provided, they observed the goings-on at a mine entrance they could barely make out in the distance. A trolley car had just been brought out and dumped, and men were shoveling and sifting the material. The hill was asymmetrically shaped, and the lawmen made their way around to view the steep side. Here they could see the preparations for Conner's hydraulic operation. Pipe was being laid on the opposite hillside and came to a stop about a third of the way from the bottom, the idea being that was close enough to be able to spray water high enough onto the hillside. Having already come this far around to indulge their curiosity, they continued on the long way to Conner's to see what else they might. Mr. Conner would forgive them for being a little late, but they didn't intend to be very late.

As they wandered further through the hills, trusting that they were heading in more or less the right direction, Stephens was surveying the country with less of an admiring gaze and more of professional inspection.

"Do you see something?" Jones inquired.

"Not yet. But I'm hopeful."

"Hopeful of what?"

"Something that isn't supposed to be there."

"Should I keep asking questions or wait for you to rest your eyes?"

"I've heard stories from States farther West that have more canyons and rocks, where caves, cutouts, and even small canyons were discovered by pure happenstance because they were carved out and formed in such a way that only the birds knew about them by flying over them. Who's to say that in country like this, there may not be the same sort of thing? It ain't made up of mesas and deep canyons, but there's enough rock and overlapping hills that something might be invisible to casual eyes."

"I should've known," Jones replied with a grin. It was for such input and ideas that Jones had known Stephens should come on this trip.

As they approached a wooded area going up the hill, they continued their hypothesizing.

"What do you think the odds are of finding such a secret escape? After all these years, someone would have found it."

"I'm sure they would've, maybe several people over the years, over the centuries. That doesn't mean they advertised it. All the gold in California might've belonged to just a few people if they had kept their mouths shut. Some people are smart enough to realize that. Besides, if—"

He was interrupted by the sound of a loud snap, a yelp of pain, and then a thud. He jerked around in his saddle as he reached for his pistol. He saw Jones lying on the ground with a long whip wrapped around his arms and body. He was about to spin his horse around to attack the masked man at the other end of the whip when a loud whistle made him look forward again. His eyes barely had time to come into focus when a sizeable tree limb that had been bent around away from him was released. The limb smacked into his chest and catapulted him out of the saddle and onto the ground. He knew no more of what had happened to himself or Jones until he awoke sometime later.

Chapter 13

Stephens's mind was full of images blurring in and out as they cycled through his mind. He saw memories of past events from years ago, and gradually, newer and newer images replaced the older ones. The first time he had grappled with a Comanche, scared to death and wild with the will to survive. The first time his party of rangers had hung a gang of rustlers who had killed innocent ranchers. Countless recurring instances of him tracking outlaws and villains and fighting for and protecting the people of his state. He saw Rico swinging an ax at him in England after he had stormed the Mallory mansion. Then he saw Katelyn fall off a horse into the river as he lay in wait to ambush her kidnappers. Now he had Katelyn in his arms, smiling at him as they danced at their wedding reception. She had said she was proud to call herself Mrs. Wayne Stephens…Stephens…Stephens…

"Stephens…Stephens."

Stephens slowly emerged from his lifetime dream to the sound of a low voice saying his name. He realized that he was lying down and tried to convince his arms to work toward raising himself up as he did the same with his eyelids.

"Stephens, are you awake?" Jones asked him when he saw a hint of movement.

"I think so, more or less," he answered as he gradually brought himself up to a sitting position. As he did, he felt pain in his chest, and he rubbed it as he talked, "Either I'm awake or Katelyn developed a lower voice in my dreams."

He blinked as if he were still trying to get his eyes to open, but they were open with nothing to see. It was dark where they were except for a faint light reflecting from down what appeared to be a tunnel. Evidently, they were at the lower end of it.

"Where the heck are we, and how did we get here?"

"We seem to be in some sort of mine shaft, at least that would be my guess. When your eyes adjust, you'll be able to see that the tunnel is too square to be natural. When you were knocked off your horse, you hit your head and were knocked unconscious. I was still trying to get out of that confounded whip when someone knocked me out too. Next thing I knew, I was waking up here, and you were still out cold. I thought I heard someone farther up the tunnel laugh a little while ago, but otherwise, nothing has happened. I started trying to wake you up so we could figure how to get out of here, but you are as stubborn asleep as you are awake."

This last statement caused a small grin to form on the ranger's face as he leaned back against the tunnel wall, but it was short-lived as Jones's story reactivated Stephens's own memories, and his blood pressure began to gradually rise.

"I don't remember the last time I was knocked out like that. Maybe my head is getting a little soft." He winced as he touched the sore spot on the back of his head, and Jones gave him a look of disbelief.

"I find that highly doubtful. As hard as you hit the ground, there's probably a permanent crater in it."

"Either way, it's my own stupid fault. That was a sucker punch move."

"What do you mean?"

"I saw you on the ground, I saw the man who snagged you with his face covered, and I knew things were going bad, and what did I do? Someone whistled at me in the middle of it all, and I actually turned to look. My first instinct should've been to jump to the ground, but I didn't. Nobody is going to whistle at you in a fight with good intentions."

Jones shrugged. "You're just out of practice. When was the last time you were whistled at?" Jones said with a grin.

"It's been a while, my legs ain't what they used to be."

They both snickered.

"Not that I would rather you be a mess of panic, but you don't seem overly worried about our situation."

"Well, one of the many things I've learned from being around you is that circumstances are rarely as hopeless and grim as they may first appear. I am concerned, and I would be greatly worried if you weren't here, but since we are here together, I've resolved to not panic until we are actually looking death in the face."

"Your confidence in me is touching. I don't suppose you've bothered to scout up the tunnel to see what we're up against?"

"I'm afraid I can't, and neither can you."

"What do you mean?"

In response, Jones kicked his heel on the ground, and a metallic jingling sound was heard. As Stephens peered closer in the darkness, he saw that both he and Jones had the ends of a chain secured around one of their ankles with a lock. Further inspection revealed that the middle portion of the chain had been wrapped around a massive wooded beam set against the tunnel wall helping hold up the section of tunnel they occupied.

"I'm surprised you didn't notice it already."

Before Stephens could answer him, their attention was drawn to the sound of footsteps approaching them. They gathered the strength to stand up and steady themselves to meet their captors. A light was also approaching and growing brighter as the footsteps grew louder. At last, a lantern appeared around the corner held aloft by one of three men. The lawmen blinked and squinted as their eyes struggled to adjust to the sudden increase of light glaring at them. After a moment, the man holding the lantern lowered it from directly in front of his eyes, and Stephens lunged at him, nearly being yanked off his feet by the chain around his ankle. The man was just a few feet beyond the ranger's reach, which proved that the stone-faced Dobson was not quite as brainless as he had appeared since he was careful to stay beyond the reach of his prisoners.

"You dirty, stinking…" Stephens's insults trailed off as he couldn't quite decide on the right combination of adjectives to describe this man who had betrayed the trust of his employer and consequently betrayed them.

"Save your breath, Yank, you won't be taking it in much longer."

Stephens lunged at him again and this time was yanked off his feet by the chain.

"Stay down there, or I'll grind you down into the dirt."

Stephens did as he was told and glared up at Dobson.

"Are you glad to find what you were looking for, Inspector Jones?"

Jones and Stephens both betrayed looks of apprehension at the revelation that at least Jones's identity was known.

"How do you know me?" Jones asked.

"Your reputation has preceded you. We've attracted a lot of attention over the last few years. It was just a matter of time before the mighty and pompous Great Britain sent someone to find us. What an obvious choice they made in sending you, Inspector Caleb Jones, renown for breaking up a great opium smuggling gang with the help of an American officer and several more cases since then. News travels far and fast in the British Empire. Next time you want to go unnoticed, at least go by a different name. That's assuming you were going to live long enough to have a next time."

Even though Dobson seemed more eloquent than he had been yesterday, it still seemed that not all his words were his own. Stephens and Jones shared this thought and tried to take advantage of it.

"You poke fun at us," Stephens popped off to Dobson from his position on the floor with a contemptuous tone, "but for all your sneakiness, you've got to be some of the dumbest bandits I've ever heard of. What outlaw worth the name would steal as much gold as you have and not spend at least a little bit of it? If you were to get caught or killed tomorrow, you would die without having enjoyed any of your spoils."

"How do you know we don't enjoy it?" Dobson's voice rang out defiantly, and a little dust fell from the ceiling at the vibration. "We all get a little cut to go spend on women, liquor, horses, or whatever. And there's always plenty more to be had."

"If you get cuts and don't give them, then you ain't the boss," Stephens remarked. "That ain't no surprise."

Rather than get angry, Dobson shrugged. "So what if I'm not the boss? I'm next to the boss, and after he has his way, I'll be the second boss over the whole country."

Now it was Jones's turn to chime in, going off what Dobson had just said and the feeling of public displeasure.

"Do you really think that hoarding a mountain of gold will enable you to break away from England? You're just a handful of highway robbers. Even if you were any kind of respectable gentry, you couldn't buy this country with all the gold that it holds. And the few of you certainly can't fight for it. You would've done better to spend the gold and enjoy life as much as you can before you hang."

"It's no concern of yours whether I hang or not. If I do, you won't be there to see it. When the time comes, it'll be the police and constables that swing for a change if they won't fight with us."

One of the other men tugged at Dobson's sleeve, indicating that he was either saying too much, or they needed to leave, or both. He gave them another sneering grin and went back up the tunnel with the other two following him. Stephens sat back against the wall, and Jones sank down beside him.

"Well, part of me is surprised that Dobson is in on this, and part of me isn't," Jones commented as he settled back into a thoughtful slump. "Do you think Conner suspects anything?"

"Who knows. If he did, I don't see how he could still be foreman, unless Conner wanted to keep a closer eye on him. Or the big dummy routine may have him fooled altogether."

Stephens talked as he watched the lights fade as it moved farther up the tunnel.

"I guess anything may be possible," Jones continued. "I'm not complaining, but I would be very interested to know why they left us alive."

"I don't know," Stephens said, and a grin grew on his face, "but it ain't their first mistake."

"What do you mean?"

"You're wearing shoes, right?"

"Ankle boots, but yes, they're like shoes. Why?"

"So this chain is touching your leg?"

"Yes, with my pant leg in between. Why do you ask?"

"Whoever chained us up didn't think very hard about what he was doing. They wrapped my chain around my boot leg and not very tight. When I jumped at Dobson, I felt a little give. That's why I jumped at him again. The force got my foot through the chain. That's why I stayed on the ground."

"You mean…" Jones cut off his question as he saw the ranger pull his foot out of the chained boot. He slipped his boot out of the chain, put it back on his foot, and stood up.

"Now then, let's see about you."

Chapter 14

In the darkness of the tunnel, which was ever so slightly illuminated by the light of a lantern somewhere around the corner, the lawmen contemplated what to do. There had been just enough of a gap between the stone wall and the wooden beam to get the chain through originally. Now that there was a lock attached to it, getting the chain back through and unwrapped from the beam was going to be difficult. Jones and Stephens relied more on what they could feel with their fingers than what they could see. The chain had been pulled through twice and was lying on top of itself. They separated the top loop and pulled through the four or five feet of chain until the lock caught in the gap. They stopped and listened. The faint sound of voices they could hear gave no indication that they had drawn any attention. Stephens looked at his partner.

"Twist the chain up some," Stephens whispered, "and pull it tight so it won't make so much noise. I'll do the same on my end and keep tension on it. When I say, try to yank the lock trough the gap."

Jones nodded and slowly twisted up the section of chain between his grip and the beam. Stephens gripped the loop in the chain tight and nodded to Jones. Jones jerked the chain as hard as he could, but the lock still caught in the gap. They froze and listened and more dust and small rocks fell from the ceiling, but still no sound of alarm from up the tunnel. Stephens nodded to Jones again, and again he jerked the chain for all he was worth, but with the same result. After another pause, they tried again without success. This time a flat piece of rock that had been pinned by the upper part of the beam fell and clattered on the stone floor. A break in the rhythm of the voices told them that someone had took notice, and a moment later, the faint sound of footsteps reached them.

"Let the chain back through!" Stephens said with urgency, and they pulled the chain back around the beam until it was like it had been.

Stephens sat with the foot that should be chained hidden from view and the chain itself lying on the floor leading up to him. No sooner had they gotten into position than a man with a lantern came around the corner to check on them. He came just close enough to be able to see the prisoners, who hung their heads and squinted at the light. Stephens, unable to resist an act of defiance, turned a squinting glare at their captor. The glare became more pronounced and the anger behind it genuine as he realized that this man was wearing the ranger's hat and gun belt. After a few seconds of inspection, the man turned and disappeared back up the tunnel, and Stephens looked to Jones.

"We can't get you free without making too much noise, and even then, we'd have to drag or carry the chain with us. So you just sit tight, and I'll be right back."

With that Stephens got to his feet and slowly began moving up the tunnel as quietly as he could manage. Jones had no better idea to suggest and sat and watched the ranger slip around the corner of the tunnel. From then on, he strained his hearing to detect what was going on. Stephens took great care not to make noise as he slowly walked toward the sound of voices. He set the heel of his boot down gently on the stone floor as he took a step, and then rolled his foot down instead of letting it fall flat, and this was how he crept up the tunnel. After he rounded the first corner, he could see a lantern hanging from the wall about twenty-five or thirty yards ahead of him at another bend in the tunnel path. Their captors must be just around the bend with how much louder their voices were. Stephens crossed to the inside wall and flattened himself against it to peer around the corner at what was next.

The next portion of the tunnel wasn't a tunnel, but rather a small cavern formed naturally in the rock of the hillside. The cavern was about the size of an average hotel sitting room, just large enough for a handful of people to be comfortable with some chairs, a table, a couple of chests, and a small fireplace that was probably only used for small cooking fires; to have it lit any more than that would increase the risk of someone detecting the smoke. At the far end of the cavern, an opening, what must be the doorway, let in a little bit of daylight. The opening must be mostly shaded on the outside, which would help keep it hidden. Stephens remembered what he and Jones had been discussing before they were ambushed, and he was both proud and annoyed at the same time that he should've guessed so close to the truth about the thieves' hideout.

There were three thieves sitting around the table, none sitting on the side facing straight toward him, holding cards in their hands and grumbling to themselves. The man who had donned his hat and gun belt was sitting with his back to him. On the table next to one of the other thieves was his shoulder holster with his short pistol and Jones's double-action Colt. On the wall behind the third thief was Stephens's rifle. These bushrangers had divided up their weapons and might have even been gambling for them. He was right, for as he looked on with one eye peeping around the corner, the group laid down their hands, and the bushranger with the gun belt laughed.

"Ha-ha! I win again. Hand over that short pistol, Flynn."

Flynn grumbled louder and slid Stephens's short pistol across the table.

"That's two for you, Fletch, but I'm keeping this one here, I done playing."

Fletch laughed again, and the third shrugged off his monetary loss.

"You rogues can have the pistols," said the third bushranger as he reached around and patted the rifle behind him with a smile. "A six-shot pistol is a six-shot pistol. But this repeating rifle will make those old red coat martinis look like muskets."

"That's a proper rifle all right, but these are proper pistols too. Not bloody conversions like we've had up 'til now." He pulled out the peacemaker and gazed at it admiringly, almost worshipfully, while the others did likewise with their own prizes.

They were as distracted as they were likely to be, and so Stephens inched his way around the corner. His hand grasped something wooden, and he clinched his fist tightly to keep it from falling. It was the handle of a shovel. Of course—what was a mine without a shovel? He stepped away from the wall to give himself swinging room, which also alerted the thieves to his presence, but he had the drop on them. He swung the shovel up in an arch from its resting place and back down again on Fletch's head with a thud. Then he reversed his pull and hit Flynn square in the face. That was two out of three down, but now the third was on his feet. Stephens stepped back from two mighty swings from the bushranger, and when he reared back to swing again, Stephens swung the handle of the shovel into his stomach. With the air knocked out of him and he bent over double, Stephens brought the shovel down with another thud on the back of his head.

Stephens dropped the shovel, grinning and dusting off his hands in triumph when the doorway became filled with the figure of a fourth man. A lookout presumably, aroused by the sound of battle, had come to investigate with his gun drawn. Stephens grabbed one of the guns off the table and fell to the floor in a roll as a shot from the bushranger rang out and sent fragments of rock flying from the wall. Stephens came up from his roll to a sitting position and fired at his assailant. The man stumbled backward, and Stephens fired again, and the man fell with his boots just visible at the foot of the door. Stephens's ears were ringing with the sounds of the shots fired inside the cavern, or else he would've heard Jones yell his name. Jones hoped that the shots meant that Stephens had succeeded rather than failed; he always did, but some assurance would've been welcome. He was continuing his attempts to force the lock around the beam when Stephens reappeared a few minutes later.

After getting his gun belt and hat back, Stephens had rummaged through the thieves' pockets until he found some keys. One of the keys opened the lock on the chain around Jones's leg, and they proceeded back up to the cavern. Stephens explained what had happened as they regained the rest of their gear, and Stephens used the other keys to open the chests. They were disappointed to find that they held nothing but some extra guns, ammunition, and tools.

"What do you think?" Stephens asked.

"Well, Dobson believes we're no threat to him now, and it would seem that these four are the only ones here. We've only been concerned with escaping, now that we have, maybe we should search the rest of the mine."

"That might be a good idea, but let's make sure we don't get trapped here again."

While Jones began to nose around other corners, Stephens cautiously pulled the body inside and ventured out of the doorway. In keeping with his theory, the doorway was concealed within an alcove of rocks planted in the hillside. In a cluster of trees just below the rocks, a lean-to had been constructed among the branches. In the lean-to there appeared to be half a dozen horses. He was about to go back inside to help Jones when a slight movement caught his attention, and after a pause, he ducked inside.

"Jones, it's time to go, company is coming!"

Jones came running back up from the tunnel with a lantern, which he put down on the table before following Stephens back out the door.

"There are some men riding this way about a quarter of a mile out, and I don't think we should wait around to meet them."

They grabbed their own horses and freed the others as they galloped off. A quarter of a mile was not a long way on horseback, and they did not escape the notice of the horsemen coming at them. The lawmen urged their horses to exert all their speed as they headed in the direction that would take them to the main road. Stephens's years of ranging had taught him to read terrain, but he had never been where he was before, and the bushrangers' familiarity with the country worked in their favor. The lawmen turned up a path that took them out of sight of their pursuers, and they reasoned that now they could lose them, but as they emerged again onto more open ground, they found that the bushrangers were coming up on them not even two hundred yards away.

When you can't outrun who's after you, head for high ground. Stephens knew this, and he began steering a course up into the hills. They were nearing Conner's mining operation again, and Stephens and Jones headed up into the rockier areas. They went up a narrow path that led onto a ledge behind some boulders, which seemed like a good place to make a stand. They dismounted, shoved their horses back as far out of sight as possible, and knelt to peer between the rocks, Stephens with his rifle and Jones with his pistol. There were five men steering their horses to climb the path the lawmen had taken. The first man was nudging his horse forward when Stephens squeezed the trigger and a .45-caliber bullet flew into his chest. As he hit the ground and his horse ran from the sound of the shot, the other bushrangers wheeled their horse around to find cover. Though Stephens had more ammunition in his saddlebags, it would not last forever, and he was reasonably sure that he couldn't find 45-70 ammunition on this continent. So he was going to be careful with his shots and take none he didn't need to.

There were four men still below to block their escape. There was no guarantee that this trail going up would come back down elsewhere, and if they tried to climb higher now, they would be easy targets. If the three unconscious men in the cavern came to and managed to catch up with these, then their odds would get dimmer. This left two choices: sit quietly and wait for their enemies to try to come up or find a way to take the fight to them on their own terms, and neither Wayne Stephens or Caleb Jones was the type of ranger to sit and wait for a fight.

Chapter 15

The sun was beginning to sink lower and lower toward the horizon, and its rays were hitting lawman and outlaw alike at an ever-flattening angle from the side. The lawmen could barely do more than sit up straight in their current position of cover without presenting enough of a target for their enemies to offer shots at. Every minute or two, when one of them shuffled around, a handful of bullets would come smashing into the rocks around them, throwing up little bits or rock and dust. Time was running short, and darkness would work in their adversaries' favor. When there was no more light, the bushrangers could slowly feel their way up the path in reasonable safety since the lawmen would not be able to see what or where to shoot. Then the bushrangers could either come up on them in the dark and trust in their numbers to overpower them or wait for what little moonlight there would be when it rose and hope to shoot the lawmen without cover before they shot first. These were the eventualities that Stephens and Jones discussed in their hunkered position. It was in their best interest to make a move before the enemy below gained more of an advantage.

"We don't want them to get too comfortable down there," Stephens said as he looked around them. "We need to make them stay concerned about losing their own heads besides trying to shoot off ours." He set his rifle aside and gripped both of his pistols. "When I say, reach over the top and let loose a few shots."

Jones nodded and poised himself to act.

"Now!"

Jones reached over the rocks with his double-action pistol and pulled the trigger three times while Stephens sat up straight on his heels and shot both his pistols twice. None of their shots did any more damage to their enemy than they had received, but most of their shots hit close enough to cause the bushrangers to duck down and swear. Stephens grinned at his partner, and his expression said that a part of him enjoyed causing trouble for the men who were troubling them.

After a few moments passed in silence, Stephens nodded to Jones. "Again!"

And again, they stuck their guns over the rocks that protected them and sent out another volley. These shots had interrupted the bushrangers just as they were about to return fire, and the surprise of it made them swear worse as they squinted their eyes in the rocky debris.

Jones's pistol was now empty, and he sat back down flat on the ground to reload from Stephens's belt. The handful of spare cartridges he had kept in his coat pocket had escaped onto the ground when he had been pulled off his horse and captured. Stephens still grinned as he continued to crouch in readiness.

"Have you always felt excitement in near-death situations?" Jones asked him as he put fresh cartridges into his weapon with relatively steady hands. As he finished speaking, outlaw bullets smashed into the rocks, and Stephens answered the shot before he answered the question.

"This ain't as bad as it might be. When a renegade Comanche sneaks up on you and tries to give you a haircut down to the bone, then it's no laughing matter. But right now, I'm just getting a kick out of letting these skunks know that they're going to have to work hard to get us. They're realizing that they're not the only ones that know how to fight."

Another bullet hit the rocks, and again Stephens answered with his own.

"Besides, to answer your question more directly, I've been a ranger for twenty years, and a man has to find some satisfaction in his work."

Another bullet hit, and this time Stephens answered with two, emptying his own guns.

"So you're saying that you're enjoying getting shot at and are not just a little worried that we might get killed?" Jones asked, not out of frightened disbelief, but out of curiosity at what his friend would say in reply.

"I'm concerned, you might say a little scared, but I'm not going to panic, just like you didn't panic in the tunnel. You know as well as I know that the worst thing to do is to curl up and give up, so why did you ask me that?"

"Oh, just idle curiosity, and I didn't want you to get bored waiting to make whatever move you're concocting."

"And just what am I concocting, Professor Jones?" Stephens grinned at the thought that if anyone heard them going back and forth like this in such a situation, they would probably be considered insane.

"Knowing you," Jones began as he turned to peep through the rocks as he spoke, "you're probably going to wait until the light is a little dimmer and then have me pop up like a fool and shoot at them by myself while you try to slide down the hill with your rifle. If we're both lucky, the flashes may affect their vision enough so that you can get close, or at least in a good position, and bring them down easy when they start to shoot back."

Stephens grin grew wider still as he put the last round in his second pistol and closed the loading gate. "I was actually going to give them a few parting shots myself, but since you're volunteering…"

Jones reached out with his left hand and took the larger pistol from Stephens's hand.

"Don't forget which one of those is which, and when you spot your target, close your eyes so the flash doesn't mess up your eyesight."

Jones smiled as he replied, "I'll do my best, and you do your best not to get killed. If you do, it won't matter if I survive because Katelyn will kill me herself." He looked at his friend. "Good luck."

Stephens picked up his rifle and nodded, and once again they popped up and showered bullets at their enemy, Jones banging away with two pistols while Stephens's rifle boomed twice before he took off farther up the path about twenty yards away and then jumped over the edge. It was not a sheer drop but just steep enough that no one but a mountain goat could walk up it. Stephens slid down the hillside, holding his rifle above his head and pumping his feet to slow himself down as he approached the ground. Every few seconds, he could hear the bang of a gun, which drowned out the sound of him and rocks falling to the ground. He came to a stop and crouched for a few seconds to make sure he was undetected before he began creeping hunched over toward the bushrangers' position. He had slid down the hill at an angle away from them, and the curve of the hill had landed him more than fifty yards way. That was short range for his rifle, but he had to obtain a line of sight first. The last glow of the sun was coloring the sky, and he had to act fast before any gun became useless beyond point-blank range.

He crept closer and closer as the gunshots echoed around him, and he still looked for a good position to shoot from that wouldn't leave him completely exposed to return fire. The ranger looked off to his right and noticed a tree just where the opposite slope began to rise away from them. That was about as good as it was going to get, and it would put him a little above the outlaws. At the next gunshot, he sped toward the tree and fell down behind it. Still no indication that he had been detected. He stood up, raise his rifle, and pressed the side of the barrel against the tree to steady it, keeping most of his body covered. All the outlaws were crouched behind one long sloping rock, and all but the farthest one was in easy view. A shot from Jones hit the rock, and a moment later, the outlaws popped up to fire back. The ranger's rifle boomed, and the man on the end fell over the rock. The man next to him had just noticed the body to his side when the rifle boomed again, and the second outlaw lay beside his cohort. The third outlaw turned around to face the new danger when he was hit and fell backward against the rock and to the ground.

The fourth jumped back out of sight as the third man fell, but as he did, he grabbed the dead man's pistol and now fired both guns at the tree. Stephens ducked behind the wooden mass as multiple bullets sent splinters flying around him. He was pinned behind the tree, and the remaining bushranger now had several guns, but they had both momentarily forgotten Jones. He had come running back down the path, and as the outlaw fired a bullet that sent a splinter into Stephens's arm, Jones stopped and fired both his pistols into the last adversary. The man's body jerked and went slightly up with the power of the two bullets hitting him before he fell to the ground. Stephens plucked the thin piece of wood from his arm and went down to meet his partner.

"Not a moment too soon," Stephens said as he came up to him.

"Or you either," Jones replied, "those were the last two bullets I had."

They squinted in the growing darkness at the bodies around them. None of them were Dobson, so evidently, he had returned to Conner's station and sent these to take care of business.

"What do you think?" Stephens asked Jones. "We're closer to Conner's place than town, but who knows how many of his men are in with Dobson. If we go back to town, we'll either have to camp somewhere or arrive in the early morning. Either way we run the risk of being found by more bushrangers."

"Conner's station offers the greatest guarantee of safety. Some of his men may be turncoats, but most will be good men, and Conner himself will be a powerful ally. Besides, Dobson may not even be there."

"Very well, let's go."

They retrieved their horses from up the path, gathered up the guns of their enemies, and used what light the half-moon offered to make their way back through the rolling country until they finally found the main road they had deviated from earlier.

It was almost ten o'clock when the approached the buildings of Conner's stationed outlined by a score of lamps, lanterns, and glowing windows. About a hundred feet from the gate in the fence that ran around the compound, a voice yelled a challenge.

"Who goes there? Answer me, or I'll shoot."

"Mr. Jones and Mr. Stephens," Jones yelled back, both of them gripping their guns in case they were unwelcome. "Mr. Conner has been expecting us."

A moment later, the sentry yelled back, "Come on up, but come slow and easy."

They nudged their horses forward and could just make out a second figure running toward the big house in the middle of the compound. As the sentry shut the gate behind them, they stopped to let him catch up. If he was surprised at their presence, he didn't show it.

"You're late," he said in an Irish accent similar to most of the people they had encountered in this country. "Mr. Conner thought you would've been here hours ago. He's been thinking that you decided to not come at all."

"We would've been here sooner," Jones replied, "but we were detained with other matters."

"Well then," said the sentry, looking up at him, "let's get you up to the house, and I'll see that your horses are looked after."

They walked their horses up to the house with the sentry walking along beside them. At the foot of the front steps, they dismounted and gave their reins to the sentry, who paused as he turned to lead them away at the sight of Stephens taking his rifle out of the scabbard.

"It's an old habit," the ranger said grinning. "I never go anywhere without it."

The sentry turned without another word and marched off toward the stables as the lawmen walked up to the front door.

Chapter 16

A knock on the door was instantly answered by what appeared to be an Aboriginal servant. He held a hand out to his side as he held the door in a gesture for them to enter in.

Once the door was closed behind them, the servant said with a very deep accent, "Follow me please."

They followed him down a hallway, which would've led to the dining room, but Mr. Conner appeared at the other end and came toward them, cutting off their advance.

"Welcome, gentlemen, I'm glad to see you here safe at last. I had given up hope of your arrival."

"We would have arrived some hours ago, Mr. Conner, but we got a bit…sidetracked," Jones replied with a tone that hinted that there was more meaning to this casual excuse.

"I see," Conner replied with a thoughtful expression. "One moment and you can tell me all about it. If you would step into my study, just here." Conner now held out a hand, indicating a door immediately next to them, and turned to his servant as they entered. "That will be all for tonight, give your wife my compliments for the dinner."

The servant grinned and bowed before walking off to the back of the house. Conner stepped inside the study and shut the door.

"His wife is my cook, and he is as near to a butler as he can manage," Conner said, now speaking to his guests again.

"You truly seem to live up to your reputation as a man willing to help anyone," Jones commented with a tone of approval.

"As you have probably heard, I was born into the selector class of people in this country. I grew up seeing people ground down into the dirt who only wanted half a chance to live a decent life worth living. And the Aboriginals were no exception, they had it worse than we did in the white man's world, which I didn't think was possible when I was growing up." He crossed to a bookshelf which housed a decanter on one of its shelves along with a few glasses and poured himself a small measure of the brown liquor. "Would you like a drink, gentlemen?"

Both lawmen mumbled a polite refusal, and Conner sat down with his glass behind his desk.

"Now then, tell me of your little misadventure."

"We actually set out at first light this morning," Jones began. "We decided to take our time and go at a leisurely pace to enjoy the countryside and make sure we didn't take any wrong turns. We eventually came to your mining operation and saw where you're preparing for hydraulic mining. If we had pushed straight on from there, we would have probably arrived here in short order without incident. However, we decided to deviate to the west and explore the far side of the hill in order to get a better orientation of your property. We hadn't gone far when we were ambushed."

"Ambushed!" Conner exclaimed.

"Ambushed," Stephens echoed in affirmation, still gripping his rifle across his lap.

"Yes, Mr. Conner. My friend was knocked to the ground by a bent-around tree limb after I was jerked off my horse with a whip. Stephens was knocked unconscious when he hit, and I was knocked out by one of the masked men that attacked us. The next thing we knew, we woke up what must've been a couple of hours later and were chained to a reinforcement beam in a hidden mine shaft. With a little luck, we were able to escape and reclaim our horses just outside the cave but had to escape again from some more outlaws that were approaching the cave and were just close enough to see us. They chased us for some time until we took cover up on the stony side of your mine. We had to fight our way back down again and overcome the gang. That being done, we were able to finally make it here."

"My stars!" said Conner as he sat back in his desk chair and took another swallow from his glass. Then after a moment, he looked back at his guests. "At first you said a mine shaft, but then you used the word *cave*. What do you mean?"

"It appeared that a mine was dug out of the back wall of a small natural cavern," Stephens replied. "The entrance is well concealed in a cluster of rocks and trees. It's the sort of thing you wouldn't know was there if you didn't find it for yourself."

"And this mine is on my property?"

"As near as we can determine," Stephens replied again. "We don't know how deep it is or if it yields anything, we were more concerned with getting out, not farther in."

"Of course, of course. I never suspected that such a thing existed on my property, much less that vandals were using it as a hideout."

"I'm afraid that's not the worst of it, Mr. Conner," Jones continued.

Conner shifted his gaze to Jones again and appeared to be in a mix of dread and anticipation.

"This appears to be at least a part of the bushranger gang that has been stealing your gold, and your man Dobson is one of them."

"What's that you say, Mr. Jones?"

"When we were in the mine, he talked to us. Since he assumed that we would never leave there alive, he must not have been too concerned with anonymity. However, when we overcame the force that chased us, he wasn't among them."

Conner stood up and began looking around the room and then paced behind his desk. His face showed a mix of anger and confusion. Jones and Stephens watched him go back and forth, and Stephens threw periodic glances at the study door, his hand ever on his rifle and ready for action in case any of Dobson's confederates at the station tried something ill-advised. At last, Conner put his hands on the back of his desk chair and leaned on it as he spoke to his guests.

"I am not altogether a fool, gentlemen. I've known what you must have gathered from Dobson's appearances, that he is not overly bright or resourceful. Not what one would look for in a station manager. How much of that is actually true of him based on what you've just told me, who can say. He's either the greatest actor on the continent, or he has just enough cunning to be a two-faced agent."

"Based on our encounter with him in the cave, I'd have to go with the second option," Stephens said, still glancing at the door. "But what's this two-faced agent business? You don't believe he's operating on his own?"

"No, I do not," Conner replied. "Not after a moment's consideration. As you might well expect, when I bought this property and established myself as a prominent landowner and miner, many of the old squatters didn't approve. Some harsh words were spoken, and even a few punches thrown, but I didn't give in. Like it or not, they finally seemed to accept the fact that they couldn't get rid of me, and we left each other alone. One of the orneriest of the old squatters is a man named Otis Cavanaugh. He was the one who recommended Dobson to me. He wanted to put aside our differences, a gesture of good faith, he said, and he said Dobson had learned much from his manager and would be a good one for me. Now I can only assume that he did it to sabotage my endeavors. All this time Dobson has been in the perfect position to organize attacks on my property and people and work toward my failure for the benefit of the squatters. Why can't they just let us be?" Conner's hands began to shake with anger as he began pacing again.

"What you say sounds plausible," Jones began, "but can you be absolutely sure of that? There is the possibility that Mr. Cavanaugh was as ignorant as you to Dobson's true character."

"I suppose there is always a chance, Mr. Jones, but I'm a gambler, and my gut tells me that Cavanaugh is behind this mischief. I would bet on it."

"Is that how you got this place," Stephens asked, "by gambling? It's no secret that you came from the selector class of people. If the squatters oppressed you as much as you say, how were you able to afford an estate like this?"

"You're right, Mr. Stephens. Years ago, I ran with rough people trying to survive. They drank hard, fought hard, and played hard. One night we were playing cards, and I drew the hand of a lifetime. I bet everything I had to my name. Since I hadn't won all night, my friends thought I must be bluffing and called me. I won practically everything they owned except the clothes they stood in. While I didn't leave them destitute or stranded, I didn't give up my winnings, and they weren't really my friends after that. I got as far away from them as I could and hocked their various belongings for money, more than I had ever had before. If Lady Luck had decided to smile on me, I wasn't going to squander it. I got some new clothes and began playing in pubs and clubs in the cities. I swear I never cheated a single hand. I waited for the best hand to come to me and struck. I got better and richer, and when this place came up for sale, I walked in and paid for it with bags of gold that couldn't be turned away because of my background. And now here I am."

The two lawmen just continued to stare as the story completed.

"That's quite a tale," Stephens commented and looked at his partner.

Jones nodded to him, and they stood up. "I wonder if Cavanaugh will be able to tell one as good when we talk to him."

Conner stared at him, then at Jones, and then back to the ranger.

"Why should you go talk to him? This is a matter for the constables, if they will actually stand up to him."

Now Jones answered him, "We will stand up to him, Mr. Conner, because I am not a businessman. I am Inspector Caleb Jones of Scotland Yard, and I was sent here with the specific purpose of putting down these bushrangers."

Conner said nothing but stared at Jones while he digested what had been said, then turned his gaze to Stephens.

"We don't have bushrangers in England, Mr. Conner, nor the frontier of Australia. My friend here is more familiar with such things than I am."

"But surely you are not a Scotland Yard Inspector?" Conner asked of Stephens.

"No, sir, I am neither an inspector nor a bushranger, I am a Texas Ranger who has worked with Jones in the past. Jones here also holds that honorary title for some work he did a couple of years back."

Conner continued to stare and absorb the information.

"Texas Rangers..." Conner repeated.

"Uh-huh. I would love to tell you some stories to satisfy your obvious curiosity, Mr. Conner, but it's been a long day, and tomorrow may be longer. If you will show us where we can sleep tonight, we'll settle in and then be on our way in the morning."

Conner roused himself back to being the good host. "Of course, gentlemen, please follow me." He led the way out of the study and up the stairs to two rooms where they could clean up and rest.

Stephens advised Jones to sleep with a chair under the doorknob, and they lay down to sleep in their beds.

Chapter 17

The next day the lawmen were up at dawn. They quickly shaved, doctored their bumps and bruises, and got dressed; they had meticulously cleaned their guns the night before so that they were in prime condition to face the new day. The sun had barely risen above the horizon when they came downstairs. As they stepped onto the ground floor, they heard the clank of silverware as Conner finished eating his breakfast in the dining room. The chair scraped the floor, and he came down the hallway to meet them.

"Good morning, gentlemen, I trust you slept well?"

"Well enough, thank you, sir," Stephens replied.

Conner gave a look of concern, and Stephens elaborated, "The beds were quite comfortable, and we had everything we needed. Your hospitality has been flawless. It's just hard to enjoy a good night's sleep after you've been bushwhacked, left to die, and had to fight for your life. As exhausting as that may sound, it's hard to keep your mind from guessing what's going to happen next and when."

"I would think that would make you desirous of sleep."

"It would," Jones replied, "if we weren't on our guard against any friends of Dobson that may still be on your property."

"I guess I can't blame you for that," Conner allowed. "Well, I know you want to be on your way. I've had fresh horses saddled for you and waiting outside. But first sit down and have some breakfast before you go."

Stephens looked at Jones, who nodded, and they accepted the invitation. After having their fill of the same food as Conner had eaten, they headed out the door. Outside they saw the two horses Conner had provided. Still gripping his rifle, Stephens did a thorough examination of each horse to make sure they were as fit as Conner claimed. Being satisfied with the animals, he then looked to their gear that had been taken off their horses the night before. All their tack seemed to be in good shape, and all their supplies, including their ammunition, was untouched. They were about to mount when Conner came walking up to them from across the compound.

"Where will you go from here, gentlemen? Back to Bathurst?"

"No," Jones replied, "we would like to see this man Cavanaugh as soon as possible. How do we get to his station from here?"

The Cavanaugh station was due east from Conner's, and with a few tips about roads and tracks, the lawmen mounted up and took off.

According to the directions Conner had given them, they should've been able to arrive at the Cavanaugh station within a few hours, given that Cavanaugh was Conner's next-door neighbor as it were. Even allowing for the fact that the lawmen would have to find their way on paths they had never traveled, it would be expected they would arrive before three o'clock that afternoon. Nevertheless, they took their time and purposely took wrong trails. They would lose themselves, watch for pursuit or trackers, and then return to the road to repeat the process at the next opportunity. They did everything in their power to confuse and evade anyone who might possibly come after them for whatever reason. Whenever possible, they looked for high vantage points from which they could scan the road ahead. They judged stealth to be of greater importance than speed. There had been virtually no lapse in time between their arrival at Conner's station and everyone there knowing who they were and that they were alive and more or less well. Possibly within a matter of minutes of them walking into Conner's house, Dobson and his cronies had been informed.

Likewise, an unknown listener in Conner's hallway, possibly the butler or some other servant, able to evade even the seasoned ranger's powers of perception, might have already tipped the bushrangers off to the fact the lawmen were heading to Cavanaugh's station. Presuming such to be the case—that outlaws had raced ahead to meet them on their way to, or at, Cavanaugh's station—meant the most safety was to come from going slow and cautious. Their remark to Conner that they wanted to see Cavanaugh as soon as possible would work in favor of this strategy, hopefully causing their enemies to push ahead without much caution and make them easier to detect. By necessity, this would mean their enemies would be waiting for them, if not on the road, then at Cavanaugh's station. This could not be helped and was expected. Suspecting Cavanaugh of possibly being the saboteur mastermind meant that with or without Dobson's interventions, they would approach Cavanaugh's property like beekeepers collecting honey.

The lawmen were certainly nervous as they neared Cavanaugh's station. All the detouring and doubling back helped to distract them to some extent, despite the cause for their maneuvers, and helped give them a better understanding of the country in that direction. It was all temporary, however, for when they topped a ridge, they looked down and perceived far in the distance the outline of Cavanaugh's station compound. From the main house and a couple of other buildings, whiffs of smoke could faintly be detected rising into the air from their chimneys. There was still one more dip and rise in the road before they came to the station gates, and they saw no reason to rush any more than they had already toward their objective. Their maneuvers had caused them to arrive in the late afternoon, and the sun would be at their backs as they came up on the place, and the lower the sun was behind them, the more advantage it would be over those having to look into it.

Jones and Stephens were approaching the top of the last hill that would bring them back into view of the station and start their final descent when the horses' ears twitched and their heads lifted with halting steps. The lawmen reined in and strained their ears, and a second later, they heard what the horses heard—gunshots. They kicked their horses into motion again and raced up the rest of the hill to see what was happening. Just before they came into view of the expanse below that held the compound, they noticed the sky was much darker than it had been minutes before. A second later, they knew why. The roofs that just a short time before they had seen to be issuing smoke from fireplace, stove, and forge were now completely engulfed in flame. Black smoke from burning timber and shingles were filling the sky all above the place so that if the sun had been high in the middle of the day, it would have been blotted out. The popping and booming of rifle and pistol fire continued, and they could see down below figures mounted on horseback running around and through the maze of buildings exchanging shots with other figures on foot scurrying around. The blazes were intensifying, and men were becoming more afraid of burning than being shot, and they ran out into the open, trying to find some safer cover from both threats.

Jones and Stephens kicked their horses again, and they shot down the hill and across the prairie as fast as their horses would carry them. As they neared the encircling fence they diverged, Jones rode toward the open gate to the left, and Stephens headed toward the big house where the station hands seemed to be trying to get to. As Stephens approached, he gripped the reins tight and drew his pistol. As he did, he saw a man take off running from a building that had flames crawling down the walls. The man covered about ten yards before turning around to shoot at something hidden by the outbuilding. No sooner had he fired than he was flung backward onto the ground by a bullet hitting his chest. Then a horseman appeared from the other side of the building and ran up to and over the shot man. Stephens clenched his teeth and gave his horse another kick and leaned backward as the powerful animal sailed over the fence and straight toward the murdering horseman.

The ranger's blood was up now, and any fear that he would've naturally harbored was momentarily replaced with indignation, as well as a hint of satisfaction at the thought of turning the tide of this one-sided battle against the evildoers. The horseman he had just witnessed had no notion that another rider was coming at him, and the ranger never slowed down his advance. It wasn't until the last second when the horseman turned his horse in search of a new victim that he saw the ranger on top of him. He had no time to react, no time for any thought at all in the second of time that showed the ranger to him and ended with a pistol barrel striking his forehead.

The ranger charged on, passing other men on foot who were startled to see an apparently friendly horseman coming from behind them. Adversaries were equally startled when they appeared from around corners, and their attention was drawn from ground level back up to in front of them. One such horseman came from between two buildings, chasing after a victim, and looked up just in time to be shot square in the chest. In the fuss and noise of such a scrap, the ranger never heard the metallic thud of the bullet finding its mark, but seeing his enemy not instantly go down, he had time to fire another shot before he flew past him. On either side of him as he galloped through the mixed crowd, he fired at anyone he saw on horseback as he made his way toward the gate where Jones could be found.

By rights, in accordance with any number of similar skirmishes he had been involved in over the years, he should have accounted for at least a handful of his adversaries killed or wounded. However, as he neared the gate, he wheeled his horse around and was stunned to see the number of his enemies had not diminished. Some were bent over like they were hurt, but none seemed to be incapacitated. They were collecting themselves now, nearly a dozen masked faces looking toward him and relishing the prospect of cutting him down, when Jones appeared. He had already entered by the gate and now shot across the space between ranger and outlaw, crossing from burning building to burning building. As he did, he shot three times into the mass of targets presented to him. Jones was not nearly so skillful at firing from horseback, but it was enough to interrupt the proceedings. Jones had barely gotten out of the line of fire before Stephens drew his second pistol and fired in his turn into the crowd.

The outlaws were unsettled now; in the middle of their easy assault, two daunting adversaries had appeared to challenge them, first one and now the other. They still held numerical superiority over these two, as well as their apparent invulnerability to bullets, but how many more would show up besides these two? As Stephens began to fire, someone in the crowd yelled through his mask and gesticulated the retreat. As he did, Stephens saw yet another one of his bullets hit the target without causing permanent harm. It was always easiest and usually effective to aim at the mass of a man's main body, but that was not working in this case. The next shot Stephens was careful to aim at the leg of the man nearest to him, and this time it yielded the unmistakable evidence of blood spatter. The man yelled as he threw his head back and groped for his leg. With the other leg, he kicked his horse and took off to escape this unanticipated threat.

With this new development, Stephens grabbed his rifle and jumped from his horse. Jones reemerged and threw two more shots at the retreating group before he looked back at Stephens. Upon seeing him kneel to take aim, Jones pulled his horse back out of the way. Stephens steadied and waited for the right moment. It came when one of the rear riders turned to fire at any pursuit, and as he turned broadside to the ranger, the rifle boomed. The massive bullet slammed into the outlaw's leg and continued through leg and saddle leather to backbone of his unfortunate steed. The horse collapsed to the ground on top of its rider and barely twitched. Stephens ran toward the wounded animal with

Jones trotting alongside. As he drew near, Stephens saw one of the horse's hooves kick, which caused the ranger to stop short and fire another bullet into the poor beast's head rather than let him suffer.

With that he ran on up to the man pinned beneath the animal. It was his hope to get some answers and information out of him. An examination of the man might indeed yield answers and information, but the lawmen would have to deduce it on their own, for the rider of the horse lay perfectly still in the dust with his head at so sharp an angle to his shoulders that there could be no question. His neck had been broken in the fall cleaner than any hangman's knot could've performed.

Chapter 18

Jones walked his horse up behind Stephens as the ranger knelt down to examine the body closer. He verified that his eyes had not deceived him; the man's neck was undoubtedly broken. He held his hand above the outlaw's face for some moments and then pulled it back; there was no breath to detect. Then he looked down at the outlaw's shirt, and his eyes focused on a spot low and to the right of the left pocket.

"Jones, come look at this."

Jones dismounted, and as he knelt beside his friend, Stephens pointed to a hole in the cloth. They saw not the color of skin or blood but the dull gray shade of steel. Stephens grabbed the two halves of the skirt and ripped them apart, sending buttons shooting onto the ground. There was a curved steel plate, like a shallow pan, on the front of the man's body. It had rounded corners and did not protrude and was held in place by leather straps that attached through slots cut near the corners of the plate. It managed to cover the vast majority of the man's front, and at just under a quarter of an inch thick, it could protect the wearer from all but the most powerful projectiles. Protect him from death, but not necessarily from harm. Where the bullet hole in the shirt had been, they now saw a crater in the plate where the bullet had struck and forced the metal inward. The impact must have caused the outlaw great pain, but he had still been alive. Stephens recalled how in the split-second when he looked at all the outlaws he thought he had shot; many of them looked to be contending with pain as they made ready to shoot him down in their turn.

"Jones, didn't you tell me at one point when this crazy journey began that the bushranger gang had called themselves Iron Shirts?"

"Yes, I did," Jones answered, looking at his friend in understanding.

Stephens continued expressing his thoughts, "It appears that name is more literal than we imagined. All those men must've been wearing these plates. If they hadn't, then there would be a lot more of them on the ground than this one."

"You're right. And you'll recall I told you about another bushranger, considered to be the last of the great bushranger names, who had made for himself and his companions crude armor that covered all but their legs. It seems these fellows saw some advantage to that."

"Yeah, cover the part that is most often shot at and leave the rest to chance."

Just then, one of the station hands came running up with his pistol pointed at them.

"Don't...don't move," said one of them out of breath and evidently still shaken by what had just happened.

Jones lifted his hands palm outward and stood up slowly.

"Calm yourself," Jones said softly, "we're not the ones that attacked you, we're here to help."

The man still pointed his pistol at the inspector, and his arm stiffened when Jones took a step toward him. Jones wanted to reassure the man that they were no threat, but he wasn't being persuaded, and Stephens was in no mood for dull wits, however justified. He shot up onto his feet again and turned a hot glare at the man.

"Don't act like such a fool, you idiot. If we had wanted you dead, we would've shot you before we ever got off our horses. We could still kill you now since you're dumb enough to point an empty pistol at us."

The man's eyes widened in surprise, and he took his pistol in both hands to examine it. As soon as the man dropped his eyes, Stephens took two long strides and punched the man so that he flew backward onto the ground. Jones looked at him and let his hands drop to his sides; he was long past the point of being surprised by anything that happened when the ranger was around.

"Was his gun really empty?"

"I don't know. All the chambers I saw in the cylinder were empty, but there may have been a live one under the hammer."

"I see. Well, better he has a sore head than we got shot by accident."

"My thoughts exactly."

Just then another man came walking up to them. He held no gun and seemed to be in better control of his mind. His face was melancholy and dejected, but he looked them in the eye as he held out his hand to them in turn.

"Thank you, thank you for helping us when you did. I'm Brophy, the foreman here."

"My name is Caleb Jones, and this is Wayne Stephens. We were coming to see Mr. Cavanaugh when we heard the shooting. What started this mess? Why did they attack you like this?"

"I have no idea. We've been plagued like every other station with bushrangers stealing from us, livestock mostly, and there have been a few scraps with shooting, but this is something else. I never knew there were so many of them as this or imagined they would attack the station in broad daylight. Such a thing hasn't happened in decades, since there was trouble with Aborigines in my father's time."

He paused and looked back over his shoulder at the big house where the wounded were being looked after by their friends on the porch.

"I'm afraid if you've come to see Mr. Cavanaugh, you will be disappointed. He was sitting on the porch when it all started. It seems he ran inside to fetch a rifle, but he never fired it. There are a lot of bullet holes in him."

Jones and Stephens looked at each other in disappointment and aggravation at the fact that instead of getting answers, they were left with still more questions, and bodies.

"Someone needs to get the law out here," Stephens said, "while there is still time to make any sense of it."

"I've already sent one of the lads to town for the constables," said Brophy.

"All the same, I think maybe we should go too," Stephens replied. "They rode off the opposite way, but some of those bushrangers may be watching the road. We'll either bring them back or come back with them if they're already on their way. Until then, keep everyone gathered at the house, and be prepared in case the outlaws come back before we do. I doubt they will, but the last few days have been full of surprises."

Brophy nodded and strode off back to the house.

The two lawmen caught their horses wandering around the scene of destruction and started them down the road that would lead them back to Bathurst. They didn't push their animals too hard since they had already made a good journey to the Cavanaugh station, and it would be well after midnight before they reached the town in any event. As they rode, they now had much more to ponder about the case and the turn it had taken. Dobson had stated the reason for all the uproar they were causing, even the killing of innocents, was to stir up dissent against England and try to cause the countryside to revolt. This most recent and bloody attack on the Cavanaugh station and the killing of Cavanaugh himself, a prominent citizen in the area, would certainly work to fan the sparks that might flame into rebellion. Such an act must certainly prompt a more thorough investigation than had been conducted thus far and warrant a request for additional manpower as well. The immediate goal must be to find the bushrangers and stop the killing; they both wanted to know the finer details of why all this was happening, but that could wait if need be until the outlaws were caught.

But how long would it take to find them? They had discovered the cave hideout and could find their way back to it with a little looking, but that was one secret place in a big country. They had been ambushed and pursued by a handful of men, but the station had been attacked by more than a dozen. So many men must have more than one or even two places to hide around the country. Was it possible they had a secret benefactor that offered them protection? They had wondered if Dobson, who had posed as the bushranger leader, was a buffoon being used as a puppet or an intelligent man practiced at playing the fool. If he was a buffoon, then why would someone use him for such crucial assignments? If he was acting, why didn't he kill them outright when he discovered their identity and the threat they posed? A smart leader would've eliminated such a threat as quickly and secretly as possible, and being hidden in a cave was certainly secret. Maybe secrecy wasn't what he wanted for them. Maybe they were meant to be killed in a staged accident that would not cause Scotland Yard to retaliate quickly and harshly. The discussion carried on as night fell on them.

"At this point, it's still all speculation," Jones said as they trotted along. "We have no evidence other than what happened in the cave, and that tells us nothing for certain. We don't have a living bushranger in custody to question, and now we can't even see if Cavanaugh would've refuted Conner's story."

"So something in you expected Conner's story to be false?" Stephens asked.

"I don't know. It's not unheard of for a man to make his fortune on a gamble, maybe I just wish it hadn't been so easy. Maybe his story is false."

"Or maybe he only knows the story Dobson told when he was hired on. If you suspect him of being involved, why did you reveal who we were, I thought the idea was to stay quiet about it?"

"I guess I have no real evidence to prove he's false yet. And after the day we'd had, I suppose I thought announcing our identity would've provoked him into a rash action revealing his sinister intensions, if he had them."

"Jones, you wouldn't be getting more reckless in your maturing years, would you?"

"If I am, you have no one to blame but yourself."

"Humph. Well, back to business. Do you recall whether Conner said he actually spoke to Cavanaugh or if he just received the word from him?"

"I don't think he made the distinction, just what Cavanaugh told him. That could've been a story from Dobson, like you say, or even a forged letter. We'll have to find out later."

"Yep. Maybe some of those men back there could've backed up one story or another, but I don't think any of them would've been much use to us just now. When we get back, maybe we can get answers."

Their horses had taken no more than a few strides in silence when a crowd of lights popped up on both sides of the road. The two lawmen drew their weapons to face the pistol and rifle barrels that reflected the lamplight.

Chapter 19

The two horsemen faced the group on foot in silence for a few seconds before one man stepped forward from the crowd.

"Lower your weapons in the name of the crown."

As their focus came off the guns pointed at them, the lawmen realized this man was dressed in a suit and most of the others were dressed in the uniform of the police. They lowered their pistols but remained cautious for a trick.

The man spoke again, "Who are you, and what is your business?"

"My name is Caleb Jones, and this is my friend Wayne Stephens. We are on our way to Bathurst to report an attack on the Cavanaugh station. There are many dead and wounded there, including Mr. Cavanaugh himself."

"We have already been informed of the attack and are on our way there now," the man replied. "What were you doing there?"

"We were traveling there from the Conner station to discuss business with Mr. Cavanaugh when we heard shooting in the distance. We rushed to the aid of those being attacked but were too late to save Mr. Cavanaugh from being killed. We drove off the outlaws and, after seeing things under control, started off to make sure word of the attack was delivered."

The leader turned to some of his companions in regular clothes and talked low for a moment.

"These two men are the ones who brought the news, and they don't recognize you."

"They were sent before we talked to anyone at the station, and we had not been there before, so there's no reason why they would," Jones replied.

"All the same, how were the two of you able to overcome a number of outlaws as large as what I was told of?"

"The outlaws were busy chasing surprised and beaten men on foot," replied Stephens, becoming impatient. "We surprised them on horseback from the rear and the flank. Now, if that is enough of an answer for you, maybe you'll tell us who the devil you are."

The leader stiffened at this. "I am Inspector Harrington, in charge of the constable station in Bathurst. Now that you know who I am, is there anything else you can tell me about this business?"

"There might be," replied Stephens again, "but we would prefer to talk to you in private and not in the middle of nowhere with your lanterns giving away our position to anyone who might want to take a shot at us. We've been shot at quite enough the last couple of days."

This statement intrigued the inspector, but he had another duty to see to first.

"I'm afraid I cannot accommodate you at the moment, my first duty is to investigate matters at the Cavanaugh station. However, if you will consent to let one of my men accompany you back to town, we can discuss this further when I return."

After a moment's consideration, they consented, and they continued silently to Bathurst with a constable riding beside them. The young man was silent the entire trip aside from an occasional cough or indicating an alteration in direction, but the lawmen would catch him randomly cutting his eyes at them as if he wanted to satisfy his curiosities. Evidently, he dared not sidestep his superior and ask questions pertinent to recent events without Harrington being present. It was late when they arrived back in Bathurst. They informed the young policeman of where they were staying for when Harrington returned and that they intended to stay in town for the immediate future.

They managed to get a few hours of sleep before sunrise. The sun was already in the sky when they rose to begin a new day, but they were in no hurry to do much moving around. During the last couple of days, they had been beat on, chained up, and dodged more bullets than they had for the last couple of years. The notion of taking a little easy time to recoup from their cuts, bumps, and bruises was a welcome one, and they acted on it. When they finally emerged from their quarters, they went in search of facilities where they could get a hot bath and decent shave. After this, they were refreshed and a little less sore, and they wandered into a café on the main street to have a hot breakfast. When they had finished and were sipping at their coffee, Harrington came through the door and looked around until he saw them and casually walked over and sat at their table.

"Good morning, gentlemen," he said with the cordiality of a man fulfilling his duty when he would rather be elsewhere.

"Good morning, sir," replied Stephens with the same dose of cordiality.

He and Jones were now obviously in better shape than Harrington, who had been up all night and morning trying to make sense of the horrific acts of yesterday. Even so, the ranger was still in no mood to be friendly toward anyone who might potentially be involved in the mess they were trying to clean up. Jones was of the same mind, if not the same attitude. He thought it best not to trust Harrington or his men until they had evidence of his trustworthiness, but he would put on a smile for the man who was evidently exhausted.

"How are you this fine morning, Mr. Harrington?" A rhetorical question, but in keeping with common friendly conversation.

"I would be better for a good night's sleep, I must say," the officer replied. "But with such a horrendous crime on my shoulders, I fear I can't rest until I have made a little more progress. I have heard several accounts of what took place at the Cavanaugh station, and given the state of the men giving them, I could safely say they more or less coincide. However, I would be grateful if I could now have your account of events. To have been so directly involved, you seem to be much less…shall we say, overwhelmed by events. And I would like to hear more details of other events you mentioned last night on the road."

Jones ordered them all more coffee and began to talk. He stuck with their prearranged back story of searching for business investments and hunting. He told of meeting Conner in Sydney and so on until every detail of their recent adventures up to the previous night had been told minus any reference to their true identity. The policeman listened with acute attention, despite his apparent fatigue, and when it was over, he sat for a long while, considering this mass of information.

At last, he spoke, "You gentlemen are either very skilled or very lucky, or both, to have made it through so much. I have never heard of this bushranger gang kidnapping people before, this is a new wrinkle. What on earth would make them consider you such a threat? Efforts to bring them to justice have been growing and growing with little effect." Harrington was starting to digress from being inquisitive to exasperated.

"You need sleep, Inspector," Stephens declared with a less-icy tone than he had used before. "Get some, and when your brain can think straight, then we'll talk again. At this point, I doubt you'd be able to make much sense of anything else we discuss."

"He's right, Mr. Harrington," Jones agreed. "Take it from me that a man has to make time to rest himself, or he will never make progress."

"Very well, gentlemen. I believe I will take your advice. When I am in a better frame of mind, I will come find you or leave word for you." He pushed himself up and walked out of the café.

After watching him leave, Stephens nudged Jones.

"I think we may regret telling Conner who we really are if Harrington checks our story with him. If Harrington is crooked, then it will just put more people after us. If he's honest, then he might resent our not coming to him in the first place and then lying to him."

Jones made no reply except for a glance, which revealed his belief that this was most likely true. They finished their coffee as leisurely as they could manage, but already restless thoughts about the past and the future were spinning in their minds. As they got up to leave, they noticed that outside people were becoming excited and congregating in groups of discussion. Exiting the café, they casually walked down the sidewalk and strained their ears to pick up as many comments as possible. It didn't take long to determine the cause of public unrest: news of the attack on the Cavanaugh station, despite any efforts that might have been made to conceal it, had come to the attention of the people of Bathurst.

Some people were devastated and heartbroken by the news, wondering if friends of theirs were included among the dead or wounded. Some were just simply mad at such a large scale and blatant act of violence. And some reacted with a mixture of emotion that ultimately led to declarations of displeasure and impatience with the law and the government for not being able to put a stop to the bushrangers after so long a while. These lines of conversation were particularly disturbing to the lawmen, but they said nothing until they reached their room.

"I don't like the feel of things out there," Jones said once the door was shut behind them. "People who are that angry and passionate have the power to cause serious trouble and invite unforeseen consequences. Such hostility against the government, especially in this charged climate of labor disputes, could have disastrous effects. And honestly, after what's happened to us, I can't really blame them."

"It would be difficult for anyone to blame them," Stephens replied. "People fighting and scratching to make life work seeing theft, murder, and mayhem all around them want justice and a sense of order. When they don't get it, they will naturally start looking for someone to blame and then for someone else who can give them what they want. With such a large portion of the country being affected for so long, it would seem natural they be upset at the government. But understandable or not, I agree that it makes for a volatile environment. One person who can tap into the people's emotions can send them toward war, civil war ultimately, with the English government."

They both sat in silent contemplation of the fact they were the ones sent to deal with these issues to prevent these eventualities, but what to do next? It was decided to do as they had planned and take the day to rest from their adventures. They had no immediate leads to follow or people to talk to, and it would be just as well to wait until the people's charged moods were calmed. They ensured their weapons were freshly cleaned and loaded. They reassessed the state of their saddlebags, which were packed tight with supplies for an emergency. And they put much effort into not worrying pointlessly about circumstances they could not alter.

The day dragged on to evening, and they had decided they could not linger any longer and would go back out into the town when there came a knock at their door.

Chapter 20

Both men looked intently at the door when they heard the knock. Stephens gripped the handle of his pistol, and Jones gripped the doorknob. They gave each other a nod of agreement, and Jones opened the door and was relieved to see a constable standing on the other side. If memory served, he was one of the men with Harrington when they met him on the road the previous night. Stephens relaxed the grip on his pistol as Jones greeted the constable.

"Good evening, Constable, what can I do for you?"

The young man looked from one man to the other with a blank professional expression on this face.

"Good evening, gentlemen. Inspector Harrington sent me to request you come to the station for an interview."

The lawmen looked at each other and again nodded in agreement before Jones responded.

"Of course, Constable. If you would give us a minute to collect ourselves, we'll be right with you."

The constable gave a stiff nod of assent and turned aside from the door as if to watch passersby on the street while waiting for his charges.

Jones closed the door gently and turned to his partner. "What do you think?"

"From watching Harrington at breakfast, I think he's honest. The more I think about it, the more I'm convinced a crooked inspector would not have been so obviously exhausted trying to piece together a crime he was indirectly connected with. If nothing happens when we see him to alter that impression, then I think we should come out and tell him what we're up to."

"I think you're right. I'm not sure how much more we can dig without help. There will only be so much more we can do before people start getting suspicious, or we start following gossip."

They both holstered their freshly cleaned pistols, and Stephens shoved his rifle under the mattress of his bed before they went out the door for their interview. The constable was all business; he didn't say a word to the lawmen beyond asking them to follow him. They did and took note of the streets they traveled to end up at the station where Harrington had his office.

"Right in here, sirs," declared the constable as he opened the door for them to go in ahead of him.

The sun was setting, and the front room they walked into was dark with only a couple of oil lamps burning low. No sooner had the door shut behind them than they heard the familiar sound of pistol hammers being cocked, several of them around the room. The lawmen's instant reaction was to draw their own weapons, but they just as instantly froze their movements as they both realized it would be suicide to draw against so many weapons already pointed at them. A moment later, the lamps were turned up, and the light increased to reveal they were surrounded by five constables, including the one who had fetched them. The pistols remained pointed at them as one of constables moved to light two more lamps. Then two of them stepped forward to take Stephens's and Jones's weapons before ushering them toward two chairs.

"What is the meaning of this?" Jones asked angrily as they were pushed down into their seats. "What have we done to be treated in this manner?"

A sergeant stepped forward to answer his question, "You, sirs, have been implicated as being party to the attack on the Cavanaugh station and so in the murders and violence performed there."

"That is absurd!" replied Jones. "Where is Inspector Harrington?"

"Inspector Harrington left the office a couple of hours ago to investigate possible leads to other potential suspects. In his absence, I am charged with the peace and well-being of this community."

Jones opened his mouth to continue his protest, but before he could say another word, the sergeant spoke again.

"Were you or were you not at the Cavanaugh station yesterday afternoon?"

"Yes, we were. But we…"

"Did or did you not discharge firearms into crowds of people?"

"Technically, yes, we did, but we fired at horsemen already…"

"Did anyone at the Cavanaugh station invite you or expect you that day?"

"No, Sergeant, we were arriving unannounced as far as we know."

"Then how can you prove you were not involved in this malicious attack?

"Sergeant, my name is Caleb Jones, and I am an inspector from Scotland Yard in London. I have been sent here to investigate the rampage of bushranger crimes that has persisted over the last two years. My colleague is an American law officer of impeccable repute who has agreed to assist me. If you will return with us to our room, I can prove it to your satisfaction."

The sergeant's expression remained unchanged and unimpressed to the surprise of both lawmen.

"I had already been informed that you would fabricate such a tale to cover your actions. You will not so easily escape the consequences of your offenses."

Jones was dumbstruck just enough to blurt out the question, "Who informed you ahead of time of what I would tell you?"

As he said it, Stephens's heart began to sink as a dark realization began to form in his mind. As if to signify the notion hitting rock-bottom, a heavy footstep sounded, and they both looked toward the dark doorway of the next room. More footsteps followed as a tall figure emerged with his head bowed. He came to a stop and lifted his head to reveal the face of Jeffery Conner. He had a solemn expression on his face as he revealed himself. Jones was speechless as he stared at Conner's face. Stephens closed his eyes and shook his head slightly to himself. The sergeant watched their expressions and then turned to Conner.

"Are these the men you were referring to, Mr. Conner?" he asked.

"Yes, Sergeant, they are. As I told you, they first came to me offering to invest in my mining operations. At first, I was intrigued, but then I started getting reports of several attacks on my men shortly thereafter. And then they appeared at my station after apparently being in a fight. The next morning, they said they were going to the Cavanaugh station, and the same afternoon the station was attacked and Cavanaugh killed. I can't imagine all this to be mere coincidence."

"Do you think these men are part of the bushranger gang that has been operating in the area?"

"I can't say for sure. There's always a possibility, I suppose, but I'm inclined to think not. By all accounts, these men are strangers. Perhaps they are newcomers trying to take advantage of the turmoil the bushrangers are causing to reap their own spoils."

"I see, sir. We'll lock them up all the same until the truth is determined. We appreciate your cooperation, and I'll see Inspector Harrington is fully informed on this return."

As he said these last words, the sound of multiple voices became audible from outside, and the sergeant's face grew harder as if he suspected some new mischief. He gave orders for the prisoners to be put in a cell while the rest of them manned the windows. Conner trailed behind the constable, who led them to a cell in the back room, and after the door had been locked, he turned to constable.

"Why don't you go on out and assist the sergeant, I'll wait here. I'm sure I'll be all right with the door secure."

The constable nodded after a moment's consideration and went back into the front room and shut the door behind him. After watching him leave, Conner hung his head again and turned toward the cell.

"I am sorry for your misfortune, gentlemen, but actions have consequences, I'm afraid."

Jones took a step forward and slowly gripped the bars as he spoke. "Mr. Conner, do you truly believe we are somehow the villains in what has transpired in the last few days? I'll tell you, as I told the sergeant, that a visit to our room will yield the evidence of our innocence."

He was referring to a letter he had hidden in his luggage from Scotland Yard explaining his orders and authority to investigate the activities of the bushrangers. A moment passed before Conner shook his head.

"That won't be necessary…Inspector."

When he said this last word, both lawmen looked more intently at him, and as he raised his head, they noticed a slight grin at the corners of his mouth.

"It is unnecessary because the time has passed where it could help you. You see, my word, like my reputation, is above question in this region, and I already have the sergeant convinced of your guilt. It will merely be a formality to have you accused and convicted, if there were time for it."

He stopped speaking and glanced at the door. From the other side of it and beyond, the sound of a disgruntled crowd grew louder.

He turned back to his captive audience. "You see, while we've been entertaining the police, my men have been going through the town telling the news that the men responsible for yesterday's atrocity are being held here and that they will likely be released. This news to people who are so angry at the loss of their friends and neighbors will not sit well at all."

"Your men," Stephens said when he paused. "Your men are not cow hands and miners, are they? They are the bushrangers. You are a bushranger, ain't you?"

Conner nodded, "I am indeed."

"And I suppose the tip Harrington is following will lead him to the same cave we were invited to?"

"Correct again. It's a shame really, Harrington is a good man, and brighter than the sergeant, but after coming in contact with you two, he has become too much of a liability. If he survives the night, I will use my influence to have the sergeant elevated to inspector to replace Harrington."

"And why would he not survive if you want him to be your pawn?" asked Jones.

"The crowd," Stephens answered. "His men are whipping the crowd up into a mob. He wants them to lynch us so we can't talk anymore, and the sergeant and his men will have to fight them off or die trying."

"Very good, Mr. Stephens. Again, I say it is a shame a man of your parts has been brought into this."

"Why, Conner?" Jones asked in cold fury. "You've told us this much, so tell us why. You are a successful business man and landowner. Why do you need to steal from others?"

"The point isn't theft, Inspector. The point in dissention. I grew up in the middle of the squatter and selector feuds, as I told you. What I didn't tell you was that I have been a bushranger for years. When I was a boy, I rode with Thunderbolt, the man who called himself Captain Thunderbolt, and I was proud of it. I was proud of the fact that ultimately, we were striking back at the landlords who ground people like me under their heel. I was one of the last boys to join him, and so the law knew nothing about me. And when Thunderbolt was killed, I was left on my own again, and the life I described to you began.

"Then Ned Kelly shook New South Wales and Victoria to the core. He made it known that if people were willing to fight, we could change the world as it stood around us. The night they planned to attack the train, I was one of a group of men waiting for Ned—men who were willing to fight, not to scratch up a bare existence, but to give ourselves a chance at a worthwhile life. But the train job didn't go as planned, and Ned came to us and told us to run and wait for the right opportunity. He went back to fight with his brother, and we ran like he told us to. He lost and was hanged, but I never lost the hope he gave us.

"I gained my good fortune not in a card game but by stumbling half starved onto the very cave where you were held. The gold in that cave gave me my stake to start over, and I did. I acquired the station, and I drew men to me who had believed in Kelly and other oppressed selectors who wanted a chance at a decent life. My good name grew with my success, and I became a man of the people."

He paused for breath, and Stephens stared at him.

"Man of the people? Some role model, your bushranger attacks caused the death of people who worked for you and other innocent people who had nothing to do with your hardships. How in thunder do you think you can change the world like that?"

"You don't see everything yet? I'm surprised, Mr. Stephens. But I'll indulge you a little longer, the crowd isn't loud enough yet. You see, most of us in that crowd back then were outlaws and of little account to anyone. And with the death of Kelly and bushrangers in general, we slipped into the pages of history. Now the attacks and robberies were not to steal and kill, these are unfortunate side effects of war. The true purpose is to create so much dissention among the good people that they all rise up to throw off a yoke, the yoke of a British Empire, so far removed as to not give a hang about its lowly subjects. Britain only cares about its profit and influence, but now we're almost to the point we can spark a true and just war to free ourselves and all be able to live the way men should." He paused again for breath and listened to the noise from outside.

Chapter 21

As they listened, the noise of an angry crowd got ever louder and louder. It was evident now that the crowd was assembled outside the front door and the constables were struggling to keep them at bay. Conner grinned as he turned to them one last time.

"That mob of good people out there now sees you as the source of their grief. They believe you attacked the Cavanaugh station and you are bushrangers. The police may believe differently, but it makes no difference now. They will be unable to contain the mob, and once they've lynched you, I will be able to influence them that the only way we can have true justice now and forever is to be independent. So your unexpected and unwanted arrival will prove to be beneficial after all. Good luck, gentlemen, and good evening."

With that, he opened the door and summoned a constable. After expressing his concerns, the two of them came back past the cells to a heavily locked door. The constable fumbled with a set of keys to unlock it and allow Conner to slip out after checking to see that no one was in the alley. When he had gone, the constable relocked the door and started to walk back into the front room but hesitated. He was scared, so scared that his hand trembled slightly as he hooked the key ring back onto his belt. He was a young man and probably unfamiliar with the violence brewing out in the street. Conner's men had done their job well, and from the cells, the lawmen could hear the terrible things being yelled by citizens thirsty for revenge on the supposed murderers. The young man stood still with wide eyes as he bolstered himself to go back and face the crowd. In the eyes of the lawmen in the cell, he was to be respected for not turning and running as he obviously wanted to do. It was not his fault he or they were in this position, and he was prepared to do his duty. However, an opportunity was an opportunity, and Stephens knew he had to take advantage of it if this twisted situation was to ever be set straight.

"Excuse me, son," he said just as the constable was about to take a step.

He stopped and turned to the prisoner. "What do you want?" he asked.

"Just to know if you and your friends out there will be able to keep us alive for another ten minutes? It sounds like you've got your hands full."

The young man lifted his chin in a defiant air. "Yes, sir, as long as we draw breath, we will defend you and keep you in custody, however maddening a thought it may be."

"How's that?" asked the ranger, looking surprised.

"The death, destruction, and pain you have caused to this community and territory would make me want to join the mob outside if it were not for the position I hold. I knew many people who worked for Cavanaugh, and if you had anything to do with the attack, then good riddance to you."

"My dear boy," continued Stephens, looking more hurt and surprised, "if you would give us half a chance to explain things to you, I bet you would see plainly that we are innocent. Certainly, a growing boy such as yourself would be bright enough to realize the truth." He laid a slight emphasis on the word *boy* this time but continued naturally.

The constable's frown deepened, and he glared at Stephens as he continued, "And once you've realized the truth, even such a young man as yourself would see the sense in letting us go rather than submitting to the wild hoard outside."

This subtle antagonizing of the young man's age was angering him, as it was supposed to, and the suggestion that he would violate his duty so blatantly as to release them was infuriating.

"How dare you!" he said harshly. "My age has absolutely nothing to do with my capacity to think or perform my duty." He pointed his finger at the prisoner. "And I'll tell you another thing…"

Before he could utter another syllable, Stephens had grabbed the outstretched hand and yanked it through the bars. The young constable flew forward and rammed his head against the cell door. Keeping his grip on his arm, Stephens lowered the unconscious constable to the floor. That done, he unhooked the keys from their resting place and began trying keys until one worked. They eased the door open as quietly as possible and slipped out and over the figure in the floor. They fumbled with the keys again until they found the one that opened the back door, and they slipped out into the alley.

As stealthily as possible, they made their way back to their room. It was evident that someone had been their going through their things. Not the mob, as they would have torn the place apart, but someone had meticulously searched their belongings. Most likely some of Conner's men looking for evidence or planting it. A quick search showed that nothing had been added, but Jones's letter of authority was missing, no doubt taken to prevent Jones from proving their identity and causing more trouble. Stephens reached under his bed and was relieved to find his rifle still there. The rifle, along with his short pistol he had hidden under the small dresser, were the only weapons they had left. Both their other pistols had been taken from them by the constables. He gave the pistol to Jones, and they quickly stuffed everything back into their saddlebags before throwing them over their shoulders and slipping back out onto the street.

The street was deserted with most of the population gathered at the constables' station, and so it was easy for them to slip down to the stable. There, only one man sat on a stool to tend the horses overnight. A quick tap to the drowsy man's head with the butt of the pistol and he was no threat to them. They quickly picked out a couple of good horses and saddled them, but then stopped to deliberate their next move.

"Somehow, I don't think it would do us much good to head back to Sydney," said Stephens in a half-sarcastic tone.

"Doubtless," agreed Jones. "If we could somehow go straight there without stopping anywhere along the way, we might have a chance. But we don't have the supplies, and the news of what's happened would travel faster than we can to the towns along the road. So I suppose we can either go in a different direction to a town we haven't been to and make our way to a different port, or we can try to prove our innocence here somehow."

"The only way to prove our innocence to that dense sergeant and put an end to this madness is to get to Conner."

As he said this, they could hear a fresh clamor up the street. They peeked out and saw people running around like they were searching for something. Presumably the young constable had come to and made it known they had escaped.

"We've got to go, and what's more, we've got to find that cave again. The only person who might listen to us is Harrington, and the way Conner talked, they'll probably have him there like they did us. Come on."

With that, they mounted their horses and eased them out the stable door. They walked them casually down side streets, not wanting the sound of running horses to draw attention. They had almost reached the edge of the city when someone started yelling down the street behind them. They didn't stop to look but kicked their horses into a run to disappear into the darkness. Once they were far away from the lights of the town, they turned away from the main road to head as straight for the area where the cave was as they could recon. When they came to the top of a hill, they stopped to rest the horses and take in their surroundings. Stephens pulled a compass out of his saddlebags and lit a match cupped in his hand to study it.

"I wish I had tried to get a map from somebody when we got here," he said. "All right, I think we need to veer a little more to the left. We turned pretty sharp to the left when we left the road to end up there the first time."

Jones nodded, deferring to the ranger's superior navigating skills, and they remounted. Going at a trot instead of a gallop, and always listening for sounds of pursuit from behind, they continued into the night. It was approaching dawn when they came across some familiar rocks and picked out part of a trail they had followed on their previous trip. This they followed cautiously for some time. The eastern sky was just starting to lighten when they stopped their horses. There, at the edge of their sight, was the large rock face that hid the entrance to that dreaded cave.

They dismounted and tied their horses' reins securely to a tree and then advanced on foot. As they drew nearer, their eyes picked up the faint light of what must've been a dying fire inside the entrance. They stopped and listened. Faint snores could be heard coming from inside, and the two lawmen were about to take the opportunity to sneak in when one of the snores was broken by a cough. The cough brought the man to wakefulness, and after another cough and some groans, they heard a set of boots hit the floor. They took a few steps and stopped before the man spoke in an Irish accent the lawmen had become accustomed to.

"Wake up, you lout!" he said loudly, evidently to another man who was still snoring. Then they heard the thud of a boot kicking wood. "Get on your feet, we've got to get that copper out of here and laid out so the boss can have his show."

There was another series of grunts and groans, and then another set of boots hit the stone floor.

"I'm up, you bog scum. Couldn't you have waited until the sun was full up?"

"No, we should've had it done last night, but you drank too much, and I couldn't handle him by myself. Now we've got to do him in and get him out where someone will find him without being seen ourselves."

"I wouldn't worry too much. If the plan went off and the boss got the town to lynch them other two, then everybody'll be too given out to be on the road this early."

"We can't take no chances. The boss wasn't too happy that those two got away from us last time, so we gotta take care with this job, or he'll skin us both. Come on."

As they started to walk back down into the cave, Stephens and Jones rushed in the entrance. The two outlaws turned at the noise, and when they saw the intruders, their expressions were a mix of anger and surprise. Stephens shouldered his rifle and aimed it at the larger of the two men, while Jones covered the other as Stephens spoke.

"Take us to Harrington, and take us now if you ever want to see the light of day again."

The look on his face combined with the huge rifle barrel staring starring at them strangled any response they might have made. After Jones stepped forward and disarmed them, they turned and continued their way into the cave and the tunnel. In almost the exact same spot where they themselves had been held prisoner, they found Harrington bound and groggy on the hard floor. Jones stooped to untie him and help him up while Stephens covered the outlaws. Jones pulled Harrington to his feet and held him up as they walked back to the front of the cave.

Chapter 22

Jones found a canteen hanging on the wall and held it to Harrington's lips to drink the water and sat him down in a chair by the entrance so he could breathe fresh air. Stephens told the outlaws to sit on the floor in the corner while Harrington revived himself. Finally, the inspector spoke.

"Thank you…thank you," he said between gulp of water and deep breaths of air. "If you hadn't come, I'm sure they would've killed me."

"They would've," replied Stephens, "we just overheard them discussing your funeral arrangement." He kept his rifle trained on the outlaws as Harrington looked from him to Jones and back to him.

"How exactly did you two happen to come here?"

"We told you yesterday, we had our turn here as prisoners," Jones replied, "which is how we knew where to come to find you, or at least where to start looking. Why we knew to come look for you will be a little more complicated to explain. First, I should tell you we are not who we claimed to be. I am Inspector Caleb Jones of Scotland Yard."

This announcement did much to finish clearing Harrington's head. He looked at Jones for a moment and then looked down at the floor in thought.

"Caleb Jones…I know that name, don't I? Yes, didn't I hear about you a few years ago, something about breaking up a smuggling ring from India? That was big news at the time if I recall."

"That's correct, it was," said Jones with a grin. "But I can't take all the credit for that accomplishment. Did the news stories here mention anything else?"

"Yes, come to think of it. It made mention of some American law officer, which the London papers said to be particularly destructive." He paused for a moment and then looked back at Stephens. "You?" he said with faint disbelief.

"Congratulations, Inspector, you've figured it out. Jones is a Scotland Yard inspector, and I'm a Texas Ranger, which is why he dragged me along on this expedition."

This statement made Harrington's line of thought come back to present circumstances.

"But what are you both doing here?" he asked.

"Scotland Yard sent me to investigate the bushrangers and their unchecked outlawry. It was felt that a fresh pair of untainted eyes was needed to seek them out and stop them. Given this county's closer similarity to the American Western territories than to the English countryside, I recruited Mr. Stephens to accompany me and help me."

This last statement drew a snicker from Stephens, who kept his eyes on his prisoners.

"We had no idea whom we could trust down here, which is why we didn't tell you the truth yesterday, and recent events have shown us we should've been even more careful."

Harrington's wits had returned quickly, and though he was initially irked at Jones's statement of not knowing whom to trust, it only took a second for him to concede the point to himself that for the bushranger gang to have been so successful for so long, local authorities might be suspected of collusion.

"What do you mean?" he asked in response to Jones's last statement.

With that Jones began the entire story all over again. He told the entirely truthful version of the story they had told the day before and continued it with all the events of the last evening with Conner's full confession and future intensions. This sufficed to answer Harrington's first question of how they came to rescue him. He let his head fall into his hands, and he rubbed his face, and he digested everything he just heard.

"Conner," he said to himself. "Good ol' Conner who tries to help everyone. Conner, who preached peace between social groups. Conner, who has stood as a pillar of the community, has actually been working to tear it apart." He shook his head in his hands as Jones spoke.

"Not tear it apart, but rather set it and the whole territory up to be torn away, from England. He wants a revolution to establish an independent country in Australia that he can be king over, it would seem."

Harrington stood to his feet, still a little wobbly. "We have to stop him," he proclaimed.

"Of course we do, and we will," Jones replied, pulling him back down to the chair, "but first, we need to get you some food and figure out what exactly we're going to do."

Stephens signaled for Jones to watch the prisoners while he began to rummage through the boxes and shelves along the cave wall. To his delight, he found a brown paper package that was about half full of bacon. He threw some wood on the dying embers of the fire, and when he had it blazing again, he got a frying pan out of the same box and began to fry the bacon. When it was done to a crisp, they all sat and nibbled the hot meat. New life and energy began to stream through their tired bodies, and their dispositions improved. Over in the corner, the outlaws groaned at smelling the food and not getting any. Stephens glared at them, and they made no more noise.

When they had finished, they sat and wondered about what their next move should be.

"We can't risk going back to town," said Jones. "After the frenzy the people were in last night, they would kill us instantly. And if any of Conner's men spots us or you out in the open, they will kill us all on the spot."

"Conner has been ahead of us all throughout this scheme of his," said Harrington. "It will be difficult to do anything effective against him without knowing what exactly he plans to do next."

With that, Stephens began to think back to when they first arrived. One of the outlaws had mentioned the boss, who must be Conner, having a show. The ranger stood up, pulled one of the confiscated pistols out of his belt, and walked over to the prisoners.

"Okay, boys," the ranger said, staring down at them, "I'll ask once nicely. What is the show your boss is wanting to have?"

They just stared back up at him and didn't twitch. Stephens glared at them and waited another moment. When he still didn't get a response, he backed up a step and put his thumb on the hammer of the pistol.

"Are y'all sure you want to do it this way?"

Still, neither one of the outlaws said anything, and the bigger of the two cracked a grin as if he didn't believe this American would actually do anything.

Stephens shook his head and said, "Okay then," and cocked the hammer on the pistol.

Harrington stirred in his chair and started to stand up, but Jones put a hand on his shoulder and stopped him. Jones put his fingers in his ears, and though he didn't understand why, Harrington did the same.

"One more time, son," Stephens said to the big outlaw who had grinned. "What exactly is the show Conner is planning?"

"Why don't you go jump down a well, Yank…"

Bang.

He had barely said the last word when the pistol fired. The whole cave reverberated with the noise; the outlaws covered their ears with their hands, and the big one folded his legs up tighter after the bullet hit the floor between his feet.

"What in the blazes is wrong with you?"

"I hate it when people call me a Yank. If I'm anything, I'd be a Reb, but to you, I'm a ranger, a Texas Ranger, and I don't have patience with people who waste my time. What is the show?"

"Bugger off!"

Bang.

The cave reverberated again, and both men ducked as the next bullet hit the wall between their heads.

"Bloody…"

The big man let out a string of oaths, and the other man began to tremble. Stephens took a step toward them and raised the pistol again. The smaller man lifted his shaking hands and fidgeted.

"Okay, okay, I'll tell you, just stop shooting."

"Shut your gob!" yelled the big man, but then the barrel of the pistol made contact with his skull, and he said no more as he lay on the floor.

"All right," said Stephens, "tell me what the show is."

"It's not a show really, it's a gathering. Conner said when he felt the people's attitude was right, he would call for them to gather at his station and urge them to fight for freedom and the ability to fend for themselves. To fight for justice for themselves without having to rely on the old empire on the other side of the world."

"So he was telling the truth, and all this time the bushrangers weren't stealing for themselves but to create strife?"

"Yeah, that's it. He said if he could make the people mad enough, make the whole territory sick of the English government not able to stop them, then it would be easy to get them to fight."

All three lawmen listened intently as this man verified with more detail what Conner had already said.

"And he thinks he actually has the weight to make this happen?"

"Sure, he said plenty of people were ready to rise up back in Kelly's day, and he was going to do it, but he got caught, and the people got discouraged. Most of his lads are part of the mob who waited for old Ned to come that night. He had us rob him as well so he could be a-aggrieved with everyone else, and all the gold we've took is hidden in different places so we can use it to buy guns and supplies when the fight comes."

This all made sense, but Stephens wanted more current plans.

"When is this gathering supposed to take place?"

"He never set a particular time until yesterday. He said with you two stirring things up and causing him to hit Cavanaugh, things have gotten hot faster than he expected."

"When?" Stephens shouted impatiently and raised the pistol again.

"T-t-this evening. He said he would let everything cool down from last night and then send some lads to post papers and spread the word that he wants people to come out to discuss the future of the territory."

So that was it then; they had a matter of hours, half a day maybe, to figure out what to do and do it. Stephens walked over to Jones and Harington.

Chapter 23

"Well, that's that," said the ranger as he leaned against the wall where he could still see the prisoners out of the corner of his eye. "Conner's going to give a rabble-rousing speech this evening at his station, his home ground, with all his men handy, and rip these people into another fighting frenzy. What about it?"

"We can't send for help," said Harrington. "Ideally, I'd like to bring in the army, but any garrison is too far away to be of immediate help. And we can't get help from any other law officers. Just because I'm not involved in this treachery doesn't mean others might not be. And to call for any help, we would have to get back to town, and that has been established as too risky an endeavor."

"Yep, and if we show up back there again, even with you alongside, that thick-skulled sergeant of yours would probably shoot us on sight," commented Stephens in annoyance.

"Sergeant Ives may not have much imagination, but he is honest and reliable. If I could get to him, I can get him to help us with no trouble whatever. But how to get to him?"

"His duty and the duty of all your constables is to protect the people and their property," said Jones. "Do you think any of them would follow the townspeople to this gathering?"

"I'd be surprised if they didn't, unless they were needed more in town, which may be the case given what you described happened last night," replied Harrington. And then, a light began to shine. "Of course, if we can get to them at the meeting, then we'll be safe."

But then Stephens interjected, "I wouldn't call us safe yet, just maybe one step closer to it. We still have to get to Conner's, find your men, and then still get away from all Conner's men. They would still outnumber us, and Conner wants us all dead."

He stroked his chin, and they all sat in contemplation of the riddle they were set with.

After a moment, Stephens stood up straight. "An army," he said, and his companions looked at him questioningly. "You said before you would call in the army. Well, let's make our own army. If Conner gets his way, there will be a mess of mad townspeople there that he wants to make fight. Let's just get them to fight the wrong, or right, people."

"How do we accomplish that?" asked Jones.

"Conner had them ready to lynch us by making them think we were bushrangers. We have to expose Conner and his men to them as the real bushrangers."

"That's a sound concept, but again, how do we do it?" asked Harrington.

Stephens pondered to himself another few moments and then grinned. "We use their trademark."

"I beg your pardon?" asked Harrington.

"You mean their breastplates," said Jones in rising excitement.

"Right," said Stephens. "After two years, there isn't a person in the country who doesn't know about them wearing their 'iron shirts' to survive being shot. We'll use that to their disadvantage."

"How?" asked Harrington again monotonously.

"Shoot 'em!" said Stephens impatiently, who thought the answer should be obvious at this point. "We slip in, take up positions away from the crowd, and when Conner has their blood running high, we start shooting his men. The bullets will bounce off them, and the people will start to realize there are bushrangers all around them. They'll either run or fight, and in either case, we'll start bringing the bushrangers down and even the odds. Their arms, legs, and heads are still exposed."

Now all three of them were on their feet in anticipation of working out the fine details. All three were trying to speak at once when there was a noise behind them; they had taken their eyes off the one conscious prisoner, and he dashed for the cave entrance. Stephens turned and made a grab for him, but he just missed his shirt sleeve. They all darted out the door after him as the man ran down the hill. Stephens stopped with Jones beside him, and Jones drew out his pistol, but before he could use it, Stephens took his own pistol by the barrel and threw it. Jones noted that he did this with the calculation he had seen Stephens use to throw a knife, and the weapon crashed into the middle of the bushranger's back.

He cried out in pain and fell to the ground. Stephens ran to him and turned him over on the ground. The man started to cry out again, but a quick punch to the face silenced him. Looking farther down in the direction the man was running, they saw a pair of horses tied under the lean-to. This reminded them of their own horses, and Stephens told Jones to go back for them while he and Harrington brought these and the outlaw back to the cave.

"Why didn't you just let Jones shoot him?" asked Harrington. "If you had missed him, he might have escaped and warned Conner of our plan."

"If I had missed him, there would have still been time for Jones to shoot, but firing a shot out here still might have doomed us. Have you never shot a gun before?"

"Of course, I have."

"Then you should know a gunshot carries a long ways in hills like these. We don't know how close some other bushrangers might be, and if anyone hears the shot, it would mean people coming to investigate, which may or may not mean trouble. Right now, we need absolute secrecy."

Harrington nodded his understanding, and they loaded the outlaw over one of the horses and brought him back to the cave.

"I suppose they let my horse go free so if anyone found him, it would add credence to the report that I had been killed."

"Uh-huh," Stephens replied absentmindedly. He was beginning to lose patience with Harrington, more because he was tired, sore, and ready to go back home more than for any serious problem with the man, who had been through quite an ordeal himself.

Harrington picked up on this shortness and wasn't sure how to respond, with an apology, outrage, or silence. He realized he had made a few, what might seem, silly or elementary remarks about the case. And to discover the bushranger gang was headquartered in his backyard, so to speak, had not improved his humor—no matter how understandable a deception it might be dubbed. As they walked back up the hill, he decided to try a half apology to see what he got.

"I'm sorry to have put you to the trouble of saving me, Mr. Stephens. Based on the stories of your exploits, I'm sure you must have had more important business to attend to."

Stephens stopped, realizing what Harrington was getting at and turned to him.

"Young fella, you're part of the business I'm here to attend to. I take your hint that I've been short and in a bit of a bad temper, but I'll bet you're none too happy about the fact we had to pick you up off of a stone floor either. I am on the other side of the world from where I want to be, and every minute that goes by until we get this mess cleared up is a further risk of getting killed. I don't know you real well, but I don't have anything against you either, and saving you is part of the job. I would have done it if a stranger had asked me to. Too many times in the past I've been with ranger companies who were too late to save anyone, and what we found instead, you don't want to know about. I've been a ranger for twenty years, and I've gone from chasing renegade Comanches to chasing bank robbers and cattle rustlers."

He stopped and breathed deep while Harrington stared at him with mixed emotions of sympathy and curiosity. Stephens's speech was making him forget his own troubles for a brief moment.

Finally, Stephens spoke again more softly, "This is my last ride, Mr. Harrington. I came on this trip as a favor to Jones, and once this is done, I'm going home, retiring from ranging and finding a job that's a tad less strenuous that lets me stay close to home and my wife. I'll try to be less grumpy going forward if you try to be a little less closed-minded to what's right in front of you."

After a moment of digestion, Harrington nodded. Stephens nodded back, and they continued up to the cave entrance.

They retied the horses to trees, unloaded the unconscious outlaw, and dragged him inside. They had just begun to tie up the two prisoners while they couldn't resist when Jones reappeared. When they completed their task, they regrouped.

"I wish that man had given us a better time frame," said Jones. "Timing will be important. If we get there too soon, that's just more time we'll have to spend hiding from literally everyone. But if we get there too late, it may be too late to do any good."

"I don't know about being altogether too late," replied Stephens, "but we will need to time it right to get the maximum effect. I'll bet Conner is going to take advantage of all the theatrics he can muster to help push these misguided people into a revolting mood."

"The evening time will be fairly accurate," said Harrington. "Town meetings have been held before, granted never at someone's home, but still they usually take place close to seven o'clock. I would wager it will be similar in this case, which means we have some time."

"Very well," said Stephens in a satisfied tone. "Let's get some more rest and food in us, clean our guns again, tend to the horses, and make sure everything is as squared away as it can be before we head out. It won't take long to get to Conner's place, so let's leave a little before seven and see what we find."

They all agreed and commenced preparing their gear and themselves for a very dangerous encounter.

Chapter 24

At six thirty, when the sun was beginning to sink in the western sky, the three men mounted up and left the cave. The two outlaws had been attached to a support beam down the mine shaft when they woke up, similar to how Jones and Stephens had been. They circled wide of Conner's station compound so as to approach it from a less-noticeable direction and had it in sight at just about seven o'clock. They closed from the western side, which possessed a number of trees; and in their long evening shadows with the low sun glaring from behind them, the lawmen crept in, dismounted, and led their horses. From farther out, they had seen people traveling on the main road toward the compound, people in wagons and buggies or on horseback. As near as they could tell, Conner had drawn a considerable crowd, maybe over a hundred, to hear his speech.

Now they crept in closer until they reached the fence running around the perimeter of the compound. Just on the other side of it from them was a feed shed and tack room with one of Conner's men leaning up against it. While Jones and Harrington stayed crouched by the fence, Stephens crept forward low to the ground until he was right behind the man. Then, with one motion, he straightened up and hammered the butt of his small pistol into the back of the man's head. Stephens caught the man by the shoulders as he began to slump down, and he dragged him behind the shed. With the guard gone, they all peeked around the corner of the building at the scene before them. A large crowd had gathered in the middle of the compound in front of the big house, and people were separated into groups of men arguing and planning and women gossiping or sharing their sorrows over past events. In various positions around the outside of the crowd, other men belonging to Conner could be seen leaning against buildings or fence posts, sitting on horses, or wandering around small areas like sentries walking a picket. There were also a few men standing on the front porch of the big house.

In more ways than one, it was a relief to see many people carrying firearms. A reasonable precaution against a potential ambush by bushrangers on the road, and maybe some of them had guessed something big was brewing. The lawmen were happy about it because on one hand, it would make them less obtrusive moving through the crowd since Jones and Harrington had armed themselves with pistols and Martini-Henry rifles from the outlaw cave. And on the other hand, when the fighting started, people who were willing to fight would be able to, which was comforting with the assumption they would fight on the right side. The lawmen pulled back behind the shed and started whispering.

"I'm going to stay here," Stephens began. "If I take this fella's vest and hat, I might can pass off as him leaning at the corner. This spot gives me a good view of the porch and Conner when he comes out. You two should be able to move around the edge of the crowd easily enough if you keep your hats pulled down low and keep talking to each other. If anyone hears my voice out there, I'm cooked."

The others nodded, and he continued.

"Try to work your way around to the other side of the crowd to a spot where you can see most of Conner's men. Harrington, if you see any of your men, or men you feel you can rely on, pull them aside and fill them in. Tell them not to do anything until we do. Good luck."

Again, they all nodded, and Jones and Harrington slipped out into the open and casually moved to join the crowd. After they moved off, Stephens stepped out and leaned up against the corner in the same way the other man had with his rifle leaned up against the wall behind him. That rifle would've been as recognizable as his accent, so it was best to keep it out of sight.

He watched as the other two traveled around the edge of the crowd. At least twice he saw them pause next to some man or other and have a few words with him. The conversation would end with a nod, and they would continue. That made the ranger feel some better about their chances; he had counted twenty-one men twice over, who must belong to Conner. Every time Jones and Harrington stopped to talk with someone else, that meant the possibility of 7-1 odds dropping to a more reasonable number. Stephens had just lost sight of them when two things happened: a pair of men began going around lighting the lamps of the compound, and the front door of the house opened, and Conner stepped out. Someone at the front of the crowd noticed him and began to clap and cheer, which was instantly taken up in a rippling pattern by the rest of the crowd. After a moment, Conner raised his hands to call for silence, and the noise died away.

"Thank you, friends," he said loudly. "Thank you for coming here to listen to what I have to say. It is not easy to say it. As many of you are well aware, I have worked hard not just to be a successful businessman but also to mend the breach between two classes of people. Too long have we been a separated people, and we would all benefit from a strong union of effort, despite our differences. But the lawless acts of a few have all but destroyed the progress we have made. The bushrangers, once thought to be done with, have revived to plague us. The squatters blame the selectors, where most bushrangers of the past have come from. The selectors claim the squatters have oppressed and forced them into such behavior. And the bushrangers have robbed and killed and destroyed indiscriminately for their own selfish gain and added to our strain instead of easing it.

"It might be said we have all been united in one sense, which is that we look to the law and the state to safeguard us from these criminals, but for years now they have accomplished nothing. Now, I don't criticize our own brave officers who have done their best, but a few men can only do so much, here or in some other area. But what has the state done? What has the government done to help them? Nothing, nothing to signify they are actually concerned. And not just the local governing power, but what has England done to protect this vast territory it possesses? As long as it is still receiving resources to fuel its empire, what are a few dead bodies and crushed homes?"

Stephens continued to lean against the corner of the shed and listened to the speech. There was no doubt Conner had a gift of oration, and he was using it to captivate his audience. As he continued speaking, Stephens watched the crowd. Most of the expressions were of assent and agreement with what they heard. It touched their hearts to hear a person of influence, of passion and dedication to improving their circumstances, speak in such a way. They wanted relief from generations-old feuds and oppression, from hardship and trials which could be avoided if some instrumental changes could be made. If Stephens were one of the poor devils in the crowd, he would be the first to fall into line to help facilitate those changes. The ranger could easily sympathize with such people, having grown up and lived through the uncomfortable and trying period of reconstruction the Southern states had endured during the years following the civil war. The crowd had his sympathy, but he knew one thing these poor people did not: that this champion apparent who was putting them under his oratory spell was directly responsible for so much of their suffering for the purpose of furthering his own ambitions. They might already be well on their way to better times if his operations were not in existence.

With that thought, he began to prepare mentally for the job he was there to do. The sun was continuing to sink, and soon the light would begin to fade. The people were becoming tense with the anticipation of changing the future, so much so that even the men Harrington and Jones had spoken to might yet be pulled into the frenzy. The ranger gripped the barrel of his rifle and held it vertically along his leg as he took two steps to the door of the shed and stepped inside. The shed had a small window on either side of the door, and feed bags were piled all around. He stacked these up until the top was just under the window and rested his arm on them as he steadied and aimed his rifle. His rifle barrel did not protrude out of the window but was hidden in the dark room. As he aligned his sights, he remembered the plan: to begin shooting Conner's men to reveal they were the iron shirts before bringing them down. But where to start? More than anything, Stephens wanted to shoot

Conner, armor or no armor, to stop this madness from going any further, but the ranger seriously doubted Conner himself would wear an iron shirt, and his apparent "assassination" would only make matters worse.

He had about decided any man on the porch would do when another man came out the front door behind Conner. Stephens blinked and recognized him; it was Dobson, the puzzling but ruthless foreman who had chained them up in the mine. He had not laid eyes on him since, and now Stephens knew his target. As he took aim, he hoped Jones and Harrington were in position as Conner raised his voice still higher.

"My friends and neighbors, if we are to have peace and prosperity, community and justice, we must take it upon ourselves to secure it! Are you with me?"

Bang!

Stephens's rifle erupted in smoke, and the .45-caliber bullet thudded into Dobson's chest as he stood behind Conner. All were silent for a few moments as all eyes were on Dobson. He staggered back against the wall in pain, but the big man did not fall or show any signs of being mortally wounded.

Bang!

Another shot thudded into his belly, and he staggered back again and doubled over in pain, but still he stayed on his feet. A second later, another shot rang out from across the compound and hit another man on the end of the porch, and he too was not seriously harmed. Another of Conner's men who had been on picket duty behind the crowd came running up with his rifle ready. A shot rang out and hit him high on the chest, knocking him to the ground next to the crowd. Whether some sight of metal on that man was visible to the crowd, or someone began to piece the puzzle together, the ranger never knew, but suddenly a man in the crowd pounced on the fallen man and ripped his shirt open. There, now visible for everyone with a line of sight to see, was a steel breastplate strapped the man's chest with a fresh dent in it.

"Iron shirts!" they began to yell. "They're bushrangers, the bushrangers are here!"

With that the crowd began to scatter as the lawmen had predicted. A prophecy could not have come closer to reality. Women, children, and families began to rush for their vehicles to escape danger. A group of the men who had exposed the armored man began to fire on other bushrangers scattered around the compound, and the chaos of battle erupted. Their first objective accomplished, Stephens moved on to phase 2. He chambered a fresh round and fired it into one of Dobson's legs. This time the man screamed in pain like a wild animal and fell to the floor of the porch. Stephens moved on to another target crouched down behind the porch railing and put a round splintering through the wood and into the man's shin. He too fell with a cry, and the ranger turned his attention back to Conner.

When the shooting had begun, he had been taken completely by surprise. And trying to recover, he had waved his hands and shouted, "Friends! Friends! Listen to me please!"

He had been desperate to regain control of his would-be army, but his own calling card, his trademark, had betrayed him. The catalyst of all these people's recent suffering was the iron-shirt bushrangers, and once it was discovered these outlaws were standing right next to them, it was all-out war. Conner realized this and realized it wouldn't take long for some of these people to come after him, even if they didn't grasp his full involvement. But even as these fears overtook him, rage overtook his fear. Rage and fury at his plans and dreams being ruined in an instant. Even as bullets whizzed around him, his sharp mind recalled where the first shot had come from, the faint hint of smoke in the shed window. He drew a pistol from inside his coat and began to blast at the window, even as Stephens took aim at him.

Splinters flew as bullets hit around the window, and one round hit a grain sack as the ranger dropped to the floor, the grain raining down on him. Conner emptied his pistol, dropped it, and took another from Dobson's belt. Stephens jumped up and looked out in time to see Conner enter the front door of the house and slam it behind him.

Chapter 25

Stephens burst out of the door of the shed and threw off his borrowed hat, lest he still be mistaken for one of Conner's hands. He ran for the house, ducking through and around men fighting and running and yelling, "Jones! Jones! Get behind the house!"

He had no way of knowing if Jones could hear him or not, but it was all he could do. He jumped onto the porch and kicked the front door with all his momentum. The door flew open with a slam against the inner wall, and the ranger charged in. He ran through the house to the kitchen and found the butler and his wife, the cook, huddled on the floor and shaking with fear.

"Where's Conner?" Stephens demanded, but they only shuddered harder and looked away from him.

Stephens threw open the back door and saw nothing. As far as he could see in the fading light, there was no sign of man or horse. Wildly he turned in every direction, searching. He ran down the hall, peeking in every room, and then ran upstairs and did the same. No sign of Conner. He came back downstairs and into the kitchen to once again look out the back door, and still seeing nothing, he slammed his fist against the doorframe and hung his head in anger and disgust. By now, the noise of the battle outside was dying down, and he was about to go check on Jones when he noticed something. As he turned to walk with his head still hanging down, he saw the light coming up through paper-thin cracks in the floorboards. He stared at the floor another moment and then looked at the butler still sitting on the floor but looking him in the eye.

"Cellar?" Stephens asked in a normal tone, pointing down.

After a second's hesitation, the butler nodded and pointed a finger at a door in the corner of the room. The ranger gripped his rifle with both hands and took a step toward the door. Before he could take another, a bullet burst up through the floorboards right in front of the ranger's foot. Stephens jumped to one side, and then another bullet came up, and another as Stephens kept jumping out of the way and finally dove across the room. He hit the floor with a groan and instantly began rolling across the floor as more bullets came his way. As he reached the wall, the shooting stopped. He jumped up and fired two shots randomly down into the cellar. His rifle was now empty, so he pulled out his short pistol and waited for a reply. His heart pounded as seconds passed, and nothing happened. He was about to start his march toward the door again when he heard a shout from outside.

"Wayne!"

That was Jones's voice, sure enough. The ranger ran out the back door and to the corner of the house. He stopped as he looked around the corner at what awaited him. Conner was there, standing close to a wagon near the coral, and in front of him held close was a girl. The wagon belonged to a family who had come out to hear the speech. When the shooting started, they had tried to load up and run away, but a stray bullet hit one of their two horses, which now lay dead on the ground. Until the horse could be disconnected from the wagon so as to allow the other horse to pull it, that wagon wasn't going anywhere. The family had hidden in the coral until the shooting had died away, and it looked as if the father had been trying to cut away the traces of the dead horse when Conner had appeared and grabbed the thirteen-year-old daughter. He must have crawled out of a window at ground level, which allowed natural light into the cellar by day. Now he used the girl as a shield against Jones and Harrington and a few other men who were steadily approaching the scene with their weapons raised. He still had a pistol, which must be presumed to be loaded, and he swung it from side to side, trying to keep all his adversaries covered as he sheltered behind his captive.

Stephens opened the action of his rifle and loaded a round into the chamber and stepped out from behind the house. Conner saw him and turned his gun toward him but was careful to never present himself as a clear target to anyone. The ranger kept walking toward him with slow, steady steps, his rifle at the ready position. Not quite straight toward Conner. He walked in a line that would take him past Conner if he continued on it. He wanted to edge to his left and so spread the arc Conner had to watch as far as possible. Conner kept his gun on him as he shot glances back the other way to keep everyone in check, and in the background, the angry father of the girl was gripping the almost-hysterical mother who would otherwise charge full steam at the man threatening her daughter's life. Stephens actually wished she would slip free so as to give him an opportunity. He kept marching slowly forward until Conner yelled for him to stop.

"What do you think you're going to do, Conner?" the ranger asked. "Grab a horse, slip away, and hide out in the bush like you did before?"

"Why not? It worked before, it can again."

"Ha!" Stephens roared and laughed so intently that to Jones, Conner seemed to get very disturbed and angry.

"What do you know about surviving in the Australian bush? By the time I show myself again, no one will even recognize me."

"Doesn't matter," Stephens replied. "After this, the whole country will be after your hide. By the time you're able to show your ugly face again, you'll have already starved to death. Just get it over with now, or surrender."

"Not a chance," Conner laughed, grinning now at the suggestion he would actually surrender. "You underestimate me, everyone always underestimated me in the past, but I'll survive, I'll return, and I will continue the work I started. It's just a matter of time until I bring down the hypocrites and bureaucrats of the tyrannical governments ruining people's lives."

"Don't you ever get tired of giving speeches?" Stephens asked, who was genuinely becoming annoyed. "I've had enough," he said at last.

Oddly, he released his right hand from his rifle and let it swing down to his side in his left hand as he began to walk briskly toward Conner. Jones had been watching the exchange very closely, swinging his gaze from one man to the other, but in the twilight, it was becoming more difficult to make out details. However, there was no mistaking that as he walked, Stephens made a pistol of his right hand like a young boy playing and acted like he was pulling the trigger. Jones could only take this as a signal for him and refocused on Conner. There was no way he could take a shot without grave danger to the girl, Stephens must know that, so if he shot, he would have to miss to avoid the girl. But maybe that was what the ranger wanted, so he made ready.

Stephens was closing in on Conner, mere yards away, and Conner began to tense up. It would be nothing to him to shoot this Yank if he had to. He'd killed before and could again, and at this range, he couldn't miss.

Stephens saw the resolve form on Conner's face, and he yelled out, "SHOOT!"

Jones pulled the trigger, and a shot roared out from his pistol accompanied by a flash of light in the darkness, and the bullet crashed into a post of the coral fence, throwing out splinters. Instinct kicked in, and Conner whirled at the sound of the shot to face the most immediate threat, swinging the girl around with him. His eyes were fixed on Jones as the shooter, and he took aim with his pistol to return fire. Jones was still in no position to shoot Conner, who was about to shoot him, but he didn't have time to worry about it. Another shot rang out, and Conner's whole body recoiled and shivered. He released his grip on the girl, and she ran bawling to her parents. When Conner had turned to face Jones, he unconsciously revealed his uncovered side to the ranger. Though still a narrow target, it was the most Stephens would get and was enough at this range. With practiced speed, the ranger drew his pistol, cocked it, aimed it, and fired. The shot hit in the middle of Conner's side and ripped through his body to the other side and came to rest against a left rib.

Most likely, with so many vital organs damaged or destroyed, Conner was dead before he hit the ground, and a quick examination proved he was dead. So the would-be leader of a false, pretense rebellion was no more. Stephens, Jones, Harrington, and the men who had stayed to fight began to clean up the battlefield. Dead men were laid out together in a row on the ground, while the bushrangers who were still alive were huddled into the barn where their wounds could be treated while they were held prisoner. Miraculously, none of the citizens had been killed, and only a few received slight wounds. Some of them grumbled and wondered why they should bother caring for the outlaws. Harrington quickly rebuked them for wanting to circumvent the rule of law they had previously been ready to start a war over. The men's words and tempers died away, and they did as they were told.

They stayed at the station overnight, and the next morning, Harrington's sergeant and constables arrived. The three lawmen walked to meet them, but despite Harrington's presence, the sergeant started to draw his weapon when he saw the other two men who were formerly his prisoners. His movement was arrested when Stephens whipped out his short pistol first and cocked the hammer.

"Stand down, Sergeant!" yelled Harrington. "These men are not criminals."

Quickly Harrington related the series of events of the previous day and confirmed Jones's and Stephens's identities. The sergeant found the prospect of making such a serious mistake very disagreeable, but nothing could be done about it now except to formally apologize. He dismounted and did so, very formally and very stiffly. The two lawmen said nothing. Jones looked to Stephens, who was looking at the ground, and then Stephens raised his head, looked the sergeant straight in the eye, and punched him in the nose. Not hard enough to break it, just bend it a little, then he spoke as Jones tried to conceal a smile.

"Apology accepted, Sergeant, on the condition that next time a person is accused of something, you take the time to find out the facts before passing your own judgment. Your blind belief in Conner's story almost got us and Harrington killed because you refused to look at and listen to all sides of the matter."

The sergeant was still rubbing and holding his aching nose when he looked back at the ranger. "Yes, sir, I'll do that."

Then he signaled for the constables to follow him to the house. The bodies were buried, and the survivors loaded into a wagon and hauled back to town to be locked up until trial and punishment could take place. The mission Stephens and Jones had set out to accomplish was completed. The true and complete story of the rebellion that almost occurred, however, was kept secret. There was still no shortage of unrest for one reason or another throughout the country, and it was believed that if the truth were known, then other Conners might be encouraged to take advantage of other people in the same manner. Most of the people of Bathurst had no objection to the secret since most were embarrassed and ashamed of how completely they had been duped and manipulated. So it was simply circulated that the case of the iron-shirt bushrangers had been suddenly cracked and the outlaws captured or dispatched.

Of the surviving bushrangers, it could not be proven who did or did not actually participate in any killing that had been done, so it was doubtful any of them could escape the noose. However, this did not keep them from trying by giving up information. As suspected, Conner had arranged for his own gold shipments to be robbed so that he could not be suspected of collusion and could claim grievance and so gain support and sympathy from the community. The overall plan had been, when the time was right, to strike a spark of rebellion in Bathurst. This would presumably spread to Orange and the whole area and eventually overtake the entire territory of New South Wales. If later on Victoria or other territories could be convinced to join, then so much the better.

A thorough search of the cave hideout did, in fact, yield up some of the missing gold hidden way down at the end of a couple of tunnels. The prisoners also told of other hideouts spread around the edges of Conner's property, including the one which the famed midnight wagon heist had been conducted from, which also proved to have gold hidden in them. It would take countless hours of calculation and reviewing of old records and reports to determine if all the stolen gold was found and what portions of it went to whom, but that was someone else's problem. The bushranger menace had been dealt with.

Stephens had seen some beautiful country during his brief time in Australia, and he didn't doubt he would enjoy seeing more of it. However, as interesting and beautiful as the country might be, and however enticing the prospect of actually doing some hunting, it would have to wait for another time. Right now, all Stephens and Jones wanted to do was go home. When their business was concluded, they packed their belongings, including the pistols confiscated by the sergeant, and boarded a train to return to Sidney. Once back in the port city, they arranged passage on the first available ship back to the United States. They had to spend two nights in the city waiting for their ship to leave, but the rest and comfort was welcome, and soon they were steaming back home.

Stephens thought more and more frequently about Katelyn, as did Jones about Emma. If they could have gotten out and pushed the boat to make it go faster, they would have. But knowing they could do no such silly thing, they settled in to enjoy the trip as much as possible. Interacting with other guests, telling stories, and comparing adventures with people who had been to Africa, India, and China was always a stimulating way to pass the time. Days and weeks passed, as before, and at long last, the ship came into view of the California coast. This ship's destination was San Francisco, which put them farther to the north than where they set out from, but at least they were back. The first thing they did was send off a telegraph message to Katelyn, which would reach her long before they did, telling her they were back safe and on their way. With that, they began the last stage of their journey traveling by train and coach back to Texas and the Stephens ranch.

It was midafternoon when the stagecoach dropped them off at the familiar crossroads near the ranch where they were met by a ranch hand in a buckboard to fetch them and their luggage. Stephens was practically giddy with anticipation of seeing Katelyn again and being able to stay with her from now on. The buckboard pulled up outside of Stephens's house, and they got down and unloaded their gear. It was odd though. Katelyn didn't come out to meet them. The buckboard was proof that their arrival was anticipated. In a moment, Stephens passed from exhilaration to dark suspicion, and leaving everything on the porch, he hurried through the door with Jones right behind him. They walked through to the kitchen and found Katelyn tending the stove with her back to them.

Stephens was about to give a cry of relief when Katelyn turned around at the sound of their feet. Her face showed joy at having her husband back home, but her husband's expression was strange, as if he were confused, and he just stared at her. Even after being gone for what equaled about four months or so, he didn't go to her. Jones had a look of astonishment on his face as he also stood still with his mouth open. Finally, Stephens found his voice.

"Katie, the whole time I've known you, you've always been about the same size. Why is it now, you look like you swallowed a five-pound sack of potatoes?"

Jones turned his wide eyes from Katelyn to Stephens, not knowing which one to be more astonished at. Katelyn didn't know whether this husband of hers was being ignorant or acting childish, but in any event, she cocked one hand on her hip, and her expression reformed from a broad smile to a look of mixed aggravation and amusement as she answered him, "Wayne Stephens, you idiot, you're going to be a father!"

About the Author

J. Stephen Miles was born and raised in Corsicana, Texas. He graduated high school in 2005 and attended Navarro College and Sam Houston State University. He has been married to his wife, Krystal, for six years and has one daughter. With interest in mystery, history, and a strong touch of Texas state pride, he first tried his hand at writing a story, blending these interests, in early 2013. With much support from family and friends, he completed not one but three stories involving a strange coupling of heroes from different worlds. Stephen has always had an interest in history and enjoyed a variety of literature from Louis L'Amour westerns to Sherlock Holmes mysteries, from Tolkien's fantasies to Forester's seafaring historical fictions. Stephen has been a Christian all his life and openly gives God praise for giving him a talent in forming phrases and telling stories.

CPSIA information can be obtained
at www.ICGtesting.com
Printed in the USA
LVHW101307100223
739184LV00001B/2

9 781639 034895